Chasing the Sun
with Henry

D1428778

Chasing the Sun
with Henry

Gary Brockwell

Matador
9 Priory Business Park,
Wistow Road, Kibworth Beauchamp,
Leicestershire. LE8 0RX
Tel: 0116 279 2299
Email: books@troubador.co.uk
Web: www.troubador.co.uk/matador
Twitter: @matadorbooks

ISBN 978 1788039 062

British Library Cataloguing in Publication Data.
A catalogue record for this book is available from the British Library.

Printed and bound in the UK by TJ International, Padstow, Cornwall
Typeset in 11pt Adobe Garamond Pro by Troubador Publishing Ltd, Leicester, UK

Matador is an imprint of Troubador Publishing Ltd

For Betty, who knows we all deserve our second chance.

Chapter 1

A Local Beach

Before I even turned the key in the front-door lock, I knew the words that were going to greet me from within.

'Make sure that dog's feet are clean, I've just washed the floor,' she boomed, as I pushed the door open and Henry rushed in.

These are the words she always utters, each Saturday on our return from our early-morning forays onto the beach. And I always reply the same.

'Sally, why wash the floor before we return?'

At this point, she always sighs deeply and mutters under her breath, while Henry stands patiently, panting, tongue protruding, waiting for one of us to replenish his drinking bowl with water.

But not today – today was different. Today, I simply smiled and said brightly, 'I am sorry' as I bent down, picked up the bowl, filled it with water and returned it to the floor in front of Henry. I gave him an affectionate pat on his flank, the action of which dislodged sand and introduced that 'wet-dog smell' into the room.

Henry moved forward, his large ears hiding the bowl, and began his lapping and slobbering at the fresh water, his tail keeping a steady rhythm along with his slurps.

'Well, just think next time,' she said, waiting for Henry to finish, so she could commence mopping up the water displaced around his bowl.

With his thirst quenched, Henry wandered to his basket in the corner of the room, a trail of water droplets from his jowls marking his way. He turned and took up a position on his cushion to entice a deep sleep unto him.

'Don't forget, Jenny is coming tonight,' she stated.

This statement is also repeated weekly and normally results in my heart sinking and a sarcastic response muttered over my lips.

But not today.

'Of course, how is she?'

Sally stopped mopping the floor and looked up, tilting her head to one side at my reply.

'Are you feeling all right?'

'Certainly, just asking how your friend is,' I answered.

'How do you think she is? She is lonely.'

'She has got the dogs.'

'That's right, make fun of my friend.'

'I wasn't, Sally!' I responded, with palms showing.

I really meant what I said. Today I felt no malice toward Jennifer Rees. I sincerely believed this benevolence of calm would remain with me even in her formidable presence later that evening. When, whilst eating cake after cake, biscuit after biscuit, she is accustomed to bemoaning my entire gender and complaining that she is never destined to be happy. And all the while Sally nods in agreement, confirming Jennifer's victim status while offering more biscuits and more cakes, which are greedily received, through her sobs and wails.

The climax to this ritual occurs during *Match of the Day*, when I am forced to increase the volume on the TV to enjoy the post-match analysis, and to compensate for Jennifer's sugar-induced outbursts. The look Sally throws to me indicates that she is unwilling to compete against commentary on why the league leaders should never play with a lone striker, and is enough to make me turn off the TV. With a heavy sigh, I always retire from the room. Henry shows his male solidarity and accompanies me. My parting scowl is never delivered back in the direction of the lounge until I am hidden safely in the hallway. I always view the remainder of the programme, glumly, on a portable TV in the kitchen from a wooden breakfast-bar stool, with the noise of Henry's snores emanating from his basket.

But perhaps this evening, I will watch TV in the kitchen all night, give them the opportunity to really talk. Today, after our walk on the beach, I feel happy.

Despite what Sally thinks, I am correct about Jennifer's dogs being company for her. She has three; all rescue dogs, which is commendable. They deserve a second chance to be happy, content and loved. I don't agree with them sleeping on her bed, but guess as they are all small terriers, they wouldn't take up that much room. I do fully understand the companionship she draws from them sharing her home, though.

Perhaps, if she walked them, exercised more, she could break the circle of unhappiness which keeps her weight a constant problem for her. And perhaps, at the same time, she could meet someone too.

That's what happened to me today on the beach. Our beach, Henry's and mine, our normally deserted beach.

At the time of the morning we are there, we own every last grain of sand, every pebble and weathered piece of driftwood that we see. To reach our beach we have to pass through towering sand dunes that have stood proudly for centuries, and marram grass covers their faces with a coarse, unkempt stubble. The dunes are so impregnable that you hear the crashing of the surf long before the shoreline comes into view.

Our entire kingdom, on account of the flora and fauna, is deemed an area of special scientific interest. In Henry's world, it is but an area of special smells of interest, all of which are examined thoroughly, before he cocks a back leg where his nose had just been and leaves his own seal of approval. Watching him running back and forth, sniffing, urinating and sniffing some more, it seems he never tires of this place, and neither do I.

As we pass between the last dunes before the shore, the view that makes this, in my eyes, a special place comes into focus for the first time – the mountains, their huge bulk hidden until now; their enormity a total surprise when they suddenly appear without warning. Rising straight out of the sea and piercing the sky, they force the cloud cover to sag below their conical summits. But now, after years of exposure to this, my initial pleasant shock has matured into a feeling of wonder at how much these gentle giants have witnessed over countless millennia.

Such conundrums do not concern Henry. He merely gets lost in the pleasure of the new smells that overload his senses, blown on the wind to him from the shore.

Henry saw them first; or rather he sensed them first. His keen nose involuntarily moved his entire face from the shore to his left. Then his excited bark drew my attention and announced their arrival into our perfect morning ritual.

With a single backward glance at me, he was off, pounding the sand hard, anxious to meet the onward-rushing dog whose owner watched from an equal distance to me.

They greeted with wagging tails and sniffed each other's noses and faces for some time, causing me to smile. After this initial, cordial introduction, I willed Henry, as I got closer, not to embarrass himself or me, but then he did it. He couldn't help himself. In one swift movement he positioned himself to the rear of his new acquaintance and sniffed and licked her anus intently. His forwardness resulted in a growl and a flash of teeth from the recipient and a barking command from me for him to come back. Which in fairness to him, he did immediately, scampering over the sand, knowing by my tone of voice he was in trouble, but equally not understanding why.

As I attempted to hook the leash onto his collar, he stood, his tail between his legs, his sad eyes staring up at me.

'Why did you do that?' I said gently, melting in the face of his submission.

He noted my change of tone and acknowledged my forgiveness with a double lick to the back of my hand. The action of which instantly made me recoil and drop his lead, as I remembered where his face had been moments before.

'You might want to wash your hand!' the voice laughed in front of me.

I look up and saw her, she gave a warm smile, revealing perfect teeth. Her hair blonde, tied into a ponytail, her face fresh, bereft of any make-up. Her body formless, dressed in a blue fleece, jeans and wellies.

'I am sorry about that,' I muttered, embarrassment sweeping over me. 'He is normally well behaved,' I added, knowing I was lying, as my mind recalled Henry's multiple misdemeanours.

I stood awkwardly, hoping the situation was not going to deteriorate further.

'Don't be sorry – Phoebe has forgiven him.' She gestured with her hand at the two dogs, now playing chase across the sands. 'Actually, she probably liked it, but didn't want him to know! Think of it as a kind of lady-dog prerogative!'

'Perhaps!' I laughed. 'She is a beautiful dog – pure Lab?' I continued.

She nodded. 'A gift from my husband, he seemed to misunderstand my need for companionship,' she stated, without a hint of irony.

'Phoebe is a –lovely name,' I said.

We stood watching the dogs as they bounded into the breaking waves together. No small talk, no discussion about the weather, just watching the dogs play, momentarily connecting with their world of no worries or concerns.

'Well, I am heading back now, been out a while. Which way are you heading?' she said eventually.

I didn't reply.

'Actually, we could walk with you,' I suddenly blurted out, 'if that's okay?' I added quickly, 'In fact, to be honest, it would be good for Henry; he doesn't normally get on with other dogs and he really is enjoying Phoebe's company.'

'I thought you said he was normally well behaved?' she injected.

'Well actually, this is why we come here early. We had just got here, to have the place to ourselves, to make it easy for Henry. I was surprised and slightly uncomfortable to see someone else here at this hour.'

'Oh, I thought this was a public beach; we won't encroach again,' she stated, and started to walk away from me.

'No, no, I didn't mean anything like that,' I responded anxiously.

She stopped and turned to face me, a smile forming across her lips.

I realised she was teasing me again, and found her playfulness caused my breath to quicken.

We walked over the sands together – the dunes to our left, the shore to our right and the mountains watching our progress from behind us.

'I am actually glad he has bonded with Phoebe, I'd like him to do normal doggy stuff.'

She didn't reply.

'My neighbour told me about this place,' she suddenly said. 'But she didn't mention how the mountains just appear before you; it's amazing!'

I smiled to myself, remembering my first encounter, but in my case, I had no one to share the experience with.

'Yep, we like to keep them to ourselves – local mountains, for local people!' I responded.

She looked at me, saw my smile and returned her own.

'Okay, I am an outsider – moved two weeks ago, still finding my way around. You locals might get blasé about them but to me they are amazing.'

It felt good to be equally playful with her.

'Perhaps Henry and I could show you and Phoebe around,' I continued, feeling confidence rushing through me.

She stopped and looked at me.

'And what would my husband and your wife think of that?' she asked with a straight face.

'Just being welcoming to a new member of the community,' I replied with a smile. 'And anyway, who said I was married?'

She laughed, but I was not sure if this was in response to my statement or my question.

'Anyway, I am not a "new member of the community" – I live miles away. My neighbour said it was worth the drive, and it truly is,' she said, spinning around greedily, taking in the whole scene.

We continued in silence for some minutes, the wind fresh on our faces and our footsteps in unison across the firm sands. The dogs continued their own walk.

'What about Henry? He's a collie-and-spaniel cross, isn't he?' she enquired.

'Yep, a right mixture! He's a rescue dog; dumped in the middle of town as a pup by his previous "owners". I use this term loosely. They were seen calmly opening the tailgate of their car, leading him out and tying him to a lamp post before driving away.'

'That's so awful.'

I nodded.

'He ended up in the dog pound and was going to be put down.'

'He was lucky that you were there at the time, to save him.'

Instinctively I threw a wounded look in her direction as the reason for me being at the pound that day caught me. The same as it always does when I allow myself to remember the circumstances of Henry coming into my life.

'Are you okay?' she asked with a half-smile.

'Yes, sure,' I replied, regaining my composure. 'He actually chose me,' I continued. 'All sealed with a look over his shoulder and a lick to the back of my hand, through the bars of his cage.'

'Don't forget to wash it!' she reminded me.

I chuckled as I remembered her first words to me.

We stopped at the only small break in the dunes, at this end of the beach, the gap was just wide enough to allow a narrow duckboard path to rise and dip beyond our view. She called for Phoebe, who returned on her command, closely followed by Henry.

'That was a really wonderful thing to do, to let Henry into your heart. I can see he loves you,' she stated, tickling his ears. 'Are you going to carry on walking?' she asked, hooking the leash onto Phoebe's collar. 'My car is through that way – I think!' She laughed, pointing toward the path between the dunes.

I took it that her words were not intended to form an invitation for me to escort her back to her car.

'No, I think I will head back now. He has had more than enough exercise today – I don't think he can believe his luck. Besides, the rest of the world is now rising; he really should be off the beach!'

'Think about obedience classes. He is a smart dog, and if he were trained he could do that "doggy stuff", as you say.'

I was pleased to have this advice to take away; it showed she had listened to me and didn't see Henry as a hopeless case.

We watched in silence as both the dogs recovered from the exertion, forcing huge quantities of air into their lungs, and periodically licked their lips in that satisfied way only happy dogs do.

'Oh, by the way, I am Eddie, Eddie Dungiven. I would shake your hand but…' I trailed off, laughing.

She giggled, exposing her perfect teeth again through her smile.

'Cerys Sindon. Nice to meet you, Eddie. Maybe I will see you again on "your" beach!' she teased.

'You are welcome any time, we're always here, every Saturday,' I responded.

As I watched, she turned and headed toward the dunes, but stopped abruptly and looked back at me.

'You are a good man, Eddie Dungiven, a good man,' she said, smiling.

'Thank you!' I replied.

And with that, she retreated from my view.

Our walk back along the beach captured the mountains in our view, but for once, I did not see them. Instead, I replayed the words uttered to me by a beautiful, gregarious, fresh-faced woman who I had only just met, but who refused to vacate my thoughts. *You are a good man, Eddie Dungiven.*

Chapter 2

Chinese Burns

Later, I sat on a kitchen bar stool, the Saturday paper and supplements spread out before me on the work surface. As intended by the art editor of the article I was reading, my eyes were drawn to the matching white-linen-trousered, bare-footed couple, entwined lovingly on a wooden floor. Their backs rested against a clean-lined leather sofa while natural light flooded the scene from behind them through a floor-to-ceiling, gable-shaped window. I stared at this alien world and realised I would need to substantially increase my income to emulate Pippa and Max's *dream self-build* in the New Forest. The only thing I could see from the photograph that we all had in common was a dog.

'I am worried about her.'

'Who?'

'Jenny, of course,' tutted Sally, her hands cleaning the sink. 'She needs a break,' she continued.

'Sally, she needs to get a job. She needs to feel like she's worth something.'

I was also thinking she needed to lose her attitude and excess weight, but knew to keep this opinion to myself.

'Yes, she does need to feel like she's worth something, so I am letting her use the downstairs guest room as a studio.'

I looked up from the paper.

'I am sorry.' Sally stopped washing the draining board and turned to face me. 'You know she is keen on photography; she has bought lots of equipment over the years, but hasn't the room at her place. We've got the room for a photo studio and I told her we can help her out.'

'Should we not have discussed this first?' I asked, trying to control my voice.

'Eddie, she's a friend; you help friends out.'

'No, Sally, she is *your* friend,' I replied. 'And we should have discussed this. Have you really thought this through? When is she going to be in there? All hours? Every weekend? Are you happy with people marching through here day and night?'

'It's not people, silly; it's pets she will be photographing. She loves animals, you know that.'

'And what? These pets drive themselves here, do they?'

Sally shook her head and closed her eyes in frustration.

'Also, where are these pets, or pet owners, going to park?'

'There is room on the driveway for four vehicles, Eddie,' she replied.

'Okay, what about Henry?'

'What about him?'

'There are bound to be dogs in these bloody photo shoots. How is he going to cope with that?'

'He will have to get used to it.'

Henry lifted his head and wagged his tail from his basket in response to hearing his name.

'That isn't fair on him!' I shouted.

'That's just you, thinking more about that dog than helping someone in need,' Sally yelled back at me.

I exhaled deeply, trying to regain my composure.

'So, how much is she paying you for the room?'

'What?'

'You are charging her for it?'

'She is a friend, Eddie! I can't charge her,' shouted Sally, throwing the cleaning cloth into the sink.

'This is our home,' I replied slowly.

'No, this where we live,' she retorted, with flint in her voice.

From her position, she stared out of the window, her hands splayed across the draining board. I continued to sit, my eyes focused on her back, angry with her for not discussing these plans with me, and for her last cutting comment. And angry with myself for not knowing how to make the situation better. She eventually turned and left the room without looking at me.

'I need to clean the bathroom,' she muttered at the doorway to the hall.

I continued my silent anger, now solely directed at myself. *Leave the bathroom and talk to me!* I yelled at her in my head. But I didn't physically move; instead I just let my inability to communicate with my wife and her with me drift away from me as it had many times before.

The *clip-clip* of Henry's claws on the tiles drew my attention as he wandered over to me, taking up a position at my feet with a deep sigh. I looked down at him and wondered what, if anything, he was actually thinking; whatever it was, it must be easier, I thought, than the emotions that tumbled and turned in my mind. Again my eye was caught by the couple smiling at me from the paper supplement.

'Smug bastards,' I uttered under my breath, before

pushing the pages across the work surface and onto the floor.

We always have a takeaway on a Saturday night, and always the same dishes. Sally always orders; I always collect. Sally has chicken chow mein and I have Singapore noodles, and we share sweet-and-sour chicken Hong Kong-style between us. This evening was no different, although tonight we ate in silence. My thoughts returned again and again to my encounter on the beach that morning and my argument with Sally that afternoon. Sally's thoughts remained her own.

After twenty years of marriage, Sally remains a good-looking woman. Every Saturday afternoon she has her hair blow dried by Marco, owner of the nearest hair salon, and today was no exception. On every fourth Saturday she has a colour run-through. I am not sure what a colour run-through entails, but judging by the car Marco drives it is rewarding for him.

Normally she returns home with flowers she has bought from the market. She discards the previous week's blooms, pours the stale water from the vase and arranges the new spray before adding fresh water. She always places the vase on the kitchen table, steps back and smiles to herself. But not today. Today the wilting blooms remained, the fresh set still cocooned in the plastic sleeve, sat in the sink.

Sally, without exception, always wears make-up. To go shopping, to go out, to stay in, to tend her bees – her face is always fully hidden beneath a layer of foundation, blusher, mascara and lipstick. I've always wished that sometimes she would not feel the need to do this, although I have never said. Instead I just feel weary when on occasion her make-up is deposited on my clothes as she brushes past me.

I put down my knife and fork, the noise of metal on ceramic amplified by our vow of silence. We had both had our fill. The remaining food glistened and congealed in the three tinfoil containers on the table between us. What had appeared appetising and comforting had now degenerated into a repulsive sight neither of us could bear to look upon any more.

'Sally,' I began, 'about earlier – I've been thinking. I overreacted; we have the room and you are right, it is good to help Jennifer out.' The words flowed from me quickly and breathlessly.

'Thank you, Eddie.' She smiled. 'You are right; I should have discussed it though.'

She pushed back the breakfast-bar stool and collected the tinfoil trays from the worktop, before turning towards Henry's bowl.

And that I accepted as the final comment on the incident. I could live with me starting the brief exchange of dialogue, me being the only one to apologise, even Sally's assured righteousness at my submission. What I could not accept was her refusing to retract her cutting remark regarding our relationship – this house being where we lived, not our home. On each occasion she uses this weapon it drives a wedge between us; a wedge that always draws me into myself and reminds me how we came to be the people that we are now. And it makes me seethe silently and my heart ache afresh each time.

'You shouldn't feed him the leftovers,' I lamented,

mentally dragging myself back into the room. 'Carbs are not his friend, Sally,' I continued.

'Oh, he loves it, silly,' she giggled, as she deposited the remains of our meal into Henry's bowl.

I sighed inwardly, knowing it would fall to me to clean up his forthcoming multiple loose movements from the garden.

'What time is Jennifer coming?' I asked, watching Henry lapping up noodles and salty soy sauce.

'Normal time – eight o'clock. Why?'

'I thought I'd stay out of the way; let you have a proper chat with her about the studio. I am working tomorrow; I need to load up the van. Then I can watch the TV in here.'

'I am worried about you, Eddie; this is the second time today you have been considerate towards Jenny. What happened on that beach?!' she teased.

'Nothing – just want to do what's right,' I stated, as a memory of that perfect smile and fresh face formed once again in my mind.

Sally turned toward the sink, lifted the flowers out, ran the water and added washing-up liquid, ready to clean the dirty dishes.

'Um, I am not complaining, just commenting. It's good you realise we should help people. Good you listened.' Her voice sounded extremely soft and muffled by the jetting water and soapsuds forming.

She turned off the water and submerged the plates in the bowl.

'By the way, I am seeing Greg in the morning.'

'Oh,' I replied.

'Yes, he has a business idea.'

'Not another one, Sally. What is it this time – selling sand to the Saudis?'

'No. And don't be rude; I know you don't like him, but he is my brother.'

'I wasn't being rude at all; I just don't want you taken in by some hare-brained idea.'

'His ideas are good, Eddie. He thought of the bees, didn't he?' Her voice sounded strained as she crashed a soaped-up dish onto the draining board.

To say Greg Dixon and I do not see eye to eye is an understatement. Within minutes of our first meeting all those years ago when I started to date his sister, it was apparent we had little in common. In fact our views differ so greatly that silence is by far the most congenial method of communication the two of us have discovered over the years. These days, our contact is restricted to occasional family gatherings, where thankfully the seating arrangements at the event, or the sheer number of guests, ensures we maintain our respective distance from each other. If eye contact is met, a mere respectful nod of the head is exchanged.

I do remember that first time I was introduced to Greg. Sally arranged it on our fourth date. We met up in a bar. I was with Sally; Greg with his girlfriend at the time – Judith, I think she was called. I was introduced to Judith – no, Ruth, it was; that was her name – who stood up and gave me a hug and a smile.

Sally turned to her brother. 'Greg, this is Eddie,' she said. I extended my hand to him warmly. He remained seated and slowly put his arm out toward me. I shook his hand firmly and was rewarded with a limp grasp and no eye contact for my efforts.

On sitting down and sipping our first drinks, I wondered what the attraction was between Ruth and Greg. She was talkative, giggly and full of life. Greg, in comparison, sat and said nothing – the difference between them was staggering. In the eyes of others, first impressions really do establish a person's character.

After the first round of drinks, the girls headed off to the toilets, as girls do, leaving Greg and me together. We sat at opposite sides of the table and on the girls' departure his body language seemingly bristled with annoyance as he crossed his arms tightly over his chest and looked outward towards the bar.

'Did you hear the football results this afternoon? I missed them,' I enquired, sipping my drink, trying to fill the silence between us.

'Can't stand the game. Golf is my passion,' Greg revealed. 'Do you play yourself?' he continued.

'No, I don't. I've never really got it to be honest. When watching, it is just hours and hours of televised sky, isn't it? What did Winston Churchill say about it? "Golf is a good walk ruined"!' I joked feebly.

'It was Mark Twain, not Churchill, and both were fools,' came the taut reply.

I felt helpless at this point to try to establish some common ground and we returned to the silence struck at the girls' departure and remained in this state until their return, at which point the girls again led the conversation for the remainder of the evening.

Later, as we travelled home, Sally asked me what I

thought of Greg. I lied and said I thought he was a great guy. This pleased her; she said it was important to her that we got on.

And so the nature of my future relationship with Greg Dixon was set. Over the years I have gotten to know Greg I have learned that he resents immigrants taking 'our' jobs. Even when those jobs are cleaning dank underground toilets on a twelve-hour shift with no daylight, clearing the streets of litter in biting January winds and driving rain, or patrolling desolate building sites in the early hours of the morning, armed only with a torch and a mobile phone. His intolerance extends to immigrants who have the audacity to open shops selling 'their' goods. He believes this takes away the opportunity to open a shop from 'our' people. The fact the shop owners contribute locally by providing jobs and paying taxes is somehow lost on him. He thinks it is a disgrace that people are allowed to practise their faith openly when it is different to 'his' religion, even though he has never voluntarily set foot in a place of worship without being part of a baptism, wedding or funeral congregation.

He applauds the openly elitist, sexist and hidden racist attitudes of his golf club; that enclave he escapes to each weekend to fuel and justify his views and opinions. The place where the car that you drive, albeit loaned to you by your employers for tax purposes or obtained via a hire purchase; that you will never really own, is important. And the ability to drive home in these vehicles after a heavy evening of drinking and backslapping is thoroughly respected. In fact, the more that is drunk, the more boastful the claims are made that the ability to control a vehicle is not affected by alcohol consumption at all.

Greg has no time for benefit scroungers, work-shy layabouts or those who claim to be unable to work or function within society due to depression or anxiety. In his opinion, this is all in the mind and the people should just get on with things. After all, as he says, we all have problems thrown at us. He maintains that people who cannot deal with what life deals them are, in his eyes, weak.

Of all his differing opinions to mine, this is the one attitude of Greg's I find the most difficult to accept. We both witnessed, hopelessly, along with others, his sister's dark journey through depression over many months a few short years ago. We witnessed her isolation, her days on end curled under the covers of her bed in a darkened room, her not bathing, not eating, her hours of crying and anguish until she eventually journeyed back to being the person she was. And with her return, Greg forgot the professional care, help, support and medication that had been administered day by day on her road back to recovery. He merely said that she was back because she had pulled herself together.

He is head of sales in a faceless software firm and has been for the last ten years – before this, he tried for five years to rise to this pinnacle that would result in his own office, secretary and embossed business cards. I can only imagine the tricks and dealings he performed to secure this position that in his eyes exudes responsibility and respectability. He networks at client golfing days, point-to-point races and cricket matches.

Outside of this corporate world, he has had business ideas. Two of which have seen Sally part with money from her inheritance from her father's will. In both cases I pleaded with her not to invest, but she did not take heed. The first was frankly ridiculous: teaching people to plough fields, sow, cut hedgerows, and harvest. Greg argued he had seen something similar when away in Hungary on business, and that city people at home would love to spend the weekend in the country doing similar activities. He could not understand that city people just wanted to relax in the countryside and that smelling of slurry or being cold and wet while attaching gear to a tractor just wasn't that appealing. Nevertheless, he leased the machinery, rented the land and hired the labour; a man called Marius from southern Poland. His employment, Greg argued, was not hypocritical considering his beliefs. He selected Marius on the grounds of him being an extremely gifted ploughman and willing to work for a rate considerably lower than that demanded by his British counterparts. However, the entire operation was discontinued within two months after receiving no bookings at all, and Sally lost her money.

His second venture was more in keeping with what city people would want when in the country. He leased six cars, four classic and two performance models, which clients could use for the weekends. It started well, with the Ferrari Enzo and the E-Type Jaguar proving to be the most popular to roar around the country lanes in. That was until the Enzo was involved in a collision with a drystone wall hidden behind a hedge and written off. The driver, one of Greg's software clients, fared better than the car and received only cuts, bruises and a damaged ego. But in preparing the insurance claim, it became apparent that due to the young age of the driver, the conditions of the lease did not cover this type of write-off.

While Greg was contesting the hidden breach of his

agreement with the leasing company, the Jaguar was hired on a Saturday afternoon by a Mr Johnson, who never returned as agreed on the Sunday evening. When the credit card used to make the deposit was found to have been stolen, Greg passed the address of the client, copied from his driving licence, to the police. In the two days it took the constabulary to trace Mr Johnson, he aged forty-three years, shrank and became wheelchair-bound. No longer the strapping, able-bodied twenty-six-year-old man who had ducked into the E-Type and set the wheels spinning away from Greg in a plume of grit and dust. Suffice to say, clients using stolen identities was also in breach of Greg's leasing agreement. Again, Sally lost her money.

However, I have to concede, albeit begrudgingly, that he was correct about keeping bees. Although, it must be pointed out that on this occasion it was Sally alone who funded the venture. I presume Greg's burnt fingers were still stinging too much from his previous misadventures into the world of entrepreneurs for him to release his own capital. Greg's contribution to the enterprise was the use of his land to keep the hives and an outhouse to prepare the harvested honey. In return, he takes (what with Sally being his sister), only a fifteen per cent cut of any profits raised from honey sales.

Sally bought into the idea of keeping bees wholeheartedly from the start. She sought out an experienced beekeeper from the area and watched and learned from him over time the basic skills and principles of beekeeping. As with all competent apiarists, he was pleased to pass on his knowledge to a willing pupil. When he agreed she was ready, she purchased her first hive in eager anticipation of the arrival of a swarming colony. Her patience was tried for months until, on a sunny afternoon in late July, a swarm was removed from a garden by the apiarist who had tutored Sally. He expertly relocated the bees into her new hive. Since then, she has grown to own twelve colonies and has not experienced a single swarm away from her hives; such is the skill with which she manages her bees. Her honey sales have also increased in popularity, from the humble beginnings of a handwritten sign outside our front door, to monthly farmers' markets, to local shops buying weekly. Her reputation and the quality of the product have lately come to the attention of a national supermarket chain, who are enquiring about stocking her honey in a number of their stores, although their pricing demands leave Greg's fifteen per cent cut seeming almost modest and on the verge of benevolence.

I believe the name she chose for the company is partly the reason it is successful. She called it Bee's Knees Honey.

'So, what is his new idea?' I asked.

'Solar panels.'

'Solar panels? What does Greg know about solar panels?' I quizzed.

"More than you do!'

I snorted loudly as a reply.

Sally ignored my sarcasm and continued, 'Oil is going to run out, Eddie – you are aware of this? The summers are getting hotter – this you *definitely* know; look at the upturn in your bookings. We need to use sustainable energy, solar power being one of the options. He has done research; there is a gap in the market.'

'What research? Where is there a gap?'

'This is what we are going to discuss tomorrow. Eco-Lites is the name we have decided on.'

'So you are not meeting up to discuss how you can lose more money again?'

'Eddie!' she responded irritably.

'Well, how much is it going to cost? We don't have a bottomless pit of money to waste, you know.'

'I don't know how much, that's why we are meeting up.'

'I thought you were meeting up to discuss the "gap in the market"?'

Sally rolled her eyes and went to speak, but I interrupted her.

'So, is he putting his own money in this time? Fifty-fifty? Sixty-forty? What was it, Sally?'

'That is my business!'

'It's our money!'

'No, it's *my* money!' she spat.

The discussion was rapidly turning angry.

'I always thought it strange how all these "once-in-a-lifetime" opportunities only materialised in Greg's mind after your father's death. Nothing when he was alive.'

'Eddie, he is my brother, it is my money; I will do what I want!' she yelled at me.

'Sally, it is *our* money,' I repeated.

'Mine! Mine! Mine!'

'Oh, that is a very grown-up response, Sally,' I returned, knowing it would hit her. She deplores being told she is immature.

'At least he is trying to do something; he's got ideas. Not like you, doing your card tricks and balloon animals for years and years!'

For the second time today, she stood with her back to me at the sink, before turning and walking past me out of the kitchen in silence.

And at this point, as on so many other numerous occasions, I felt a perverse level of comfort in the degradation thrown out by her to me. I stood, my eyes unfocused on the world around me, my mind and memories again tumbling and turning.

'Coming to load the van, boy?' I asked Henry brightly, trying to raise myself from the crumpled position the argument had left me in.

Henry lifted his head and beat his tail on his bedding five times before regaining his previous blissful pose on his side.

'Traitor!' I cursed at him as I retreated through the back door to my van on the driveway.

I looked at the graphics painted on the wing of the van – the bouncy castle, the balloon models and the words *The Party King* in red and yellow letters – and banged my fist hard against it, stirring a low thud in the empty hollow inside. I opened the driver's door, pulled it shut with force and on sitting down, repeatedly thumped the steering wheel in my pent-up frustration.

'Now who is being immature?' I eventually asked myself as I turned the ignition and missed first gear with a grinding crunch.

Chapter 3

Summer Fete Bouncer

The drive to the lock-up takes about ten minutes. I was alone, but even if I had had company, I would not have bothered with conversation. My thoughts consumed me, tormented me, leaving me unable to explore the path to reconciling my differences with Sally.

Yet, as I drove, my mood lifted partially, so that by the time I swung the van into Clifford's yard and parked up, the words *You are a good man, Eddie Dungiven* came back to me again, uttered in my mind from a beautiful mouth with perfect teeth.

Clifford Wilson has rented the lock-up to me for the past sixteen years. Well, I say 'rented' to me in the loosest possible sense. My payments over the years have included performing magic shows for his two nephews at Christmases and birthdays and lending my equipment for free at the annual farmers' country show. Clifford and his wife Mary do not have any children themselves.

I met Clifford for the first time on Christmas Day morning seventeen years ago, our first Christmas in the house, a month after we had moved in. Obviously, this was long before Henry was around to announce any arrivals at our property and Clifford guided his Land Rover to the back door without us being aware, although we were in the kitchen, preparing the Christmas lunch. Only the sound of the car door closing and heavy feet upon the gravel alerted us to the fact that we had a visitor. I opened the back door with curiosity and was confronted with the presence of a formidable man. His outstretched hand and smile confirmed the goodwill of this stranger. As we exchanged a solid handshake, my hand was dwarfed in his as he introduced himself. The hardness and roughness of the skin on his fingers and hand hinted at the manual and outdoor work his life path had included.

Clifford's appearance that day was to welcome us to the community and to invite us up to his farm for food and drinks during the Christmas holidays. We took him up on the offer and headed out the day after St Stephen's Day and found Clifford and Mary to be perfect hosts. Their welcome was totally genuine, their farmhouse warm and cosy as logs crackled and spat in the wood-burning stove as the December wind howled and screeched into the dark, cold night outside. It was after turkey and ham sandwiches, home-made cakes and tea that the opening of a bottle of single malt occurred and Clifford asked me what I did for a living. As Sally looked on proudly, I told Mary and him that I was a children's entertainer, the Party King, performing at birthday parties, Christmas and special occasions. Clifford slapped his huge hand hard on his thigh and bellowed an enormous, happy laugh, as he tilted his head toward the ceiling. He suddenly sat forward and asked excitedly what my act entailed, while Mary smiled next to him, looking at me.

'Well, I begin with a magic show – making things disappear and reappear, card tricks, coin tricks and balloon modelling – and I finish with a disco,' I stated, feeling suddenly awkward in front of this 'man's man' of a farmer and his polite wife.

'That's wonderful!' he laughed. 'Show us a trick, Eddie!'

'I don't have any props with me, Clifford,' I protested.

'Mary! Where is that pack of cards we never use?'

'Why don't you have a man's look for them, Clifford?' Mary teased her husband.

He attempted to retaliate, but stopped as Mary got up with a chuckle and tapped his knee playfully before heading out of the room.

She returned in a few minutes sheepishly claiming the pack could not be found. Clifford was extremely disappointed at this. So I offered to go out to my van, where I knew I had a new gaff pack in the glove compartment, this news brought a smile to Clifford's face. I raced out into the foul weather as quickly as possible to retrieve the pack but when back in the warmth of the farm house, I felt incredibly nervous as Clifford and Mary stared at me expectedly. Sally noted my apprehension and squeezed my arm for reassurance. Performing to primary school children who would applaud anything remotely exciting was a very different proposition to two adults watching intently my every single move.

I took the cards in my hand, and as I began to shuffle them, all my fears evaporated as the performance commenced. I decided to perform Sally's favourite trick, simple but effective.

After laying out four aces face up in separate piles and adding three additional cards on top of each, Clifford was left holding, as intended, four aces, which he had seen form part of the separate piles moments before.

'That was brilliant!' Clifford, Mary and Sally clapped.

'Thank you – it's called McDonald's Aces!' I responded.

'Do another for us?' requested Mary.

Three card tricks later, and with Mary and Clifford muttering to each other, 'I don't know how he did that', I decided to stop.

'I don't know about kiddies, you should perform to adults,' Clifford commented.

'Really?'

'Certainly!' came back Clifford, with Mary nodding by his side.

'I've told him this before!' interjected Sally.

'Okay, okay! I will think about it!'

'You should, really, it's a talent,' stated Mary.

'Actually, I was thinking of expanding and starting doing bouncy castles and inflatables as well for the parties,' I stated, trying to change the subject.

'I've seen those things!' laughed Clifford. 'Sounds like a great idea, would love to have a go on one myself!'

We all laughed at the thought of this huge man bouncing up and down on a rubber castle painted with storybook characters.

'It's the storage of the things that is the problem. I don't have the room,' I said.

'Well, I have here. Lots of space: the barn, outhouses, a lock-up. You are welcome to use it.'

'That's very kind, but we can't do that!' said Sally.

'Nonsense! It is my pleasure. I would show you the space tonight, but that wind out there is something else.'

'Okay, let's talk about it all properly in the New Year, Clifford.'

'What is there to talk about?'

'Well, rent to begin with – how much do you want for it?' I asked.

'Oh, we will work something out.' Clifford waved the question away. 'In the meantime,' he continued with a giggle, 'how about showing us another magic trick?!'

And since that first encounter, Clifford's enthusiasm for the tricks has not in any way diminished. It really was his drive and persistence that convinced me to branch out and perform magic shows for an adult audience too, and I advertised in the following spring. It took time for the bookings to start to build, but now a third of my work takes me to birthday, engagement and anniversary celebrations in restaurants, pubs and retirement homes.

Up until two years ago, at the annual country show, he was always the first person to throw off his shoes, clamber on board an inflatable and bounce wildly with arms flailing around, giggling like a small child. You could have called it a kind of a tradition. But last summer, he wasn't standing next to me, willing the bouncy castle to life. Although it was strange for him to not be by my side as the inflatable reached its full height and became ready for the inaugural bounce, I presumed he was busy elsewhere, doing something else at the show. I delayed as long as possible, sending out two messages over the public address system for Clifford to head over to the bouncy castle, which only seemed to attract children to the area, who proceeded to circle the inflatable like ravenous sharks. I am used to keeping children entertained, but eventually I realised that jokes, songs and silly voices could no longer compete with a forty-foot yellow slide with separate bouncing area, I had to allow the children on.

I selected a troop of excited preschoolers first, knowing their interest would be minimal and they would want to come off before the bigger children invaded and conquered the structure. Clifford arrived moments later, claiming he had not heard the messages. However, his timing of arrival was so precise, it was as if he had been watching and waiting. He did sound genuinely disappointed to have missed 'his turn', but argued it was not fair for the waiting kiddies if he had a go at that point. Exactly the same scenario occurred this summer too.

By the time I had turned off the engine and opened the door, Clifford was walking across the yard toward me. After fifteen extra years of summer sun and winter wind and rain, his face now resembles the texture of knarred wood, every crease and wrinkle seemingly crafted by the effects of the weather.

'How are you, Eddie?' he asked as I closed the door.

'Okay,' I lied, trying to keep my true feelings to myself as I walked toward the lock-up.

Clifford looked into the cab. 'Not got your pup with you?' he asked with disappointment.

After five years Clifford still refers to Henry as a pup. This is probably due to his continued immaturity, which Clifford does exploit with his use of key words to send Henry into a frenzy whenever he sees him. To Henry the phrases 'Where's your ball?' and 'Are you coming?', uttered in a hurried, excited voice, are enough to send him rushing around the yard before stopping and staring at us, his head tilted to one side with his tongue half exposed over his jaws, before he continues his erratic chase once more. Clifford is the one person who doesn't mind Henry's behaviour toward his own dogs. He actually laughs at Henry's stand-offs with his Border collie, Ben. Ben, being much older and set in his ways, is used to working with sheep that always run from him. He is curious about the younger male's attitude, but not thrilled with the nips he endures when the cross-breed gets excited. As Ben submits, Clifford always tells him to not be such a wimp. His other dogs do not really bother much with Henry, keeping themselves in the barn or on the far side of the yard, sniffing and investigating; content within their own worlds.

It was Clifford who persuaded me to give Henry a home. He believes that in country life all animals have a job to do and they are not pets. On Clifford's farm, Ben works with him controlling the sheep, in particular moving the ewes and the lambs up to higher ground in the late spring to feast on the newly shooting heather on the slopes that surround his home. This effort gives the lambs' meat a tender taste when they are sold for slaughter later in the year.

A younger Border collie, Alfie, now rides in the Land Rover with Ben and Clifford too. He will in time take over from Ben. Clifford maintains that within any litter of Border collies, one will be an exceptional sheepdog, while the others will not have the temperament necessary to trust them entirely with lambs. Alfie has already demonstrated that he has the attributes to succeed Ben. Although I have asked Clifford, I have never been sure what happens to the remaining rejected puppies from a litter.

In Clifford's barn, three Jack Russells live. Patch, Bobby

and Molly deter rats, drawn by the abundance of animal feed, from being around the yard, and if any are caught they are killed swiftly in the dogs' jaws with a violent shake of the head that breaks the rats' necks. The three never tire of their duty.

Two cats patrol the barn and outhouses for smaller vermin — and are rewarded daily with substantial leftovers from Mary's kitchen.

A peep of chickens provide fresh eggs for Clifford, Mary and their friends and neighbours, and three geese act as boundary protection, their territorial instinct a perfect deterrent to any unsuspecting intruder.

In Clifford's eyes Henry also served a job. Not a job that could be categorised in his own domain, but a job nonetheless: to provide Sally and me with a focus to love and enable us to move on. But to me he is a pet.

'No, he's not with me today, Clifford. Henry couldn't be bothered to get up,' I stated, pulling up the steel shutter of the lock-up.

'You have him ruined, letting him sleep inside! He has a thick coat for a reason, you know,' replied Clifford with a grin.

I ignored his response and flicked on the light switch inside and waited for the fluorescent lighting to flash and buzz into life, its power illuminating the contents within. The world of the Party King.

'Are you around tomorrow, Eddie? I want to ask you a favour,' continued Clifford, seemingly unaware of my mood.

'I have three jobs tomorrow: two bouncy castles and a magic show. Why, what's up?'

'I need to replace some fence posts in the back field; sheep going in. Meant to do it weeks ago, but you know me, sidetracked by all manner of other things around the place. I wondered if you would use the post driver , as my shoulder is still playing up.'

'If I am back in time, certainly – if not is Monday okay?'

Clifford nodded in response, and I knew and respected that the excuse of his shoulder injury was to cover up the shortness of breath the medical professionals call 'the angina symptoms' he was sure to endure in continually lifting and pounding the driver -onto the tops of the posts. The same symptoms that have sadly confined his summer fete bouncing to memory.

Not so many years ago, he would have been able to keep up with me in any manual task despite the thirty-year age gap between us. But in recent years a lifetime's diet of fried food, weekends drinking bitter and working with harsh chemicals around the farm have caught up with him to such an extent that he has to be careful of the level of work he can undertake. Thankfully for Mary and the doctors he has been sensible in his approach and will use a younger, more able workforce when necessary. This is only fair and just for someone who has spent the first part of their life looking after and helping others.

'Come on in for tea and a chat with us when you are done, Eddie,' requested Clifford, heading toward the back door of the farmhouse.

'Will do, Clifford,' I shouted after him.

I also remember a time when he would have eagerly helped me load the van, his body built perfectly for the physical exertion required. Health is fragile, precious and utterly taken for granted.

I surveyed the lock-up, mentally rechecking what I needed for tomorrow, before heading for the decks and stand and placing them in the far end of the van. Next I added the lights and amp for the disco. I rechecked the bookings in the diary in the cab, before heading back into the lock-up and loading up the first of the two inflatables, a standard square castle, on my sack truck and transferring it to the van. I returned to load the second, the one I wanted to check in the diary, still not convinced that the forty-foot obstacle course would fit into the garden it was booked for. But it was what the customer insisted they wanted on the telephone; in their mind, I am assuming, the biggest and the most expensive had to be the best for their precious child. I hoped they had a contingency plan if, as I suspected, it didn't fit into their garden. I wheeled it out to the van and struggled to load it inside, and returned for three air fans, ground pegs and a repair kit. Finally, I searched for the accessories I needed for the magic show: my folding table, satin cloth, magic cloak for the birthday child to wear as they performed a trick, wands, top hat, playing cards, rope trick, ring trick, handkerchiefs, modelling balloons and Eric the Psychic Duck – all were loaded into my red props box marked in yellow on the side with *The Party King* and pushed into the back of the van.

I returned to the lock-up and reached to turn off the lights, my eyes focused, as on so many other occasions, on the neatly folded inflatable stored against the far wall. Dust hung loosely over the surface. The pink turrets were hidden and the faces and wings of the leaping painted characters were cut in two by the neat creases of the folds, the full majesty of the fairy castle not seen in an inflated state for the past seven years. I sighed as darkness invaded, inviting a silent, constant void once more.

Turning toward the farmhouse, I made a mental note to pick up more modelling balloons on Monday from the wholesaler's. I always make balloon models to be given out with the party bags whilst the children eat their food. Pink cats for the girls, blue pirate swords for the boys. Experience has taught me to try and finish this task, hand over the models in a cardboard box to the parents and depart before the effects of sugary drinks and artificially coloured party food combine to induce an unnatural upsurge of energy in the children. If I do not manage this before they have consumed their fill, invariably their attention returns to me, and their chemical imbalances ensure the party ends abruptly to the sound of fighting pirates, screaming girls, exploding balloons and crying. Shouting, stressed-out parents apologise to me, swearing that their child and their friends are not normally like this. The explanation is always the same: 'They must be tired from the excitement of the day.'

The flowerpots guarding the kitchen door to the farmhouse reflected the change in season, like dusk, when the light to a driver is neither one thing nor another. The winter pansies' blooms lay tired, faded and torn, preparing to hand over the custody of colour to the spring bulb tubers that beneath the soil frantically threw their green spears ever upwards, the tips still concealing the energy that would burst through as swaying yellow trumpets in a few weeks' time.

'Hello, Eddie,' called Mary from the kitchen. 'Tea?'

I spied her camel coat; her best coat, draped over a chair at the table and presumed she was on her way out for the evening.

'You off out, Mary?'

'So you are going, then?' Clifford barked in agitation as he entered the kitchen.

I looked at him in confusion, surprised by the tone of his voice.

'She's seeing that bloody medium,' he continued.

'Now, Clifford, stop that!' replied Mary in annoyance.

'He's a fake, trading on people's vulnerability,' stated Clifford gruffly.

'Sorry, who is?'

'I am going to see Ignatius McKenzie, the medium, at the village hall tonight, Eddie. He doesn't approve,' said Mary, nodding at Clifford while pouring the boiled water from the kettle into the teapot.

'Who?' I questioned.

'Ignatius McKenzie, you must have heard of him?' said Mary.

I shook my head.

'Why won't you listen? It's a waste of time and money. Nothing but saying what people want to hear. It's wrong,' Clifford said.

'Well, that's your opinion, Clifford, but I know he has a gift. I know two people he has got messages to, and he relayed to them things that no one else would know about them. Maybe Robert can come through for me.'

'I've told you, the dead should be left in peace, including your brother,' responded Clifford in a tone that indicated the conversation was ending.

Mary started to speak, but stopped herself and instead reached for her coat over the back of the chair. She turned to me with tears forming in her eyes, said goodbye and walked out of the back door without a further word to Clifford.

In all my years of knowing them, I had never seen or heard Clifford and Mary have a cross word. But this exchange and exit fused the impression that this disagreement had been simmering for some time.

Clifford and I now stood in the kitchen in silence, him looking at the floor, me staring into the oncoming night through the back-door window. This current situation left me feeling uncomfortable, and like Mary, I too wanted to inject balance into Clifford's last statement, but felt compelled to remain silent.

'I am going to head off, Clifford,' I eventually said, without the tea being poured from the pot, and he merely nodded in response, still looking at the floor as I moved through the back door.

On the journey home I broke my silence in my mind and formed my response to Clifford's retort. Yes, the dead should be left in peace, but so too should those of us left behind.

Chapter 4

Sugar Rush

The sobbing had started.

From the kitchen, I could hear Jennifer and Sally in the living room; Jennifer, I presumed, was bemoaning the whole world being against her, while Sally soothingly attempted to prove otherwise. Contrary to what I had decided earlier, I was now compelled to not stay in the kitchen for the evening; I wanted to let Jennifer know that it was fine to set up a studio, that the world was not against her – I concluded nobody should ever feel that lonely. Plus, I entirely agreed with the look Henry gave me as he wandered over to my side. *Make it stop*, he pleaded with his eyes.

'I know, boy,' I reassured him. 'Let's go in.'

In an attempted to encourage a level of decorum to descend unto the scene beyond the closed living-room door, I announced our arrival from within the safety of the hallway with a cheery and noisy, 'C'mon, boy' to Henry and waited for a few moments to ensure our entrance was not unexpected.

In the living room, less than half a sponge cake was presented on a large plate on the coffee table. Sitting solidly on Jennifer's substantial thighs was a smaller plate, decorated only with crumbs, providing firm evidence as to the whereabouts of the remainder of the cake.

'Hello, Jennifer,' I stated brightly.

'Eddie,' she mumbled.

'How are you doing?'

Sally threw me a look that screamed, *Why did you ask that?*, and my neutral words seemed to simultaneously invite the wailing from deep inside Jennifer to recommence.

'Jenny, is it okay if I tell Eddie?' soothed Sally, holding her friend's hand.

'Sure, he can have a laugh about it too,' she sobbed.

'Eddie will not laugh.'

'Really?' snorted Jennifer.

'You know he won't.'

'Come on, Sally, it'll be a huge joke to him, I know everyone is laughing behind my back about it.'

'You are upset, naturally, but no one is laughing at you, no one is being unkind, Jenny. Can I tell him?' she continued.

I stood watching this exchange about me as if I wasn't actually in the room. It was as if my character was being alternately torn and defended before my very eyes.

Jennifer leaned forward and cut herself another substantial slice of cake, transferred it to her smaller plate and sighed deeply as she drew it toward her mouth.

'You have no option but to tell him now,' she replied through a mouthful of cake.

Sally looked up at me.

'Jenny has been working voluntarily at the animal sanctuary and rescue centre,' began Sally, looking toward her friend, seeking reassurance to continue. 'She went there one day after she'd struck a cat that ran out in front of her car about a mile out from the place and wanted to see what they could do for it. They were short-staffed and she ended up trying to save the cat with the vet there. The cat didn't survive, had to be put down, which of course upset her, but she enjoyed the experience of teamwork and being that close to animals, so she agreed to return to help out in the future. It was the first time she had been back to the centre after she brought home her last rescue terrier. Initially, she went for one afternoon a week, but that soon increased to six days a week – dog-walking, cat-grooming, mucking out and generally being kind. How long did you say you have been doing this?'

'Four months,' stated Jennifer through tightly shut lips, hiding the final piece of cake now in her mouth.

I nodded in interest.

'Why did you not tell anyone, Jenny?'

Jennifer just shrugged her shoulders.

'Jenny was enjoying it at first, gaining confidence in herself. Although she struggled with interacting with the other members of staff, in particular a stilted man, Faruk, who seemed incapable and unwilling to speak to her at all in the office, which they manned together on a regular basis. Instead, she took every opportunity to enthusiastically show people the cats and dogs that needed to be rehomed.'

'After a couple of weeks a Mr Wallace came to the centre wanting to rehome a dog. It was unusual for a man to be there looking for a dog for himself and not accompanied by children to choose a family pet. As always, Faruk appeared to be busy – doing what, Jenny was not sure. So she took the initiative and showed him around the pens. As they walked, they chatted about the dogs inside the cages and the sad reasons why many of them are there. He eventually decided on a young spaniel cross and Jenny arranged, as always, for a home check visit to be carried out the following week, prior to adoption.

'The checks came back fine, didn't they Jenny and he returned to complete the paper work and pick up the dog the next day?'

Jennifer nodded in agreement.

'Two days later, a bouquet of flowers was delivered to the centre for Jenny, from a Mr Wallace as a thank-you for her help in choosing the dog. Jenny had never had flowers bought for her before and she blushed when anyone came into the reception area and marvelled at them, but she thought Faruk seemed agitated by the repeated spectacle, although he would not say a word.

'The next week Mr Wallace appeared once again and asked to see another dog for company for the first – he had named him Harvey. He specifically requested Jenny to accompany him and told her on leaving the reception area that Harvey had adjusted so quickly to his new life; that he felt compelled to return to try and help another dog. Again, he chatted to Jenny, their conversation easy and relaxed as they examined the pens, and again, Mr Wallace settled for another spaniel cross,' Sally explained. 'And this time, there was no need for checks, so he took him straight away, this is correct isn't it, Jenny?'

Jennifer nodded.

'Do you want to carry on?' enquired Sally.

'No, no, you.' Jennifer waved the suggestion away.

'He came back a couple of weeks later, as the centre was closing. Jenny told him she couldn't help, but he replied he was there to take her out. Jenny was flabbergasted and argued no. Mr Wallace would not take no for an answer, but conceded that if she wanted to go home and change first, he would pick her up at 7.30. She made excuse after excuse; her dogs at home needed to be seen to, she needed to hang out her washing, needed to go food shopping. But in the end she gave way, knowing her resistance was futile, as Mr Wallace rejected each excuse with logic and reasoning. She went home, fed the dogs, showered, dried her hair, applied a little make-up and struggled to decide what clothes to wear.'

I looked at Sally quizzically on hearing that last statement.

'You wouldn't understand, Eddie, it's a woman thing,' stated Sally with a smile, which also produced a half-grin from Jennifer.

'He picked her up and they went out to dinner. He was charming, complimentary and asked to take her out again soon. He returned to the centre once more a few days later, again looking to rehome a rescue dog. He said the amount of joy the dogs had given him was immeasurable. This time he chose a beagle cross and arranged another date. Jenny,' continued Sally, 'how many times did you go out with him?'

'Seven,' came the reply, after some thought.

'On the sixth date, he was unusually quiet. When Jenny quizzed him, he mentioned he had money worries. Real money worries – he owed a considerable amount to a betting syndicate and payment was overdue. He needed a cash injection to enable him to manage this, or else his property was in danger. Jenny offered to put some money forward – she wanted to help, she had found someone she trusted and who shared her love of animals. He thanked her, said he hadn't told her for that reason and declined the offer. But Jenny insisted she wanted to help and this time it was her that wouldn't take no for an answer. He eventually, and seemingly reluctantly, agreed to accept her assistance. She agreed to transfer £18,000 into a bank account the next day.'

'How much?!' I exclaimed loudly, before realising what I had said.

Jennifer looked down at her hands in her lap.

'Why?' I added, gaining a level of composure.

Sally looked at her friend to check the wailing was not about to begin again as the rawness was exposed once more.

'I've already said, Eddie: Jenny had found someone she trusted; she'd never had that before in a relationship. It was a lot of money, most of Jenny's savings, but she did it on trust, because he made her feel good about herself and was he was kind to animals – you know that means a lot to her.'

I knew what was coming. Knew Jennifer's naivety had left her £18,000 short in her bank account. I knew that 'Mr Wallace', once he had the money, would never have been heard from again. But then I remembered that Sally said this occurred on the sixth date – they had dated seven times.

'The day the money arrived in his account, he met Jenny at the centre. With her help, he chose another dog, a collie this time, and said he realised he enjoyed having a pack around him, with himself as the alpha male. He took her to lunch and was back to being his normal charming self – he thanked her for her generosity and advised her he would pay back the money in full with interest by the end of the month. Jenny argued there was no hurry, she was glad to help. He dropped her off at the centre and picked up the collie.'

Sally went quiet.

'And?' I enquired.

Silence.

'I am guessing you haven't seen him since?' I stated, trying to not sound judgemental or condescending.

'Eddie, it's worse than that,' said Sally, looking up.

'Oh?'

'It's true; Jenny hasn't seen him since then. And yes, she is hurt and feels humiliated. But it's what happened yesterday that is worrying.'

Jennifer leant forward and placed her head in her hands and stated to sob. Henry sat closer to me, sensing the crescendo might increase.

'Jenny had a visit at her home yesterday from the RSPCA and police. She was asked to voluntarily accompany the officers to the police station to help with their enquiries.'

'Enquires into what?' I asked.

'That is what she asked. She was told it was a serious matter involving a Mr Wallace. As soon as she heard the name, she asked anxiously if he was okay, and her worried tone was noted by the two police officers and the RSPCA inspector. She was asked again to voluntarily accompany the police officers – one male, one female – to the police station. She agreed to go.

'Once in the interview room, she was asked what her relationship with Mr Wallace was. Jenny responded that he was a friend with whom she had connected through their mutual love of animals. She sensed the attitude of the police officers change with her statement. The female officer switched on the TV monitor sitting on the table between them and connected a laptop to it.'

Sally turned to Jennifer. 'Are you okay if I tell Eddie?' she probed.

Jennifer sighed and looked up at the ceiling. I had no idea what was going on.

'No, Sally, I'll tell him,' she said eventually. 'The image was grainy; I couldn't make it out at first. Then I realised it was a dog, hanging, swaying from a metal bar held in its jaws. After a few minutes, I wondered why they were showing me this. Then the image changed suddenly. Without warning, the same dog was in a pen when another dog was thrown in by an unseen man. The first dog became instantly aggressive at this intrusion and lunged toward the other in a frenzied attack. an I was horrified and closed my eyes, but they shouted at me to look at the screen. It was tearing it to pieces, it wouldn't stop. I looked away, but they again shouted at me to keep watching. I cannot get the image to leave my mind nor the sound of the pitiful whimpers. It was then I realised the dog being torn apart was Harvey, the dog Mr Wallace had first rehomed. On the monitor it lay motionless as the other dog walked away, blood and saliva caught around its muzzle.

'The filming stopped abruptly and was replaced by another of carnage inflicted by the same dog on the second dog Mr Wallace took. The scene was repeated twice more. I wanted to cry and scream, but nothing came out at all. Then the female officer asked me if I recognised any of the dogs in the videos. I told her I recognised all of them from the rescue centre.

'She erupted in anger and said she couldn't believe my attitude. I didn't understand what was happening. She then said, "Did you, or did you not, supply those dogs to Elliot Wallace, knowing they were to be butchered as part of a barbaric training regime for his illegal fighting dog?"

'I answered no! But she stated, "That isn't what he says." She continued, "He is in custody and has said you selected the dogs with him in the centre. Is that not true?"

'I answered, "Yes, but he wanted to rehome the dogs, give them another chance"; I argued I would never be involved in something like that – I love animals.

'The male officer snorted at this answer, before asking, "So you love animals? If that is so, why did you place a bet of £18,000 for his dog to win its next fight?" I pleaded my innocence, but then remembered he'd requested I wired the payment to a "DG Syndicate" bank account, not his own – he said it would be easier to pay the money direct to the creditors.'

Jennifer stopped speaking and looked down at the floor.

'But they have let you go? The police, I mean,' I asked.

'Pending further enquires,' Jennifer and Sally replied in unison.

'What does that actually mean?' I wondered aloud.

'I was allowed to leave the station when they were convinced I didn't know anyone from DG Syndicate, but only on condition I didn't leave the country. They drove me home and made me hand over my passport to them. This is so serious, Eddie; I don't know what to do.'

And with her final words the wailing began again, as intense and as raw as that I had witnessed from the sanctuary of the kitchen. It appeared Jennifer had reached this same point of her story, the enormity of it catching her again just as it had as I had innocently uttered, 'How are you doing?' to her on my arrival in the living room.

'Jennifer, we will get this sorted,' I stated, trying to sound upbeat.

Jennifer dabbed her eyes with the cuff of her sleeve. The entire situation did indeed sound hopeless. But there had to be a way; had to be proof for the police that Jennifer was merely naive and not involved in some dog-fighting gang. I struggled to understand how someone could willingly be that cruel to another person or animal.

'What about the people you work with – they could vouch for you? What was the man called that worked with you on the desk; he must be able to help?' I enquired.

'Faruk, you mean?' replied Jennifer.

'Yes, that's the name – he could help you.'

'Huh, I don't think so. He never really spoke to me, gave the impression I was an irritant to him. Our working relationship deteriorated from me initiating conversation and him replying with yes/no answers, to complete silence between us,' remembered Jennifer.

I was struggling now. Sally was so much better at navigating through an extraordinary situation than I was, but she seemed content for me to continue, for me to take the lead. But I just sat, not knowing what to do or say next.

Henry relieved me of my duty. He suddenly awoke, wandered over to Jennifer and placed his head on her knees and looked up at her.

'Hello, Henry,' she cooed through a smile as she gently patted his forehead.

With the change in mood sparked by Henry's craving for attention, I felt empowered to continue.

'Jennifer,' I began, 'Sally told me about the plan of using the spare room as a studio. I think it is a great idea, it would be really rewarding for you. You can set it up any time you like.'

'Not going to be any good to me in prison, is it, Eddie?' she replied, still patting Henry and not looking at me.

'You are not going to prison!' I responded.

'You are not, Jenny,' concurred Sally.

'We'll see,' Jennifer sighed.

'How are you going to prison when you are not guilty of any crime?' pleaded Sally. 'It will be okay, Jenny.'

'But Sally, I let the attention and flattery get in the way of my judgement. I should have known; I should have seen what was going on. Instead I ignored it all and basked in the illusion of being wanted,' stated Jennifer calmly and with reason, in contrast to her previous reaction.

'That's very easy to say with hindsight, Jenny,' stated Sally with confidence. 'But how were you to know what was... going on?' she concluded meekly, reluctant to unleash into the room once again the image of dogs chosen for torture and execution, for fear of the imminent eruption from Jennifer.

The moment passed, thankfully without incident, and silence descended on the room. With Henry now contentedly asleep at Jennifer's feet the task of invoking a change of mood lay firmly with Sally and me. But again I struggled with what to say, and looked toward Sally for guidance.

Silently, Sally placed a hand in her friend's palms and with her other began to gently rub her back between the shoulder blades. Jennifer breathed deeply edas her shoulders visibly lowered at the soothing touch. I watched, transfixed, as this simple gesture appeared to remove a degree of the stress and discomfort that tormented Jennifer. I wondered to myself, as Jennifer laid her head upon Sally's shoulder, if I ever could be receptive to such a technique, or would my ingrained instinct of ignorance and denial form an impregnable barrier that could not be breached or broken?

'Shall I make some more tea?' I uttered.

Both women nodded and I retreated to the kitchen. I heard the familiar sound of Henry's claws clipping on the tiles in the hallway as I reached the sink.

I made the tea, delivered it to the living room and retreated back to the kitchen. I remained there, watching *Match of the Day*, to the sound of Henry's snoring, until I heard Jennifer saying goodbye to Sally.

Jennifer popped her head around the door and said goodbye to me, and I walked out into the hallway as she left through the front door. Sally closed the door, locked it and turned back into the hallway.

'That was lovely to say to her, Eddie, thank you,' gushed Sally, striding toward me.

'She looked like she needed help.'

'Thank you,' she said again.

I smiled in reply, but remembered the unpleasantness that had passed between us earlier that evening.

'I am going to go up and have a relaxing bath. Why not come and join me?' Sally asked, kissing me lightly on the cheek.

'I need to sort him out and double-check the van,' I stated, as the *Match of the Day* theme music drifted through from the kitchen.

'Oh, I had better wash up the cups and plates in the living room,' remembered Sally with disappointment in her voice.

'I'll do them,' I responded.

'Okay, but don't be long and come to bed,' she soothed, climbing the stairs.

I took out Henry's leash from its place in the cupboard under the stairs. Miraculously, his doggy sixth sense sprang into action: before I had even closed the cupboard door, or called him for that matter, he appeared, his tail wagging the entire back half of his body with excitement, knowing we were heading out.

I don't have Henry on the leash at this time of night; instead I carry it and give him freedom to explore and only attach the leash if we meet any vehicles travelling the road, which is very rare. We have two routes we can take. From the house we turn left and travel twenty metres to where the lane forks. Henry always runs on in front and waits at the fork, waiting for me to decide our direction. Tonight I chose the right-hand lane, the longest route.

Later, he couldn't believe his luck, as he stood waiting for me halfway along the lane. His breathing was heavy with his constant inquisitiveness, willing him to search the darkened hedgerows with his powerful snout. I waved him on further; in contrast, normally at this point we turn for home. We journeyed on and he stopped periodically, looking at me, knowing this was to be longer adventure than those he is accustomed to at this hour and not sure whether or not he should carry on.

Back home, I gave Henry some fresh water, carried the plates and cups from the living room and washed and rinsed them all very thoroughly in the sink. In contrast to my usual behaviour, tonight I dried them all and put them away in their appropriate places.

I patted Henry goodnight, turned off the kitchen light and headed across the hallway and up the stairs.

I crept into the darkened bedroom and discovered Sally's sleeping form on the left side of the bed. I quietly undressed and slipped under the duvet beside her. I could feel she was naked and had been waiting for me. But the unmistakable musky odour of sex emanating from beneath the covers indicated she had satisfied her needs some time ago, without me even being there.

I heard her breathing lightly through the darkness next to me and yearned to know what she was dreaming. Closing my eyes tightly, wishing the recurring image of the discarded bouncy castle to leave me, I tried to pray, to urge the desire for physical love with my wife to somehow return. Instead, as my eyes stung with the effort of squeezing them shut, the words came back to me yet again from earlier today. *You are a good man, Eddie Dungiven* was uttered in my mind, from the same beautiful mouth with perfect teeth.

Chapter 5

A Book of Perfect Brilliance

I always start the day with a cup of tea. Ceylon tea always taken black. I always sip looking out of the French doors, focusing and contemplating the day ahead. I blew over the top of the mug; a sudden miniature mist was deposited on the door by my action and as it cleared I sensed myself becoming distracted by the spring explosion of growth and life displayed outside, behind the glass. This domain was all Sally's work, all Sally's vision.

I remember when we moved into the house seventeen years ago, standing bemused just the other side of the glass I now stared through on a foggy, dead morning in November. Sally jumped around excitedly, planning and plotting, her breath hanging visibly in the dense air as she spoke excitedly.

'Sorry, Sally, I just cannot see it,' I confessed truthfully, staring at the mud and the tired, feeble grass.

'It's a blank canvas, Eddie, just look at it!' she said, her glee and frustration merging into one emotion.

I shrugged my shoulders, indicating my indifference, as I stared at where she now pointed, partly as I was enjoying the playful interaction between us, but mostly because I honestly couldn't see her vision.

'That's where the vegetables will go,' she said, pointing helpfully to make me feel part of it. 'And over there will be—'

'What vegetables?' I demanded, interrupting her.

She looked up, as though jolted from a dream; suddenly her brow began to crease, hinting at the thought process my words may have instigated. Then her mouth opened to form words.

'And don't say *lots* of vegetables,' I teased, knowing what her answer could be.

Her mouth closed and she smiled at me.

'I need to do a bit of research!' She laughed. 'But that's where they are going to go,' she added, as if the content of the beds was mere detail and the location was the important decision.

She looked on again.

'Over there we will have borders – I don't want them uniform, like Dad's are, I want a wavy edge to them and –toward the back of the garden, I want some trees, trees that blossom in the spring and burn red with the arrival of autumn.'

'Anything else – an ornate fountain perhaps? A half-ruined folly?' I added sarcastically.

'No, no, nothing like that, Eddie,' she replied, reading my sarcasm as a genuine suggestion. 'I want to create an environment to entice wildlife. Plants and cover to draw in lots of insects – caterpillars, flies and beetles – to encourage the birds to visit and feed too, and bees, lots of bees to pollinate the flowers that will produce seeds that will replenish the borders. I want to be out in the sunshine, picking salad leaves and beans and popping them on a plate within minutes, or digging out potatoes from the ice-cold ground ready for our Christmas dinner.'

Suddenly, my cynicism evaporated.

'It all works, doesn't it?' I stated as I finally allowed Sally's vision to reveal itself to me.

She nodded excitedly.

'Eddie, I am going to take photographs and keep them in a scrapbook, as it develops – it is going to be perfectly brilliant!'

With the plan decided, we turned to head back inside, the cold soaking into us. Once inside, the weather let its feelings be known for not being consulted in the process. It rained and rained and rained, day after day after day.

Two weeks later, I lay in a bath of steaming hot, lavender-infused water, trying to revive my back, to coax my vertebrae into their normal positions. My body was used to modelling balloons, not turning sods of heavy, waterlogged clay, and that was all I had done for the entire day.

As I headed out for the second day of toil, Sally joined me. She had spent the previous evening, as I sat trying to ignore the dull throb that pulsated deep inside my lower back, engrossed in a gardening book she had borrowed from the library, taking notes, looking through the index, checking and double-checking – for what, I could not be sure, but she didn't stop until exhaustion brought her study to an end for the night.

As I dug, Sally was hovering, waiting, as if she had something to say. Something she wasn't sure how to broach.

I turned over the clay in silence. I did not want to talk, did not want to invite any dialogue to begin; instead I tried to ignore my back as it screamed with every movement and simply broke up the earth with a garden fork, a sharp stabbing sound reflecting my labour as I stuck the soil with the back of the fork, breaking the silence. Huge lumps of clay clung the soles of my shoes as I worked, and oozed upward and over their tops, soaking my socks, as I stood in the area I had dug over the day before.

'Eddie?' said Sally probingly.

'Um-hmm?' I replied, trying to sound casual.

'I don't know how to say this.'

'Say what?' I asked, still digging, still turning over, still aching.

'The vegetables cannot go there,' she replied hurriedly.

I didn't answer, nor stop. I just kept on digging.

'I said, the vegetables cannot—'

'I heard you,' I said, trying to dislodge a piece of sticky clay stuck fast between the prongs and remain calm.

'I read it last night: any vegetable needs maximum sunlight to thrive. They will not have a chance to reach their potential unless we change their position; this area is too shady; it faces east.'

The clay would not move from the fork as I hit it repeatedly, ever harder, flat into the ground. I gave up and thrust the fork vertically into the soil.

'Why didn't you tell me last night? Save me doing all this?' I nodded viciously toward the ground, my voice raising.

'That's what I was checking, over and over last night; I wanted to see if there were any that would grow comfortably in that space. When I discovered there weren't, I didn't know how to tell you, so I went to bed.'

I didn't reply.

'What, nothing will grow in there?' I finally asked.

'Not comfortably, but Beetroot and Brussels sprouts will tolerate it.'

And with these words, I knew she had me. I detested both and she knew this, but Sally loves sprouts and enjoys beetroot.

My loathing is drawn from my childhood, when at numerous Christmas dinners I engaged in a stand-off with Father, culminating with, and I quote, 'No dessert for you, lad, until those bloody things are all eaten up.' Knowing I couldn't win the argument, I forced down every piece and with each chew and swallow of sprout, I held off the need to retch, until eventually the plate was clear. But to be honest, enduring the cold, soggy vegetables was bearable when a bowlful of hot, sweet, rich Christmas pudding and custard was my reward.

On the other hand, beetroot was in a different league altogether. For some reason, it was always a school day when I would pass round the side of the house to the back door and my heart would sink as the earthy, pungent odour attacked my nostrils without mercy, indicating the beets had boiled for hours already just to soften their skins. I visualised an imaginary purple haze drifting from the pan, rising like a poisonous gas over a battlefield. The real battle was yet to commence with my father at the table as the dinner was served, but the outcome was never good. To this day, I maintain that beetroot smells like earth, tastes like earth and is not a colour that should be eaten. Furthermore, anything that takes that long to prepare to become 'edible' should really be left alone. In summary, it is just plain wrong!

'This won't go to waste, though,' Sally added helpfully, looking at the bare earth I had exposed.

She seemed oblivious to my annoyance; to the time I had wasted. But being the way she was, I let it go.

'What will it be, then?'

'Another border, there are plants that seek shadier areas – I read that too! Plants like ferns, hostas and viburnum would love it in there. We can prepare it in the early spring; get it ready for them then.'

'We could plant your suggestions in there,' I offered, unable to utter the names of the hated vegetables.

'And what, have you moan like a child with every mouthful? I don't think so,' Sally teased.

I couldn't help but smile to myself, but tried to remain stern.

I stood, staring at the dug earth, the fork standing proud, and then upwards to the remainder of the garden.

'Where then?' I asked quietly.

'Back there.' Sally indicated toward the rear of the garden.

We walked out an area together and rubbed our boots into the grass at right angles, to indicate the corners of the plot.

With the task complete, I moved into position, ready to cultivate an area the gardening experts agreed was a superior space. Before I began, I moved the wheelbarrow next to the area I was now set to work, to enable the capture of the turf I would first attempt to skim off the bed, before turning the soil. I lifted the fork, preparing to split the ground, when Sally yelled.

'Wait!'

I turned around, alarmed at the tone of her voice, and saw her rushing in through the French doors into the house.

'Hang on, Eddie!' she shouted over her shoulder.

I waited, unsure of her intention. I looked toward the house and patiently stood, waiting for her form to emerge from the interior. As I continued to stand, I felt the winter cold cling to me as my mind and body became unoccupied. It seemed a considerable time since she had retreated, and I moved my feet in the damp grass and rubbed my hands together in a futile effort to generate heat. As the minutes swept by, I forced myself not to go in search of her, knowing she had not fallen or had an accident whilst inside. Instead, the necessity of staying warm eventually overtook all other thoughts and I decided to recommence the dig.

As I lifted the fork to puncture the ground, I heard her voice.

'Hang on, Eddie! Hang on! I couldn't find it!'

With her words, I loosened my grip on the fork and looked up to witness her waving our camera triumphantly in her hand as she strode toward me.

'I need to get a shot of you turning over this bed. It will be the first picture in the book!'

I shook my head and smiled at her.

'What about the ground over there?' I stated, nodding towards the area I had previously dug.

'That doesn't count. It was a practice area!' she laughed, raising the camera up to her face.

'Practice?'

'Yes, practice. Now pose and smile!' she commanded.

And I obliged her with the fork resting on the ground,

my right boot raised, ready to push the instrument through into the heavy clay soil and a static smile fixed upon my face.

'One more!' she requested.

'Sally, I am freezing!' I protested through my exposed teeth.

'Just one more!'

Photo shoot over, I began to dig in earnest, as Sally watched and surveyed the garden.

'We can take pictures through the seasons, show how the garden sleeps and awakes and all the time grows and matures. Also take pictures of birds and insects that visit, and build up the book!' she said excitely.

I looked up and smiled at her.

'I was thinking we could build a pergola too, have honeysuckle and jasmine growing up and over it,' she said.

'Do you want me to do that after this, or before?' I teased, thrusting the fork into the earth and taking a rest.

'No, silly, this will be in the future, with a deck underneath it for us to use. The bees and butterflies will love the jasmine in the daylight, and in the evening when the heat of the day is still trapped in the garden, moths will be drawn to the sweet scent of the honeysuckle.'

'What if they boycott it? What if they decide they can get their insectoid nectar pleasures elsewhere?' I proposed.

'Not possible, they will not be able to resist! It will be the talk of many an arthropod soiree,' came her confident reply.

'Arthropod soirees?' I asked.

'Oh yes, extremely popular occasions. Dancing, drinking, snacks – sugary varieties obviously. The dancing can be with multiple partners at any one time, on account of each guest having three pairs of limbs.'

'Really?'

'Yep, really. You should read more, Eddie; then you would know about such things!'

We both laughed at the absurdity of the discussion.

'Do you want to see where we can set it now? I am guessing it would be nice to have late-evening sunlight falling on it. What about over there?' I pointed at the far corner of the west flank of the garden. It was hard to imagine how this cold, dead environment could possibly be warmed by the summer sun again.

'You stick to your digger job for now,' she said, kissing me lightly on the cheek.

I picked up the fork and broke into the soil.

'Actually, Eddie, I am feeling quite tired now; I think I will head inside,' said Sally.

'You okay?' I asked.

'Yes, just feel tired, that's all.'

And she turned and walked back to the house.

Alone, I built up quite a rhythm and started to work quicker through the task. My effort was suddenly disturbed by shrill notes that seemed to come from directly behind my shoulder. I turned around and saw the robin, perched on one of the handles of the wheelbarrow, its' body bobbing up and down. It sang again at me, a beautiful lilt that lit up the dank afternoon, and hopped down confidently among the soil I had prepared to pick out a grub of some description with a spring-and-stab motion. Task complete, it held the morsel in its beak for a moment; then bobbed up and down, before returning to the wheelbarrow handle with a small flap of his wings and devouring the insect in one swallow. This was repeated over and over, the little bob up and down and the spring and stab. Eventually, I began to locate worms and larvae as I turned over the soil and tossed them toward the bird to pick up, which it did greedily on every occasion. And periodically throughout this, the silence was perpetuated by the robin's voice, solid and reassuring.

Each day after that, when I worked on a bed, the robin came, sang, ate greedily and bobbed. It became almost tame. I told Sally about it after the third occasion, which prompted her to go the next day to the local fishing tackle shop – not the chain stores that stock everything these days; this was years ago – and purchase a box of live mealworms.

I argued, 'Why waste your money? The bird enjoys the grubs I find it just as much, for free.' But as the insects were turned out into a saucer and placed on the bare earth, I was amazed, and a little saddened to be honest, as the robin rejected my recently revealed grub and instead headed, beak first, straight for the wiggling mass of mealworms.

We watched together for a while.

'Take some in your hand, I am sure it will come to you,' instructed Sally.

'Of course it won't,' I scoffed.

I knew the bird; I was the one that had shared its company. We had a connection; I knew its limitations, how close it would come.

'Smile,' commanded Sally moments later, her camera obscuring her face, as the little creature pecked greedily at the mealworms in my palm.

I watched intently as repeatedly the featherweight bird performed unimaginable violence against the mealworms. I moved my hand closer to my face, eager to view from a different angle. If the mealworms gave an audible shriek when held in the bird's beak, instead of a pathetic, silent wriggle, would I be as keen to control both their worlds at this time?

'This picture will be called *Eddie and Bob*,' she stated, still snapping away.

'Bob?' I questioned.

'Of course, on account of its little weak knees that keep buckling under it' she reasoned. 'This will be one of the star pictures in my scrapbook!' she added.

She said that for every photograph taken over the years, from the petite watering can and matching boots, to the towering sweet peas and sunflowers, to the butterfly garden, which technically wasn't in the garden outside but instead sealed within its own world, but which nevertheless warranted inclusion in any scrapbook. Sally captured the full life cycle of the butterflies on film, from unfeasibly hungry caterpillars, through a macabre pupation stage of motionless, hanging tombs, to the bursting forth of new life as the butterflies, their virgin wings dripping with pure, delicate beauty, emerged triumphantly from their cocoons. She kept them captive in the 'garden' for a couple of days to observe them, before releasing outside on a still, warm summer's afternoon.

That first spring after Bob had been sustained through those winter months was, quite simply, a disaster. We planted out onions, carrots, peas and lettuce in May and checked every day after the first week for signs of life breaking through the thick soil. After three weeks, we witnessed the first fragile spears of green pushing up from the surface. We were ecstatic and hugged each other, and Sally took many photos for her *Book of Perfect Brilliance*. Unfortunately, when developed, the images revealed only dark soil; so small were the seedlings that they could not be seen. It was at this point things that started to go wrong – very wrong. We watered them well and the spring sunshine ensured constant warmth, but the few plants that had emerged were not growing. We continued with our offerings of water, but our efforts could be described as pathetic at best; at worst, a failure.

After six weeks, we gave up completely, as the last visible shoots withered away to nothing before our bewildered eyes. We had travelled from elation to despair in a few short weeks and there was nothing we could do.

Over a subdued Sunday lunch, I presented the last option available to us, while cutting through shop-bought carrots on my plate.

'We could ask your dad for advice?' I suggested nonchalantly, before resuming my silence.

Sally didn't answer. She purposely had not sought her father's help or advice, wanting to do it her way. Sally found her father domineering, always critical with his opinions. This was her project, but it was his hobby and had been for many years.

'I will ring him later,' she said finally, and returned to silence.

'We could concentrate on the flower beds and borders; maybe they would be more successful,' I put forward.

Sally nodded slightly.

After lunch, we headed back outside and looked at the first bed I had initially begun to dig the previous November. It needed work, to be stripped of invading weeds, to be prepared and made ready.

'I'll start on it now,' I said.

'Let's do it together,' said Sally.

'Are you sure you are up to it?'

Sally nodded, but within twenty minutes, I was digging alone.

Sally appeared outside again, and judging by the look on her face, she had evidently called her father.

I said nothing, just kept turning over the soil, waiting for her to speak.

'He'll be over at four,' she said flatly.

'Okay,' I said, not knowing what else to say.

'I am popping up to the garden centre to pick up hostas and viburnum for here,' Sally stated, pointing at the earth I was revealing.

Within the hour, she was back with an array of pots containing various leafed plants, which she brought to the bed I was digging over, two at a time, and placed them in sets of three, still in their pots, on the soil.

'These will look good!' she exclaimed, sounding more upbeat, standing back and surveying her arrangement.

I noticed him first, stepping out of the French doors. Sally's expression changed as she instinctively knew what had drawn my attention.

'George,' I said as he approached us.

'Hello, Dad,' said Sally.

'Eddie.' He nodded toward me. 'What's my girl been up to?' he asked, his voice bright.

I sensed Sally squirming. Her father appeared oblivious to his daughter's discomfort.

'Where are they?' George asked.

We both nodded toward the far end of the garden. And I for one now felt embarrassed by the purpose of his visit.

'Not good, are they?' he stated obviously, surveying the 'vegetable patch'.

We shook our heads, feeling very young, very foolish and very insignificant.

'How much manure did you use in here?'

'Manure?' I asked.

'Yes, horse shit. The soil seems very heavy, how much did you put in?' he asked crossly.

'None,' answered Sally.

'None?!' he exclaimed. 'Compost, then?'

This time I answered with a shake of the head.

'Bone meal?'

We both shook our heads.

'Well, I am surprised you got as far as you did, then,' George concluded, nodding toward the lame crop at his feet.

We looked blankly on.

He sighed and blew out his cheeks, his agitation not disguised.

'You are a silly girl,' he stated.

I wanted to remind him where he was, to show some respect, but instead I remained silent, my respect for him barely holding.

'Soil needs to be broken down and nutrients added to get a good crop,' he stated. 'I suggest you put in studs now, over the whole plot – it's a bit late, but you should be okay – and lift them in October. They will work the soil for you. Add plenty of manure in December and plant spuds again next March, and add more manure. After two years, the ground should be broken and well nourished, ready for these crops.' He waved disapprovingly at the existing vegetation.

'Okay, thanks,' I answered, trying to sound bright and upbeat.

He shook his head and laughed to himself, completing Sally's humiliation.

'I can't believe you didn't know to work that soil,' George stated, his annoyance audible, but I wasn't sure why he was so angry.

With nothing more to say, we all turned and headed back toward the house.

'Would you like a cuppa, Dad?' asked Sally.

'No, I need to see your brother. Want to borrow his chainsaw before he heads to the golf club tonight,' George replied.

It was apparent that George, as usual, preferred to spend time with his other child.

'What's going in here, hostas?' he asked as we passed the newly-dug flowerbed.

'Yes,' said Sally excitedly.

'Huh, good luck with that; it'll be slug paradise in there within the week. There'll be nothing left but stalks; you're wasting your time,' George 'helpfully' advised.

He waved a nonchalant goodbye as he headed through the house to the front door. The door slammed shut behind him, I presumed due to the airflow from the open French doors.

He had physically left, but an uneasy presence remained.

While I continued to dig over the ground, Sally followed, planting her hostas with a trowel in the groups of three. We worked in silence.

Three weeks later, I awokefrom my dreams to discover

the empty indent on Sally's side of the bed. I glanced at the clock and panicked when the time 3.20am came into focus.

I rushed from the room in search of her, trying to keep my anxiety hidden. Upstairs checked, I called her name softly as I headed downstairs, met only by silence. Living, cloak and dining rooms searched, I finally entered the kitchen. Looking through the French doors, my eyes were drawn to a moving beam of light in the garden. Unsure of what I would find outside, I opened the knife drawer and chose the carving knife to be my last defence if necessary.

I ventured onto the patio, leaving the door open in case I needed to make a hurried retreat. As I stared, I calculated the beam of light was a handheld torch, not moving toward or away from me, but merely arcing over the ground. I walked purposefully but silently toward the light, my bare feet instantly soaked by the dew covering the grass.

Halfway across the grass, relief embraced me as I recognised Sally's form, her back to me, in the starlight. I smiled to myself as the tension of not knowing where she was and who this figure was evaporated. The knife in my hand suddenly made me feel extremely foolish.

'Sally?' I said as I reached her.

She turned around on hearing my voice, dropping the flashlight.

'Sorry, I didn't mean to wake you,' she said.

'What are you doing out here?' I asked, wanting to disguise the panic I had felt on waking and seeing the figure in the garden.

'Taking care of these,' Sally replied, picking up the torch and shining the beam onto her recently planted hostas.

As predicted by her father, the lush green foliage of

the daylight hours had been invaded by multiple slugs of differing sizes, colours and general grotesqueness. I didn't know there were so many varieties.

'Could you hold the torch for me, Eddie? It will be easier,' she said.

I took the torch from her as instructed and pointed the beam over the dark soil.

'We don't have any pellets, do we?' I said.

'I am not using pellets,' she replied, as I noticed for the first time the bucket at her feet.

With nimble fingers, she plucked at one leaf hosting seven slugs and shook the molluscs into her other hand, before dropping them into the bucket. I shone the light inside to witness a writhing, slimy mass of movement, as the entire floor of the bucket was covered in slugs.

I moved the beam over the soil away from us, to where Sally's hostas, planted so proudly, were all under attack by slugs in classic pincer movements.

'What are you going to do with them?' I asked.

Sally gave me a little laugh, as she worked on the next leaf.

'Take them down to the bottom there,' she replied, pointing to the end of the garden.

'And do what with them?'

'Release them.'

'Release them? Why?'

'It's the right thing to do, Eddie.'

'All they will do is come back here,' I stated.

Sally raised an eyebrow at me.

'Okay, albeit very slowly!' I laughed. 'Still think you should use pellets,' I added.

'Eddie, use pellets and the hedgehogs and birds ingest them too when they eat the slugs. Harriers and hawks then eat the birds and the poison passes to them. They all deserve to live.'

We carried on working. Sally on slug collection; me as lighting director. But soon the inevitable occurred and Sally began to slow down considerably.

'I am running out of puff, Eddie,' she said.

'Do you want me to finish it off?'

'I feel bad asking you.'

'It's almost done,' I said, deliberately flashing the light fleetingly across the ground to disguise the many slugs still feasting.

'Thanks, Eddie,' she said, and gave me a hug and a kiss on the cheek. 'Remember to put them at the bottom of the garden.'

'Sure.'

Touching them was disgusting, so I worked quickly. I regularly had to flick potential escapees from the sides of the bucket back down to the bottom.

Eventually, the last mollusc had been evicted, mid-banquet, and relocated to the bucket.

I picked it up, but changed my mind and put it back down, and instead headed for the kitchen quietly, so as to not wake Sally. I searched in a couple of cupboards in my hunt and returned outside with a container. I wasn't sure how much to use, so poured over half of the contents onto the slugs, covering the top layer. I picked up the bucket and walked to the end of the garden as instructed by Sally, and only there did I shine the torch inside to see the result. I was actually horrified at the scene I had created.

I understood that the water contained in the slugs' bodies would be drawn toward the salt crystals I had sprinkled over them, but I did not envisage the twisting and turning of apparent agony that would be unleashed, nor the bubbling and hissing as they very slowly and painfully died before me.

Looking on, I felt ashamed in that garden.

I dug a hole in the soil and emptied the contents of the bucket into it before spreading the soil on top, all without the use of the torch to illuminate the mass grave.

With the soil patted down, the scene returned to normal; it was as if the violent act had never occurred. I collected the container of salt on the way back into the house.

Back in the bedroom, Sally stirred as I got under the covers.

'Did you put them at the bottom of the garden, Eddie?' she asked sleepily.

'Yes,' I answered truthfully.

I sensed her smiling as she whispered, 'Good, thank you' into the darkness.

I said nothing more.

Now all these years later, the garden has matured and the wildlife haven Sally visualised has materialised. The hostas, once so fragile and limited, have to be divided every couple of years, for space. They are still fragile, but their sheer numbers mean they can coexist with the slugs. A proportion of our vegetable crops are given away to neighbours, as opposed to going to seed or rotting away.

I am not sure what happened to Sally's *Book of Perfect Brilliance*, put away some years ago. It would be good to look through it, to see how things have changed, and if our memory of events matches the photographs.

Sipping my Ceylon tea, staring through the French doors, I remind myself I still need to build that pergola and decking, and plant the jasmine and honeysuckle at its posts.

Chapter 6

Chasing the Sun with Henry

Six weeks; six Saturdays. Six early-morning walks on our beach. Nothing. Each time as I parked in the main car park, the nervous expectation sitting with me was replaced by frustrating disappointment when I returned having had only Henry's company for the duration of each walk. My progression back to the van was interrupted each time by an insistence on turning and looking behind me every ten paces or so, to see if any figure, human or canine, would make their presence known, but always the beach remained deserted. Each time I turned the key in the ignition, an element of foolishness accompanied my disappointment as I headed back to the house. Yet this feeling of absurdity was never present when I returned to the beach seven days later, just a quickening heart rate and a dry mouth to greet me among the sand dunes.

Conscious of the possibility of another encounter, I bought a new fleece and walking boots on the Thursday before my first return to the beach. I spent a considerable time in the newly opened outdoor pursuits store, not only considering the items' durability, but also, for the first time in years, how they actually looked and would be perceived by others. It had to be said that the 'help' I received from the extremely keen assistant consisted only of informing me that the fleece also came in black. My direct questions regarding break-in time for the boots and the true waterproof ability of the fleece were greeted with an 'I am not sure' response, so with this limited advice forthcoming, I used my own judgement.

I fully intended to head straight upstairs on my return to the house and store the items in my wardrobe, but Sally appeared in the hallway as I arrived and innocently enquired what was in the bags, such was the rarity of me purchasing anything not related to the Party King. I felt compelled to show her the contents, and on viewing, she appeared genuinely impressed with my choices.

'Does this mean I can finally throw away that tatty, threadbare jumper you insist on wearing and the boots with the different-coloured laces?' she asked with a smile.

I said nothing.

On the third Saturday, as I pulled up the handbrake on the van, my windscreen wipers were on maximum speed, as they had been since we left home. With the engine switched off and the wipers still, the rain formed an instant shield on the glass and simultaneously rapped violently on the metal above our heads and behind us. Henry lives for his walks, but on this occasion he gave me a look that seemed to plead, *You must be joking?* Reluctantly, he jumped down from the cab as I held the door open for him, and his sense that the bad weather viewed from inside the van would be considerably worse outside was immediately confirmed as he stood on the soaked duckboard, his tail tucked pathetically between his hind legs.

We lasted approximately ten minutes before the stinging horizontal rain forced us to retreat. The journey back with the rain pounding our backs was only marginally less gruelling, albeit more so for me than Henry, with the necessity of turning around and checking the beach every few paces a burden on me alone.

Judging by the damp ache flooding through my shoulders and elbows as I began to drive away from the car park, I concluded the fleece, as indicated on its information tag in the shop, was indeed only showerproof. It pays to read and understand the signs that surround you.

Yesterday was fine. The sun was warming as we strode out onto the beach. The light was so pure on the mountains that we could pick out individual trees on the slopes, and the numerous streams tumbling down glistened like silver thread.

Henry raced down toward the shore, his intent obvious to me. The water's edge had retreated to its furthest point away, leaving a considerable expanse of dark, wet sand between us and a troop of wading birds, hungrily searching for food in the exposed flats. Still a full thirty metres away from the oncoming Henry and sensing danger, the entire flock took flight in unison, almost like a collective leap, landing a safe distance away from him, his pounding paws and his curiosity, to continue their feeding. This was repeated again and again. Be it wading birds or even the sun (which he has been known to chase on occasion when there isn't any life form in his vicinity), Henry never tired of this activity, the wind full on his face, ears trailing in his wake, his lungs drawing in huge quantities of life-giving air. Although what he would actually do with a bird, or indeed even a heavenly body for that matter, if he were ever to be successful in his pursuit, remained a mystery. The chase is everything.

His attention was drawn away from the birds by the tatty, chewed green tennis ball that flashed into his line of vision from the left and skimmed and bounced across the beach. I still held the slingshot responsible in the point of release as he instantly changed direction and mind to pursue his new quarry.

In contrast, my memory of why my heart had quickened and my mouth had dried as I parked up had slowly dulled in my mind's eye as I walked, admitting to myself that there would be no movement from among the dunes, no figure in wellingtons or chocolate Labrador coming into focus. I looked toward the horizon, where the sky met the sea, for an answer. Was she really that beautiful, as gregarious as I remembered? If she had suddenly walked into my view, would the Cerys in my mind still fit the image physically presented to me? Had I exaggerated and honed her perfect smile, her laugh, her fresh face into an image recognisable to me and me alone? Perhaps I had even passed her since that first encounter, that *only* encounter – walking in the street, driving on the road or in Malacy's Bar – and did not give the real Cerys a second glance.

Thetennis ball, now soaked in dog saliva and sand, was rolled at my feet and drew my attention away from my own preoccupation. The arrival of the ball was accompanied by frantic panting, punctuated by a regular licking of lips by a long, thin tongue, desperately searching for water around the jaws, and a pair of obsessed brown eyes trained expertly upon the ball's resting place, almost willing it to move again of its own accord, to enable the chase to commence once more.

This exercise was repeated again and again until Henry's physical strength gave way and he lay down at my feet.

"Got ya!" I teased as I bent down and rubbed his ears.

After a few minutes, he was on his feet again and we headed back toward the dunes and the van beyond. The mountains still looked magnificent in front of us; not a hint of cloud obstructed the face of them, which in turn meant the view from along their ancient and exposed backbones would be unsurpassed in all directions – out to sea, inland to the city on the far horizon, and closer, much closer, into the secret lakes held within their cupped hands that would shimmer green and blue and call those present who had made the effort to enter this hidden kingdom to drink deeply from their pools; then when their thirst was quenched, to sit back and listen to the deafening silence that resounded in this place.

I made a mental note to tell Gus I wouldn't be around this Thursday, the day we head into the mountains. The day we are shouted at by the silence.

Chapter 7

Pub Quiz Playboy

Gus Eastley is a complex man. Not in the sense that he is deep or studious, or an artistic sort, creating difficult prose that academics debate the meaning of and struggle to understand. Nor is he prone to episodes of depression, or someone whose energy is directed toward fighting for good causes. No, his complexity is more to do with the fact that no one really knows anything about him as a person. Certainly, we know him as he appears among us, but the journey he made to be at this point is a complete mystery to us all.

Gus has had a colourful life; or rather he mentions episodes from a past that seems a million miles away from here. His stories have never failed to raise a wry smile from his audience, and I can honestly say, I cannot remember being privy to the same story more than once. The wry smiles that ensue are the result of disbelief in what is being conveyed. The fanciful nature of the tales seems so improbable that in your first few encounters with Gus you could be excused for deeming him a liar, a charlatan, or nothing but an eccentric oddball. I know I certainly did.

My introduction to Gus Eastley was here, in Malacy's Bar on a summer's evening five years ago. I had arranged to meet Sally after I picked up the last of the bouncy castles from that day's parties and she had tended her bees. I should have been there a good thirty minutes before her but was running quite late due to a group of adults insisting on having a turn on the bouncy castle after the children had all gone home, an event that took a considerable time to organise and execute.

I eventually walked in and found Sally seated, her back to me, talking to a stranger at the far end of the bar. She laughed loudly and hard before I reached her and the stranger looked over her shoulder at me as I approached, a warm smile on his face, seemingly savouring making another man's wife laugh so freely.

'Sally?' I said.

She turned around on her stool and faced me, smiling broadly; still affected by the influence this man had had upon her.

'Eddie, this is Gus,' she gushed. 'He has moved into the area. Bought Kathleen's old place.'

'Please to meet you,' said Gus, raising his glass.

'Likewise.'

'Can I get you a drink?'

'No, no, I am fine.'

'Oh come on, Eddie, have a drink with us,' pleaded Sally. 'Gus has some wonderful stories. Tell Eddie about your shoes and the Prime Minister!'

Gus put up his hand as if to stop the story being told.

'No, really, I am okay,' I stated.

'One drink. Gus has been keeping me company; you know I hate being here on my own. What kept you, anyway?'

'Just got delayed, that's all,' I said.

Sally did not like entering or being in a bar on her own; she always thought people would look at her as being cheap, common, and would always choose to stand in her own company, despite the fact that she knew a good majority of the clientele as neighbours. But if entering with me or in a group, or meeting someone with me by her side, her girlish nature quickly bubbled to the surface. Contrary to her usual arrival, this girlish bubble expanded easily the day we met the stranger Gus Eastley and was holding her mood buoyant as she willed me to stay with her eyes.

'Okay, I'll take a pint, please,' I said to Gus.

'My pleasure – a pint of what?'

'Malacy knows.'

Gus nodded slowly. He caught Malacy's eye and asked for my usual.

'Ah, a stout man,' he uttered as he witnessed Malacy filling a pint glass half full with the dark liquid and letting it settle. 'Lager for me in the summer months, bitter when the clocks go back in the autumn and stout during the Six Nations,' he uttered fluently.

'Why?' I asked, warming to him.

'Tradition!' he responded, handing a £10 note to Malacy before telling the bar owner to take a drink himself out of it.

'Tradition?' Sally and I replied in unison.

'Yep, tradition.'

And that was all Gus would say about it. Whose tradition, and why those particular drinks in that particular order, he did not divulge. In fact, over the years this has been a regular occurrence with him. A snippet of information dripped into a conversation that is not backed up with any explanation or reasoning leaves you questioning and wanting to know more. Then there are the stories; the stories are something else.

My pint was placed in front of me by Malacy. I raised the glass toward Gus and uttered cheers.

'My pleasure,' He said again.

'Tell Eddie about when you met the Prime Minister!' said Sally excitedly, as I downed my first mouthfuls of liquid.

'I am sure Eddie doesn't want to hear about that!' said Gus, waving away her suggestion with his palm.

'Well, I'd love to hear it again,' she stated. 'It's hilarious!'

I put down my pint and drew air in over my teeth. I remember thinking that it was lovely to see her smiling, to see her happy after all that had happened.

'No, I'd love to hear it,' I commented with a smile.

Gus sighed. 'It's nothing really.'

'Gus!' teased Sally.

'Okay, okay, wish I hadn't told you now, as you have bigged it up so much!' he laughed. 'Years ago, when I was younger, I was in Australia. Just planned to hang out really for a few weeks, but with all the parties and sunshine, the weeks became months until eventually funds became depleted and I had to consider taking a job. A father of an acquaintance of mine put me forward for a broker's assistant role in a firm he had connections with in Sydney, overlooking the harbour. It really was just an office dogsbody role – writing tickets, ensuring prices were correct and that the reports were sent out to the regulatory board on time – but I was earning some money to top up the party fund again!' He stopped and smiled.

'Go on!' I encouraged, though not sure I understood anything about the job he was explaining, nor why such a tenuous connection as an acquaintance's father would assist him in getting it, or for that matter why he was in Australia in the first place. But I wanted him to continue, intrigued from the offset by this story that was so far removed from my own life experiences. I simply wanted him to continue because Gus was extremely likeable.

'Anyway, one afternoon, a memo comes around – this is pre-email, pre-PC,, I might add!' he stated. 'The memo advised that the British Prime Minister was to visit the office the following week as part of his tour of the country. The firm had recently opened up a satellite office in London, to start trading in Europe. These were exciting times, the era of Gordon Gekko's "greed is good" and "lunch is for wimps",' said Gus, nodding his head toward us, while I in turn looked on blankly.

'I know, Eddie, I didn't understand either,' admitted Sally quietly.

Gus continued. 'In recognition of the jobs the firm had created in the UK, the office in Sydney had the "honour" of a tour by a man whose popularity was falling so low he would grasp any photo opportunity, either at home or abroad, that resulted in positive newspaper columns, which in turn could ultimately translate into career-saving votes. Well, that was my opinion of him anyway!

'So, the big day arrived, and I was working at the desk, matching up tickets and desperately trying to decipher the mining salesman's scribbles – a career in medicine would have been appropriate for him, such was the illegibility of his handwriting. Suddenly, the entourage of PM, Minsters, chairman, CEO and various other egotistical, power-crazed fools came into my view from the left. I needed to get those tickets over to the exchange before closing and kept my efforts concentrated on this task, but I was also aware of the introductions and repeated small talk coming ever closer to my desk.'

Gus stopped and took a swig of lager.

'Now, I do not like wearing shoes, I never have,' began Gus with a smile, to which Sally burst into uncontrollable laughter. I looked on with amusement.

'If I had my way, I wouldn't wear any at all,' said Gus. 'I think it all goes back to a past life.'

'Really?' I exclaimed, not sure where this was leading.

'Yes, I was regressed once,' continued Gus, unabated. 'I was a deckhand on a triangular trade ship from the 1720s, didn't wear shoes and have hated wearing them ever since.'

Gus sensed the mood change in his audience, stopped speaking and looked at Sally and me and our puzzled stares.

'He didn't mention that part before,' whispered Sally.

'I can prove it,' he stated, overhearing her. 'But that's another story for another time. We all have been here before, or will be here again.'

Without waiting for either of us to reply to this tangential interlude, Gus continued.

'As I said, I hate wearing shoes, so, as usual I was sitting with my shoes off under my desk. I heard the voices becoming distinctly louder to my left and saw, out of the corner of my eye, Neil standing up two desks down from me, being introduced to the PM. I hurriedly began to enter the last ticket details into the terminal, eyes fixed on the screen, and desperately searched for my shoes with my feet. I pushed hard with my right foot, squeezing and wiggling my toes inside the slip-on loafer. As my feet had been "free" for a couple of hours under the desk, the shoe felt uncomfortable and restricting. I located the other shoe and pushed into it, feeling the same discomfort, just as I hit the enter key to send the trade details to the exchange.

'The screen froze just as the chairman gushed behind me, "And this is Augustus, over here with us from your part of the world, Prime Minister." With his words as my cue, I stood up, my hand out ready, and made eye contact with the politician, when really all I wanted to do was ensure the trade file has been successfully sent. We shook hands for a few moments and held eye contact until his eyes dropped down my body to the area around my feet. My eyes followed, and then I realised the reason for my discomfort. My left shoe was on my right foot, my right on my left, giving my feet an unnatural comical curve effect, pointing away from each other.

'The Prime Minster stared transfixed in silence for some moments before regaining some composure, and simply uttered, "Quite extraordinary" and moved on to the next desk without another word to me.'

I coughed on my beer as I chuckled. 'That never happened,' I argued.

Gus put his hands up in surrender. 'I swear that it did.'

We quickly learned that he always ended his stories with that phrase – and never explained himself further. From that very first encounter we came to enjoy his tales and assumed them to be tall but highly entertaining.

I remember in the winter of that first year we met, he told a story more outrageous than any of the previous escapades he had shared with us. I believe the weather turning bitterly cold and the first snow flurries blowing through jogged his memory into recalling a time when supposedly he and a group of friends were on a skiing trip in St Moritz in Switzerland. During one evening of après-ski entertainment, they descended to a popular (and expensive) haunt called Roo's Bar for cocktails. After a number of rounds of margaritas someone in the party stated that the cocktails, though good, were no way up to the standard maintained consistently in a bar he knew in Florida. This point was disputed by a number of the party, who insisted the very bar that they stood in was by far superior.

The debate raged on, with pros and cons for both locations being argued enthusiastically, until it was concluded and decided by a democratic vote that there was only one way to prove the qualities of one bar's cocktail credentials over the other.

Three taxis were ordered to take the group to the airport, where return tickets for the last flight that night to Miami, via Frankfurt, were purchased. Apparently, fourteen hours later, they were watching in anticipation as the bartender at Club Nikki in Miami Beach poured the contents of a cocktail shaker into nine salt-rimmed margarita glasses.

However, the analysis did not prove conclusive and the group was split on the outcome and debated the merits of cocktails in the warm Florida moonlight against the snow-crisp coolness of Switzerland on the flight back to Frankfurt.

As usual, our incredulous looks contrastedtohis insistence of the tales validity.event.

To my astonishment, some weeks later, on heading to Gus' for the first time for Christmas drinks, the validity of his story was confirmed. As we waited in the living room, getting our bearings before Gus returned from the kitchen with our drinks, both Sally and I were drawn to two framed photographs on a table; of a group of young men in brightly coloured ski clothes all pointing and looking upward, wide smiles on each of their faces in both shots. Their attention was directed at the names of the establishments they stood in front of. One had a subtly backlit sign saying *Roo's Bar*; the other spelt out *Club Nikki* in gaudy neon strips. Studying the identical subjects and clothing, we had no reason to believe that these photographs hadn't been taken within a few hours of each other, or that the tall, slim, blond figure at the back wasn't Gus.

That is when we looked at Gus' stories in a totally different light, but still the reason why he chose to leave that lifestyle and live among us is unknown.

And now I took my seat opposite him in Malacy's Bar, as is always the case on Sunday evenings. We belong to the *Numquam Vincere* pub quiz team. Malacy only introduced the quiz night to exploit a loophole in the strict licencing hours that have been held firm on Sundays for years; whereby, if an establishment provides entertainment, they are permitted to stay open two hours longer than a standard bar. Dancing, live bands, comedy and organised quizzes are all deemed to be entertainment under this rule. Malacy, being a prudent and thrifty publican, saw the quiz option as the cheapest and easiest to organise. And so for the past four years, Sunday night has been quiz night.

Gus chose the name and informed the non-Latin-speakers amongst us, actually the rest of the team, that it meant 'The Invincibles', and we had no reason to doubt him. Although, we have never actually won!

The team is balanced. Clifford knows his geography, Mary takes control of the regular anagram and picture rounds, and Sally with her love of books is essential for any literature questions. I have a bizarre skill of remembering lyrics and band names that should be confined to the great jukebox in the sky. Gus mops up the more obscure questions – that have everyone else looking up at the ceiling, scratching their heads and puffing out their cheeks – with an ease that defies belief.

'Canada.'

'Sorry?'

'Canada,' repeated Gus as we waited for the sheets and pens to be passed around the tables in preparation for the start of the quiz. 'I was just saying to Clifford before you arrived, Canada is the place we should all think of moving to.'

I laughed, not knowing where his latest tale was leading.

'I am serious,' he continued. 'They speak English, have no quarrel with any other country and have a sound economy. It's a huge country, so real estate is cheap and there is so much to do outdoors, totally different lifestyle to here.'

'Yes, and as I said,' added Clifford, 'it is covered in snow and ice for five months of the year with temperatures way below freezing, and a quarter of the population speak French. You haven't thought it through, Gus.'

'Ah, but you are forgetting one thing,' replied Gus, sipping his drink.

'The baby seals,' said Mary.

'What?' we responded in unison.

'The baby seals, they are really cruel to baby seals. Track them over the ice and club them until they are dead. It's awful.'

'Yes, I have seen that, Gus,' I admitted.

'Forget about the seals for a moment,' retorted Gus, trying to not lose his audience.

'But it's cruel, Gus,' stated Mary again.

'I appreciate that, but here is the thing,' continued Gus, undeterred. 'Global warming is going to warm Canada up! So Clifford's point of five months of snow and ice will become a thing of the past. Add that to the other positives – the English-speaking parts of the country, the peaceful people, the huge expanses of land to buy and build on – and it is sounds near perfect,' summed up Gus, as if in front of members of a Crown Court jury.

'What about the dog mess?' enquired Clifford, unimpressed.

'Clifford!' shouted Mary at her husband. 'That's enough of that.'

'What are you talking about?!' demanded Gus with a chuckle.

'I will tell you,' began Clifford, looking warily at Mary. 'In the winter, because it is so cold, when people walk their dogs in the cities and towns, they do not bother to pick up the mess their dogs make. Instead it freezes and gets buried under the snow, not to be seen again. Well, not to be seen again until the springtime when the ground warms up and the snow melts, as does the dogs' mess – unbelievable stench.'

Clifford glanced toward Mary, ready to pre-empt any response.

'Yes, but that is my point: there will not be any snow or freezing conditions, so the problem will be eradicated,' stated Gus.

'But how do you know they will not continue to let their dogs do it, snow or no snow?'

'Now, Clifford, that is quite enough.'

'I was just saying, Mary,' he replied, knowing, on hearing his wife's words, to cease his participation in the conversation.

'Okay, when I get there, I will lobby for all the people who want to do this after global warming to move to the French-speaking parts. They could pretend they are in Paris!'

We all laughed hard, so much so that our competitors on the other tables looked around at the sound of the commotion.

'But what about the seals, Gus? You still need to address the problem with the baby seals,' said Mary sincerely.

'There won't be any ice, Mary, so the seals will be gone – nothing stays the same,' answered Gus flatly. 'Where's Sally?' he asked before Mary could reply.

'She had a meeting with the people from the supermarket about her honey. Thought she would be here by now,' I informed the assembled team.

'Meeting on a Sunday?' said Clifford gruffly. 'That's disgraceful of them; don't they let people have peace?'

'Clifford, that's no different to you tending your sheep on a Sunday,' Mary pointed out.

'My sheep have no brains! Need checking every day. Surely a meeting could wait until a Monday.'

'Capitalism never sleeps, Clifford!' Gus joked.

'Anyway, your sheep are in good company with you!' teased Mary, thrusting her elbow playfully into her husband's side.

'What are you two, a double act?' he retorted with mock annoyance.

'Meant to say, Gus, I cannot make the walk on Thursday,' I said quickly.

'Oh,' he replied with disappointment.

'Sorry, I have a school booking.'

'That's a shame; the weather is set to be good, would have been perfect for trekking Smugglers Path.. But I could head down to the city instead; catch up with a couple of fellas I haven't seen in a while – liquid lunch and tea!' He chuckled.

'They are fascinating, by the way,' stated Clifford to no one in particular.

'Sorry?' replied Mary. 'Who is fascinating?'

I shook my head and wondered too what Clifford was bringing to the conversation.

'Bees!' he stated, raising his voice.

'No need to shout, you old fool, you!' hissed Mary back at him.

'Why is that, Clifford?' asked Gus.

Clifford folded his arm over his chest, content he now had a captured audience.

'Well, let me tell you,' he began. 'Inside each hive, they have a perfect society: every bee has a role, a duty, and every bee has a purpose – for a worker this changes during her lifespan. Did you know; they perform a dance that gives directions to a new source of nectar for the others to follow?' He waited for a response, but none was forthcoming, so he carried on regardless. 'The hierarchy inside,' he continued, 'always holds, and every bee will defend a nest to the end. In their minds they are still forest-dwellers, so when a keeper puffs smoke into a hive to commence an inspection, they assume the colony is under attack from a forest fire and aim to protect the hive and the most important thing in it.'

'The queen?' I suggested helpfully.

'Yes, exactly,' answered Clifford, not really listening to me. 'No! No! Not the queen!' he corrected himself. 'Although she is extremely important. No, they protect the *honey* they have produced and stored as a food source, taped up in combs. Guess how they protect it?'

'Little bee-sized guns!' came Mary's suggestion.

'And maybe buzz bombs?' chipped in Gus.

'Little bee-sized guns? Buzz bombs?' replied an agitated Clifford. 'No, they eat it up, as fast as they can, to ensure their life's work is not destroyed. And in doing this, they experience a sugar rush that makes them initially energised, but quickly very sleepy, very docile, so the keeper can examine their hive while preserving their safety and the bees'. If you manage a hive properly the colony will be content to stay. They are forgiving and will tolerate the regular removal of a portion of their honey, the attack on their home, the partial destruction of the cells they have built. But if a keeper neglects the bees, they will have nothing to repair and will outgrow the hive and abandon it, merge into a swarm to find a new home. Sally must be skilled at keeping her bees happy; she's never had a swarm, has she?'

'No,' I replied.

'Why are you boring us about this anyway?' asked Mary matter-of-factly.

'I will tell you why: guess how they attack invaders to their hive?' asked Clifford, smiling knowingly. 'And no, it doesn't involve buzz bombs,' he added.

'Sting them?' suggested Mary wearily.

'Can't be, they die if they use their sting,' I contributed.

'Exactly,' said Clifford. 'That is a very, *very* last resort.'

The table went quiet.

'Shall I tell you?'

'If you must,' sighed Mary.

'They cover the intruder completely and rapidly vibrate their bodies, causing the temperature around the victim to rise very quickly.' Clifford nodded excitedly as we looked on.

'So?' Mary shrugged.

'They cook them alive! Anything that gets too close to their hive,' he proclaimed. 'Imagine that: little bees being able to work such a thing out? Such an effective method, they really are amazing.'

'I've never heard such nonsense!' replied Mary.

Clifford put up his hands. 'Gus, you are a clever chap, you tell her,' he pleaded.

'Well, I have heard they will attack hornets that raid the hive in this way, but not any other creature, to be honest,' confessed Gus.

'It's *any* creature,' insisted Clifford, 'people included.'

We all looked at each other and collectively laughed.

'They don't cover people and attack them, Clifford!' I insisted.

'Yes they do, you mark my words!' he replied, trying to keep the upper hand over those of us who found his statement impossible to believe.

'Here she is now,' said Mary through her laughter, looking over my shoulder as Sally walked in through the door.

She took her seat next to me and greeted everyone across the table in her usual cheery way.

'My round,' declared Gus, standing up and heading to the bar.

'How did the meeting go?' asked Mary politely.

'Pardon?' replied Sally, seemingly startled.

'The meeting, Eddie said you were seeing that supermarket about buying your honey. How did it go?'

'Oh, you know, facts, figures, that kind of thing. Think we will have to meet again to finalise everything,' stated Sally vaguely.

'Well,' injected Clifford, 'I still think it is wrong they made you do it on a Sunday.'

'Oh, Clifford, go and talk to your sheep! She's a woman trying to get on. Baaaaa!' Mary added for good measure. That made me laugh, and eventually cracked Clifford's face into a smile.

'Sorry, I don't understand,' replied Sally, looking confused at Mary and Clifford, but not at me.

'Everything okay?' I asked instinctively out of the side of my mouth, but not knowing why I wanted to check.

'Yes, yes, why shouldn't it be?' Sally replied, not looking at me.

'Okay, first question, people!' The quizmaster's voice came over the microphone.

I couldn't understand this feeling of uneasiness I was sensing from Sally, or why she was avoiding eye contact with me. She seemed fine when she left earlier today to meet with the supermarket representative.

'Who shot Ronald Reagan, the fortieth President of the United States?'

All four of us sat around, looking at each other, then up to the ceiling for inspiration.

The quizmaster repeated the question a further three times. And with each reading, our ability to extract the answer from among us did not improve.

'John Hinckley Junior, March 30th 1981,' Gus whispered nonchalantly, returning with the drinks on a tray.

'Of course!' said Clifford, writing down the answer on our behalf.

Chapter 8

Clive

My flesh-coloured wig cap is always the first thing I put on. Then I concentrate on applying the make-up in front of the bathroom mirror: left eye, followed by the right – red ovals, outlined in black. To be honest, it took me a couple of years to perfect the shape and outline, finally making me appreciate why Sally can take so long to get ready. Not that her face looks like my own creation after she has applied her make-up, you understand. I apply the same colours to my mouth to create an exaggerated smile and finish with a red circle on the tip of my nose.

Next the costume: stripy socks – I have a white vest on already – and black jacket and trousers, two sizes too short in the arms and legs. Next garment is a bowler hat with a ginger wig sown in, which hangs down on over my ears and neck when worn . I still do not know why, but the bowler hat and ginger wig combination always makes me smile when I see it. It also extracts a multitude of double-takes from people in vehicles and pedestrians whenever I drive to a venue.

My audiences also delight in the hat, when during the show I casually take it off and scratch my head, revealing to them my 'bald' head. They shout and point at me while I pretend to not understand what the issue is until I look at my hat and notice the hair inside. At which point I throw the hat into the air in shock and catch it on my head – well, most of the time. But if I am not successful and the hat rolls around on the floor at my feet, my audiences are always forgiving. Primary-school children are always forgiving.

I reach for the final item, an oversized stripy bow tie that matches my socks. I secure it around my neck and my transformation is complete. I look deeply into the mirror and Clive the Clown stares back.

Admittedly, Clive is not a name usually associated with clowns; it is more in keeping with the image of a steady accountant type or an institutionalised government employee. True, there was Clive of India and his fabled chronicles of derring-do, but Clive was his family name and therefore I do not count it as actually being in the Clive mould.

I wanted to choose a name that was safe, secure and subject to alliteration. Clive works – plus, and most importantly, under-elevens find the sound amusing.

Clive has no road sense. In fact, he has no sense or memory retention at all. With each show he discovers anew, and the audience are reminded of, when and where to cross a road safely.

I incorporate a zebra crossing, flashing Belisha beacons and three pedal cars into the performance, powered by selected children from the audience. Eric the Psychic Duck from my birthday party magic show makes a cameo performance as Clive's friend; simply called 'Duck', who quacks loudly each time Clive is in danger when attempting to cross the road. Duck's frantic quacking alerts the children to also warn Clive.

To be honest, Clive is initially so hopeless crossing the road he shouldn't really be trusted to dress himself, let alone be out unaccompanied. Before each calamity, Duck plays a scene from an information DVD to demonstrate to Clive what he should do to cross a road safely. Clive nods to confirm he understands and then subsequently fails to conform. Resulting, as already mentioned, in much quacking from Duck and shouting from the children present.

During the show the scenario of running out onto a road from behind parked cars is played out. Two pedal cars are parked up, and true to form, Clive, forgetting the message revealed to him moments before on the DVD, decides to stand between the cars and cross the road into the path of the third car that is being driven. Suffice to say, Duck and the audience prevent certain carnage once again. With the increased decibel count, Clive realises his mistake and moves away from behind the cars and heads toward the zebra crossing instead.

If one child finds themself in the position of attempting to cross a road from behind parked cars and sees in their mind my stripy socks, oversized bow tie and bowler hat with ginger hair protruding underneath and stops, thinks and moves away to a safe crossing place, then my metamorphosis into Clive is justified.

I obviously have no way of knowing if my show has any effect in achieving this, so I will continue to perform once a month during term time, until I have proof it is no longer required.

I checked my appearance one more time in the mirror, ensuring my tie was straight and my make-up was not streaky or smudged. Quite frankly, I looked ridiculous, and I was content for Clive to continue his crusade, to spread his message before the Easter break.

As I left the bathroom, Sally appeared in the doorway. She looked immaculate.

'You off out?'

'Meeting Trafford,' she replied, not making eye contact as she brushed past me.

'Who?'

'Trafford, the buyer from the supermarket. Need to run through some more things,' she stated, looking at her reflection in the mirror. 'I did tell you, Eddie,' she said to her image, while running her fingers through her hair, fluffing it outwards.

My past record speaks for itself; I do have a tendency to forget things I have been told. For example, I have been known to arrange to go to a football match, only to be informed we are due at one of Sally's friends and her boring husband's house for dinner on that same evening. Or I've promised to help Clifford with a job that clashes with a prior engagement with Sally's mother, choosing wallpaper or some other tedious activity which was planned 'weeks before'.

In reality, these instances occur because I am a man, and there is not very much I can do about that. But I do not recall this being mentioned – I am quite sure that, even with my failings, I would have retained a name like Trafford in my mind if I had heard it before. Not that it mattered where Sally was going or who she was meeting; she didn't have to tell me. It was just that there was something different about her appearance as she stood there, but I could not pinpoint what it was.

'I could meet you for lunch,' I stated brightly.

'Sorry, I don't know when I will be finished,' she replied, her eyes still studying her complexion.

'Oh, okay, was just a thought.'

Sally turned away from the mirror and looked at me briefly for the first time. Her mouth formed a half-smile as she diverted her gaze to the floor.

'Right, have a good day,' she uttered flatly as she passed me.

I went to speak, but remained silent.

I heard her feet hurry down the stairs, heard the front door open and close firmly. Her car door closed with a thud and moments later I heard the engine pulling her away from me.

It was at this point I realised what was different about Sally's appearance today. For the very first time I could remember, after all the years I have known her, her face was bereft of any make-up.

I drove to the venue, courting thoughts that were alien to me. Thoughts that had never invaded my consciousness before, thoughts that jostled with the others that routinely sit and cause my heart to ache. These are the same thoughts that always accompany me in the van prior to a performance by Clive. Then the journeys to the beach these past few weeks and the bitter disappointment I felt on returning to my van each time flooded my senses with a slap for my hypocrisy.

I parked up in the school car park and checked my appearance in the sun visor mirror. I still looked ridiculous, and headed to the reception area of the school to announce my arrival.

The show went well. My hat landed squarely on my head

as intended and Clive gained guidance from the children for every misdemeanour he attempted to undertake. The only issue was the selection of two overly eager seven-year-old boys who were picked to operate a pedal car each, on the merit of sitting up straight with their arms in the air. Once behind the steering wheels of their respective vehicles, they became less able than even Clive to follow simple instructions. Each egged on by the other, the proceeded to 'duel' across the assembly hall floor, accompanied by screeching sound effects when they turned at the perimeter of the hall. Until such time, after their third warning, as the year head relinquished them of their responsibilities.

'You have let yourselves down' could be heard as she let them out of the hall, back toward the classrooms and an unknown fate.

I chose again, more carefully this time. I selected two girls, again sitting up straight, who performed their duties with diligence and composure. Perhaps this episode was an indicator that females do in fact make better and safer drivers than males.

Sally was back when I returned, sitting in the living room, reading a newspaper. She greeted me with a warm smile from her chair and made eye contact. Not fleeting, not nervous, but prolonged eye contact, boring into me. My mind now confined her previous detached state to a memory, and with her facial emancipation covered under a layer of freshly applied make-up, normal service had resumed. I cursed myself for allowing my imagination to massage my thoughts.

'How was it?' I asked.

'Fine, just fine. Think we are getting somewhere. And

you? How was it?'

'Usual, went well.'

At this point, silence joined the conversation and decided to lead.

'I went to Mum's on the way back,' stated Sally eventually.

'How is she?'

'I am a bit worried about her, Eddie.'

'Oh?'

'On Sunday, she was dusting the dining-room table when she saw a bird sitting outside on the windowsill.'

I looked at Sally, trying to discover where this story uewas leading.

'It was small and white,' she continued, 'and not a species she knew – you know how she loves looking at the birds on the feeding table through her kitchen window. It didn't fly off when she came near. In fact, she says it stared at her, studied her face. It was still there the next day, and the day after that. So she decided to feed it. Throw some crumbs out, from the fan light.'

Sally paused, looking at me.

'Today, she went to the room and it was still there, sitting outside, looking in. She cannot explain why, but the way it was behaving was causing her distress and she decided, on impulse, to shoo it away. She opened the window, presuming it would fly off as the pane swung outwards, but instead, it merely flew up, fluttered its wings, and headed in through the open window. It landed on the back of a dining chair. She waved her arms at it to frighten it into leaving, but it merely flew up onto the top of her dresser and sat with its head to one side, looking at her. She knew she couldn't reach it up there, so she left the room, closed the door and decided what to do next. When she went back, it was again perched on the back of the same chair. She went to force it to leave out of the open window, but again it flew up onto the dresser. This happened four further times, with the bird always on the same chair when she came in. And that's when it hit her.'

'What did?' I asked, trying to keep up with the story, which I thought was going to end with Sally's mother experiencing a fall or injury and us discussing the installation of ramps, stairlifts and walk-in baths, or in the worst-case scenario, her moving in with us.

Sally took a deep breath.

'The bird keeps landing on Dad's seat in the dining room. You remember the seat he always sat at?'

'Yep, the one closest to the door,' I remembered out loud.

'Well, she is convinced the bird is Dad!'

I tried desperately to contort my stomach muscles to hold in my laughter, a laugh that was primitive, a sound that is buried deep inside all of us, that explodes with force and with scant regard for the situation or the feelings of those around.

Yet, I somehow held my composure.

'She thinks your dad has come back as a little white bird?' I asked flatly.

'Yes,' hissed Sally. 'She called Greg to ask him what to do. She didn't tell him she thought it was Dad, though, you know what he is like. He said he would come around and get rid of it for her. He arrived when I was there. We waited in the doorway as he entered the room and went toward the bird – it didn't fly away, but instead it launched itself at him and pecked at his outstretched hand, before defecating on it.'

'It had taste, then,' I stated.

'Eddie!' snapped Sally. 'It then flew toward and out of the window,' she added. 'As it left, Mum started to cry, much to Greg's annoyance. He told her it was just a stupid bird, which made her worse and him even more annoyed.'

'Strange, I thought the fact his hand was covered in bird shit would be making him annoyed. Or perhaps that's just me,' I replied, barely hiding my sarcasm or contempt for her elder brother.

The phone in the hall began to ring. Sally ignored my comment and got out of the chair.

'While Greg washed his hands,' she stated, walking to the door to the hallway, 'Mum sobbed on my shoulder that she had sent Dad away. I am worried she misses him so much she is giving up, Eddie.'

'It's been two years though, Sally,' I offered.

She turned to look at me for a second before disappearing into the hallway.

'Oh, hi, Jenny,' she answered after her initial hello.

With Jennifer on the phone in the middle of the day, normal service had been very much resumed. I decided it was time for me to retreat upstairs and remove my make-up, for me to be cleansed of Clive until the next time.

Looking into the mirror, wiping off the make-up, I reflected upon Sally's mother's belief that her dead husband had visited her. Who was I to question the physical improbability of his manifestation with no chin, feathers and a beak for a nose? She had lived with the man for over forty years; they had shared that special bond you only find with one person in your life. The bond where you know when your partner is going to ask you a question and what the topic will be; yet no one else is aware of the thoughts sparking between your minds. It is as if a telepathic link occurs between you.

Sally and I are close, but do not share that link. Her thoughts remain a mystery to me until they are spoken, by which time everyone else is aware of them too.

Maybe her mother really felt his presence in the shape of the bird; saw a resemblance of his soul reflected through the window of those beady black eyes. Then again, it could be grief attacking her in a cruel and malignant way, making a room an out-of-bounds area, forcing her eyes to instantly see his shape sitting forever at the table in his chair ; forcing her mind to retreat, coaxing her to hold the pain of loss ever closer to herself.

Sally and I have jointly been attacked by grief. But neither of us could support the other, could take the burden of the moment and hold it away, albeit for a short space of time, to enable the other to regain strength, to breathe. Instead we dissolved into our own independent voids. I do not know what is worse to face: the pressure of attempting to be outwardly strong while inside you are falling to pieces, or the helplessness of watching someone fade before your eyes into the shadows of their darkest fears and not want to be found or rescued.

My face clean, I cupped cold water in my hands and splashed upwards. The sensation banished memories. With my head partially lowered, I raised my eyes to find my reflection. Water dripped from my nose and chin as my hands held the edge of the basin. As is the norm, my reflection said nothing, nor gave away how I was feeling.

I held the pose for a moment until, with a shiver down my spine, my grandmother's voice rasped in my mind as it has for all these years. She told me when I was ten years old that if you stare at yourself in a mirror for too long, your vanity invites the Devil to your side, and without warning, you will suddenly see him sneering at you from over your left shoulder.

From the top of the landing I could see Sally sitting on the bottom stair, the phone pressed firmly to her ear. I watched for a few moments and saw that her contribution to the conversation was seemingly to listen. From my position, Jennifer's voice was audible to me but her words were not distinguishable. What disaster had sought out the unfortunate Jennifer this time, I thought? And why, as usual, did she deem it acceptable to offload the entire twisted and sorry tale into the ears of Sally?

I began to descend the stairs.

'Okay, Jenny – again, that is fantastic news. Just goes to show, good things do happen. I will let Eddie know. Bye-bye. Bye-bye,' Sally said, getting up and replacing the telephone on its cradle on the hallway table.

'Eddie!' she called loudly, not looking behind her.

'I am here,' I replied from the bottom step.

Sally physically jumped at the sound of my voice.

'Eddie! You scared me! Were you eavesdropping?' she accused.

'No, of course not, just out of the bathroom,' I countered, not knowing why I felt the need to defend myself and my actions.

'That was Jenny.'

'I gathered that. What world-ending crisis has beset her today?' I asked.

'Don't be unkind. It's nothing like that,' argued Sally. 'She was calling to tell me the police have released her from their enquires regarding that vile dog-fighter.'

'Wallace,' I added helpfully.

Sally looked at me. 'How did you remember his name?' she asked.

I shrugged my shoulders in response.

'Anyway, she's been allowed to collect her passport. You remember the man she was working with?'

'The bloke she didn't get on with?' I replied with confidence.

'Yes, what was his name?' Sally challenged.

I shrugged my shoulders again.

'Faruk,' she suddenly remembered.

'Oh yes, Faruk,' I replied knowingly.

'Well, he has come forward and vouched for her good character to the police. He has revealed the numerous times she came in early to work to clean out the dogs and walk them. How she checked every night before she left that each had enough fresh water. All of this was recorded on the centre's CCTV, and he produced a copy as backup for what he had disclosed for the police to view. He also described how on two occasions, she broke down when a dog had to be put down due to an infestation of mites.'

'Why would he do this? They didn't get on.'

'Or so Jenny thought,' corrected Sally.

'But he wouldn't speak to her.'

'I think he was just quiet. Maybe Jenny took this as being aloof.'

'Jennifer thinking a man is horrible with no tangible evidence? Surely not!' I exclaimed.

Sally ignored my churlish dig at her friend. 'He is a good man, Eddie,' she stated brightly.

My mind locked onto the words that had just resounded around me, and I battled the thoughts Sally's innocent words evoked for me.

'She is coming over tomorrow to start putting her studio together,' said Sally, leaving the hallway.

'Sorry?' I answered absent-mindedly.

Chapter 9

Are You Ready for Your Close-Up?

I had a strange phone call today. Well, not strange as such, just random. Three years ago, I joined a networking group for small businesses. Gus got me into it, said it would be useful, in his words, to grow 'the empire of the Party King'. For a minimal fee the group meet monthly in a coffee shop in a local garden centre and exchange ideas, experiences and client names over freshly ground coffee and home-made cakes.

This was at a time when I was trying to branch out, market a more adult-orientated show. It was in its embryonic stage and I wanted to make it work. Delicious though the cake and beverages were, it did not take me too long to establish that this forum wasn't really conducive to expanding my particular type of business. Although Gus argued that I needed to persevere, it was obvious to me that the B&B owners, local accountants and mobile PC repair doctors all seemed to have more to gain than I did. That said, I did agree to be included in a brochure – *Be Seen* – highlighting my business; that was produced by a local photographer, who coincidentally was also a member of the networking group. But then again, all the members did this; none wanted to be seen as not wanting to promote their respective businesses. A professional photograph of me, playing cards in hand, accompanied by five hundred words, filled my page. I was £40 lighter for the privilege and, knowing a run of five thousand copies were to be placed in strategic and influential sites in the nearby towns and villages, I waited for the constant ringing of my phone to begin. Alas, it was not to be – not one call or enquiry came out of it and shortly afterwards I withdrew from the network forum.

That was until today. The voice on the phone opened the conversation by stating that they had found me in *Be Seen* and would I be interested in performing at a ladies' night? I was a little hesitant and informed him I wasn't comfortable in front of a crowd of hostile, alcohol-fuelled, catcalling women. He laughed and reassured me that it wasn't that kind of ladies' night. Instead, he disclosed he was the treasurer of a charitable organisation, the Lombarders – made up of male members only – and the event was an annual dinner and dance for members accompanied by their wives and girlfriends. I laughed with him on discovering my faux pas, and checked my diary while he was still on the phone. I confirmed I was available and asked for the venue details.

'The golf club,' he said simply.

I was only at the golf club once before, a party for Sally's brother Greg's thirtieth birthday. With my preconceived opinions of the place deeply instilled, I argued with Sally that I didn't want to go, but I already knew that my point of view, versus the occasion/birthday boy combo, had no chance of winning her over.

I reluctantly got ready and remember feeling disgruntled

that a dress code was in place, where men had to wear suits and ties. Don't get me wrong, I have no objection to wearing a suit and tie as befits the occasion – and I like to spend money on quality suit material and silk-woven ties. But I couldn't see why a birthday celebration would necessitate such a request. This dress code wasn't Greg exercising his prerogative as the centre of attention. No, this was a rule directly imposed by the golf club itself, on members and non-members alike. I still argue; why should a person with no affiliation with a club or association be subjected to such a draconian stance on what is smart and what is not?

On arriving at the venue, I was surrounded by middle-aged men, all club members, and all dressed in similar cheap suits, some of which had obtained a dull sheen on account of dry-cleaning visits, and whose 'off-white' shirt-collar edges curled comically under themselves, like stale triangular cheese sandwiches. Their look was completed by an array of insipidly coloured polyester ties. I observed in disbelief, as more and more examples of this identical look continued to arrive.

To this day, I still cannot accept how this can be deemed smart attire, when to appease the rules, I and the handful of other non-member guests had turned out immaculately dressed, in sharp suits, quality ties and polished shoes.

It was obvious that a guest could have arrived in a well-made and fitted smart plain T-shirt and been turned away because the shirt did not have a collar. In contrast, the cheese-sandwich-collar gang were received with backslapping and smiles.

This was the start of the evening, a time before any members had 'mingled' with us non-members.

I soon discovered the reason behind the mingling. They wanted to ascertain which golf club we were affiliated with, and in turn, whether an invite for a round would be forthcoming in the future. I personally took this scenario in a light-hearted way, to mean a kind of golfing 'away day fixture' for the members; the humour behind this, admittedly weak, was met with blank expressions and appeared totally lost on the two individuals I expressed it to. After this, with the mingle in full swing, when asked, I merely stated I did not belong to a club.

It did not stop there – their continued probing and my responses unleashed a misconstrued elitism in them that was further stirred by my admission that I had no knowledge of or interest in the forthcoming Ryder Cup.

The final confirmation of my inadequacies was underlined by my admitting to a member that I had never played the game, or even held a club. On this bombshell, communication ceased, culminating with a gaze into the distance and a 'Please excuse me, I need to go to the bar', after which he moved off without a second glance at me. I suppose he was at least polite in his scathing loathing.

Polite or not, with their rejection, the members forged a stance of superiority, believing that their hobby is central to life; that it is an activity that takes them to another plane, to a standing where everyone should aspire to be. In their eyes, how could anyone not subscribe to this point of view?

I once was told, 'Dismissing someone on account of your misplaced opinion is the scourge of humanity.' After enduring that night, I finally understood what that really meant.

Still, it wasn't all bad. I did manage to avoid the birthday boy for the majority of the evening, and his sneering, slurred comments and revolting attitude were only directed at me as last orders were called.

In total contrast, his credit card was set behind the bar and we became extremely well acquainted over the course of the night.

Actually, perhaps on reflection with this action, I didn't understand the meaning of misplaced opinions after all?

Still, it was a long time ago and work was work.

I was sure the calibre of guests at the Lombarders' function would not fit the mould I had observed at the venue before. They would be a good bunch of people, charitable people who performed good works throughout the community. If anyone was entitled to let their hair down and enjoy themselves, it was them. I was sure it would be a gratifying evening to be part of, and thought about the types of tricks I could perform as I said goodbye to the treasurer.

I headed for the kitchen to make a cup of tea, when a key inserted into the front-door lock caught my attention. I already knew who it was. And within moments, as I turned to face the door, the considerable build of Jennifer materialised on the threshold.

'Eddie,' she said, without making eye contact with me.

'Jennifer,' I replied, deadpan.

'Hello, Henry,' she gushed. Henry wagged his tail lamely in response.

'I am making tea, would you like one?'

'No, I am running late, I need to get set up,' she replied, lifting a large, chrome-ribbed suitcase into the hallway from behind her.

'I'll make a pot, in case you change your mind,' I said, heading into the kitchen.

She didn't answer, but I sensed her moving down the hallway behind me. Judging by her grunting and panting, I presumed the weight of the suitcase was etched firmly on her face as effort on her journey to the spare bedroom.

Jennifer had set up the studio soon after the police had dropped the charges for her involvement with the dog-fighting ring. I was intrigued to ask her if she knew what had happened to Mr Wallace – was he charged, was he in prison? I hadn't heard anything on the local news about the case and wondered if he too had been released without charge.

But it was a subject I could not broach with Jennifer – my relationship with her over the years has remained one of polite small talk at best, silent scowls at worst.

Every time I see Jennifer, I make a mental note to ask Sally if she has any idea of the situation – they are, after all, best friends. But as Sally and I have not exactly been communicating of late, my question always evaporates into nothing as I struggle to connect with my wife and share my own thoughts and worries, irrespective of outside influence.

I have to say, she has kitted out the room extremely well. I knew she was a keen photographer, but had not appreciated to what level she aspired.

The windows are professionally blacked out with fitted curtains. Within the room she has a selection of flash lighting kits, tripod-mounted and able to accommodate umbrellas or soft boxes, depending on what is required for a particular shot. Two boom arms and stands sit high above, for white, blue, silver and gold reflectors to diffuse unwanted shadows.

She has a number of interchangeable backgrounds, which

flip over a portable frame. A fantasy blue-satin cloth, which I think she regrets using on account of the dirt, hair and marks left behind by larger dogs. It takes her a considerable time to clean the material each time. As an alternative, she has two 'realistic' views – *Restful Meadow* and *Spring Woods* – for clients that choose to have their pet in a non-staged, more natural settling. Jennifer has commented that this is the most popular screen-scape for her mid-sized dog portraits – although how a restful meadow could ever be considered a natural vista for the multitude of bull terriers I have witnessed pulling their owners toward the studio door is beyond me.

Jennifer also has a selection of pliable PVC choices, in sapphire blue, glen green, dove grey and poppy, that not only form a backdrop and floor covering, but also dress a still-life table. This table is used for smaller pets – toy dogs, cats, rodents, reptiles, and her least favourites, the arachnids, in all their hairy, slow-motion, wiggly-leg forms. I have to concede admiration for Jennifer in the way she has not let her fear (I have heard her, on occasions, wail hysterically when sighting a spider scurry across the living-room floor in front of her and Sally, during those cool nights of autumn when they seek out the warmth of a house in preference to the oncoming bite of winter) compromise her service to her clients. I know she has already photographed Harry, a Chilean rose tarantula, a number of times – close up, from above, from the side and head-on, after his owner has triggered the 'threat stance' in him by prodding him with the end of a pencil.

On a table to the left of the photographic set-up, connected by an infinite amount of cabling, sits an array of electronic boxes with periodically flashing lights and a large printing machine. The purpose of all these devices, I am not going to pretend to have the first clue about. All I do understand is that the gadgetry is hooked up to a laptop, also on the table, that receives the images captured by the digital cameras she uses.

I also have to concede that the transition from spare bedroom into photographic studio was seamless. It was a good excuse to clear the room of clutter, and Jennifer did take on all the work herself.

She had business cards printed up and distributed through veterinary surgeries, pet shops and the supermarket notice board. After an initial flurry of enquires due to promotional gimmicks of half-price large prints and five portraits for the price of four, and partly due to public curiosity, the sittings have steadied. She works four days a week, ten to five on Wednesday, Friday and Saturday – with Thursday a late and popular night.

I still am not comfortable with the key situation, though – this is my house, and as is the norm, Sally did not consult me regarding the cutting of an extra key. That said, other than Thursday evenings, I am rarely here when Jennifer is; besides, how else would she get in without one – she is not going to squeeze through the letterbox! The one drawback, though: she doesn't go home on a Saturday; instead, after her last client, she camps in the living room with Sally. She doesn't appear to leave any earlier, so in fact has longer for cake consumption and bemoaning my gender in general.

'Actually, surprised to see you here, Eddie,' Jennifer stated from the kitchen doorway.

'On my way later – no inflatables today to set up, just two parties.'

'I'll catch up with you before you go.'

'I can see you this evening,' I said.

'No, I will not be here then,' she stated, shaking her head.

'Oh? That's not like you.'

'Meaning?'

'Meaning nothing,' I replied, realising my comment may have caused offence to her; it doesn't take much.

'I need to talk to you about something,' she said cryptically.

When on earth have Jennifer and I ever had a 'talk about something' – anything, actually? I thought to myself.

I muttered, 'Sure' as the kettle clicked its announcement that the water had boiled for the tea.

Drinking my tea in the kitchen, I heard the doorbell ring and resisted the urge to enter the hallway and open the door of my house to the visitor. Instead, I heard Jennifer open her studio door and head through the hallway. Judging by her cheery hello and admiring gushing noises on opening the door, I presumed the sitter this time was not Harry.

I drained my tea and headed outside to the van to check the addresses of the bookings, and if I needed to drop by the wholesaler's to pick up a new 'wobbly' wand or if it would last a few more weeks – and all the time, I pondered what it was Jennifer wanted to discuss with me and tried to not let the fact I couldn't open my own front door today without her being there bother me.

As suspected, the wand had seen better days. I got into the driver's seat; I knew I had enough time to get to the wholesaler's before the first party. *Besides*, I thought, *I should also pick up some modelling balloons – can never have enough modelling balloons.*

It hadn't helped that last week the wand was taken and used as a club by a birthday boy to beat a younger girl – his sister's friend – repeatedly about the head. His attack was accompanied by high-pitched yet menacing 'hi-yah!'s and 'take that!'s with every wobbly blow. I remember his mother tried to explain this unprovoked attack by claiming he was just excited about the party and it wasn't his normal behaviour. After a few minutes of ignoring her calling his name in a sympathetic tone, he was evidently bored and ceased the barrage, dropped the wand and ran to the other side of the community hall (where the party was being held) to wrestle with his male friends.

It was only at this point that the young girl started to cry, and cry hysterically. Still, enticed to cease the tears by the offer of a slice of birthday cake, she reverted to being as obnoxious as him, picking up the discarded wand and hitting another innocent victim across the shoulders. This transformation occurred after only a few licks of the blue buttercream icing that generously entombed the cake that was now clasped in her hand.

En route to the wholesaler's, I took a call from the parent organising the first party. They had to cancel. It was two hours before the event. They stated their daughter had a vomiting bug and had been sick all night and that morning. They apologised, but did not offer to pay a fee, a token, as means of compensation to me. Instead there was a deathly silence as neither side spoke. Eventually, they commented again that their daughter was genuinely ill. I told them I was sorry about it and hung up.

Driving back, new wand and balloons purchased, I mulled over the fact that I didn't insist on a cancellation fee. I told myself that for the next booking I took I would inform the parents that there was a cancellation policy. But I knew that I wouldn't.

I pulled into my road and was dismayed to see a car parked in my space on the drive. Still annoyed with myself for not insisting on a cancellation fee, this breach of my personal space channelled my anger further. I parked up on the road outside, slammed the van door hard on exiting and walked all of ten paces to the boundary of the property. Heading through the front door, I marched toward Jennifer's studio, my anger evaporating with every step, until I decided at the studio door that a firm-but-fair stance was required and that I would ask the person to move their vehicle so I could park.

As my hand hovered as a fist, centimetres from the door, I froze, stopped in my tracks by one word uttered from within.

'Phoebe! Phoebe!' encouraged Jennifer shrilly.

I continued to listen, my head pressed gently against the wood, trying to coax and channel the now-muffled tones into recognisable words for my ear to process, but it proved impossible to decipher what was being said.

Standing there, concentrating, my mind formed an image of the car parked on the driveway. A dark-coloured saloon car. I dismissed it as not being a car Cerys would drive. This was ridiculous! How on earth could I possibly conclude what car she drove?

I closed my eyes; the darkness of my eyelids transported me into the studio, where I could see Cerys standing out of the camera shot as Phoebe sat looking head-on at the camera.

Tea – come away and make some tea, I told myself.

I moved away from the door and headed into the kitchen. What to do, what to do? Perhaps I should knock on the door and ask Jennifer if she would like a cup of tea. Then I could casually say hello to Cerys. I dismissed the idea as quickly as I thought of it, as I realised that if I did so, Cerys would presume Jennifer and I were an item, a couple, married. No, I would wait in the kitchen until I heard them leaving the studio and then enter the hallway in the same instant; timing was going to be everything. Again, I would make my greeting casual. The fact Cerys would still consider Jennifer and I a couple was blind to me in my "improved" plan.

I checked my reflection in the kettle on the worktop, but it was impossible to tell what I looked like in the convex image. I decided I couldn't run the risk of heading upstairs to the bathroom to use the mirror, in case they emerged from the studio at the same time. My stampede down the stairs would be perceived as odd at the very least.

At this point my phone rang and all my planning and thoughts of a rendezvous with Cerys were shot to pieces. On the other end of the line, the father of the second birthday child of the day explained they had a dilemma. They understood they had booked my show for 4pm, but had sent out the invitations in error with a party start of 2pm and wondered if I could come right now. They would of course, they stated, compensate me for my trouble. I was surprised, as always, by how people react differently when faced with situations.

I put down the phone, agreeing to be there in twenty minutes, secretly thinking that there was no mix-up with the times; rather, they assumed they could entertain twelve party-fuelled under-six-year-olds for two hours and discovered rapidly that they couldn't. Still, I couldn't judge.

I made up my mind. It was simple now. I would knock on the door and tell Jennifer I was leaving and did she have a moment to talk to me as arranged? In the room, I would see Cerys and say hello (again, casually) and mention I hadn't seen her on the beach for some time. That was as far as my plan had been hatched; from that point onwards, I was going to improvise. I really just wanted to see her.

Rehearsing in my mind, I saw but took no notice of Henry as he moved from his bed to do his doggy stretching. First down on his front paws, his chest resting on the floor, his hindquarters high in the air. On standing up, he walked off; pushing first his left, then his right rear leg individually into straight points behind him.

I left the kitchen, and in moments I was by the door. Should I grin, smile or look uninterested on entering? I really couldn't decide.

In one fluid motion, I knocked and entered.

'Jennif…' I started to say, but my voice trailed off at the sight presented before me.

Sitting facing me on a stool on the fantasy blue satin cloth was a middle-aged man, naked, with a perfectly groomed and cuttoy poodle arranged on his lap. The poodle's fur was dyed pink.

The man obviously looked embarrassed, the poodle yapped a croaky bark at me as poodles do, and Jennifer yelled at me crossly to leave. But I was fixed to the spot. *This isn't Phoebe*, I thought to myself, *and you are not Cerys*, I added dumbly. And all the while I held the door open and did not hear the clipping of Henry's claws making their way to the studio to discover the source of the barking and the reason for Jennifer's raised voice.

The next few minutes were a blur. But suffice to say, Henry did not take kindly to Phoebe the poodle being in his territory and proceeded to bark and snarl in her direction. In reaction, she wriggled from her owner's lap to defend herself, which exposed the owner's pubic region to me, dyed the same shocking pink colour as the dog. It was a sight I never imagined I would ever see, and is something I wish I could forget.

The dogs then began to chase around the studio, accompanied by frantic barking, knocking over equipment and causing lamps to spark and die as they crashed to the floor.

As Phoebe became entangled in the cables from the equipment on the table, we all yelled at them to stop, our combined voices seemingly making the situation even more fraught.

The sitter got up, retrieved his clothes and hurriedly put on his trousers (commando-style, I noted, my eyes drawn once again to the explosion of pink below his waist), as I finally caught Henry and dragged him by the collar into the kitchen and shut the door.

On my return, the room looked even worse.

'Jennifer, I am so sorry,' I began.

'Just get out, Eddie!' she screamed at me, surveying the damage to her studio.

I stood in silence as the client left with a now-calm Phoebe under his arm. She gave a final, defiant yap in my general direction for good measure as she passed me.

'I know it isn't a good time, but I have to go out now. Do you still want to talk to me about...?' I stopped in mid-sentence, reading the look on Jennifer's face as at best unapproachable, at worst genuinely hostile.

'Another time, then,' I added, moving swiftly from the studio.

Chapter 10

When the Wind Blows

If a spiralling weather system allows an easterly wind to form, its touch over the water can stimulate the brine to behave even more excitably than normal, with bigger-than-usual lines of waves relentlessly crashing and pounding against the shore of our beach.

Sometimes, if conditions are favourable the east wind also brings with it a mist that hugs close to the shore.,.

Making the turn off the main road behind the dunes, the temperature reading in the van plummeted a full twelve degrees. The brilliant summer sky, which had earlier forced Henry to pant in the cab and me to open the window, had at this point retreated behind us. It was replaced by an energy-sapping, bone-boring dampness in the shape of a sea fret, which made the dunes, as we sat looking out, appear and disappear in an ebbing and flowing mist. On occasion, the wind can remember its manners, and returns and to disburse the fog ,and in doing so, invites the warmth and summer to return. But today, in my opinion, the wind was not prepared to show any signs of benevolence and I concluded our walk would be swift and merely a mechanism for Henry to exercise and empty his bowls.

Such was the density of the fog, I imagined, that if the

waves had retreated to their furthest point away, the water's edge would be hard to detect, lost inside a soft fade, with the sound of fuming surf, muffled to my ears, the only tangible indicator as to where land and sea merged. And the mountains would be totally obscured, their majestic slopes, woods and waterfalls all secrets, veiled and hidden.

If anyone had found this place for the very first time today, had walked between the dunes and arrived at the seafront, the scene, or lack of it, I felt would determine they sadly were not destined to ever return. The beauty of the place would never be revealed to them, the retelling of how the mountains appear suddenly in view would not be divulged excitedly when they eventually returned to their home. The hundreds of wading birds pecking and stabbing the wet sands and changing direction in unison would not be marvelled at. Nor would they feel the freshness of the air penetrating deep into their alveoli, encouraging their entire body to grasp the possibilities of life with vigour; a feeling that would leave them awakened with an immeasurable sense of well-being.

Henry yawned, stood up on his seat and shook himself from tail to head, his large ears flaring comically around his face. I opened the driver's door and immediately the deathly dank air flooded in. I checked the dashboard to ensure the headlights were switched off, knowing that keeping them on with no engine running in these conditions would culminate in single clicks from the ignition as I turned the key on our return, and an unplanned extended stay on the beach. Only Clifford and a set of jump leads would release us from our entrapment.

'This proves I love you,' I told Henry as he jumped down after me through the open driver's side door.

He ignored me and headed toward a patch of marram grass, studying and sniffing the tough blades intently, though for what purpose, I will never fathom.

I took my fleece from the cab and zipped it up all the way to just under my chin, but the cold already had a hold. It had already claimed me.

'It's supposed to be summer,' I muttered incredulously, heading through the dunes.

The walk was miserable. Not only because the swirling fog crept into my eyes, under my fleece and even through the tongues on my boots, but more so because of the previous evening I had shared with Sally, the consequence of which still played on my mind this morning.

Sally had come home late again, which has become a regular occurrence over the past three months. I obviously have no issue with her coming back late, none whatsoever. It is the atmosphere she carries back with her to the house that I find unacceptable. With each return, the situation appears more fraught. Her silence on entering is broken each time by the set of keys she drops noisily on the hallway table. Such is her seeming disinterest in my presence that I have now got to the stage where I do not even bother to get up to greet her. And when I do engage conversation, it is acknowledged, if at all, with snapped words of one syllable, usually yes or no. Yet within an hour or two of being in the house, the old Sally, my Sally, returns. The Sally who is kind, talkative and constantly on the go, who cleans the mantelpiece, the windows, washes up or washes the floor, the Sally who speaks excitedly and with passion about her bees and gardening.

Yet when she arrives back each time after a business

meeting with Trafford, she doesn't want to discuss her bees, nor indulge what has been agreed regarding marketing, or the projected increased production of honey. Nor can I mention the costings involved; I am sure a big supermarket chain tries to squeeze every last bit of profit from the producer for their own advantage. I want to ease some of the pressure off her, but I take her silence stance, although a new characteristic of Sally's, to be a coping mechanism in the face of the pressure she presumably feels.

That was until last night, when, after thirty minutes of silence, I mentioned that while she had been away, I had done some research regarding commercial hives. I had seen how much they cost, whether they would be viable for her, and I had the details saved on the computer.

She cut me down in mid-sentence, saying, 'For fuck's sake, Eddie, give it a rest!' with distinct irritation in her voice.

In all the years I have known her, Sally has never sworn at me before, and I was truly lost for words.

She walked out of the room without saying anything else. My instinct was to stay in the room, to pretend all was normal, that my wife was still with me. Yet, I found myself rising from my chair and heading out into the hall to find her – as though I was somebody else. I found her in the kitchen, staring out of the window into her garden beyond.

I spoke before I realised any words would come.

'What's going on, Sally?' I shouted with a passion erupting from deep inside me that I did not remember ever directing me before.

She didn't answer, but remained still, her back to me, her thoughts and visage trained on the window.

'I asked you, what is going on?' I repeated with equal passion.

'Nothing,' came the obvious mumbled response.

'Nothing? Nothing?!' I shouted.. I moved around to face her. 'You ignore me, here and then use that language at me?'

'It's you, Eddie, the way you are!' she hissed into my face.

'What does that mean, "the way I am"?'

She went to move, and as she did, I grabbed hold of her wrists.

'Don't walk away!'

You're hurting me!' she yelled, with genuine pain in her voice.

I looked down and saw my hands locked around her wrists far more tightly than I had realised, and released my grip instantly.

Sally rubbed her reddening wrists together and stared at me, smarting.

'What's happened to us?' I asked, calmness trying and failing to return to my voice. 'I was just trying to support you, to help,' I added.

After twenty years of marriage, within minutes of each other she had sworn at me and I had physically hurt her for the first time.

Sally continued to soothe her wrists and stared at me, like a wounded animal.

'Sally, what is going on?' I repeated again, calmly this time. 'You come back,don't speak for hours and then you are fine. I am not sure what has happened to us.'

'Huh – "fine". "Fine"; what does that mean? That I clean and cook and fall into the same old routine? Is that what you mean, Eddie?'

'No, I mean…' I trailed off, unable to finish the sentence.

'So that is what you mean!'

'I am trying to support you,' I responded. 'You never speak about the meetings, how the negotiations are going. You just come back silent and I have to wait for you to be you again. And the amount of time that takes is become longer and longer each time.'

'What is there to say? They are business meetings, they will be finalised when they are finalised.'

'Okay, but negotiations have been going on for a considerable time, months in fact.'

'Meaning?' Sally snapped.

'Meaning nothing, just… are you getting close to an agreement? I hate seeing you stressed.'

'I am not "stressed",' she replied. 'And you know nothing about it. If you want to support me, just stick to your balloon modelling,' added Sally with venom.

With her words, I was crushed and Sally returned her gaze to the window.

'That was unkind, Sally. I only want to help you with the burden,' I finally stated, trying to keep my voice from cracking.

She didn't reply.

'Why is it taking so long? We cannot survive like this. What happens when they are pressing you to produce more and more honey? Then the pressure will be on.' I spoke my thoughts loudly and in quick succession. 'But I forgot, I am just a balloon modeller who knows nothing,' I spat. 'But I'll tell you something…' I paused until Sally had resumed eye contact with me. 'This balloon modeller would do anything for you. Anything.'

Sally touched the side of my face with her hand. 'Oh, Eddie,' she said gently.

I reached up and cupped my hand over hers.

We stayed like this for some time until the expression on Sally's face changed.

'Eddie, I need to tell you something,' she said, pulling her hand free.

I looked at her anxiously, driven by the change in her expression and the words she had just uttered.

She composed herself and looked out of the window for inspiration or a choice of words. Either way, I stood with the instinct that my heart was about to be broken consuming me.

'I haven't always been at meetings.'

'Sorry?'

Sally sighed. 'Over the past few weeks, I haven't always been at a meeting about the business,' she confessed.

I stood in silence; letting the words sink into me, absorb me.

'So where were you, Sally?' I asked flatly, looking at my feet.

Sally did not answer, and I felt my heart starting to race.

'I said, where were you, Sally?' I repeated, my voice rising and each syllable emphasised.

'I didn't want to tell you, but you have put me into a corner. I've been seeing someone.' She paused. 'Ignatius McKenzie,' she added.

'What do you mean, "seeing someone"?' I didn't give her a chance to respond, and continued, 'I knew it; I am not stupid, Sally. He's the supermarket buyer, isn't he?"

'What?, No that is Trafford Jones.' she said with irritation now back in her voice. 'Why do you never listen to me?'

'How long and why, Sally? Why?' I asked, without listening to her reply.

Sally started to cry and attempted to move out of the kitchen.

'That's right, you get found out, so you turn on the waterworks and try to leave the room. No way are you going! No way!' I shouted, blocking her path. 'We are staying here until you give me every detail and answers to every question. I knew it, knew it!'

She did not reply.

We stood in silence. Sally looking up at the ceiling, me at the floor.

'I ask again, how long has been going on? I've been worried about you taking on all this pressure, when all along you have been carrying on. You've made a right mug out of me.'

Sally breathed deeply and regained her composure.

'Eddie, you have got it all wrong.'

'I've got it all wrong?!' I shouted. 'You just told me you have been seeing someone else. How have I got that wrong?'

'Ignatius McKenzie is a medium. Mary gave me his name.'

'I don't understand.'

'She gave me his name, said he could help me make sense of things. He's been helping me to come to terms with things. Showing me a different angle.'

I remembered now – Ignatius McKenzie; that was the person Mary was going to see when she and Clifford had words in their kitchen a few months back.

'But hang on, Sally, he does shows, big theatre venues. How can that help you, with all those people there?'

'He does private sittings at his house too,' she replied with tears flowing from her eyes.

'And that's where you have been going?' I asked softly.

She nodded without making eye contact.

'But how come you behave the way you do when you come back? How are you feeling when you return here?'

Sally shrugged.

'And is it helping you, seeing him?'

Sally shrugged again,

'Eddie, just hold me please,' she said with her arms outstretched toward me, her cheeks wet with tears.

We embraced and I felt her body go limp in my arms, then her shoulders shaking. We stayed like that for some time, before I gently kissed her forehead and stroked her hair away from her eyes. She looked up at me and then focused her gaze on my lips. Our mouths came together and we kissed slowly at first, probing, almost testing, then with more urgency, until we were consumed with an abandon we had not experienced together for years.

Then it happened: the cause of my trouble this morning.

In one fluid movement Sally dropped from my view. Her hands unfastened my belt buckle, followed slowly by the zip and lastly the clasp; then she pulled my trousers and boxer shorts downward. Before I could respond or speak, the warmth of her mouth drew the breath sharply from me. This was not Sally.

Don't get me wrong, Sally has performed fellatio on me before, but without sounding cruel, she wasn't very good at it; the act just consisted of a lot of slurping noises and my tip just inside her mouth, in front of her teeth. Nor, for that matter, has it ever been performed in the middle of the kitchen floor at 6pm. I have always been too polite, or maybe just not confident enough to suggest this wasn't really working for me. But this was very different: she slowly ran her protruding tongue around the tip, before heading downwards and licking the entire length of the now-inflated shaft, while all the time, her eyes stared into mine. She then concentrated at the base, lapping with her tongue at a place underneath that I never knew until that point actually existed on my body. Then she took the whole length into her mouth in a way that made me shudder, until she finally concentrated on the top third with a rhythmical motion from her mouth and hands. I closed my eyes and instinctively ran my hands through her hair, which triggered her to pull even deeper with her mouth, her movement eventually encouraging my hips to begin thrusting in unison with her.

As the sensation intensified I tried to pull back. But within seconds I pushed down on her shoulders for support as I lost control, my physical excitement heightened by her continued hold. In fact her efforts intensified as the familiar burn poured from within me into her willing and wanting mouth, her momentum only relenting long after my last surge had past. It was then Sally stood up and kissed me, a salty taste of my semen still very much on her lips, but the majority of the liquid swallowed and consumed. This was not *my* Sally.

She turned and headed out of the room without another word to me. I stood trying to take in what had just occurred, the pure pleasure of the event overwhelming me. It was then I saw Henry sitting in his bed under the breakfast bar, staring at me. I had forgotten when I came in searching for Sally that he was in there. There was me standing with my trousers and boxer shorts around my ankles and the air circulating around my deflating loins. I realised he must have witnessed everything, and the doggy disapproval on his face left me feeling strangely embarrassed.

Here on the beach, the events kept churning over in my mind. At last I knew why she had been going out so often and why she came back in such low spirits – she was trying to make sense of everything that had happened around the death of her father. But this did not answer why she had chosen to swear at me and belittle my occupation, nor did it explain the spontaneous act in the kitchen. Then a voice in my head reminded me of the old proverb 'don't look a gift horse in the mouth' – very apt, I chuckled to myself, but the nagging doubt as to where Sally's skills had been honed remained. It was not something I could readily ask her.

After twenty minutes of damp walking and multiple chase-and-retrieves, I turned around to face the dunes, to see if the fret was showing any sign of clearing. Their bulk remained hidden, confirming summer's influence was unable to penetrate and it was time to head home.

Then, through the mist, I saw her.

Well, I thought I saw her, fleetingly, in the distance; it was hard to say for sure.

Henry for once was not a warning device to confirm my suspicions; instead he waited expectantly by my feet for the ball to fly once more across the expanse of sand.

Suddenly, the fret swirled around itself, leaving a pocket of clean air in its wake, into which the figure strode, near to me. A fleece, wellingtons and a ponytail all became abundantly clear.

Without hesitation I called out and waved.

'Cerys! Cerys!'

With the last syllable uttered, I realised my voice hadn't sounded as I wanted. I was going for man-of-the-world casual, but instead created in my larynx tones reminiscent of a high-pitched, excitable teenage boy in my urgency to make contact again.

My effort, however it was perceived by her, was rewarded with a wave; two-handed over her head, no less, in return.

Henry looked over, wagged his tail for a few moments and continued his hypnotic stare at the tennis ball in the slingshot.

That's strange, I thought; *last time, he was way over the sand chasing Phoebe and embarrassing himself and me.*

We continued walking toward each other. I smiled, waiting for a reaction – which came in the form of another wave.

We continued walking until that moment when I could see the whites of her eyes. I never fully appreciated what that phrase meant until that point. The expression, the inner being, the person are all revealed, naked and exposed.

Her eyes looked haunted, void of the gregarious sparkle that I remembered.

We met in front of each other – the fog swirling around us.

'Cerys, are you okay?' I asked with feeling.

She smiled her warm smile, revealing her perfect teeth, and with it applied a mask.

'Hello, Eddie,' she replied. 'I am fine.'

I stood, unable to find words. Not a single syllable would form in my vocal cords. The many times I had rehearsed my witty dialogue over and over on these very sands deserted me at this, the critical moment. Instead I smiled with a gormless expression, unsure of what to do.

'It's supposed to be summer!' I finally blurted, and regretted saying it instantly and returned to my mute state.

'It is back there,' replied Cerys, pointing her head over her shoulder toward the dunes.

She bent forward and tickled Henry's ears playfully as he continued to stare patiently at the ball in the slingshot in my hand.

I then realised Phoebe was nowhere to be seen. I concluded she wasn't with Cerys at all.

'Where is Phoebe? Is she not with you?' I asked with surprise.

Cerys drew her lips into her mouth and bullied them into a white, bloodless submission.

I stared at her, not fully understanding what my observation had conjured within her.

Her anxiety appeared to reach a climax and she blew out her cheeks, and with the action released her lips, with a small popping sound.

'I shouldn't have come,' she uttered, before spinning around and running up toward the dunes.

'Cerys! Cerys! Wait!' I shouted.

I ran after her, caught up and pleaded with her to stop – and her run changed to a fast walk, as I jogged backwards next to her.

'What has happened, Cerys? Stop!' I pleaded, as I managed to stand in front of her, halting her progress.

Even though we stood close together, she made no eye contact, her focus held on the dunes somewhere beyond the mist.

'He took Phoebe away,' she whispered over my shoulder.

'I am sorry, Cerys, who took Phoebe away?'

'He did, he said he would.'

I tried to make sense of her words, her behaviour, but couldn't determine a reason why she was there at all without her chocolate Labrador. And I concluded that after all these months of wanting to see her, of fantasising about meeting again, now the moment had arrived I was in reality standing on a cold, desolate beach with a complete stranger, whose erratic behaviour was causing a growing level of concern to rise within me, as the minutes ticked by.

'Cerys, I do not understand. Who has taken Phoebe from you? Did it happen in the car park? We can look for her, Henry and I, or I can call the police,' I offered in rapid succession.

I do not know if it was my questioning or something else that jolted Cerys, but her expression changed. The manic stare into the distance evaporated, as if she had been transported back into the here and now, and an air of normality swept over her face. She looked into my eyes and a smile spread across her lips.

'I am sorry, Eddie –it's just that seeing you with Henry made it all come back,' she blurted, and with these words, the smile retreated from her mouth.

I decided not to respond, to see if she would divulge any further details, or if I could make sense of the situation. But she fell quiet, keeping her remaining thoughts to herself.

We stood facing each other in silence – me in the direction of the shore, she toward the dunes. Henry now lay by my side, resigned to the fact that the chase session was without a doubt over.

Cerys' teeth chattered and she trembled visibly beneath the layer of her turquoise fleece. I simply stood not knowing what to say or do. *Should I offer my fleece*, I thought, *which, though a chivalrous act of epic proportions, could doom my T-shirt-clad body to a state of hypothermia? Well, maybe that is a slight exaggeration, but it would certainly leave me feeling very cold indeed. Should I take her arm and suggest we walk up to the car park, get warm in the van?* But I concluded I had to find the correct words to ensure the sentence didn't sound creepy – after all, my efforts at communication thus far had made me sound like a lovesick teenager, and then my observation had caused her to run away from me. No, the words had to be right, I thought as I continued to dither.

'It's so cold!' she exclaimed. 'I've got a hot flask in the car, shall we go?' she added, laughing, and started to walk.

And that was that. I had dithered; Cerys had taken control with her hot drink for sharing scenario.

Yet I stood my ground as she passed me.

'You coming, Eddie?' she called after her.

I turned to face her, but still made no attempt to follow. Don't get me wrong, I was tempted; I wanted to spend time with her. But equally, I was wary as to how someone could switch in a moment from an anxious, wounded state to inviting me to share the inside of their car.

She turned, bent down and clasped her hands to her knees.

'Henry! C'mon, boy!' she shouted cheerfully.

In a moment, with his name recognised, he was off, padding gleefully across the sand toward her, his tail wagging happily.

'You fickle, fickle little shit!' I hissed at him.

'C'mon, Eddie, it's cold,' she pleaded as Henry sniffed around her legs.

I followed.

With my movement, Henry remembered who his master was and waited for me, letting Cerys lead the way up toward the duckboards and through the dunes.

I caught her up and we walked side by side in silence, our footsteps in unison, just as they had been during that first meeting on the beach.

'Is that your van?' she enquired as we reached the car park.

'Is that your Range Rover?' I replied sarcastically, looking at the only other vehicle parked up.

She giggled slightly.

'Dumb question, wasn't it?' she asked.

I didn't answer; I did not think I was supposed to.

'*The Party King, bringing magic to every special occasion,*' she read aloud. 'Who's the glamorous assistant, then, you or Henry?' she teased.

'Oh, me, naturally,' I replied.

From the fraught and tense atmosphere we had experienced out on the sands, here we seemed to connect once more. The mood felt relaxed, jovial, as it had during that first encounter.

She clicked open the vehicle with her key and went around the back and pulled the tailgate up.

Responding to two pats of her hand on the bumper, Henry jumped in and began sniffing the blanket laid out in the cavernous boot. Cerys reached for a stainless steel bowl stowed behind the wheel arch and laid it out in front of Henry, before searching under the blanket and retrieving a plastic two-litre milk bottle. She opened the bottle and poured the cooling water held within into the bowl with a satisfying rhythmical glug, ready for Henry to lap up, which he did greedily once Cerys moved away.

'Don't worry, yours won't be served in a bowl!' she told me as we moved to the front of the car, she to the right and me to the left.

I smiled, enjoying her company once more, yet I was still concerned as to the whereabouts of her dog and the reason she was here at all this early on a Saturday morning.

I climbed into the passenger seat, conscious of the immaculate cream leather upholstery and trim that contrasted with my van's cab, which was covered in dirt, dog hairs, dog saliva and car parking tickets.

Cerys clambered into the driver's seat and closed the door, but still the cold encircled us.

'Will Henry be okay if I close the tailgate? I forgot to do it,' she asked, looking over her shoulder toward the back of the car.

'Sure, he will be fine. I'll do it,' I replied, opening the passenger door.

Henry had made himself right at home and was curled happily on the blanket. I stroked his head before pulling down the tailgate and returning to the front.

'I wasn't sure what you drank, so I made two,' said Cerys, smiling, holding up two flasks.

I looked at her, then at the flasks, then back at Cerys, slightly unnerved by the situation, but at the same time felt an urge to laugh welling up inside of me. I could be sat here in a car with a serial killer, my dog held captive in the boot, but all I could think was that at least I was out of the cold!

'Tea? Coffee?' she enquired brightly.

I looked at the flasks presented before me and then up to her face. Our locked gaze released a smile and a little shake of encouragement of both flasks in her outstretched hands, to aid my decision.

Her smile was the same that first time I saw her all those months ago; a sense of playfulness, life and fun radiated from it and my uneasiness evaporated in this confined space.

'Do you always bring two flasks out with you? Do you get that thirsty?' I enquired teasingly.

She laughed loudly. 'It is a bit stalker-like, isn't it? I don't usually make a habit of it, but thought I might see you and didn't know if you liked tea or coffee,' she added with what I took to be honesty.

'Wow, really?'

She nodded. We looked at each other in silence.

'It is a bit stalker-like, though!' I stated suddenly.

'Right, for that you are getting tea, whether you like it or not!' she replied, putting down one flask and unscrewing the lid from the other.

'I was going to choose tea anyway.'

'Oh, really?' she asked, pouring the liquid into the cup.

'Yes, really.'

We both laughed and she handed the drink to me. Milky tea; I knew I had to be polite and drink it.

With her own drink poured and cooling in the cup in her hands, we stared out of the windscreen toward the dunes, their shape elusive through the churning mist.

In the ensuing silence, I debated whether to confess that she had been on my mind since that first meeting, but concluded such a statement would surely put me back into 'creepy man' territory again, much as it had as I struggled to find the words out on the beach.

'It's funny,' I started. 'Every week we've been down here, I have looked out for you and have been disappointed not to see you.'

She didn't answer.

'Because I really enjoyed our chat,' I added, trying to justify my opening words.

She still didn't reply.

Damn, I must in fact be in 'creepy man' territory, I concluded to myself. *Best not to say anything else.*

'Same here,' she finally said, looking over to me.

'Sorry?'

'I've been down here a few times,' she replied with a faint smile. 'First time I have found this car park though,' she added.

She returned her gaze to the windscreen and blew over the top of her tea, coaxing the steam from the liquid, inviting it to cool down.

Did she enjoy that first meeting; did she feel disappointment at not seeing me too? I had no way of knowing from her answer and was not going to ask outright – such action, I felt, would put me on the path to narcissism; not a place I have ever fancied going to. In my life, I have seen many travel there quite happily and shout, on arrival, how wonderful the view is. I am guessing the top is surrounded by mirrors. Greg, Sally's brother, and his golf-club chums spring to mind as examples.

'Cerys,' I said softly.

She turned and looked at me, sipping her tea.

'What has happened to Phoebe? It might help to talk about it.'

'Where do I start?'

'Anywhere you think is appropriate,' I replied.

'Well, when I was four…' she started with sincerity, but then paused.

'Go on,' I encouraged, not knowing where this was leading.

'My sister pulled off the head of my favourite doll!' she continued sarcastically, before laughing.

'I sound like a dodgy therapist, don't I?' I admitted, with mock realisation drawn over my face.

She nodded and wrinkled up her nose.

'Sorry,' I said simply, smiling.

'That's okay,' she replied.

She took on a passive look and stared down at her tea.

'Oh, I don't know, Eddie,' she began. 'Things have been bad at home for a long time – I guess taking Phoebe away was his ultimate way of hurting me.'

'Who? Your husband?'

She nodded.

'I am fine about it now, but seeing you earlier, out there, brought it all back. I'd had her for nearly five years.'

'I see,' I replied flatly, not knowing what else to say.

'Apologies if I was erratic,' she added, nodding in the direction of the beach.

'No, no, not at all,' I lied.

'Eddie, I was! You are a very sweet man,' she giggled.

'I don't know about that, I am just sorry you don't have your dog.'

She lifted her shoulders in a shrug and released them.

'Can I ask you a question? But tell me to be quiet if you don't want to answer.'

'Sure,' she replied.

'Why would your husband take Phoebe away? She wasn't his to take.'

'Fair question,' she began. 'He did it because he could. Cole, my husband, is a very controlling person. He is very successful in business, used to getting his own way.'

With the words 'very successful in business' I felt inferior to a man I did not know.

'I've put up with this for a long time. He believes his success means he can dictate where we go, who we see and when we see them. But I have started to push back. I've started to say no to things I do not agree with. He knows deep down I don't really care about the car I drive, the holidays, or the clothes his money provides – yes, they are nice to have, but taking them away will not affect me. But he also knows that Phoebe is the only thing he has ever bought that really means something to me. That's why he took her. He threatened he would and he did.'

I was still licking my wounds of my internal sense of inferiority when I realised Cerys had stopped speaking.

'What are you going to do?' I asked, breaking the silence.

'Bide my time, Eddie,' she replied.

'That sounds a bit sinister!'

'Hell hath no fury and all that.'

'Now it's plain scary!'

'You are married, Eddie, aren't you?' she asked quickly, ignoring my last comment.

'Yes,' I replied, guilt spilling involuntarily out of my mouth along with the word. Guilt for sitting in this car with this woman, guilt for wanting to be sitting in this car, guilt for wanting this moment to be reality from that very first time walking on the beach with her.

'How long for?'

I paused before answering, not comfortable with this shift of attention from Cerys.

'Almost twenty years,' I finally uttered.

'Wow! So you know even better than me, then, how hard it is sometimes. How hard it is to keep feeling alive, to not fall under the spell of repetition, where we kid ourselves we feel safe and are not panicked by the limited time that remains to be us.'

I merely nodded, understanding exactly what she meant.

'Is that how you feel?' I asked eventually.

'I think you know the answer.'

I chuckled to myself at her reply.

My untouched tea was now cold in the cup as I placed it to my lips for the first time.

'What has made you push back on your husband?' I blurted out suddenly.

She replied, 'Sorry?' as I tried to understand where this forward question had come from within me.

'You said earlier your husband was controlling, but you are saying no now – why is that?' I replied with equal forwardness.

She pushed a button on the driver's door and the window retracted with a whir, inviting the mist into our sanctuary as she reached across and retrieved my cup. She threw the liquid out of the window in one motion and turned to face me, before leaning forward and placing the two cups on the dashboard.

She returned her gaze to me, her fingers parting her hair, her right elbow resting on the steering wheel.

'Because I met you,' she said gently.

Now it was my turn to say, 'Sorry?'

'That first time, you seemed so alive!' she stated as an explanation.

I looked at her dumbly, not sure of what to say.

'I was tongue-tied!' I finally admitted.

She ignored my confession.

'You get up early to be in this beautiful place. You gave a dog a second chance, a home. You've reminded me there is something out there, something good. These simple actions are the ones that matter. Not the chasing of things we do not really need. And now today, I find you are a magician, making people question what is real and what is fantasy by your actions. You bring them joy, Eddie, which in my eyes is amazing.'

I didn't know how to answer, so I spoke as I saw it.

'I walk Henry this early because, as you know from past experience, he cannot be trusted to behave. I perform magic not because I like it, but because it is all I know how to do. I'll never have a car like this, or holiday in faraway places, or own a fabulous house like the one I am sure you live in with en suites, a swimming pool and a sauna. That to me would be amazing,' I replied with honesty.

I wanted to say more, to convey what I was *really* thinking, tell her how I was feeling, but at this point, Cerys interrupted me.

'Eddie, these things you list are part of what we chase, but are ultimately unimportant. They come at a price, a heavy price for our lives and relationships.'

'That's easy to say when you have them, when you don't have to struggle financially,' I retorted.

'True, I confess, a lack of financial worries makes aspects of life manageable. But these are aspects we create ourselves. It's so easy to get sucked into a world where a "friend" has a five-bedroom house, so you buy a six-bedroom one. It's a world where another has a daughter that rides a pony, so you buy a stable in retaliation. Where you subscribe to a magazine not because you enjoy the features, or agree with their editorial leaning, but because you think it is what must be seen on your coffee table. It's superficial, Eddie, all of it.'

'I would still like a crack at it! Make my own mind up,' I responded playfully.

Cerys smiled, reached for my hands and cupped them. The action seemed so normal, almost like a reflex. Yet that first gentle touch made the skin on the backs of my hands tingle and my groin throb.

'To reply to your other statement, yes, Henry can be naughty, but without him being like this we would never have met. I was only on the beach because I was fed up of being on my own, of rattling around an even bigger house that my husband insisted we needed, with even more materialistic, fluffy padding than the previous one. Fed up of the rows and the "Look at what I have provided for you" speeches from Cole, on the odd occasion he is actually home. Then I meet you: someone who has the important things in life sorted.' She squeezed my hands in hers. 'It was fate we met,' she giggled.

The sound of friction alerted us both to the direction of the dashboard and we instinctively grabbed for the cup as it fell toward the floor.

I caught it cleanly as it approached the gearstick, while her little finger closed around the handle. Within that split second our faces came together, and a second later, so too our lips. My senses were bombarded with messages and absorbed information that exploded in waves of pleasure as I experienced and explored a new kiss for the first time in almost twenty years. Like that kiss with Sally yesterday, it started first as probing, almost testing, but soon was stripped back to bare passion, when only that all-consuming moment in time matters. Our tongues darted, our hands ran through each other's hair, and I was a teenager all over again.

Chapter 11

Lost in Translation

'Why the Whispering Rocks today, Gus? The weather is good, we could go higher,' I said, tying up my boots.

'No real reason, just fancied it – an easy day after last week,' came the honest reply.

We take it in turns to decide the route. Last week I decided on a difficult approach that enables a walker to explore four ridges, all at a similar elevation, that reward you with nothing but mountain views for 360 degrees for the duration of the walk, approximately twelve kilometres from the first ridge to the fourth. But getting to this position is the problem – as I said, the approach is difficult, and that is where the effort lies. It takes two hours on a continuous incline before the first ridge is reached. And last week, this incline was lashed with horizontal rain driven by a furious wind every few hundred metres we climbed. The culprits, shower clouds relentlessly swooping low, deposited their offerings, hungrily sucked up from the vast ocean days before. Even with wet-weather gear on, our progress was miserable. We both knew that had we been on our own, we would have turned back. But with the encouragement of the other funnelling a desire to continue, we worked through it. Until, one hundred metres from the start of the first ridge, the wind died to a whimper and the clouded sky that we knew was set above the sea became illuminated with a brilliant light.

Gus commented that the weather was going to change for the better, although the cloud cover in my opinion still looked menacing. I asked him why he was so sure.

He pointed to the smallest of breaks in the cloud, far off toward the horizon, and said, 'If there is enough blue in the sky to patch a sailor's trousers, the weather will soon be fine.'

'And where did this sound meteorological theory originate, Gus?' I asked mordantly.

'From an old Scottish fisherman I encountered when in Mozambique,' he replied nonchalantly.

I didn't want to respond, but I couldn't resist; my curiosity got the better of me.

'What were you doing in Mozambique, Gus?' I ventured.

'I was trying to get a passage on a boat to Mauritius to see the Seven Coloured Earths. I had a bet on about them,' explained Gus, with all the confidence of a rational and obvious explanation, but as was his way, no further information was forthcoming.

I had no idea what he was talking about, nor, as has become the norm, did I have any reason not to believe him. No reason to question that this encounter had indeed taken place.

'I see.' I nodded, unconvinced, as the sky darkened once more. I definitely doubted the validity of the old fisherman's weather forecasting.

Yet, within twenty minutes, we stored our wet-weather clothes in the dry compartments of our bags, had our sunglasses firmly on our faces and contemplated removing our fleeces, as the sun happily beat down upon us.

Today's walk would be very different. We hadn't walked this side of the mountains, Gus' choice, for a long time – over a year, in fact. In the winter, when the weather can be wet for weeks on end, the approach through ancient sheepfolds can turn to bogland that needs careful navigation, step by step, sometimes forcing one to move, crablike, over many metres before continuing forward and repeating the process over and over. Combine this with the fact that the subsequent path to be negotiated after the bog follows a channel that is swollen with freezing run-off rushing from the mountains, which leaves part of it almost impassable during those colder months, making it a bleak experience. In the summer, though, it is a very different place. The channel is dry and the walk can consist of taking the path, or alternatively, scrambling over the now-exposed boulders and rocks that had formed the riverbed. It is a reasonably slight elevation, the path route undemanding, the challenge coming from picking a route through the boulders.

But it is the view that is the reward on arriving at the Whispering Rocks. The rocks are a collection of huge granite boulders, which are suspended and balanced together at impossible angles that seemingly defy the known laws of physics. They form a narrow vista that ends in a sheer drop that reveals a stretch of water known as the Blue Lough, far below. Directly opposite the Whispering Rocks, a waterfall flows over a mountaintop, depositing a constant supply of water into the lough.

Legend has it that long ago, a giant, in fear of an even fiercer and stronger neighbour, used this desolate place to store his wealth of gold and jewels. The story tells that it took many months, under the cover of darkness, for him to carry huge quantities of the treasure at a time here. With each visit, he tunnelled and buried it deep into the ground. When he had finished his labour, he marked the place of his stash by building up the stones that now form the Whispering Rocks into a large mound.

Content with his work and satisfied that his wealth could never be stolen, he did not return for two years, in which time his rival was slain (although that is another story in itself). But to his dismay, on the day he returned, when he attempted to dig, he found the ground where his treasure was buried had given way under the sheer weight of the gold and jewels buried there. In searching, he found coins and precious stones strewn down the side of a cavernous pit, exposed in the landslide. With two winters now past, the pit was filled with deep water and he assumed the majority of his treasure had slid into it.

In his rage he began to dismantle the marking place with his hands and kick at it with his feet, and in doing so, he moved the boulders into impossible angles. Still not content, he proceeded to throw a succession of the rocks from the mound into the lake below.

His anger was unabated, and he lifted the largest boulder from the mound and with considerable effort hurled it downwards into the water, accompanied with a deafening roar from his throat, which spread for miles around. The impact of this huge lump of granite threw up such a vast volume of water that it headed up and over the mountain opposite, causing a rainbow to materialise. The beauty and suddenness of its appearance calmed the giant into a more serene state.

Surveying the damage he had caused, he slowly turned and walked away, never to venture to the place ever again.

This is how folklore explains the erratic suspension of the Whispering Rocks, the creation of the Blue Lough below and how the water displaced by the final boulder the giant launched trickles back to this day into the lough as the waterfall on the opposite side of the valley. And why – most importantly, some say – gold and jewels (well, quartz actually) can still be found on the steep slope beneath the Whispering Rocks.

In reality, the landscape was formed by intense and violent glacial activity thousands of years ago. Although, Gus and I always want to believe the secretive dealings and vile temper of that giant long ago are the true cause.

We normally hold our own thoughts during a walk, only communicating when we see something of interest, or need to consult the map. Today the map, though packed, was not really needed; the boulders of the riverbed were our guides. Interest was provided by the mountain hares and the circling buzzards playing a life-and-death version of hide-and-seek with each other. And of course, the sheer beauty of the mountains that surrounded us on our journey toward the Whispering Rocks.

My mind was occupied, as it had been since Saturday, with the events that had unfolded on that misty beach. The thought that kept coming back, time and again, was that while my first encounter with Cerys had been remembered as nearly perfect, it had now had dimmed into insignificance compared with the recent events. We only kissed. I say only; it was a prolonged, passionate and intense experience that left me giddy and smothered in guilt, yet I was also walking on cloud nine, because it felt so good, so right.

In between kisses, we cuddled, stroked each other's hair and talked. Cerys admitted that, like me, she had been there every Saturday since our first encounter – firstly walking with Phoebe, then after she was taken, alone. I confessed how disappointed I was when I trudged back every time to the van with just Henry for company, and then got annoyed with myself for being so irrational, so obsessed, so out of character. She laughed and replied excitedly that she knew exactly what I meant. She told me that on each occasion, not just that day, she had brought two flasks, one tea, one coffee, with her, and always a container of water and a bowl for Henry too. And on arriving back at her car alone, each time she had poured the liquid contents out over the duckboards with a heavy heart. At this we both laughed and concluded that the whole situation was crazy. The kissing commenced again at this point.

We touched only briefly on the details of our lives. From my perspective, I was concerned that revelations of my life would destroy the mystery, the excitement of the encounter – she would see the man before her. Also, I was reluctant to probe, as the inadequacy I felt at knowing her husband was successful would only be intensified.

I did mention that I would have loved to have seen the world, but it will always remain just a pipe dream.

'Why?' she enquired.

'Why? Cost!' I replied flatly.

'It doesn't have to be expensive, you know.'

'Really? I am sure you don't travel like that,' I commented, glancing around the roof of the Range Rover.

'My husband loves the luxury. The five-star service, the marble, the infinity pools, the being waited on hand and foot. Personally, I'd prefer to be with real people and see the real country.'

'But as I said, you do travel like that,' I responded.

'Not my choice – it is what he wants,' she replied curtly.

We kissed again and then fell silent, holding each other.

'Honestly,' she finally said over my shoulder, 'with your passport, a credit card as backup and a bottle of grapefruit seed extract, you can go pretty much anywhere you please in the world.'

'Anywhere?' I said, lifting my head and searching her eyes.

'Yep, anywhere.'

'I should put that theory to the test. Obviously, I will let you know when I am holed up somewhere in a filthy prison in far-flung corner of the earth with only rats for company!'

'That isn't going to happen, silly. Besides,' she continued, 'I'll be with you.'

I let her words sink in. Spoken matter-of-factly and with no hint of irony, almost as if this were already planned, preordained, destined to happen. And with this, the uneasiness I felt on the two flasks being presented to me retuned. This wasn't normal. Well, to me it wasn't normal: to be making holiday plans – no, life-changing travel plans, albeit loosely – with a stranger. In fact, sitting in the car was still not lying well with part of me.

'So, what is grapefruit seed extract for?' I asked, intrigued, trying to go with the situation.

'Drink water from a street vendor in Delhi and you find out!' came her cryptic reply.

We kissed again. *This* part I had gotten used to, had accepted, and through the action, proved the existence of evolution by demonstrating our ability to adapt to situations!

With a final, gentle, lingering kiss goodbye, accompanied by the pressing together of our foreheads and a promise to meet again there at the same time next week, we reluctantly parted. I collected Henry and walked the few steps over to my van. Once in, we waved, smiled and blew kisses at each other through our door windows, before Cerys reversed her vehicle and I followed. At the end of the car park approach road, Cerys indicated left and I headed right.

By the time I had run through my gear set, from one up to five, the weather was clearing and I opened my window welcoming the sunlight to to infiltrate the cab.

It was at this point that I glanced at the clock in the dashboard and momentarily assumed the display was wrong, but with reason reinstated, I quickly concluded that I had in fact been in Cerys' company for almost two hours. Guilt racked me. I was only sixty minutes later than usual. Yet, I found I was making elaborate excuses in my mind to relay to Sally on my return. A deer hit the van. No good – no sign of damage. Temporary traffic lights on the shore road – but this was also the route to her mother's house, and what if she had driven along it herself that morning? I could have argued it was emergency roadworks to mend a burst water pipe and the crew were just packing up when I got there, so the scene was total chaos. But I then reconsidered, as no one lives on the shore road for a seven-mile stretch, reducing the need for a water main to fantasy. It then struck me: what if a tourist was hopelessly lost, wanting to be on the other side of the mountains? I could have led via the back roads and tracks, while they followed; that would easily put an hour on my morning. But then Sally knows me. That action would be so out of character that she would know I would not do this.

Every excuse was rehearsed in my mind with an upbeat tone, an air of 'que sera sera' – I don't know why, but as much as I tried, I couldn't stop it. Yet again, Sally would know this wasn't true. If I am late, quite simply, I moan.

Yet the most plausible explanation for my delayed return was not even considered, only to be rejected: I never thought to simply say, 'Henry and I spent longer on the beach.'

As I turned the corner into the road where the house sits, I decided my plan of action: I would do exactly as Sally does on her return from trips out and say nothing.

I swung the van into the drive, with my mind primed and focused like a crouched Olympian waiting in those final, dragging seconds for the starter pistol. The gun fired and my game plan fell to pieces as I was faced with an empty space where I presumed Sally's car would be.

A rushing sensation of fear washed over me, causing me to exhale deeply. What if she had followed me to the beach? What if she was looking for me now? What if she had seen us and was in state of despair? What if she had seen us and had followed Cerys home? And with the last scenario still prodding my brain, it invited logic to come back. *She is probably out at the shops, or just out somewhere*, I concluded, taking the keys out of the ignition.

Yet, I still felt a sense of trepidation on entering the house with my cheery hellos met by silence. I searched every room, calling out as I went. I even checked the spare bedroom, and only relaxed when it became abundantly clear that Sally was not at home.

Later, I sat in the kitchen drinking tea and confessed to myself, as my heart rate returned to normal, that I was rubbish at this, at the act of deceit. Yet I also knew I had been seduced by that most basic of human needs: the feeling of contentment, the joy of happiness. And the afterglow that still enveloped me at this point far outweighed the malfeasance of the situation. I knew that after this second encounter, I couldn't wait until the following Saturday; I yearned to be back in the Range Rover again, or walking on the beach. This feeling was verging on becoming an addiction.

We always have a good lunch. Today was no exception. Today we feasted on ham from locally reared pigs, apparently happy pigs – well, happy until they were placed between the slices of fresh, crusty bakery bread that Gus and I chewed on. Tomatoes and salad onions from his garden completed the sandwiches. Apples and bananas from the greengrocer followed for dessert. Personally, I would have been equally pleased with a pork pie, a Scotch egg and a packet of crisps. But I know this consumption, gorgeous though it would be, would be counterproductive considering the exercise we had participated in for the past two and a half hours.

We sat within the Whispering Rocks, side by side, the sun on our backs, the Blue Lough far below us, shimmering with silver and white lights. The silence of the setting was only broken from time to time by Gus munching on an apple.

'I've met someone, Gus,' I blurted out.

'Oh,' came the reply as he took another bite from the apple in his hand.

'"Oh" – is that all you have to say?'

'What do you want me to say?'

'I don't know; I thought you would have an opinion, give me some advice.'

'You are a grown man, Eddie. You can make your own decisions. You don't need my approval.'

I felt embarrassed; ashamed above all else that Gus would react like this. But really, what did I expect – why did I even tell him? Did I expect him to slap me on the back, tell me well done, wanting to know all the details about her? Or to chastise me for the choice I had voluntarily made? No, I realised I had told him in an attempt to offload some of the guilt I felt that was tightly intertwined with the pleasure of visualising Cerys. The need to unload this guilt left me blind to his reaction.

'It's all just happened so quickly, I can't think of anything else,' I finally said.

He didn't answer, but still looked straight ahead, chewing on the fruit.

'I was once at a reception at the French Ambassador's residence in Kensington Palace Gardens,' he began, still not looking at me. 'He – the ambassador – was retiring after many years in service and his wife hosted a series of farewell lunches. This was the final one; I was seated on the top table, three seats down from her. The conversation was light, congenial, with the ambassador's wife retelling stories, in a delicious French accent, of the many wonderful people she had encountered over the years her husband had been in residence. Each story concluded with polite laughter and smiles along the entire length of the table.

'The person next to her, a retired lieutenant general who had worked with the FFI in the lead-up to the liberation of Paris in 1944, had a booming baritone voice and asked her, while tucking into the fish course, what she was most looking forward to now that her husband was retiring from his long and distinguished career.

'The ambassador's wife, in a reflective mood, paused for some time before she addressed the hushed line of diners, who had all turned to face her. She nodded an acknowledgement toward them, smiled and started to speak. "The thing I am most looking forward to now my husband is retiring is… a penis."

'The sound of coughing and choking and the sight of a multitude of hands reaching for wine glasses filled the room, before a silence descended, as each half-eaten piece of fish on each plate was thoroughly inspected by each diner with their knives and forks.

After a couple of minutes the retired lieutenant general leant in close to the ambassador's wife and said deeply, yet softly, "I think Madame will find the pronunciation is 'happiness' with a 'hah'."'

We both burst into fits of laughter.

'Gus, what were you doing at the French Ambassador's reception? Did they serve chocolates on a tray?' I asked, trying to regain my composure.

Gus ignored my comment, and as is his way, did not elaborate further on the story. Instead he turned to face me, with a serious look on his face.

'Does she make you happy? I am presuming they are a she…?'

'Yes! And yes, it's early days though. She makes me feel alive!' I replied cheerfully, keeping the actual number of meetings to myself.

'Well, that is important, really important,' he said, looking intently at me. 'We all deserve to be happy, Eddie.'

'Thanks, Gus. I wanted to tell someone, and thank you for not being judgemental.'

'Why would I be?' he said quietly.

'I don't know. Just thought—'

'Like I said,' he interrupted, 'we all deserve to be happy. That includes Sally,' he added, his voice even lower.

The choice of name for this place was finally revealed as the rocks whispered the words 'that includes Sally' back to me, over and over. The handiwork of that giant, driven by rage, all those years ago, triggered my conscience to act as an antidote to my fledgling addiction.

Our troop back was as uncommunicative as the journey to the Whispering Rocks had been. Although this time, my thoughts refused to summon Cerys. Instead, twenty years of marriage filled the space, each image pausing just long enough to evoke recognition, before being replaced by another like a flickering slide show.

With each click I saw our first argument, post wedding, a petty misunderstanding and the frantic physical reconciliation that followed. I recalled cream teas in Devon, whisky-tasting in Skye and blistered toes on Hadrian's Wall. Candlelit carols at midnight Mass, where the only way I could endure it was the promise of devils on horseback and a fine Rioja at her parents' house after 1am. I smiled at the way she still dreads summer storms, their unpredictable power causing her to recoil and squeeze my arm tightly with every thunderclap, followed by her counting the time between the next flash of lightning and rumble and informing me where the storm is in relation to our world.

My smile retreated with the image of that Friday afternoon, which brought the worst storm of all. The police car surprisingly parked outside on my return. The policewoman sat on the sofa, cradling Sally's limp form to her chest. The turmoil which forced its way into our lives on that vile night led Sally blindly into darkness and my own lonely journey to denial. Finally, with a frown on my brow, I came up to date and reflected on the lost years that have followed and the emptiness they have brought.

Within sight of the car park, my phone burst into life in my backpack. Its tone lifted the house lights, confirming the slide show was over.

Normally, I would leave it; investigate only when back at the van, with walking boots and fleece off, driving shoes on. But not today – instinctively, I reached around my back and swung the bag off my arm, before retrieving my mobile. Looking at the screen, the text revealed I had a voice message.

The opening silence spoke volumes. Eventually, Mary's voice came through, frail and distant.

'Eddie, it's me,' the message began. 'Clifford's been taken into the Royal, it's his breathing.' She paused for a short while, before adding, 'Okay? Bye, Eddie.'

She evidently assumed she had replaced her phone correctly on its cradle, as I am sure the three minutes of tormented sobbing that followed were not intended for my ears.

I plodded on in silence, my phone held tightly to my ear. The sound of her distress amplified with every step, and only ceased at my phone's insistence that the message had ended, cancelling the connection.

'Message left today at 11.42,' my phone concluded.

I cursed the mountains, my beautiful mountains, for entrapping Mary in her misery alone for the past five hours. For all I knew, her tears had continued to flow for all that time.

'What is it, Eddie?' asked Gus, trying to gauge my mood.

'It's Clifford, I think he is dying.'

'Let's go straight to the hospital,' he replied. He didn't say any more, he didn't try to make it better; he just spoke matter-of-factly.

I merely nodded.

At the van, I hurriedly tried to change out of my boots, but the laces became twisted and entwined, as my coordination fell to pieces. As I fumbled with the knots, I found the sound of Mary's cries had transformed into tears in the corners of my eyes.

Chapter 12

Formation Flying

The golf club hadn't changed. Well, to be precise, the car park hadn't changed; the same elitist parking hierarchy existed as I remembered from my previous visit to celebrate Greg Dixon's thirtieth birthday.

The four spaces nearest the clubhouse were exactly as before. Each bay had two metal rods near the kerb supporting horizontal chains, from which swung weathered white wooden signs. From nearest the entrance extending out to the left, the signs read *Captain*, *Vice-Captain*, *Secretary* and *Lady Captain*.

I wondered what the penalty was for parking in these spaces without permission. I reasoned that this had to be one of the worst violations in the etiquette of golf – a total lack of respect for rules and tradition – and therefore, an infringement of such severity would warrant a punishment the average golfer would find intolerable. Perhaps a ban on wearing multicoloured knitwear, or being shunned in the clubhouse bar would haunt the guilty and allow them time to reflect upon what had occurred.

The four spaces aside, the remainder of the car park, I reasoned, was a free-for-all for all and sundry. I was only performing close magic for the evening, so therefore did not require the van to transport my props or equipment. But I drove it just the same; reasoning that if the evening went well, people would see the van with its red-and-yellow insignia and maybe enquire about future bookings.

I did not, however, consider the tight space and limited manoeuvring capabilities within the car park and took an age to position the van in a prominent spot, as near to the entrance as I could.

Once inside, I was again reminded of the protocol I had read before here – *No spikes or course footwear to be worn beyond this mark* read a notice on the wall several metres away from the male changing rooms. And further along the corridor toward the bar, another sign announced, *Members are reminded, guests must be signed in, appear appropriately dressed and be accompanied at all times on these premises.*

Very welcoming! I thought to myself as I strolled past the sign and entered the bar area.

The bar itself covered the majority of the far wall. Towards the back, a vast array of bottles of strong liquor were bracketed high up on a mirrored wall and secured to optics. Multiple bottles of the same varieties of gin, vodka, brandy and whisky sat lined up, waiting, expecting, ready to release their liquids on contact from a teasing glass rim, in return for a rush of upwardly mobile bubbles seeking the top of each bottle upon the glass' withdrawal. In front, a solid oak counter formed the bar itself, and fixed to this were a lesser number of beer pumps. The overall view of the bar presented a strong indication of the drinking preferences of the regular clientele.

I noticed among the optics, hung up on the mirror, yet another sign reminding members that the bar no longer accepted cash transactions; instead each member's security card would need to be loaded with cash to pay for beverages. I gave a second look to the date at the bottom of the sign and correctly calculated, twice, that seven years had passed since its placement. Either business was extremely slow or the sign was hiding a crack in the mirror.

To the left of the bar, a pair of double doors attempted to hold back the muffled sounds of the function room being prepared for the evening's event. The top halves held sandblasted glass that spelt the name of the club in swirling fake Celtic characters, and through this the laying of tables with cutlery, crockery, glassware and balloons could be seen, complementing the trapped noise.

I pushed through the doors, my presence not even raising a lift of a head from the busy catering staff. The round tables in the room each had twelve chairs positioned around them, and on closer inspection of the completed tables, each crisp white tablecloth was adorned with sparkles and confetti and each place setting also held a beautiful wrapped present for the named guest.

In all of this activity I sought the treasurer to whom I had spoken first on that infamous day when Phoebe the poodle came to Jennifer's studio. We had conversed on a few occasions since, but never met. And there, standing near the kitchen doors, I spied two men talking. One looked very much in control, speaking fluently, emphasising his points with relaxed hand gestures in front of him and a controlled finger sweeping over his shoulder to the centre of the room. I presumed he was the banqueting manager. The other man looked stressed, very stressed, and with ninety minutes to go before the evening commenced I presumed him to be Mike Saunders the treasurer.

I wandered over to introduce myself.

'Mike?' I enquired.

'Yes,' he replied hurriedly as the other man continued to assure him all would be fine.

'Eddie, Eddie Dungiven,' I explained, holding out my arm for a handshake.

'Eddie Dungiven?'

'The magician for this evening,' I encouraged, smiling.

'Oh yes, yes, of course! Please forgive me, a little stressed!' he replied, gripping my outstretched hand tightly.

'So, if you think of anything else, Mr Saunders, please let me know,' added the banqueting manager before turning to head into the centre of the room to inspect and approve a newly completed table.

'Okay, okay,' Mike said, still squeezing my hand.

'Sorry, I am a little early I know,' I confessed, pulling free.

He nodded and looked around, preoccupied. I don't know why but I felt compelled to try to put this man at ease.

'These guys are professional; they do this all the time. I've performed at many of these events – trust me, it will all run like clockwork. Just relax. It will be fun!'

He merely nodded in response.

Yet, I knew deep down I was really trying to reassure myself with my words. My innards always turn to jelly prior to the start of these events. That was the reason I was here so early, to give myself time to process and work through the nerves within the venue itself. The thought of an abusive heckler, a drunk snatching the cards and spilling them all over the floor, or forgetting the card they had chosen, always played on my mind and I needed to visualise it happening to enable me to prepare. But I also knew it was this fear that kept a performance sharp, tight and focused.

'What will you do? How does it work?' asked Mike.

'As in the tricks?' I replied.

Again he nodded his head in response.

'Are you having a drinks reception first?'

Another nod.

'Well, in that case, when people are relaxing with drinks, I will approach their table or group if they are standing and select an individual and ask if they would like to see a trick.'

'I do not want our guests hassled,' he injected, looking alarmed.

I had heard this so many times before and replied with my tried and tested response.

'Understood, and you are totally correct, they should not be harassed.'

He again nodded a response.

'Generally,' I continued, 'it is relatively easy to choose a receptive individual by reading their faces.'

Mike stared at me intently.

'Really? How do you do that?!' he asked with interest.

'Ah, Mike, can't tell you that, that's a trick of the trade!' I teased.

He chuckled and seemed more at ease.

'I will perform simple, effective close magic card and coin tricks, where a guest feels in control and makes a choice. When dinner is called, I will go to tables between courses and perform again. Obviously, when food begins to arrive, I will move on to another table.'

'Go on.'

'After dinner, I will take more time, perform more elaborate tricks; sit with the guests at the table.'

Mike raised his hand to stop me and looked worried. 'We have a number of speeches at the end of the meal, so I do not think this will be possible,' he said.

'That's okay; I can do these after the speeches.'

'Well, we have a comedy hypnotist after the speeches, then a disco – I am not sure there will be time...' He trailed off, thinking as he spoke.

'We'll work something out,' I reassured him.

I wondered who the comedy hypnotist was, and was taken aback that they were actually back in vogue. I presumed their day had come and gone. This is not performer snobbery; I know some people do not like card tricks and close magic, but at least with a trick it is harmless fun and inclusive for all. Not some grubby secret to be used to feel better about yourself at the expense of an unsuspecting other.

'Okay,' he replied in a tone that indicated our conversation had drawn to a close.

'Oh, I meant to ask you, Mike – out of interest, who are the Lombarders?'

Mike and smiled at my question, seemingly pleased to oblige me.

'We are a group of local businessmen who meet up once a week for dinner and a chat. On top of this, four times a year, we go away for, shall we say, a boys' weekend, usually somewhere in Europe. It's not all fun, though! There is a serious side too: we organise Christmas food parcels and an annual party for the elderly. This takes up a lot of time, means we are away from home a lot, raising funds, sourcing goodies. So this event tonight is our way of saying thank you to our partners for all their patience through the year. We also invite friends that we think could bring something to our organisation. A chance before they join, for them to see how we roll. This is the first I have organised, nerve-racking is not the word!' he added.

'So, it's not to appease your partners for your jollies around Europe then?' I teased.

Mike merely smiled at my suggestion and gave me a wink in response.

Content with the presentation, the banqueting manager left the final table and was striding back toward us.

'I really need to get on now,' said Mike, sensing his time was about to be occupied once more. 'By the way,' he added, 'there is a meal for you in the kitchen.'

'Thank you, I'll take it later,' I replied, knowing my nerves would ensure the food would return within the hour if I ate it at this point in time.

I walked back toward the bar, looking around the room as I travelled, running through all the possible issues that could spring forth in this place in the coming hours. Content I had all covered, I headed outside to the van to listen to the football reports while I waited for the guests to arrive.

Within moments of sitting down, turning on the radio and hearing a disgruntled fan bemoaning his team's poor start to the season, I thought about Cerys.

Our time together had slipped into a routine. I was surprised how quickly, after only three meetings, this had occurred. Even illicit encounters require a level of order, it seems.

I always arrive first; always wait in my vehicle until Cerys is parked up alongside. In the interim period, I am presented with the prospect of listening to Henry's whining and moaning to be let outside. He knows he is at the beach, he knows why he is at the beach, but cannot understand why he isn't actually allowed onto the beach.

Why did we persist with this arrangement? I couldn't be sure of the answer as I sat in the golf club car park. ; oirPerhaps it was what it was – a component of a situation which didn't make sense, but felt so right.

Whatever it was, on each meeting, in the cocoon of Cerys' Range Rover, we smiled warmly, hugged and kissed deeply.

We always walked out across the sands, half an arm's length apart. Although the beach was always deserted, guilt made us keep our distance.

'I love this beach, Eddie,' she said happily, while spinning around to take in the expanse of sand, the mountains and the flat line of water.

I smiled to myself, and to Henry, just waiting for his ball to be thrown, anticipating the rush past him and the bounce, bounce, bounce toward the sea.

To add to the moment, the sun broke from behind its morning clouds and I felt compelled to ask a question in this relaxed atmosphere.

'Cerys?'

'Mmm?'

'What does your husband do?'

Cerys stopped walking and looked at me, puzzlement on her face.

'That's a strange question to ask, Eddie. Where did that come from?'

I had to agree, it was strange, but it had been with me, eating me up, since that first meeting afterPhoebe had gone.

'I guess,' I offered, 'I was just curious. You said he was successful, I wondered what in.'

'Are you jealous, Mr Dungiven?'

'No,' I lied.

'Good, because you shouldn't be.'

We walked together in silence. I knew I couldn't ask again, knowing it would make me seem jealous. But now that it was out there, it was tormenting me so much that to keep from thinking about it was near impossible.

I turned around to see the footprints left in our wake and strode backwards, and now she spoke.

'He's a florist,' she said.

'A florist, as in flowers?' I exclaimed.

'Yes! As in flowers, what other kind do you know? The only similar word has a "U"a Tin it and would see him playing in an orchestra.'

I noted her rapid and sarcastic response.

'Just surprised, that's all,' I responded.

'Why?'

'Because you said he was a successful businessman. It's not what I imagined.'

'Huge money to be made in flowers,' she replied, again rapidly, seemingly defending him. 'People will always die,' Cerys continued. 'Will always have birthdays, people will always screw up and need to say sorry. Perhaps people will always get married – and in all cases, people will always want flowers.'

'True,' I conceded.

'He's got five shops and wants more, always more,' she added, deadpan; seemingly in contrast to her earlier revelation of her husband's career choice.

'Five?' I repeated, feeling my inadequacies returning.

'Yep. That's where I met him, in his first shop. I went in to arrange a bouquet for my friend's mother's funeral; it was apt, being the middle of November – the month of the dead. I was in a rush, miles away from where I lived, and stumbled upon the shop. He took the order and made up the flowers; put them on the counter and started to busy himself with another arrangement. had I asked him if I could pay for the bouquet, I was in a hurry, but he ignored me. Instead he continued to spin roses, carnations and foliage into an ever-increasing creation.

'Eventually he stopped, stood back and smiled. "That's £25," he said. I reached for my purse from my bag and paid him. He handed over the flowers with a smile and I intended to let his bizarre behaviour go without explanation and turned to leave. "Excuse me," he called. I turned around and saw him holding the second bouquet in front of him. "And these are for you," he said, peering around the blooms.

'I said, "I don't know what to say."

'"Thank you is enough," he said. He then asked for my mobile number, which I, totally out of character, gave to him with a smile and left the shop. After which he texted me in the street, and repeatedly as I drove. I remember it was raining very hard.'

Cerys suddenly stopped speaking.

'Sounds all very romantic,' I suggested, not knowing why she had shared this information with me, or why she had stopped her recollection at that point.

'I was flattered, yes,' replied Cerys honestly.

She seemed unaware what effect this revelation was having on me. Quite simply, I didn't want to know any more. Although what could I do – I had, after all, instigated the discussion by asking her about her husband's line of business.

'I was in a bad place though, Eddie,' she added.

'Oh?'

'Vulnerable.'

'I see,' I replied, though not understanding.

'My father had died a few months before. I was really close to my dad. I think through the flattery, I saw a bit of my father's strength and dependability that had been missing for me since he'd been gone.'

'And he filled this?' I uttered helpfully.

'Unconsciously for me, yes. Cole is quite a bit older than me, same build and around the same height as my father was.'

I couldn't offer anything else. And we continued in silence, less Henry's desperate panting as he waited to chase the now-soggy, sand-coated tennis ball held in the slingshot again.

'What about yours?' Cerys suddenly asked.

'Sorry?'

'Your wife, what does she do?'

'She's an apiarist.'

'What, she studies gorillas?!' teased Cerys.

'No, she is a b—'

'A beekeeper! I know what it is, Eddie,' interrupted Cerys in a curt tone. 'I really know nothing about bees, but wish I did,' she continued.

'Everyone says that!' I replied.

'That's good, proves I am normal then, doesn't it?!'

'Cerys, why are we talking like this, about this stuff?' I bleated out.

She stopped and looked at me, around my face, deeply into my eyes, and concentrated before answering.

'We get on really well and getting to know each other means getting to know about all aspects of the other's life. And we both obviously have problems in our relationships or we wouldn't be meeting here,' she said softly. 'I am just trying to be honest, Eddie, something I haven't been able to be before in a relationship.'

I didn't answer her.

'Do you not think I am right?' she asked, walking again over the sands.

'Of course you are.'

'I said before, a few weeks ago, about feeling alive in a relationship. Mine started to go wrong a good number of years ago now.'

'Did it?' I asked.

'Yes, when the age gap between us really started to show. I realised I had married a father figure who had become obsessed with making money and nothing else. That I could take, until a few years ago when my mind, without warning, turned maternal and instinct took over me and nothing could alter my train of thought. I guess ours is a familiar story for eventual breakdown.'

She turned to face me as we walked.

'Quite simply, I wanted a child, Eddie, but he didn't.'

She looked at me, wounded, and I struggled with what to say. So, as a man, I opted to remain silent.

After some time, her face regained a level of composure.

'I am over it now. Well, that's not strictly true – I am resigned to the fact that it will never happen and clasp resentment close to my heart for him, in a place where love for a child should be.'

I wasn't comfortable with this conversation, and sensed where it was heading.

'What about you?' she uttered predictably.

'What about me?'

'Do you have any children, Eddie? Bet you would be a great dad, what with all the bouncy castles and balloon tricks!'

'No, I don't,' I replied flatly.

'Did you not want any? What about your wife?'

I prepared the answer I had recited before in the face of people's curiosity.

'No, nothing like that. I guess it just wasn't meant to be.'

Cerys nodded and looked at me. In the distance, heading toward us, a figure walked with two dogs off their leashes.

'We best head back,' I stated, evaluating the situation and for once relieved to see someone else walking on the beach, allowing me to move the conversation away from the current subject.

'Sure,' replied Cerys.

We carried on in silence for some time, enjoying the sunshine and breeze upon our faces, until Cerys spoke once more.

'Eddie, can I ask you something?'

'Mmm?'

'If it wasn't the family issue that drew you to be here, what was it?'

I paused and thought carefully before replying. 'I don't know. Guess we just accepted what life had become. We got into the routine you spoke about before. Meeting someone by chance makes you look at it differently. And she is always out tending to her bees, more so than ever these days.'

It was Cerys' turn to not reply.

'What's your wife's name?' she eventually asked.

'Why?'

'I am just curious.'

'Sally.'

'Sally,' she repeated. 'Pretty name.'

And with that the heavy conversation slipped away from us, replaced by lists of our favourite foods, drinks and films. It soon became clear Cerys had seen many more movies than I, and we established that her favourite genre was sci-fi. She tried to convince me of the merits of these movies and explain the various time-travel plots that have been threaded through so many blockbusters, all of which went over my head, much to her amusement, and through much laughter she tried over and over to make me understand.

But I know what I know – you cannot turn back time. Things happen and time moves on regardless. And all the while we kept our respective distance from each other.

All this changed again back in the Range Rover. The kissing, whispering and caressing returned and reached a crescendo of abandonment that if witnessed from the outside would have been impossible to deny – but such was our detachment from reality that we scarcely cared.

We had found saying goodbye increasing difficult, with neither wanting to break the moment with the dreaded phrase 'I have to go.' That was until today, when Cerys glanced at the clock on her dashboard and announced abruptly that she had to leave. I was quite surprised by this, and she added she was out tonight and was getting her hair cutt by way of an explanation.

With a final kiss, I left the car feeling deflated, the emotion kicking me as I heard Cerys turn the key in the ignition. I worked to keep my disappointment hidden deep within myself. I also wanted to know where she was going and with whom, but knew these questions were not mine to ask and my jealousy must remain leashed. Instead, I sat waving through my cab window as she reversed away prematurely, a cheery smile fixed upon my face, while in reality my mind was beginning to search for what I had done wrong to bring this morning's liaison to a sudden end.

Now, in the golf club car park, with darkness falling, instead of running through my set of tricks to perform, I found myself sitting in my cab, my mind again pushing a suggestion to the front to be considered as the reason for Cerys' hurried departure earlier. I concluded with despair that the failure to develop our teenage embraces further was reason enough for her to cut short our time together this morning. A pattern had formed – we kissed and kissed with urgency; then stopped and talked for a time before beginning the cycle again. My inability to be forceful, assertive, to move the relationship forward, to take the lead had simply driven her to make a polite excuse to get away.

The possibility that she actually was visiting Marco's salon for a booked appointment for a colour, cut and straightening session and had simply lost track of time in my company was suppressed in my mind. My thoughts preferred to spin my imagined failings out of control.

Clifford suddenly came into my mind, or rather, the shell that is now Clifford did. Even after two weeks of daily visits, I am still shocked by how small this huge man looks, trapped in his hospital bed. His substantial frame dwarfed by the array of machines and monitors that surround him – pulsing their information, both visually and audibly in a language that no one who sits by his bedside can understand. On the occasions, the regular occasions, when a piece of equipment suddenly drones out a shrill single note, we, Clifford's visitors, look at each other, waiting for a member of staff to arrive to investigate. But always, in moments, with concern etched across all of our faces, one of us will retire to find a nurse. They will arrive, press a red or green button a number of times to reset the monitor in question and banish the sound. Turning their attention to Clifford, they take hold of his tired hand and ask if he feels comfortable. And always, the farmer simply nods his head meekly.

Today's visit had a different feel. For the past fortnight, he has had two small plastic tubes taped to his cheeks that meet beneath his nostrils. These, we have been told, help get oxygen into his lungs easily. It was deemed a temporary measure, as they wait for his body to respond to the antibiotics that have been administrated to clear the lung infection that brought him here in the first place.

But today the plastic tubes were gone, replaced by a full face mask, clamped around his head with elastic. The clear plastic form resembled an imagined futuristic fighter pilot of yesteryear movies.

Now today we have been told that Clifford has not responded well to the antibiotics, so a different course will be tried.

The mask is, again, supposedly a temporary measure, in place to ease the strain on his heart and lungs. Yet with all this reassurance from the medical professionals, I watched today as his barrel chest heaved up and down in shallow breaths, attempting to use the pure oxygen pumped from the wall behind him.

He can speak with the mask on, but cannot be heard. With the mask off he can be heard, but very quickly runs out of breath and needs the mask replaced.

Eating, I have seen, is extremely challenging for him. The summer fete bouncer is reduced to taking a few mouthfuls of soup from a spoon held to his lips by Mary, before he slips the mask back over his nose and mouth to draw a breath and swallow the liquid down. And yet, the medics tell us to wait and let the antibiotics work.

Car doors closing and voices laughing brought me back into the golf club car park. I focused through the windscreen of my van and saw the car park now half full and the light beginning to fade around me. Through my wing mirror, I spied couples walking toward the clubhouse, now brightly illuminated from inside in the twilight. And all the while, my observations went unnoticed. I still hoped my initial enthusiasm for the Lombarders would hold steady, but looking at them heading en masse to the building, and with the knowledge from their treasurer of their extracurricular activities, I was reminded of moths attracted to a flame, or maybe, judging by their costumes, more like guests invited to the ugly bug ball. Their attire, manner and the venue brought me right back to that birthday celebration with Greg Dixon. Greg Dixon. My heart sank as my mind wrestled with the fact that he could be here tonight. I didn't believe he would be a member, but as Mike had said, tonight was also a recruitment exercise for new blood. I was sure Sally's brother would jump at the chance to enthuse about his beloved golf club to anyone unlucky enough to be in earshot.

I checked and straightened my bow tie slightly in the sun visor mirror, checked my new deck of cards was still firmly in the inside pocket of my dinner jacket and prepared to leave the sanctuary of my world and enter an alien one which I now foresaw would consist of rituals, toasts and tradition.

Well, I was wrong.

On stepping inside I was confronted by a scene of the ordinary; what I like to call normal people doing normal things. Groups stood around drinking, chatting, socialising. A mixture of excited chatter punctuated with regular cackles and laughter equalled a relaxed, friendly atmosphere.

I wandered around the edge of the bar searching for faces, smiling and nodding to anyone that caught my eye, choosing who to approach. I stopped when I was in close proximity to a group of four, two women and two men. All middle-aged, three listening to one of the ladies who was speaking, dressed in a shimmering black dress and patent leather high-heeled shoes. I moved around so as to be in her vision and smiled as our eyes met briefly as she continued to speak. She was aware I was listening but I knew she would conclude her story. With her anecdote delivered, they all laughed in unison and I waited for my chance. As the laughter died down to smiles I spoke.

'Excuse me for interrupting; would you like to see some magic?' I asked in a deep tone, which hinted at an air of authority. 'Real magic!' I stated in the same tone, directly at the woman in the shimmering black dress.

'Mike said there was a magician here tonight,' she replied excitedly. 'Go on, it will be fun!' she added, looking at her companions.

With the group turned to face me and smiling, I retrieved my cards from my breast pocket. I examined the pack, still in its clear plastic wrapping, turning it over and over in my hands. I looked up in mock horror at my audience, studying each of their faces individually. I cleared my throat and rubbed my fingers over my lips.

'Well, this is quite embarrassing,' I lied. 'My wife has packed a new deck of cards.'

In response, my audience smiled politely.

'I normally use my tried and tested ones,' I lamented, while in reality, I had simply sealed up a set with duplicate cards already concealed within.

At this point I knew I was losing one of the men. His withdrawn smile showed a level of contempt for me and my audacity in interrupting his evening. But it was this very reaction that gave me the buzz; to be able to pull him back and have confidence in my ability was my reason for performing.

'Well, you will have to perform real magic as you said you can!' teased the woman in black, right on cue. I had, as always, chosen well.

'Have you ever seen close magic before?' I quizzed.

Three faces shook in front of me, while the fourth stayed still.

'Me neither!' I exclaimed.

Three faces smiled; the fourth remained tight-lipped.

'You sure you don't want to see a coin trick instead?'

She shook her head at me and wrinkled her nose.

'Ah, okay. What's the worst that could happen?' I pleaded with mock distress in my voice. I cleared my throat as I unwrapped the pack. 'I have the van running in the car park just in case though,' I added quickly.

As predicted, three smiles turned into polite laughter.

I placed the plastic in my waistcoat pocket and withdrew the cards and discarded the two jokers, again into my waistcoat pocket. Keeping eye contact with the woman in the black dress, I then split the cards and shuffled them.

'Pick two cards,' I commanded, while offering the fanned-out pack to her.

I turned my head away as her fingers hovered over the cards.

'Look at them and return them to the pack, but do not show me. Done it?' I asked, already having hold of the card she had selected and returned.

'Yes, I have,' she replied, looking to her friends with a smile.

'Very good. Okay, let's…' I trailed off as a round of applause emanated from the entrance and quickly engulfed the room.

I stood, puzzled by this commotion, and searched for an explanation on the faces around me.

Then the chanting began.

Initially, only two or three male voices could be heard, which were rapidly joined by others in the room.

'Snoddy! Snodddy! Snoddy! Oi! Oi! Oi! Snoddy! Snoddy! Snoddy! Oi! Oi! Oi! Snoddy! Oi! Snoddy! Oi! Snoddy! Snoddy! Snoddy! Oi! Oi! Oi!'

And so it continued, almost tribal, above the applause and occasional wolf whistle.

A small man with wayward, thinning grey hair and a shocking yellow bow tie appeared in the centre of the room. He unashamedly milked the adoration with a playful push of his hands at the wrists, while at the same time, lifting his eyes upward. This, evidently, was 'Snoddy'. Accompanying him was a slightly younger woman who somehow had squeezed into a red dress that would have still been questionable for her to wear ten years and two sizes ago. Like Snoddy, she appeared to love the attention their entrance had commanded.

Before I could ask the group I was stood with to identify the couple, Mike the treasurer announced, loudly and to yet more thunderous applause, 'Gentlemen and lady guests, I present to you, your chairman Roger Snodd and his lovely partner Melaine.'

The couple snaked their arms around each other's waists and again held the moment for as long as was possible, both grinning broadly.

Eventually the chairman invited quiet with the repeated descent and ascent of his outstretched palm.

'Friends!' he began. 'And that includes you, Freddy!' he added, pointing to a tall, lean man standing at the far end of the bar, much to the amusement of all the guests. Freddy merely pointed back at the chairman in the same fashion, while those around him whooped their approval.

'It's been a hard year,' he continued. 'Especially that weekend in Berlin!'

His guests responded with more whooping and laughter.

'But seriously, let's not forget or lose sight of what this evening is for. To say thank you to our partners for all their support and understanding for those many, many times we could not be home during the year because of committee business.'

'Hear, hear, Snoddy!' came the murmured replies from the men present.

'And also let's also acknowledge we are all in equal partnerships,' he added.

'Hear, hear!'

'For example, I drove here tonight and the lovely Melanie is going to drive home! A perfect example of equal partnership in action!'

The room erupted in hysterical, uncontrollable male laughter, the loudest of which came from Roger Snodd himself.

And that was, I sensed, the beginning of the end of the evening for me. With the arrival of Roger Snodd they all appeared to lose any idea of decorum or maturity. I say all, when in reality it was only the male guests behaving in this manner. It was as if the chairman's arrival had ushered in a relapse into juvenile behaviour, where the males goaded and egged each other on. Being in this business for some time, you get a feel for how things will go and in these circumstances, it would be impossible for me to perform with the level of collective heckling this could release. As they were behaving like children, I could only hope they would calm down in the same way. My hopes lay with the meal and the Lombarders sitting at tables as responsible adults. Although the consumption of alcohol, if continued at the current rate, could provide even further complications in any future performances during or after dinner. I had to see how things panned out.

I knew Mike the treasurer would not mind me not performing at the reception, and I now thought I understood his nervous state as the tables were being laid out.

I decided that instead of wandering around the bar, I should go and have my meal in the kitchen. I pushed through toward the double doors leading to the dining room.

En route, through much 'Excuse me, coming through' on my part, my buttocks were pinched twice and playfully slapped three times, and on each occasion as I turned around, the male instigators merely commented, 'Sorry, thought you were someone else!' much to their own amusement and that of those around them. On the last occasion, near the swing doors, 'Another round?' was also uttered as the group downed the contents of their glasses in unison.

I was relieved to enter the dining room and found all the tables now set up, the lighting low, helium-filled balloons tied to each and every chair and copious amounts of as yet unopened wine bottles centred in the middle of each table.

Beyond the tables, in the far corner of the room, the DJ for the evening stood behind his decks, finishing his sound checks into the microphone.

'Two-two. One-two. Two-two.'

This continued, with adjustments to the EQ, for some time. However, I am not sure why he bothered; I was convinced that if his audience heard feedback, they would probably cheer. I also had a good idea of the reaction if any of the waiting staff had the misfortune to drop and break any crockery or glasses once dinner commenced.

I entered the kitchen where a number of the waiting staff sat, relaxing after eating their meal, taking the chance to be calm before the storm brewing just beyond the double doors was unleashed. I introduced myself and was asked to join them, and moments later a plate of roast dinner was presented to me by a chef, which I gladly tucked into. Outside in the dining room all had become quiet, the sound check confirmed as officially over with the appearance of the DJ in the kitchen. He didn't introduce himself to the house staff; he was the only male in the building (apart from the chefs) not wearing a dinner jacket and bow tie, instead sporting a short-sleeved purple shirt, bootleg jeans and tan cowboy boots. He had a mobile DJ air about him. He nodded hello to me, before he too tackled the food presented to him.

The waiting staff stood as one and headed out into the dining room for a final brief from the banqueting manager, leaving the DJ and me to eat our food in peace. We didn't speakas we ate, the only sounds were the constant, frantic noise of cooking behind us.

'Steve Monroe,' he finally said to me while putting down his knife and fork on his now-empty plate.

'Eddie Dungiven,' I replied, and we shook hands.

'You are the magician, right?'

'Yes, although not sure how much I can do with a crowd like this,' I stated, nodding my head toward the bar.

Steve laughed. 'Just you and me tonight,' he said.

'What about the other guy? The comic hypnotist?'

'A no-show, I think! I heard the guy who booked me taking a call when I arrived.'

'Really? He seemed extremely stressed when I arrived, but back there in the bar now he's giving it full throttle like the rest of them. Not a care!'

'Maybe 'cause he knows they don't really care about the acts! No offence, Eddie.'

'None taken,' I replied.

'All they want is to let their hair down, have a laugh and a boogie. Nothing wrong in that, is there?' asked Steve.

'No, of course not.'

'But you are like me, not happy getting paid unless you feel you have actually earned it. Am I right?'

I nodded and Steve laughed.

'They booked me last year and it was an eye-opener, that's for sure. You should hear some of the songs they requested – no, actually demanded that I play. Well, you will do in a couple of hours! It's all very bizarre.'

'What songs?' I asked, intrigued.

'Wait and see! My advice,' Steve continued, 'is just go with it.'

'Are we ready?' asked the banqueting manager, poking his head around the door into the kitchen.

'Certainly, Seb,' replied the head chef – I presumed he was the head chef; he had the largest hat on, the loudest voice and appeared to sweat the most out of all the kitchen staff.

'Excellent! We need to get some food inside them out there,' replied Seb.

With that, he let the door go and in thirty seconds we could hear him announcing at the bar entrance that dinner was now served.

The predictable cheer, though muffled by the space

between us, rose up as they heard the news, accompanied by a different chant this time to the tune of *Hot Hot Hot*.

'Time for food, food, food,' was repeated over and over, and grew louder as the dining room filled.

Steve Monroe the mobile DJ was right; I had to just go with it.

I wandered out from the kitchen and hugged the wall, observing the Lombarders before me. When all had taken their seats it didn't take very long for someone at the table in front of me to untie the helium balloon attached to his chair and inhale the gas.

He turned to the lady guest to his left, tapped her on the arm and said, as she turned, in a comical, squeaky voice, 'My name's David, shall we get a room?'

The table erupted into hysterics. She took the balloon from him and inhaled deeply.

'Piss off!' she squawked back at him. That was the green light for the activity to flow to every table. And all this before the first course had even arrived from the kitchen!

Again, all attention swung to Snoddy as he and the lovely Melanie arrived minutes after all the other guests. All stood, surprisingly, in silence until he and his partner had taken their seats.

Food consumption did seem to calm them all slightly. Each course, bizarrely I thought, began and ended with a toast. It all seemed a bit excessive and overindulgent. All were asked by Snoddy to be upstanding and then recite back the name he was toasting. On each occasion, the full contents of their glasses were expected to be downed in one. I noticed, after the first few toasts, hands greedily taking a wine bottle and filling up their glasses before the next toast was announced. He began by toasting the Queen; then moved forward to ex-chairmen and onward to obscure historical individuals from New Zealand, Bermuda and Zanzibar who had connections, however loose, with the Lombarders. Before the cheese and biscuits Snoddy gave the 'gentlemen' permission to remove their jackets, which heralded whistling and hands banging on the table cloths all around the dining room.

I wandered casually toward the back of the room, looking for any signs that a table would be receptive to a trick.

A voice to my left caught my attention as I passed by.

'Excuse me, another bottle of Chablis here,' commanded a familiar voice.

I turned to see Greg Dixon, Sally's brother, smirking at me.

'My mistake, thought you were waiter!' he added sarcastically, addressing the table. He was extremely intoxicated and even more obnoxious than usual.

'He's a balloon modeller! Married to my sister,' he said loudly, pointing at me accusingly from his seat.

Some of the other guests, male and female, as drunk as him, sniggered at this statement and repeated, 'Balloon modeller' through more sniggering. Others went quiet; two got up and retired from the table altogether, sensing a growing situation.

'I didn't know you were in the Lombarders, Greg,' I commented, trying to rise above his behaviour.

'I am a guest here. Business people, my kind of people – look around. You don't fit here,' he replied, while indicating with a swaying hand, just in case I wasn't sure where his kind of people were situated around the table.

All the sniggering had now stopped. I said no more and began to walk past the table.

Greg Dixon uttered something under his breath.

'Didn't catch that,' I replied, stopping, but not looking at him.

'I said where is your wife tonight?'

I didn't answer. For the past few weeks Jennifer had not been around on a Saturday night to eat cake, moan and generally be a mood vacuum. In fact, I hadn't seen her since my encounter with Phoebe the shocking pink poodle in her photographic studio. Instead, Sally had taken to going out on a Saturday evening by herself, to spend time with Ignatius McKenzie the spiritualist. Her appointments are always around the time we eat; therefore we no longer partake in our traditional Saturday night Chinese meal – Singapore noodles for me, chicken chow mein for Sally and sweet-and-sour chicken Hong Kong-style to share. Sally now also says this food is not good for us anyway and insists that she will grab something later. However, when she returns, late in the evening, she always comments that she is not hungry. In fact, she doesn't really speak at all.

Since Clifford has been in hospital we have all stopped going to the Sunday quiz night. I spend my evening by the old farmer's bedside, while Sally tends to her bees. She says they need more attention now that the good weather is here and the evening is best to examine the hives. The day's heat trapped in the air and the oncoming dusk makes them docile, she says.

'That's you all over, silence. Perhaps you should check where she really is,' Greg spat.

'What's that supposed to mean?' I retorted, taking the bait.

'Come on, guys, we've all had a drink, time to chill,' reasoned the Lombarder to his left, using words I presumed he had learned from his teenage son.

'It means she will never change and neither will you!' Greg shouted, getting up from his seat.

Eyes from the neighbouring tables settled on us.

'C'mon, Greg, let's get you some air,' said the man next to him, taking hold of his arm at the elbow.

He walked him around the table and raised his eyes to me in sympathy before heading through the dining room and toward the double doors leading to the bar.

The remaining people seated around the table now engaged in conversations as if nothing untoward had occurred, while I stood there looking on, ignored.

Time to leave, I thought to myself, and headed toward the bar to make my excuses to Mike the treasurer, who had disappeared, to much cheering, through the doors after dessert. I was prepared to face Greg if he was in the bar; I was quite sure he wouldn't even know what he had said. But before I could reach the door a female voice called to me from the last table.

'Excuse me, are you the magician?' she asked.

'Yes I am,' I replied, trying to sound upbeat.

'Would you show us a trick, please?' she said, looking around the half-full table.

'I would love to, but I have finished for the night, I am afraid.'

'Oh, don't say that! Please, just one trick. Please!'

I realised with the size of the dining room and the multiple conversations being conducted on each table, the rest of the guests seated here were oblivious to the scene that had recently played out toward the back of the room.

'Okay, okay! Just one, though!' I answered with a smile.

The table cheered and seemed receptive. With the element of heckling absent, combined with the high level of alcohol consumed, I guessed a simple trick would be as effective as a complicated sleight of hand. In fact, I prepared to perform the trick I had commenced as Snoddy and the 'lovely' Melanie arrived.

I sat down next to her and took the pack from my inside pocket again. As I removed the cards, I asked the woman if she had ever performed magic herself.

She shook her head and smiled, already drawn in.

I false-shuffled the deck while looking at her and her fellow guests.

'Okay, what's your name?' I asked, putting the cards face down on the table.

'Kate.'

'Right, Kate, I want you to choose two cards, replace them in the middle of the pack, and by giving them a strike with your hand, force them to the bottom of the pack. Can you do this, Kate?

Kate nodded.

'Are you sure, Kate?'

Again, she nodded, laughing this time.

'Good! Oh, and if it goes wrong, I can claim you didn't hit the pack in the magical way! Gets me off the hook, so to speak!'

I fanned the cards, pushing upward slightly the two I wanted her to select. Kate waved her index finger over the cards, deep in concentration.

'C'mon, Kate! Steve Monroe wants to start the dancing by 9pm!' I teased.

She laughed lightly and grabbed the cards I intended.

'Excellent! Excellent! Okay, you chose the eight of clubs and the seven of spades,' I said, splitting the pack in half with the faces down. 'Correct?'

'Correct,' she replied.

'Okay, place them back in the pack, on top of this pile,' I instructed quickly, pointing to the left-hand pile of cards.

I placed the right pile on top of the left and sat there looking at the deck. 'This is it, Kate! This is where the magic happens!' I exclaimed, still looking at the cards.

I could feel the eyes of everyone at the table on me, and hear their collective chuckle. I looked up.

'It's your moment. Have a practice on the table. I'll show you,' I instructed.

I laid my palm out straight, centimetres from the white tablecloth, and raised and lowered it three times, before striking firmly.

'Now it's your turn.'

Kate mimicked exactly the motion I had demonstrated, before crashing her hand down hard upon the table.

'All right, Kate! All right! Take it easy!' I said, jumping back in mock surprise. 'Who is your partner?' I asked, looking around the table.

A stout middle-aged man put up his hand and smiled.

'What's your name?'

'John.'

'I wouldn't upset her, John, if I was you!' I advised wisely.

'I already know!' he teased back.

I mimicked Kate's technique and exhaled loudly.

'Okay, joking over, this is it, Kate. On the count of three I want you to strike the deck and not think it's John's head this time.'

The whole table laughed, as she got her hand in position.

'One,' I said.

'Two,' the whole table chipped in, and I knew I had won them.

'Three!' we all stated as Kate struck the cards.

With her hand released, I quickly turned over the pack and removed the two cards at the bottom.

'Kate, are these your cards?' I asked, showing her and the table the eight of spades and the seven of clubs, which had been planted there from the start.

'Yes!' she squealed.

The table applauded as I gathered up the cards, conscious as ever not to draw attention to the switching of number and suit.

'How did you do that?' asked Kate.

'I didn't do anything, it was all you!' I teased.

'But... but that's impossible,' she reasoned, looking around the table for an explanation. 'John, how did he do that?'

'I have no idea, babe, but it was fun.'

I smiled to myself as I collected up the cards.

'You can't leave now!' she stated, placing a hand on my forearm.

'I am afraid so – I said one trick, Kate!' I reasoned.

'Oh, I know, but that was fantastic. Please, just one more.'

'Yeah, go on, just one more,' murmured the other guests around the table.

I pushed the cards back into the box.

'Besides, my friend Cerys is coming back now, I am sure she would love to see a trick.'

My hand stopped on the cards I had just placed in my pocket, giving me a latter-day Napoleon look.

There, walking through the double doors toward the table, was Cerys. A Cerys I had not seen before, but still a very beautiful Cerys. Gone were the shapeless fleece, tied-back hair and fresh face. Instead she wore a black, backless, figure-hugging, full-length dress. And what a figure it celebrated – it revealed the shape and feminine magnificence of her full breasts and allowed a tantalising glimpse of cleavage, not in a vulgar way, but presented as a delicately powerful elegance. Her waist and hips were in perfect proportion to complete the hourglass effect. Marco had indeed been busy this morning. Her hair, although always tied back when we met at the beach, reached far below her shoulders, indicating that when loose, it would have tumbled in waves past the middle of her back. But now it was cut to her shoulders, bobbed and completely straight. The edge followed her jawline perfectly. For the first time since I had known her, her face was made up, giving her skin an amazing doll-like sheen that emphasised her stunning blue eyes and highlighted her slender cheekbones. She looked simply stunning as she walked around the far side of table to take the vacant seat next to Kate.

I withdrew my hand from inside my jacket and tried to look calm. What should I say? Should I greet her? Should I ignore her? Kate made my decision for me.

'Cerys! Cerys! This is… Sorry, what is your name?' asked Kate.

'Eddie'

'This is Eddie; he's a magician! He performed a trick for me. He'll do a trick for you, it's amazing, really amazing!' gushed Kate.

Cerys took her seat and looked at me across the table.

'Nice to meet you, Eddie,' she said in a friendly manner, her parted lips and half-smile revealing her perfect teeth.

'Likewise,' I replied, holding her stare, but not meaning to.

'Where have you been, anyway?' asked Kate, totally unaware of the connection between us.

'Nowhere, why do you ask?' responded Cerys accusingly.

'Oooooooh, easy!'

'Have you been a naughty girl outside with Cole?' added Kate.

This drew nudges and winks from around the table.

'Or was it someone else?!' John chipped in.

My heart sank as I had to let the thought of Cerys being intimate with another man wash over me, and on another level, not being able to defend her from this juvenile twaddle ate me up inside.

Cerys looked annoyed and trapped; my presence making it worse, I was sure, as she felt she had to explain herself.

'You lot have got dirty, dirty, minds,' she began. 'If you must know, I was outside with Cole talking to a guest, a possible business contact; the real reason he asked me, as always, was to walk me around like a show pony.'

The guests at the table laughed.

'Where is Cole now, then?' asked Kate.

'Adjusting his flies!' said a diner, to much laughter.

The urge to leap over the table and grab him by the

lapels of his jacket coursed through me. It was strange, I thought, how my reaction differed completely from hearing my drunken brother-in-law's comments about Sally.

'They are still talking, got other stuff they want to discuss – not for my ears apparently,' replied Cerys, ignoring the jibe.

'Who is it?' asked Kate.

'Elliot Wallace, I think is his name, seems a nice guy.'

No one around the table had heard the name, but it jolted something inside of me.

'Wouldn't mind having a chat with him myself, always good to network,' stated John.

'Right, has the inquisition finished now? Can this gentleman show me his magic?' said Cerys, while reaching across the table for a wine bottle.

Her movement allowed me a view of her buttocks shaped tightly beneath her dress, which I tried to register as quickly as possible to ensure no one caught me. Inspection over, there was, to my eyes, no visible panty line. With this and Cerys' words, 'Can this gentleman show me his magic?' buzzing around my mind, it was all I could do not to smile and snigger. Perhaps, I thought, I was juvenile enough to join this table after all.

I cleared my throat and prepared to speak, unsure of the range of octaves my vocal cords would present for communication. I hoped I wouldn't be that teenage boy on the beach again, as I had been during our second encounter.

'Would you prefer a card or coin trick?' I asked when she had sat back down.

'Um, let me see,' Cerys said, sipping her wine. 'A good card trick, I think. Not one of those ones where you merely swap the suits and the numbers around and pretend they are the same cards chosen. That said, I don't recall seeing a coin trick.'

'Coin trick it is, then!' I laughed, and in doing so invited the whole table to respond.

'Okay, Mr Eddie...?' began Cerys.

'Dungiven. Eddie Dungiven,' I replied, trying to keep a straight face.

'Okay, Mr Eddie Dungiven, entertain me!'

'Do you have a coin?' I asked.

'You want money off me before you start?!' she exclaimed to the table.

Cerys reached inside her clutch bag and revealed an even smaller matching purse, and from this she took a 10p piece. She stretched over Kate and placed the coin in front of me on the table.

'There you go, and I want it back!'

'Would it be better if we swapped places?' Kate said.

'Would be easier,' I confessed.

And with that Kate got up and allowed Cerys to slide into the seat next to me. She sat looking at me, a huge grin upon her face, and close enough that her perfume teased me and filled my senses.

I performed an old but timeless routine. I began with a coin roll, moving the coin over the tops of my knuckles. While looking at the guests, I commented that the trick was easy because the coin was in fact made of rubber.

With a dubious murmur coming from the table, I stopped rolling and took the coin between my hands and pulled it, and in doing so, appeared to bend it.

'See, see,' I stated. 'Here, Cerys, you feel it,' I added, handing her the coin.

She felt obliged to pull the coin in the same manner I had, but much to her amusement the metal remained solid. She looked at me, laughing, and handed back the coin.

'What's wrong?' I asked, trying to sound puzzled. And with that, I let the coin slip from my hands and onto the table with a tinkling sound. 'Cerys, what have you done?!' I exclaimed, disappointed.

'Nothing!' she chuckled.

I picked the coin up and moved it around my hands, making it disappear and reappear seemingly at will.

'Okay, I want you to look after the coin, not let me take it. Do you think you could do that? Maybe after that, you could work some magic, the same as Kate did.'

Kate smiled and looked around proudly.

'Okay,' said Cerys.

'Good, turn over your palm,' I instructed.

Cerys obliged and I reached across and placed the coin in her hand. Touching her hand in public brought an excitement that found me concentrating on my breathing. I looked into her face, sensing she felt the same. We had embraced and kissed hours before and no one in this room would ever be aware of the fact.

'Now, Cerys, you need to keep hold of the coin. Close your hand into a fist.'

Cerys followed the instruction and sat quiet and still, looking at her hand.

'Tell you what, Kate, have you ever seen her as this quiet before?' I asked.

'Never! You should be around more often, we would get some peace!' she teased.

I saw the corner of Cerys' mouth twitch as she tried to stifle a grin.

'I'll see what I can do!' I said, staring directly into Cerys' eyes as she looked up. 'Now, Cerys, I need you to…' I began to say, but stopped, looking at the right sleeve of my jacket.

I touched the top of my sleeve as a frown formed on my face, lifted my arm and shook it from side to side, until a 10p piece was dislodged from inside the sleeve and landed onto the table.

'Please open your hand, Cerys.'

And she did, slowly, playing along at being my assistant. Acting aside, she did genuinely looked surprised at the realisation that as intended, she hadn't felt me withdraw the coin before she closed her palm.

'Very good, very good indeed!' She nodded.

'Okay, let's try again,' I said.

Cerys held out her hand again.

'No, tell you what, let's make it so I cannot get anywhere near the coin,' I said, placing it in front of her on the table. 'I want you to put your hand flat on top of this, okay?'

Cerys again obliged.

'There is no way I can get that coin, is there, Cerys?'

She shook her head, but with little confidence.

'There is no way it could move through your hand into mine, is there?' I said, placing my hand lightly on top of hers as I spoke.

I felt her hand shaking slightly underneath mine, and could see her trying to control her breathing.

I took my hand away from hers and formed a fist in one fluid movement.

'Ladies and gentlemen, this is magic,' I said loudly, unfurling my hand and revealing an empty palm.

'This is magic gone wrong!' I corrected, to much laughter.

I turned to Cerys. 'Okay, take away your hand – two tricks out of three isn't bad though, is it?'

Cerys lifted her hand in a dramatic fashion and again looked surprised to find no coin.

'What have you done with my coin? I am sorry – your coin! Good job it wasn't £2!'

I stopped speaking and tilted my head, studying the left side of Cerys' neck.

'Excuse me, may I?' I enquired.

And before she could respond, I reached across with the hand that had been empty, making sure those around the table could see it still was the case, and stroked her neck and earlobe momentarily with my fingers. My imagination witnessed her nipples to stiffen beneath her tight black dress as I 'retrieved' the coin from behind her ear a second later and held it up for inspection.

The table applauded and Cerys smiled at me, her pupils dilated.

'Told you he was good!' stated Kate.

I was now really enjoying myself, and after the last tactile illusion, was thankful the light was dim in the dining room and the bottom of my dinner jacket rested on my thighs.

Cerys had asked me previously to perform a trick for her, but I had declined, anxious it might fall flat in the confines of her Range Rover. And the feeling of being inferior to her successful businessman husband had never been far away, adding to the caution.

I had decided to stay, partly to be near Cerys and partly because of the buzz I got from performing.

I reached for my cards in my jacket pocket, and as my finger curled around the box, Mike the treasurer was greeted with cheers as he re-entered the room. He held an empty wine glass in his hand and struck the side of it with a teaspoon to gain attention and silence.

When all was quiet, he spoke. 'Gentlemen and lady guests, I present to you, your chairman, Roger Snodd.'

To the sound of rapturous applause, Roger Snodd stood and surveyed the room. Again, his presence seemed to create a hypnotic effect among the guests, and as before, he milked it for all it was worth.

'Please, please, thank you,' he uttered above the din in fake surprise.

The clapping ceased and as the room filled with quietness, from Steve Monroe's decks some faint music could be picked out. It wasn't loud enough to detect the tune, but enough to place it as a military march.

'Friends,' began Roger Snodd. 'Firstly, thank you all for coming and thank you to our wonderful ladies for their gracious presence here – they all look truly beautiful.'

He paused to allow the men to respond with 'hear, hear's and banging of the tables.

'The meal, I am sure you will agree, was delicious and I'd like to take this opportunity to thank the catering staff for all their efforts.'

This statement was met with polite applause.

'You know I am a modern man, keen to do away with unnecessary protocol.'

His members whooped and oooohed at this suggestion,

whereas I was reminded of the endless toasts and granting permission for the men to remove their jackets at a point in time decided by him.

'So, so, I have decided,' he began, waving his hands for order. 'I have decided to do away with long, drawn-out speeches this year.'

'Noooooooooooooo,' came the collective response from the male guests, while the women appeared to remain silent.

'After all,' he continued, 'of what interest are they to our lady guests? Do they want to listen to line after line of in-house jokes and boys' humour? Do they want to hear our "colourful" songs? No, this will not do. So, instead I have been thinking about what our ladies really want, and I have concluded that they want to be impressed by us. How can we do this, you may ask? Well, it can be achieved in many different ways. Each takes effort, each should been seen as a sign of us attempting to impress. You could wine her, dine her, telephone her out of the blue and hug her because you can. You could hold her, surprise her, always compliment her and tell her every day how beautiful she is. You could smile at her with love in your eyes, laugh with her, cry with her and cuddle with her and let her fall asleep in your arms. Then again, you could shop with her, shower her with jewellery or buy her flowers. You could hold her hand; write love letters and poetry to her. In summary, gentlemen, go to the end of the earth and back for her.

'As I let you digest this, I will remind you of what I said on our arrival here tonight: that our relationships are equal partnerships. So if this is the case, what can our ladies do to impress us, the Lombarders? I have given this an equal amount of deliberation and can conclude with confidence that turning up naked and bringing beer just about covers everything!'

The men lost their senses at this, and guffawed and sniggered and repeated the last line of Roger Snodd's proposal over and over to each other. The women, in contrast, either laughed politely, or looked on simply embarrassed at the testosterone surging around them. Kate was in the former camp; Cerys in the latter.

Above the din, Roger Snodd spoke again. 'The music is ready, boys – you know what to do. This is one tradition that will not be disregarded on my watch!'

And with this, he indicated to Steve Monroe to increase the volume of the march. The timing was excellent, as at that very point the familiar refrain of the *Dam Busters* theme filled the room. Now I understood what Steve had meant regarding the music choice. With the stirring anthem blasting away from the corner of the dining room and the cue from Roger Snodd, three quarters of the Lombarders took flight to the dance area and with outstretched arms proceeded to run around the floor, mimicking, I presumed, Lancaster bombers in flight.

I watched in disbelief and turned to speak to Cerys, but she beat me to it.

'Just don't ask!' she said

John, Kate's partner, couldn't resist the lure of joining in the formation flying and tipped his 'wing' in salute to Roger Snodd as he flew past en route to the others.

I leant in to address Cerys. 'Is your husband in amongst them?' I teased.

'If he hears it, he will be!' she replied with a seemingly heavy heart.

Being with Cerys was wonderful, but it was all false, sitting there, watching the surreal scene play out in front of me. I had to leave; I had performed only two tricks all evening and with the music now in full swing, I could see the atmosphere only degenerating even further. The possibility of performing any more diminished, and I decided I wouldn't be looking to find Mike the treasurer for any payment.

'I think it is time I was going,' I announced to Cerys as I got up.

'Oh, okay. I understand,' she replied.

I stood and waved to Kate, and she raised her arm in return and seemed embarrassed by her partner's continued frantic movements at the far end of the room.

Once through the double doors, I was on alert in case Greg Dixon was in the bar, but all was in fact quiet; he was either outside, or had been put in a cab and taken home. Instead, just a few drunks stood by the bar, speaking loudly but not listening to what the others said, and not interested in joining the traditional 'dance' next door.

'Wait a sec.' Cerys' voice rang out behind me, her entrance bringing the *Dam Busters* theme fully into the bar for a moment. She assessed the situation before continuing to speak in hushed tones. 'I just wanted to say it was lovely surprise seeing you, though I should have guessed you were here, what with that ruddy big white van in the car park!'

'And I wanted to say how lovely you look. Your hair is beautiful,' I spilled out with ease. How could I find the words to compliment this woman and mean them, when I've never been able to tell my wife anything of the kind, not even that I loved her?

Cerys smiled warmly at the praise and then looked into my eyes as if searching for inspiration to speak.

'Cole is away in the Netherlands the week after next; he has asked me to join him midway through. My flight's booked for the early morning, so I am staying at an airport hotel overnight,' said Cerys, not pausing for breath.

I looked at her; then realised she had stopped speaking.

'Okay,' I replied in a quizzical tone.

'Eddie!' she hissed.

'Yes?'

'I've a hotel room booked,' she whispered.

And suddenly the penny dropped with me.

'Oh, oh, you want me to... right, right,' I stammered.

'I was hoping for a more positive response, you know!'

'I am sorry, of course, it's... Wow! I need...'

'I only found out today,' she stated, ignoring my tongue-tied reply. 'I was going to tell you next Saturday morning, but was conscious that the short notice might be difficult for you. But again, fate has intervened and made this possible!'

'Right, right,' I added.

'If you want to, that is,' Cerys replied, misunderstanding my attitude.

Someone wanted to be with me, someone that was beautiful; somebody full of life was attracted to me enough to wish to spend the night with me, to wake up with me. Yes, it was flattering, but equally now that the moment I had wanted to happen could become a reality, I was flabbergasted that it actually might.

'I'll have to sort some things out,' I stated obviously.

'Well, if you want it to happen, yes, you will.'

'I'd really love to kiss you,' I replied quietly, trying to rise above Cerys' dismissiveness.

'Not a good idea here, Mr Dungiven,' she said, wrinkling her nose.

The drunks in the bar had finally listened to one story and gave out a collective explosion of laughter, which ebbed, then reappeared even stronger than before.

'I know, I know.'

'See you next week, I'll have times and all that then,' Cerys said.

'Okay, see you next week.'

And with that, she turned and headed back toward the double doors and I strode toward the exit. My head felt further from my feet than ever before; my mind was occupied counting off the subsequent sleeps before the week after next; I was like an expectant child waiting for the sound of sleigh bells and reindeer hooves to arrive at the darkest point of winter. I didn't consider what I would offer to Sally as an excuse.

Such was the effect of Cerys's proposal that I hadn't noticed, until she opened the double doors and allowed the sound to flood in, that the stirring anthem had been replaced by an easy listening number. A 1930s-style singer was asking questions in successive lines – if I had ever seen a dream talking, walking or dancing. I presumed, judging by the Lombarders' raucous responses as Steve Monroe turned down the volume on each line, that he, this hopeless romantic crooner, rather smugly, had.

In the car park the music and the Lombarders could still be heard, but the sounds drifted in and out into the night, masking the madness held within the club.

I reached the van and stopped. Something was wrong.

Voices, two voices, projected from the far side of the van. Two voices shielded by the bulk of my vehicle. Two voices apparently hiding away from the party. Two voices in a darkened car park are always suspicious. With my initial thoughts of the van being stolen banished by the content of their conversation, instinct screamed at me to keep out of view.

I couldn't see them, but thankfully neither could they see me. I wasn't sure how the dialogue would have panned out if I had let my presence be known.

'Like I said, next one is in a couple of weeks,' said one voice. 'I'll give you details of the location a few hours before, can't be too careful.'

'I am tempted, you know I am, but I can't really get out of the trip, business is business,' replied the other.

'We are talking serious cash here, Cole, big players, big money.'

'How big?'

'Tens of thousands changing hands on the night. Some of these guys only partake a couple of times a year. This one is like our annual festival!'

'I know, you said that before. Let me work something out.'

'So you are in?'

'I will let you know!'

'Plenty more are interested. Is it the entrance fee?'

'No, it's not the entrance fee. I've said I am away for that week.'

'Can't really wait for an answer, I need to know now.'

'Oh, c'mon. I just need to make some calls on Monday morning.'

'There aren't many that turn down an invitation and get asked again. There are limited places, a waiting list, I can't really make exceptions.'

'Okay, okay, I am in, I'll fly back early if need be.'

'I knew you would see sense!'

They both laughed.

'I'll need the £3K entrance fee by the middle of the week.'

'Sure, take a cheque?'

They both laughed again.

Their voices were getting louder; indicating they were heading to the back of the van, back to the party and into my vision. I moved in parallel to their progress, until I was at the front of van and still out of sight.

'My boy has come on a treat; he's ready. That Lab you got me really worked him out! Complete carnage when he got going!'

I couldn't be sure if it was shock at what I had just heard or because they had neared the clubhouse, but their voices grew faint as I leant against the grille of the van, alone in the car park.

Chapter 13

First Dates and Goodbyes

I've always been of the opinion that routine is what shapes us. It's what we crave. We all need structure and order in our lives.

Daily we wake to an alarm, a shrill blast which forcibly drags us from our dreams, from our havens. Then, blinking at the numbers presented to us in sleepy disbelief, we search with a blind hand to sever the din that has tricked our minds and bodies into a kick-start and instead breathe, just breathe.

We head to the bathroom; grab at the switch, anticipating the painful light to come with tightly shut eyes, and on opening, the feeling of adjustment is always uncomfortable.

At this point, our own individual routines take hold. I personally urinate, brush my teeth, shave and shower, always in that order, never deviating. Even the act of shaving has a routine. I always wet shave, always start with an upward stroke above my lips on the left side and move to my cheek, then jawline, followed by chin, right side jaw, cheek; then full circle back above my lips.

But today I threw chaos into the mix and chose a different route around my stubble. I cannot explain why I did it; it certainly wasn't planned, wasn't the routine; I think I changed, plain and simply, because I realised I could.

As my shaving foam-covered reflection steamed up in the mirror, I raised my hand to apply, as always, the first upward stroke above my top lip, but paused, altering my direction and swept downwards instead. I moved to the right side above my lips, then right cheek, left cheek, chin and jawline right to left. The result was the same, but the experience felt fresh; I had to concentrate. It was, dare I say it, after so many shaves over so many years, almost enjoyable again; it was up there with the first novelty shaves of youth when the action removes the soft down of innocence.

It illustrated to me that change was good and should be welcomed and embraced, but sometimes it is not easy to accept. Change is always there for us to discover; we just are unable to find it hidden in our routines.

Shave concluded, I climbed into the shower and with the revelation in my mind I contemplated changing the order I soaped and washed my body. It really seemed like the first day of the rest of my life, but with the water jets running I reverted to my tried-and-tested method. Too much change, I concluded, can be unsettling, as I let the warm water run over my shoulders for a few minutes, before soaping my right armpit as I had done countless times before!

Drying off (again in my usual order), t', I heard the front door close and knew Sally had risen and gotten ready in the bathroom downstairs and left without even a 'good morning' uttered. I resigned myself in an instant to the fact that the currents we battled against, without us realising, had carried us to different parts of the shore.

And tied tightly around this thought, strangling it in fact, hung the anticipation and subsequent fallout of a night spent with Cerys. Imagery of osculation and subsequent guilt flew around my mind – undressing her, cupping her breasts, taking her nipples into my mouth, running my fingers down her back, up the inside of her thighs, hearing her moan contentedly beneath me. But I concluded it was easier to feel this guilty than to communicate with my wife, or to save an exhausted relationship that was surfacing for the last time.

Gus and I had planned to visit Clifford today instead of walking. Gus normally only visits at the weekend, but is away from tomorrow for a week. He is heading to Italy to see *Il Palio* or something; I guessed this is an opera, but didn't want to ask, to admit my ignorance, as he spoke about it with a casual confidence. He mentioned it also had to be the year of the owl, which left me completely confused.

But at least Gus visits. I have made excuse after excuse to Mary and Clifford to explain Sally's constant absence. I recall she has only visited once with me, and I believe Mary said she visited on her own one afternoon, not long after Clifford was admitted, but that is it. But they continue to ask how she is and are interested in the contract she is working toward with the supermarket, and comment that they appreciate how busy she is. Clifford always makes a point of calling her a good girl. Sometimes, it seems, the less you do, the more you are appreciated.

Gus was already at the hospital when I arrived, sitting the opposite side of the bed to Mary. Mary was there all day, every day and only left Clifford's side when he needed to be examined or in the still of the night, when she knew he was in a deep slumber. The hospital had been flexible about the times she was there to display her devotion to this colossus of a man.

Mary looked tired, worn out; the strain of her self-imposed vigil was smudged in the dark rings under her eyes and the stale smell of her clothes, captured by the hospital ward heat and multiple wears.

Clifford greeted me in the manner I had become accustomed to: he raised one of his huge paws and grabbed my forearm and shook it gently, smiling beneath his mask. He looked like he was still full of fight in his stationary, horizontal position.

Mary had asked me to bring up some fruit juice ice lollies for Clifford to suck on. He found the cold and the sweetness soothing and a welcome change to the lukewarm tap water the hospital provided in a plastic jug – strawberry was his favourite flavour, she added.

Mary was already holding a pink lolly to his lips. In her exhausted state, she had inadvertently requested that Gus bring some as well. I sensed that in the heat of the ward, mine would be little more than a sticky liquid by the end of visiting time.

'How are you doing today?' I asked Clifford, same as I always did.

He nodded an okay, as was the norm, and I took a seat.

'Mary, I need to tell you while I remember,' I began quietly, trying to not draw Clifford's attention as he listened to Gus. 'I bumped into Ted on the way here and he needs you to sign some papers for red diesel. He said you know what Finleys are like about paperwork – they won't deliver again until the "t"s are crossed and the "i"s are dotted – or something of that nature, I am sure you can guess what he really said!'

Ted Slone owned the neighbouring farm and since Clifford's admission had voluntarily taken the role of organising the local farmers to keep Clifford's place ticking over. It was hard to do, what with their commitments and the fact they were severely stretched, but they all agreed Clifford would do the same for any one of them.

'Thanks, Eddie, I will go up and see him,' said Mary over her shoulder, but I wasn't sure when she would, or even if she would remember. I made a mental note to go up to Ted's place tonight, collect the papers and bring them up to Mary tomorrow in the hospital.

'I don't know what we are going to do long term,' she whispered.

'Don't worry about that now.'

'The boys have been great, but can't keep this up,' she said. 'Perhaps you could take it on!' Mary joked.

At least I think she was joking, and let it pass.

'The consultant wants to see me later,' she stated flatly out of the side of her mouth.

'That would be good, check the progress, right?' I said.

'You away this weekend, Gus?' asked Mary, changing the subject.

'Siena,' he replied.

'Where?'

'Tuscany, Italy.'

'No, I know where it is, silly! I meant whereabouts in Siena.'

'Oh, I am staying with a friend,' Gus said vaguely, 'in the Civetta Contrade. So I have no choice but to support their mount in the Palio!'

'The horse race?' asked Mary.

Gus nodded in agreement.

'Well, I think it is cruel, Gus,' admitted Mary.

'Not as bad as the baby seals of Canada, though?' teased Gus.

'Don't get me started on that again!' she laughed.

'I understand what you say, but there is a lot more than just the race. There is the pageantry, the tradition, the whole sense of occasion,' argued Gus.

'He's right,' stated Clifford through his mask. 'I was there once, when I was in the RAF,' he said, removing his mask to enable us to hear him more clearly.

'Really?' I asked.

'Group of us headed down on leave from Germany,' he added.

'I never knew you were in the Air Force, Clifford. How come you have never said?' Gus asked.

But he had slipped his mask back on. The consumption of the fruit lolly and contributing one sentence had taken their toll.

'Oh yes, national service. Posted in Germany, well, West Germany in those days,' said Mary, taking over from Clifford. 'You had a choice: Army, Air Force or Navy, but you couldn't get out of doing it, served for eighteen months. That right, isn't it?' she said, looking at Clifford for confirmation.

Clifford nodded in agreement.

'You actually were exempt if you worked the land,' she added. 'Vital service, food production, but in those days, Clifford was training to be a vet, so had to do his time in the forces. It was only when his father died that he was pressured to take over the farm by his mother – he only had a year left to qualify too.'

We didn't reply, unsure of what to say. Both Gus and I presumed Clifford had always wanted to work the land.

'You youngsters don't know you are born!' Mary said with a laugh. 'That's when I met him. Do you remember?' she asked, stroking Clifford's cheek.

Clifford smiled and nodded in recognition.

'I should have known what I was getting into – imagine it, riding on a bus with no money!'

'Sorry?' Gus and I replied simultaneously.

Mary chuckled to herself, looked at Clifford and then continued to speak.

'I was on a bus going home, filthy night, dark, windy. How high was the rain bouncing off the pavement?' she asked Clifford for reassurance.

Clifford lifted a tired arm to an exaggerated level, before dropping it down heavily with a smile across his lips.

'Anyway, I am sitting there minding my own business, worked all day in a cafe, tired, heading back to my parents' home, when a commotion developed at the front of the bus. He,' she said, pointing her thumb toward Clifford, 'was short of his fare, not by much, but enough for the conductor to demand he got off at the next stop. I was cross and just wanted to get home, but the driver pulled over and stopped the bus, as the conductor and Clifford continued to argue. He said he was staying at a friend's home and didn't know the price of the fare. The conductor said no matter, the price of the fare was the price of the fare and you couldn't ride without it.

'Clifford then pleaded that he had travelled all day down from West Kirby. I didn't know the significance of this at the time, and nor, it seems, did the conductor, as he lifted him by the arm out of his seat to move him down the bus to the doors. He fell silent as he was marched through the bus, resigned to the shame of eviction as everyone at the front of the bus ignored him. I felt sorry for him, and before I knew what I had done I was rooting inside my bag for change and calling down to the conductor to ask by how much the fare was short.

'He gave me a look that told me he had seen all this before and I was being conned, but he still allowed me to pay the difference. He said there was paperwork that needed to be completed and a report to be filed.

'I replied, "Let's all just get home." He muttered it was regulation, not his doing, but with that, he pressed the button to sound the bell and the driver pulled off to resume the journey. Clifford took a seat at the front and sheepishly thanked me, but said no more for a while. As I passed him to get off at my stop he thanked me again, smiling this time, and asked me my name and where the stop was. I told him and jumped off the bus and hurried toward my parents' house, bent into the horizontal rain, and thought nothing more of it, apart from his lovely smile.'

'You must have been a looker, Clifford!' teased Gus, to which Clifford nodded his head in acknowledgement.

'Three weeks later, we were having tea in the kitchen, when the doorbell sounded; my brother Richard went to answer it and came back telling me there was an airman at the door asking for me. I told him to stop being an annoying little brother. But he repeated it.

'Dad got up from his tea and went out to the hallway. He was never happy having his tea interrupted, but he came back with a grin on his face and confirmed what Richard had said, and added it was best I get rid of him. I didn't know any airmen, didn't know any men, the truth be told! So I went out into the hallway in a state of confusion. Sure enough, there on the doorstep was a man dressed in the light blue uniform of the RAF. I stared at this stranger and asked if I could help him, and then he smiled and I recognised him as the bus fraudster!'

'Did you invite him in?' I asked.

'Oh no, I wanted to show him off! He looked extremely handsome in his uniform! So I told my parents I was going out, took him on my arm and proceeded to walk to the bus stop to go into town, to all the places I could think of where my friends might be. I introduced him to everyone I could find, in shops, cafes and the bus station! But I keep a tight hold of him, to ensure there was no competition. Besides, I had to take him away from the house, or my father would have grilled him to such a degree that it's doubtful I would have seen him again anyway!'

We all laughed, and in doing so, Clifford misted up his plastic mask, breaking the sombre mood of the ward.

'But how did he find you?' asked Gus.

'Well, he told me he had spent the best part of two hours knocking on every door in the area, asking if Mary was at home – he had remembered my name and the bus stop. There was some confusion at one place, when a Mary was summoned to the door by her suspicious mother, only for this peculiar stranger to reject her as the wrong Mary and then scurry away, apologising all the way down the path to the front gate!'

We laughed again, maybe a little too loudly, as the sound attracted attention from the visitors around the other beds.

Mary stopped laughing and looked at her husband.

'And here we are now,' she said, not attempting to hide the two tears suddenly forming in the corners of her eyes.

Clifford caught her hand and squeezed it gently and then reached up to wipe the tears from her eyes. He managed to displace one, but the effort was too much for him to remove the second from her other eye. His hand slumped back to his side on the bed and he stared straight ahead, his involvement in comforting his wife now confined to eye movements and a shallow heaving of his chest. This combined action seemingly sparked a signal for Mary to unwillingly shed a silent, steady flow of tears that trickled down her face.

'What time is your flight tomorrow?' I asked Gus, trying to move the situation back to something near normality. But how could this be normal? Clifford had always taken care of Mary, always protected her, always been her rock. And now in this sterile environment, the man who had worked sixteen hours a day in all weathers, had lifted and carried countless loads on his massive shoulders and frame, was slipping away to a whisper and Mary's tears were an acknowledgement that for the first time, she had given up hope.

'Mid-morning,' replied Gus, upbeat.

'Give you a lift?' I offered.

'That would be good. Thanks!'

Normality exhausted, we looked on in silence as Clifford attempted to lift his mask off his face.

'Let me help you,' we said in unison, standing up.

'No, Clifford, you've done enough,' pleaded Mary.

But the old farmer ignored our requests and cleverly pushed the mask up so that it still covered his nostrils, but allowed him movement to speak.

'How come you never settled down, Gus?' he asked.

It was the question out of nowhere, but one we all had wanted to ask for years, though we knew would never get an answer from him. Clifford had used his prerogative as a dying man to broach the subject for all of us, guessing that Gus could not deny him an answer at this point. Silently, I thanked him for it, and for moving us into a new area of normality that no one else could have revealed.

Gus kept his composure and rubbed his chin thoughtfully; if he felt cornered, he certainly didn't show it.

'It wasn't for a lack of trying, just never seemed to happen,' he put forward by way of an explanation.

We all sat in silence, watching, waiting for him to expand on this, and felt sure this wasn't enough, not this time, possibly the last time Clifford would get to know the answer.

'There was someone, a very special person. But it didn't work out.'

Again, we sat in silence, expecting more.

'Two sentences isn't enough of an explanation,' challenged Clifford, before placing his mask back over his mouth.

I was left wondering whether this action was intended to show his disappointment at still not knowing the truth and thus terminate the conversation he began, or to guilt Gus into revealing more. Gus evidently took it as the latter and raised his hands in submission, but I had no idea, in that hospital ward, what details this unassuming man was preparing to reveal.

'I met her in Kenya,' he began. 'My parents had friends over there; they didn't leave after independence, but stayed on. I don't really know the whole story, but they owned an estate in the highlands and farmed coffee. My parents spoke of them occasionally, and then after I graduated from university, it was suggested I stay out there for one season and work on the land; my father thought it would be good for me apparently, before I took a job in the city with a jobber firm he had arranged. But I would have the opportunity to explore the country too.

'In fact, after a couple of weeks it became obvious I wasn't ever going to really add anything to the workings of the estate; I was, in fact, more of a hindrance than a help, although no one ever said it! I never got the hang of laying out the cherries to dry, I couldn't master the turning of them, when to do it and when not to. Sounds simple, I know, but get it wrong and you get uneven ripeness and fermentation, which impacts the coffee's flavour. I continued to try, but I didn't improve. I was given less and less to do and found my trips of exploration took up the majority of my time.

'After a month, I started to attended the weekly coffee auction in Nairobi with the estate manager, and understood, during my first visit, the real reason for my father sending me here: to prepare me, to prime me for the world of finance I would be submerged in when I returned home. We would play out the buying and selling of the coffee before us in the auction house and the manager had an uncanny knack of striking exactly when the final bidwould be obtained. I, in contrast, was quite hopeless at it and concluded that this didn't bode well for my future career.'

Gus stopped speaking; he seemed to be remembering details, details that he was preparing to share.

'Go on,' encouraged Mary gently.

'This weekly jaunt,' he continued, 'formed, over time, into the only piece of "work" I undertook. One week, after the auction, the estate manager advised me that he had other business to attend to in the centre of Nairobi – he wasn't forthcoming and I didn't ask; he was that kind of person. He pushed me in the direction of the City Park and said he would meet me there around 4pm. He explained the park was famed for its nature trails and they really were worth exploring. We always packed a picnic to share, normally consumed on the long drive back to the estate, but today only I had supplies; he would catch some food after his meeting, he said. He also told me to watch out for the vervet monkeys in the park – they would steal any food they could, even rip it out of your hands, given the opportunity. The Sykes' monkeys, on the other hand, were extremely gentle in their requests for food and preferred to beg, palms outstretched, gazing with sad eyes.

'The park was indeed lovely. I spent a couple of hours walking the trails and then prepared to sit and take some food and snooze the afternoon away. As I sat down with my bag on the grass under the shade of a tree, a group of children emerged from the trail I had walked. I had heard their excitable voices behind me on a few occasions, but I didn't see them on account of the winding paths and lush vegetation, and now with their trail over, they proceeded to race to a clearing in front of me and play football with a tatty ball that one of them had been carrying.

'Walking, bringing up the rear, was a woman – their teacher, I presumed – who, once in the clearing, joined in the free-for-all with an equal level of enthusiasm as did her pupils. The ball came toward me a few times as I unpacked my food and I kicked it back to them, much to their delight. Hearing them laughing and shouting stirred something inside of me, and after eating a single piece of fresh fruit, I spontaneously jumped up and rushed over to them. I took the ball off a large boy and played tricks, performing pullbacks and step-overs to keep the others away from the ball. They pushed me and tackled me, attempting to get the ball away, but I managed to dance around them, and all the time the air was full of laughter and noise. I eventually gave the ball to the smallest child there. She attempted to kick it but missed and allowed an older girl to take over and run, run, run; the pack in hot pursuit of her.

'I stood still, the action moving steadily away from me, exhausted in the hot afternoon sun, but content when the teacher stood beside me and spoke. "You are a good footballer!" she said, with a beautiful smile.

'"Not really," I replied. "They made me look better than I am," I added, laughing. I suggested to her that they could organise into teams; that way they would get even more out of it, instead of hurtling around in confusion. She said she had tried but couldn't make it work and wondered, while I was here, if perhaps I would have a go. It was extremely forward of her, but I felt compelled to agree, to which she immediately cupped her mouth and called them all back to her. They turned as one entity and stampeded toward us.

'But long before they had reached us, her attention was directed toward the trees. She let out an ear-piercing shriek that made me wince, before clapping her hands. Standing, crouching and squabbling amongst my food were a multitude of monkeys. Judging by the different-coloured chests on display, it appeared that the Vervet's and Sykes' had teamed up for this raid, the latter's reputation for gentility completely dismissed as a myth. She rushed over, with me on her tail, and together we banished them with arm-waving and shouting. But it was irrelevant; they had eaten most of the food already and carried off the remainder during their noisy and frantic escape.

'The children joined us and stared quietly at the remains of my picnic. "You will have to come back with us and eat," she suddenly said, smiling. I protested, but she was insistent and so very beautiful. She introduced herself as Kamili, and again smiled warmly.

'I felt obliged to accept and found myself heading back, not to a school as I presumed, but to my surprise an orphanage. The children in the park were merely the tip of the iceberg – the dusty grounds of the orphanage teemed with life, from toddlers to adolescents, and the same number again peered through the open windows of a block of low-level buildings at this stranger, but that soon developed into smiles and waves as their natural curiosity fought and won the battle against their shyness.

'Kamili explained that she was the full-time principal, part-time nurse, and teacher of the orphanage. She shared over lunch her hopes for the future of the children who were safe in this environment, her realisation that this work merely skimmed over the surface of child poverty in the city, and her frustration at the lack of government funding. She also introduced me to Makini, the full-time cook, cookery teacher and part-time nurse, and to Amali, a man who acted as a caretaker for the orphanage and taught practical life skills to all the children. A Dr Rahma would normally have been here today too, but she was delayed treating another orphanage that had had an outbreak of measles.

'Kamili's passion and dedication swept me up; her optimism sparked in me, inspired me. Here was I, useless at every aspect of the coffee business, but paid an allowance and living in comfort, and the same would potentially still be the case when I took my place on the stock exchange floor; my shortcomings cushioned by monetary wealth. I was humbled by the selfless actions of these wonderful, gifted people. I wanted to help, felt an urge to contribute, and offered there and then to teach English to the children. Kamili's face lit up and she hugged me, and that when I knew it – I was in love.'

Gus stopped speaking again and looked up, I presume to gauge our reaction, to ascertain if he should continue. But we all just stared at him blankly; his words absorbed Mary's tears of sorrow. Of all the stories he had told down the years, this was truly the most memorable, and the one we could connect to most of all.

'I know what you are thinking – love at first sight, yeah, right! But it was; it's the only way I can explain the emotion that consumed me. On an otherwise uneventful day, that sunny afternoon, four thousand miles from home, in the middle of noisy, dusty Nairobi, I had stumbled across my purpose for existence.

'After an introduction from Kamili, I spent thirty minutes teaching a group of younger children the *I'm a Little Teapot* song and actions. You know the one?'

We all nodded as Gus placed a hand on his hip and formed a spout with his other arm.

'After the lesson ended, I headed back to the City Park, waited for the estate manager and told him I wouldn't be going back with him that day. He gave me a knowing look and said he understood totally. But he didn't understand at all; his presumption of lust leading me was misplaced. I spent the next week living, eating, teaching and sleeping in the orphanage. When the estate manager returned the following Monday, I advised him I wouldn't be back for a considerable time. I knew it wouldn't be an issue for my father; I believed I had a free rein within reason. The estate manager nodded respectfully and commented that she must be very special.

'It was that night that I was invited to share Kamili's bed for the first time, and that was where I slept for the rest of my time in Kenya. I enjoyed the teaching, the enthusiasm of the young people, the energy they radiated, and I marvelled at how they could flourish and reach their individual potential despite the terrible scenes they had witnessed or circumstances they had been dealt. As I had promised Kamili in the City Park, I organised them into three football teams. The initial coaching, if I am honest, was soul-destroying, but one by one they got it, the whole essence of the game of football. They stopped running around after the ball en masse and instead finally held the positions allotted to them and passed and moved, passed and moved their way across the pitch. I enrolled them in a city league; one team reached the semi-final of the cup competition, another finished third in the league, and the last remained, sadly, a work in progress.

'One day Kamili sat with me watching the children play and told me that over half had lost their parents to

AIDS, and that a quarter of those were themselves HIV positive. The remainder, she explained, had witnessed rape, torture, murder and abject poverty, but the repercussions of this turmoil remained trapped deep inside of them. With support from Kamili and the rest of the tireless staff, the children gladly grabbed the second chance presented to them. We lived and loved in that orphanage and didn't seek the sadness that we knew ultimately would have to be revealed as the months became weeks, the weeks became days and the days became hours before I had to break away and return home.

'Three days before my departure, as Kamili lay in my arms, listening to the nocturnal world come alive outside our window, it struck me. I didn't have to go into a profession I knew and cared little for; I had a choice, I could decide. I should apply for a work permit to return to Nairobi and make a difference to children's lives, to support these young people on a long-term basis. We could do so much more good work, but this would need funding. I decided to speak to my family, to relay all the selfless deeds done here to better the lives of others, and what a real difference it made in revealing a future where before there was none. When they were aware, I knew my family would happily donate funds to this cause I believed in so strongly. I shared my vision with Kamili and told her, excitedly, that Amali could have a proper set of tools for maintenance of the orphanage, and a workshop kitted out with workbenches to teach in. Makini would have a purpose-built kitchen and a food science area to pass on her knowledge. We could employ a full-time nurse and a counsellor to work on the children's health and all would receive a salary or allowance. The children would have new beds, new clothes, new classroom desks, new books – in fact, new everything!'

Gus went quiet again, choosing his words.

'At the airport, I told Kamili I loved her and that I would return as soon as my working visa was approved. We walked slowly to the departure gate, willing time to stop, even for a short while, and to ensure I didn't cry, I made the practical suggestion that she should set up a bank account for the orphanage, as the funds would start arriving before I returned.'

Gus stopped speaking and looked ahead, anxious.

'Imagine those ridiculous words being the last ones spoken between us,' he added.

Clifford reached for his hand and held it firmly, like a father would a child's.

'Oh, Gus,' murmured Mary.

'I never saw her again,' he whispered, confirming what we had already surmised.

We sat, wanting to know more, but not prepared to probe – it was Gus' decision whether to proceed or not.

'One week after I left, a military coup tried but failed to overthrow the National Assembly, which led to a spate of civil unrest, looting and rioting in Nairobi. Kamili, for whatever reason, was in the wrong place at the wrong time and was killed by a bullet fired from the security forces as they struggled to regain control during a riot. It took me six weeks to receive tangible confirmation that she had died; one of the older children I had taught English to wrote me a letter – this is pre-mobile phones, remember, but it was mere confirmation; inside I already knew she was gone, I just knew it.'

Gus looked up and smiled ironically. 'It's funny, you know, that first week back home, I never got the chance to tell my father about the orphanage and the funding required. Every time I prepared to discuss it, which was often, he appeared disinterested and swung the conversation around to the city etiquette I would need to adhere to. And when I knew, instinctively, watching the evening news reports coming out of Nairobi, that Kamili was dead, I made the decision to come quietly, to conform, I knew I couldn't take up the task on my own and sadly scrapped the idea of providing support, of bringing safety and refuge to those who were disadvantaged, as my – and I don't say this lightly – soulmate was no longer there; my spark, my purpose was gone. It now felt as if my spontaneous lurch into happiness had been foolish, a sign of my immaturity which I should not share with anyone, least of all my father. But inside I had died. I wanted to run away.

'A week later, I plucked up the courage to tell my father I wanted to travel for another year before I started work and surprisingly, he readily agreed. But on two conditions: I mustn't return to Kenya and I was to pay my own way; I would have only limited funds. I booked a flight on Qantas and nine weeks later touched down in Sydney. The following year was and remains a bit of a blur – Australia, Swiss Alps, Florida – but you all know the stories that I can remember!'

We laughed politely at his confession of memory loss.

The buzzer sounded, confirming visiting time was over, and seemed to conclude Gus' willingness to divulge any further personal and painful details.

Clifford moved the mask over his nostrils again in preparation to speak.

'Sorry I asked you now, son, that must be painful to retell,' he said, taking hold of Gus' hand again.

'Actually, feels good talking about it, been a long time,' Gus insisted, placing his other hand on top of Clifford's and rising.

'Have a good trip. And enjoy the race. Life is too short,' Mary stated, and regretted her choice of words instantly.

Gus smiled and walked past the bed with a wave, as Clifford placed his mask fully over his face once more. Gus stopped and looked at us all in turn.

'Do you know what the name Kamili means in Swahili?'

'No, Gus,' Mary and I said.

'It means "perfect", and she certainly was,' he said, and walked out of the ward without another glance at us.

'I'll pick you up at 8.30, Gus,' I called after him, which he acknowledged with a wave of his hand.

The three of us sat (and lay) in silence, each processing their own interpretation of Gus' doomed affair. It was obvious he still loved this woman, even after all these years. Despite what he had said to Clifford, the pain of speaking and remembering that year long ago in Africa was still intolerable for him, but I respected him for his efforts to ensure that Clifford's final time here was as comfortable as it possibly could be.

I was sure Gus wondered what life would have planned out for him and Kamili. What adventures they would have had together, how the orphanage would have grown, brought more love, more support and comfort to a stream of forgiving children. Perhaps he imagined their own family growing around them; perhaps he wondered what life would be like with Kamili by his side that very day, that very moment in time. I couldn't understand why he did not go back to the orphanage, why he did not explain to his father the need for finance and the good it would encourage. But then again, I didn't know his father, and I did know that grief taunts everyone in an individual way; in the particular way we are, as a person, most crushed – no two experiences of it are ever the same.

Movement around me and the sound of chairs being pushed back signalled that it was time for my departure too. Besides, I knew Clifford's favourite TV quiz show was scheduled to begin soon and his concentration would be fully on that.

Mary stood and wheeled over the TV to the foot of the bed in preparation and untangled the earphones caught around it. She clicked through the channels, ready for the familiar host and studio set to be revealed soon on the screen.

'I'll get those papers for you tonight, Mary,' I said, putting on my fleece.

'What papers?' she replied, offering up the earphones to Clifford.

'From Ted's, for the diesel.'

Mary shook her head in a lack of recognition.

'Don't worry, I'll sort it out, it's not a problem.'

'Mrs Wilson?'

Mary turned at the sound of her name.

'Could I have a word with you, please?' asked the consultant now standing at the foot of the bed, a laptop trapped under his arm. 'Mr Wilson,' he addressed Clifford respectfully.

Clifford nodded slowly to the white-coated man.

'We'll go to the relatives' room,' he suggested brightly.

I stood awkwardly as Mary followed the doctor slowly toward the far end of the ward before he disappeared around a corner. She stopped after a few steps and looked behind her at me. 'Eddie, will you come too, please?'

I put my hand up to Clifford, and without saying a word I followed her to a part of the ward I had not previously visited.

The relatives' room door was open, and sitting on a table with his legs swinging freely was the consultant. Beside him, he had the laptop open.

'Please, please, do come in, close the door,' he instructed us both. 'Are you the son?' he directed at me.

'No, this is Eddie, a very good friend,' said Mary as an explanation.

The consultant nodded and looked at the laptop, searching for a file on the screen.

'Okay,' he started, looking up again, 'Mr Wilson has been here for a while now. We have tried two types of antibiotics on him, to fight the infection.'

Mary nodded in agreement.

'The second course was successful.'

This time I nodded, feeling positive.

'But as you see, his condition has not improved.'

Now Mary and I looked at each other, confused, but remained silent.

'So this morning, we carried out a further CT scan on him to see what was really going on in there. I've got the results here, cracking pictures.'

He turned the laptop around to share the images of Clifford's lungs on the screen with us. He moved a finger across the control pad and animated the images back and forth, back and forth. To Mary and me, it looked like an indecipherable ink splat that expanded and receded into itself with each showing. Running it backwards or forwards made no difference to us.

The consultant stopped the animation suddenly and told us to look at the screen. He pointed to a small area that was coloured white, and turned to us.

'This is Mr Wilson's problem, here,' he said knowledgably.

'What is that?' I asked.

'Unfortunately, it shows clearly now that there is an excessive formation of CT.'

'CT?' asked Mary.

'Sorry, connective tissue build-up, otherwise known as fibrosis.'

We sat in silence, not fully understanding what was being relayed to us.

'Actually, to give it its full title, the disease is called "idiopathic pulmonary fibrosis, on account of the fact that we have no idea where it has originated from for Mr Wilson.'

We still did not understand.

'Now you know what it is, how do you treat it?' asked Mary.

'Mrs Wilson...' began the medic. He paused for a moment, before leaning forwards from his seated position. 'The prognosis is bad,' he said quietly, with compassion in his voice. 'It is not treatable, I am afraid.'

Mary put a hand up to her mouth and shook her head.

'Those white areas here are scarring,' said the doctor, pointing once again at the screen. 'They are where Mr

Wilson's lung capability has died. Whatever was in there causing it is still there, it will get worse. There is nothing we can do to halt this. I am really sorry.'

'Have you told him? Does he know? I thought it was bad, but I thought he would get better, come home,' lamented Mary.

'Yes, he does know, we spoke to him at length this morning. He wanted me to tell you tonight after visiting, wanted to make sure you had one less day to worry about it,' revealed the doctor, with a sympathetic half-smile on his lips. 'He is a very special man, Mrs Wilson,' he added.

I took hold of Mary's hand as she bowed her head. By the bedside earlier, when she appeared to give up hope, there must have been something inside her still believing that her Clifford, the summer fete bouncer, would recover, would go home. Maybe not able to work on the farm, but home in any case. But the words of the consultant had destroyed that hope and opened up a reality that she didn't want to see.

'How long?' she asked simply to the floor.

'Hard to say, really – wish I could be more specific for you. A couple of days, I would estimate.'

'And does he know that, a couple of days?' asked Mary, still staring at the floor.

'Yes he does, Mrs Wilson. Yes he does. He also wishes not to see anyone else now; only you, Mrs Wilson, it is his decision, his choice. Eddie,' he began, addressing me directly, 'this gives you an opportunity to say your goodbyes. In my experience, you should try to use this time; it will be invaluable for you all later.'

'Is he in pain?' I asked, and then felt foolish.

'He continues to struggle to take a breath. We will

give him morphine now, and this will help make him comfortable,' replied the doctor, matter-of-factly.

I nodded, not knowing what to say; the thought of saying goodbye so quickly, so rushed, so final, just wouldn't compute.

The medic allowed a respectful amount of time to pass before speaking again.

'If you have any other questions, let me know. Again, I am very sorry,' he said, closing the laptop, lifting himself off the table and heading for the door.

'I want to stay with him now. Just me and him, is that all right?' Mary asked, speaking to the doctor's back.

He spun around and smiled at her. 'Certainly it is. We can make a bed up for you,' he said.

'No, no, that's not necessary. I just want to stay with him, be next to him, close to him,' she repeated.

He nodded and walked out of the relatives' room.

We followed and wandered back over to Clifford's bed, not saying a word to each other. What was there to say?

I thought about what the consultant had suggested, that I say my goodbyes, but my mind was blank, unable to conjure up a poignant message to relay to Clifford.

Spontaneously, I leant in toward him.

'I am leaving now,' I said. 'You mean the world to me, you know that,' I added, as he nodded slightly.

As I stood up, Mary turned and kissed my cheek and we embraced. She whispered her thanks for me coming up so often, for going through the past few minutes with her in the relatives' room, and then made a revelation to me that made my words to Clifford seem inadequate.

'Clifford thinks of you as a son, Eddie,' she said gently.

And with her words, Clifford reached up, squeezed my hand over Mary's shoulder and winked a watery, tired eye at me.

Still processing her statement, I watched as she took her place beside her husband and fed one of the earphones into Clifford's left ear, then plugged the other into her right. She gently laid her cheek on his shoulder, making sure it wasn't causing him discomfort, and stroked the side of his face with the back of her left hand, and all the while their eyes were transfixed on the screen of escape, fantasy and make-believe positioned in front of them. They remained in that position, a lifetime of love, devotion and memories captured in the image.

Clifford murmured something through his mask.

'That's right, that's the answer – Manuel's "hamster" was called Basil,' repeated Mary, laughing, lifting her head slightly to find her husband's eyes with hers.

I walked away, a slight smile of understanding upon my lips; aware I had witnessed two different examples of love tonight, knowing I had been privileged to absorb both. One in the present shined pure with positivity and would do so until the inevitable end. The other burned with the unforgiving fuel of 'what if's and 'if only's. Unlike Gus, whose decisions I believed were misguided and shaped by his grief, I now understood completely that my own foolish, spontaneous lurch into happiness was not sustainable – how could it ever last? Humbled by this constant husband and wife in front of me, I finally had the sign; I finally realised I really needed to conform, to make what I had, what I shared, work. Just as Mary looked at Clifford, so I needed to really *see* Sally; it was the change I had to make.

Chapter 14

The Twenty-Second Rule

Unfortunately, Sally didn't see *me*. I arrived back to the now-customary empty house and called her to tell her about Clifford's deterioration and cursed as the line switched to voicemail. Sally replied by text an hour later, stating flatly that she was sorry to hear the news, and that she would see him Friday night and would be back within the hour. I wanted to tell her about Clifford's decision to allow no more visits, but knew I had to do this face-to-face. I needed her to listen, to empathise with my experience of my last moments with Clifford. I felt as lost and as helpless as Jennifer did following her involvement with Elliot Wallace and the dog-fighting ring. I had felt this emotion for one terrible moment before, but this time I needed to reach out to Sally, needed her to rub my back in the same soothing manner she had willingly done for Jennifer.

On Wednesday, the night before my last visit to Clifford, she was actually in the house when I arrived. She asked if I wanted some pasta – she had made enough, she explained; it just needed to be heated through again. Three months ago, Sally would have contacted me in my van as I travelled back from my last performance and asked what time I would be arriving back to begin the preparation of the meals that we ate together. She invariably would ask what I fancied; though sometimes she'd request I pick up something specific from the convenience store on the main road, ten minutes from the house, but it was always consulted, always together.

In ninety days it had deteriorated into this: us rarely being in the house together, rarely speaking, never eating meals together and me grateful to have been shown a level of consideration by being offered a portion of dried-out pasta, where Sally had made too much, I presume, for herself. The once-gleaming, in fact overly clean kitchen, along with the rest of the house, is now rapidly giving way to dirt, grime and grubbiness. I try to keep on top of it, but to be truthful, I only really seem to notice when the dishwasher is full and the cutlery drawer holds no more butter knives, or my reflection in the bathroom mirror is hidden beneath a dull sheen of splash-marks.

We do not even endure the weekly food shop together any more; instead, Sally has opened an online grocery account. At the time of booking she must have instructed for the delivery to be stacked in the wood store along the side of the house, I guess because she is out so often these days.

I have also ceased speaking about her bees with her. I have no idea how long business and contract negotiations take to conclude, but it should have been handshakes and champagne toasts by now, I reasoned to myself many times. I counteracted this by suggesting that ensuring a deal was in your favour would take time, and this is the point Sally must surely be at. There must be a stumbling block, yet Sally seems to be managing this on her own.

If she isn't tending her bees, speaking with the

supermarket, or with her brother working on the plan to conquer the solar panels market with 'Eco-Lites', she is at Ignatius McKenzie's house having spiritual sessions. From her initial weekly visits, Sally now attends two or three times a week. Last week she changed her Saturday evening sessions to Saturday afternoon instead. This was, she said, because Ignatius had a double session in the afternoon, which meant they had a greater length of time to connect. I wanted to ask how much these regular visits are costing, but held my thoughts, knowing it would not be received well; through the shouting, I would inevitably be reminded categorically that it is her money. I also wondered what effect this has on her mental health, but this was another subject I could not discuss with her. Her Saturday evenings are once again spent at home, but with Jennifer not recommencing her visits she spent her Saturday night last week soaking in the bath before retiring alone for an early night. I am sure she will do the very same this week too.

I admit that, from time to time, I have found the physical side of our relationship difficult, and Sally is fully aware of the reasons for this. With Clifford and Mary's long-standing love for each other as my benchmark, combined with Sally providing some food, albeit not to share, that night I contemplated initiating the affection she has craved on many occasions.

Sally sat reading a newspaper after I came into the living room from the kitchen; the dishwasher, full to capacity, had begun its pre-wash cycle. Henry followed on behind me and wandered over to Sally. She tickled his ears without looking at him, but soon tired of his licking and panting and instructed him to lie down, which, Henry being Henry, he dutifully ignored. He soon reacted to her stern, irritable 'Go away' though, and settled himself beside my chair.

'The pasta was great, thanks for that,' I offered into the still room.

'Are you working on Saturday?' she asked, ignoring my compliment.

'I've got two bouncy castles to set up before two, then a magic show at four, all ready and loaded up.'

Sally didn't answer. Instead, she put down the newspaper and stood up.

'I am going to bed,' she uttered, crossing the room, and left without another word.

'I'll be up in a minute,' I called after her.

And so I was.

Sally lay propped up on a couple of pillows, concentrating on a book.

'I didn't know you liked Dickens,' I said, looking at the cover of *Little Dorrit* in her hands.

'Always liked it,' she replied.

'Well, I never knew that,' I said.

Sally ignored me, pulled her pillows into a reclining position, reached to turn her bedside light out and turned her back to me. I counted the seconds in my head as I waited in the darkness for my eyes to adjust to the rapid change in light. I slipped into the bed, my weight displaced on my forearm, and moved toward her. I reached around her waist as my lips gently brushed the top of her shoulder and travelled up her neck to her jawline.

'Eddie, no! I need to be up early tomorrow,' she stated firmly, moving her head away from my advances.

With the words halting my plans before they had begun,

I removed my hand from around her waist. The crushing pain of rejection taunted my self-worth and my confidence retreated back with my body to my side of the bed.

Sally again patted her pillows flat and shuffled further away from me to the very edge of the bed. *One of us should retire to the guest room*, I thought, but I didn't want to move, I didn't want to draw any more attention to myself than I already had with my actions. I turned over onto my back and stared up at the ceiling, my eyes now fully adjusted to the darkness.

Lying next to someone that doesn't want you to be there is not healthy.

'Goodnight, Sally,' I said into the darkness.

I could now see the entire outline of the ceiling of the bedroom, and knew sleep would evade me for some considerable time yet. Should I try again with Sally? Should I try to coax my confidence back for one final push? Then the sound of Sally lightly breathing in her sleep, pretend or otherwise, made the decision for me.

In an instant I was again that very young and clumsy man in a bar, struggling to sit down in the cramped space provided by the tightly packed tables. It was the fourth bar of the evening, a long evening of pre-Christmas drinks, an evening of games, high spirits and pranks.

As I swung to manoeuvre my trailing leg into position to join my friends, it jolted the next table and forced the girl nearest to me, with her back to our table, to spill her drink over her top. She gave out a little yelp, followed by those around her table laughing at her wet shirt and my blundering approach to sitting down. I apologised profusely, but she said it was not a problem. She was extremely beautiful, her hair dark and face concealed by a perfectly applied cover of make-up. I offered to buy her a drink to make up for the one I had spilt, but she was adamant in her reply of no and gave the impression that no further conversation should take place.

Later, when it was my round, I returned from the crowded bar carrying three pints through a wall of drunk and unreceptive people. Nearing the table, she got up suddenly and swung around, jarring one of the pints out of my hand and spilling half the contents of the glass over the left side of her white top. I tried hard to resist but the combination of young hormones and drunken, weary eyes found my gaze transfixed on her small, pert left breast. Though the shirt was now horribly discoloured by a dirty wet stain, my slightly blurred vision only saw the rise of her nipple underneath, reacting to the cold liquid.

'I am so sorry,' I mumbled at her, still looking at her breast, though in my mind I was convinced I was being subtle.

'That's okay,' she replied. 'Although, my face is up here!'

I took the hint and looked into her face, and saw a big, warm smile upon her lips.

'Should I buy you that drink now?' I asked sheepishly.

'Yes, you should!' she answered as I looked beyond her and noticed that most of her table was now empty.

'You best come with me in case I spill it,' I replied, looking directly at her with confidence, while she laughed out loud.

I really had no idea where any of this was coming from. I was usually rubbish around girls. I became tongue-tied or glowed bright red with embarrassment if one spoke to me, and on many occasions, both actions occurred simultaneously. My friends, on the other hand, seemed to have no such problems and bigged themselves up with outlandish boasts and tall stories of epic proportions. I was, as far as I could be sure, the only one not to have 'scored' with a girl yet, although I kept this information to myself.

Pushing our way back to the bar, this time with this girl, seemed right.

I remember it took an age to get served – every time I caught a bartender's eye for more than a fleeting second, they decided to serve the person next to me, always a girl. Eventually the drinks came and I tipped hers toward her as if I was going to spill it, before handing it to her. She told me her name was Sally, and that she thought it was a strange chat-up technique to throw drinks over a girl, but I was very likeable, she said. I wasn't sure then, and I still am not sure what that actually meant. I almost made some outlandish boasts but held back, though I did tell one tall story of mild proportions before the 'time' bell rang, signalling the end of the evening.

We kissed tentatively outside, the cold December night air shaking the alcohol from our systems. When asked, she agreed to meet me at the cinema on the following Wednesday.

I lay in our darkened bedroom, trying for the life of me to remember the name of the movie we saw on our first 'proper' date, but try as I might, the title evaded me.

That daunting first introduction to the family followed swiftly on. On entry, the house was like a furnace! Sally's father insisted the central heating should be on in all areas of the house. I found out afterwards from Sally that he only did this to make a good impression on me; normally he was reluctant to open up the warmth to all areas of the house in order to save money, preferring instead for himself, Sally's mother and her brother to wear sweaters to compensate. Contrary to what I was led to believe, we were expected to eat a hearty meal prepared for us – this was near impossible, due to the meal we had already eaten in a cafe beforehand and the subtropical conditions we found ourselves in. I persevered, knowing that good first impression would be crucial, and even tackled the substantial pile of soft carrots, a vegetable I hate, overcooked or otherwise, that covered a quarter of the surface of my plate.

As our relationship grew, it naturally steered toward engagement, then marriage. Sally loved the idea of her 'big day', as she called it. I chose the engagement ring with her and handed over a month's salary to pay for it. She selected her wedding dress with her mother. Her father insisted on paying most of the expenses – he wasn't, in his words, going to let his only princess down, and seemed to believe that providing the lion's share of the finances enabled him and his wife to dictate how and on what the money was spent.

In those spontaneous quiet times partners have when they share and map out their dreams and future together, both Sally and I constructed a small wedding, a relaxed gathering in a village hall with a select number of friends and family in autumn, our favourite time of year, when the warmth from the previous season still radiates from the ground, the sun sits low in the sky and the world is bathed in red, brown and orange, as nature prepares to sleep. This was far removed from the actual day that was pummelled by midsummer storms, whose persistent thunderclaps made the greeting of, in my case, strangers; in Sally's case, little-known uncles, aunts and cousins difficult as they filed past, en masse, into the two hundred-seat marquee, and with each crash of thunder, Sally jumped nervously.

We purposely did not provide a wedding list; instead we asked that if people were kind enough to think of us could they please provide cash as an alternative? This was to enable us to choose the items we wanted as we started our married life together. The communication went unheeded, and the numerous wedding gifts we insisted we did not want all still had to be acknowledged with thank-you cards. Initially Sally intended to write individual cards for each gift, bearing a special message for each guest. However, after completion of the first, she succumbed to my idea of a generic approach for each replicated gift that surrounded us. When we had finished writing and were ready to envelope and stamp up, we had twelve cards of thanks for the toaster, seven enthusing about the kettle, eighteen for the mantelpiece clock and twenty-five plus expressing our gratitude for the towel set. Seven people received individual notes in recognition of the generous cash gift they provided.

My mind then turned to that day, that special day three years into our marriage, when Sally insisted we met for a pub lunch because she had news to share. She refused to divulge, until I was seated next to her, what this was – and I was glad she had been insistent as I felt my knees shake under the table when she finally spoke. Again, we had offers of financial support and advice from her family, but we knew what *we* wanted to do, and our dreams and future would now develop and change over the forthcoming months. We had tried to grow up over the past three years, to make our own decisions, to make our own path. We did take one piece of advice though, and decided to paint the spare bedroom walls 'buttercup yellow'.

And at this point, the memories became blocked as I willed sleep to find me, to take me away from further change and regrettable broken dreams behind my now-closed eyes.

My mind began to drift, to extract random thoughts and flashes; two bears on roller skates led me through a shaded alley to a sun-drenched courtyard. And as they wheeled away, leaving me alone, the title of the movie from our first date came back to me at last: *It's a Wonderful Life*, I remembered. *Yes, of course that was the name*, I thought, as sleep came to me.

Yesterday morning, I took Gus to the airport as arranged, my lack of communication easily explained as my response to Clifford's prognosis. I did not relay the actual timescale involved as per the consultant's opinion, only that Clifford would not be going home, would not be able to leave hospital. I knew if I told Gus, he would simply worry while he was away, and what could he do? What could any of us do now? I also omitted to mention Clifford's personal decision regarding no more visits. Gus genuinely seemed a little hurt that Mary had chosen to share the prognosis only with me. Or maybe he was merely regretting exposing himself so openly and leaving prematurely yesterday. Whatever the truth, we hardly spoke on the drive.

At the airport drop-off point, he suggested cancelling his trip and going straight to the hospital. I discouraged him, thinking on my feet, and told him to try and enjoy himself and take lots of photos; it would cheer Clifford up on his return. Getting out of the van, he agreed with a smile and a nod that this would be a good idea and wandered over to the terminal building, his battered holdall slung over his shoulder.

Later, I performed at two children's parties and all the while, through pass the parcel, *I Am the Music Man* and demonstrating the wobbly wand, I thought about Sally and my decision to conform, and tried to compose the speech I would deliver to Cerys on the beach the next day.

Last night, as has become the norm, I ate a late supper by myself in the kitchen, Henry in his bed, snoring, under the breakfast bar. I had phoned Sally in the early afternoon and left a voice message, asking her to meet me for dinner in a country pub – nothing fancy, just a chance to do something different together, and to talk. I didn't get a call back. I sent a couple of text messages as backup in the late afternoon and eventually received a text reply at 8pm, claiming her phone had been playing up and she had only just received my messages. She stated that she was currently with Clifford in the hospital and would be back soon, and that it was obviously too late now for a meal. Her lack of an apology was telling and I found it strangely more upsetting then the lie she had just told.

Around midnight I felt her slide into the bed next to me. I felt her carefully turn her back away, carefully keep every cell of her skin away from mine, to travel to her dreams without me. The bed might as well have been a thousand miles wide; the distance between us would have remained the same. And in the darkness, a silence of denial from me refused to see the truth revealed in her message.

In the hushed tomb of night, I heard her phone vibrate four times on the table beside her. I convinced myself that my second message from that afternoon had just got through. It was odd, though, how Sally's phone was always set to silent vibrate; something she had only been doing these past few months. the hospitalatsn:As sleep circled me, I decided as I lay there to get up early the next morning before Sally and check the phone, to make sure it was my message that had been announced in the hallway. But what would I do if it wasn't mine? I reasoned that it most probably would be Jennifer, making arrangements to meet up tonight. More importantly, how could I explain why the text had been read? It was obvious Sally wasn't asleep when it had arrived and must have heard it too.

Why could I not just confront her; ask where the missing hours of last night had gone, why she was always out, why we do not eat, speak, or even look at each other any more? But quite simply, I was frightened to ask; afraid of the answers I might hear. Like Mary reeling from the consultant's words, I dreaded hearing a truth I did not want, a change I could not control. To me, it was better to live within the wreckage of a realm, though deeply flawed, one that I knew and was perversely comfortable in; one that I was convinced I could save, bring back onto a steady course.

In reality, on waking at first light today, I looked over to see if Sally was asleep, but she was in fact already gone. I hadn't heard her get up; she must have showered in the downstairs bathroom again. I sat up, my mind already racing and alert. I really do not know how I have been sleeping; I always appear to be in the same position as when I closed my eyes six short hours before. Finally, I convinced myself I was disappointed that I now would not be able to confirm that the message received on Sally's phone was indeed mine.

Then, as I wandered into the kitchen, Cerys entered my thoughts, as did the conversation I would be having in a short while. I patted Henry good morning in his basket and shuddered as I thought about Phoebe's fate, as I had every day since overhearing the conversation by my van at the Lombarders ladies night. I noticed the paper on the work surface.

'*Seeing Greg – solar panels,*' I read aloud. *That's strange for Sally to leave a note*, I thought, and I didn't understand the unease I felt on reading it.

I made tea and mulled over the note and my forthcoming speech, sitting at the breakfast bar. Cowardly, I wished Cerys and I had exchanged phone numbers; we had made a conscious decision not to, as the temptation to contact and the explanation on discovery by our partners would be too great. But if we had done this, had allowed illicit communication to flow back and forth in the many hours we spent apart I could now present my words via a text message, the modern way, without punctuation, without a crack in the voice, ultimately avoiding the contact with the recipient's eyes that completes the message that the words only partly deliver. I dismissed the idea as quickly as I had it – not all aspects of modern life are an improvement on the practices of before. But with the use of technology I could have warned her about her husband's dark secret and with each day that passed I felt more guilty that I held the knowledge to myself.

Tea drunk and cup in the sink for washing later, I made my checks – keys, dog leash and phone that had been charging overnight in the kitchen. Disconnecting the phone from the charger, a message alert bleeped at me. I opened the message and was immediately puzzled.

Eddie, if you need to talk I can be around, the message read, received from an unknown number. I noted it was sent last night at 2.07, way past my bedtime. I stared at the phone. Was this Cerys? No, it couldn't be, we were meeting in an hour and what did she mean? What were we to talk about? Had she come to the same conclusion as me? Who else would send me a text from a number I didn't have stored as a contact? The message had to be for me; it addressed me by name. It couldn't be some random post-argument drunken text delivered to my phone by shaky fingers, viewed through bleary, bloodshot eyes.

Sorry, who is this? I typed quickly, and sent the message.

In the van as I turned over the engine, the phone bleeped once more, this time from the glove compartment. I picked up the phone, curious as to who it could be.

Eddie, it's Jenny, I was going to give you space, but I am sure you might need the support. I can be there from ten.

This didn't make any sense. I felt cold and exhaled deeply. How on earth did Jennifer know that I was heading to the beach to break up with Cerys this morning? How did she know about Cerys? I started to panic. *If Jennifer knows, Sally knows*, and with that revelation my heart pounded in my chest. The irony of the situation, the trying to make it right before it was too late, wasn't lost on me. Perhaps she was going to act as an intermediary between Sally and me, but I knew she hated men, so was probably using it as an excuse to poke and prod me, to kidney-punch me on the ropes, to further rubbish my gender for her own needs. I tried to reduce my heart rate and think. *Logically*, I reasoned, *perhaps Sally doesn't know, only Jennifer – but how?* I decided I could spend the next few hours mulling over this conundrum and concluded that I should, at this point, keep her on side. I selected 'reply' on my phone, typed, *Thanks* and sent the simple, polite message.

For the first time I dreaded the drive to the beach. The excited expectation had gone, replaced by a feeling of dread. Even the disappointment I experienced on so many Saturdays trudging back to the van after walking alone was preferable to this. What could I start with? 'I cannot see you any more', or 'Your husband is involved with a dog-fighting ring and may have given Phoebe to them'? How on earth could I tell her the latter? But she needed to know the truth, I knew this. But with Jennifer knowing, I had to ensure I went through with it, to explain why I couldn't see Cerys any more, why next Wednesday couldn't happen.

Pulling into the car park, my heart sank further. Parked up was a white Range Rover. For the first time, Cerys had arrived before me. I had no time to prepare, no time to go over my words. She waved enthusiastically from her driver's seat as I pulled in beside her, and I smiled in return. She got out of her car and came over to me, running, laughing, oblivious to what I was going to say. Cerys opened the passenger door of the van.

'Thought I'd do an away fixture today,' she said, getting in as Henry dropped to the floor and licked her hands affectionately. 'Hello, Henry!'

She leant in to kiss me, and I could do nothing but respond. Her soft lips touching mine made me melt.

'So good to see you!' she commented when we broke away. 'Now, Wednesday – the room is ready after 3pm, so I thought we could meet beforehand at the hotel and have a bite to eat, I think the restaurant is okay. That's if you can make it at that time. Been thinking about it all week, since the ball – you were brilliant, by the way; I'm not just saying that because of us, so many people commented on it. My flight is at ten so I need to leave by eight, and you can stay until twelve if you want to, no rush.'

Cerys stopped speaking and looked at me.

'I am all over the place, Eddie, aren't I? Babbling on and on, all these random thoughts in my head. Shall we go?' she added, opening the passenger door a little, causing Henry to get up and wag his tail.

I sat still, wanting it to be five minutes into the future.

Cerys finally noted my silence and spoke again.

'Everything okay, Eddie?' she asked gently.

I didn't answer.

'Eddie? What is it? What's wrong?' Cerys said, closing the door and ignoring Henry's deep sigh as the sounds and smells of outside were removed from the cab.

I turned and looked at her, wishing I had been able to send that text message after all.

'Cerys,' I began, looking straight into her eyes, 'I can't make it on Wednesday.'

'Oh, Eddie!'

Annoyance tore through her voice, and she stared me out, until I broke eye contact.

'I know, I am sorry,' I conceded meekly.

She puffed out her cheeks and exhaled deeply.

'I am just disappointed, I've thought about it all week.

252

It's not every day I do this, you know, I don't make a habit of this sort of thing,' she stated. 'May I ask why?' she added.

'Why?' I unnecessarily repeated; my planned speech destroyed before even the first word was formed.

'Yes, why you can't meet me on Wednesday.'

'I just can't make it, that's all,' I lied, hoping it would be enough.

But it obviously wasn't.

'That's not an answer, Eddie, and you know it. I gave you all this time to make arrangements – when I saw your van parked at the golf club last week, I knew this could work, I was so excited. I really wanted to tell you, to find you there and then, but knew I had to wait for the right moment to broach the subject. It was really difficult for me to ask you, but I want to be with you, fully, totally,' Cerys said, her frustration spilling out.

She then asked the question I dreaded.

'You do want to be with me, Eddie, don't you?'

'Of course I do!' I replied enthusiastically.

'Phew, for a moment there my brain thought we were breaking up!' laughed Cerys.

I didn't laugh, I didn't reply; I just stared straight ahead through the windscreen toward the dunes.

Cerys stopped laughing. I felt her eyes staring at me.

I faced her and saw the look I had wanted to avoid. The look of crushing bewilderment, the look of someone wishing they had not revealed their thoughts so openly moments before, the look of someone not wanting to hear another word, hoping the tears forming in their eyes will somehow block out the sound.

'I am sorry; I just can't do this any more,' I stated, plain and direct.

Cerys said nothing, but just turned and looked out the windscreen toward the dunes as I had done.

'It was seeing Clifford and Mary at the hospital. It just made me feel—'

'Stop! Stop!' shouted Cerys. 'I don't want to hear excuses or reasons; you made a choice, not me, don't try to justify it!'

I obeyed and remained silent, the words I wanted to say left hanging and I knew I could not tell her about Phoebe now.

I am ashamed to admit that at that point, I wanted to run, turn and flee. But this was my van, my space; I couldn't leave. Instead, I continued to sit, wishing she would go.

'So this is it then?' Cerys finally offered into the silence.

I nodded, not sure what to do next, my eyes still studying the profile of her face.

Eventually, she took hold of my hands and looked at me, tears running down her cheeks. She smiled at me, her warm, honest smile, and I returned it with my own.

'Eddie, this could have been so good, it was right. Clifford and Mary are different people; you can't live your life as another.'

I didn't answer, I didn't know if she expected or wanted me to. As Cerys said, I had made my choice.

She withdrew her hands from mine and momentarily kissed my forehead tenderly. She then patted Henry's head and told him to be good.

'Look after yourself, Eddie. I hope you find what you are looking for,' she said, opening the passenger door once more, but this time leaving.

Cerys ran to her car while I sat motionless in the van. I heard her engine start, heard the vehicle reverse and wheel-spin quickly away, heard the silence return once more, but I didn't look. I didn't dare.

When I eventually moved, I don't remember the walk on the beach. I don't remember details of the drive home. I do remember the feeling of utter despair, the urge to yell at the top of my voice until my throat was hoarse and sore, and the unrelenting feeling of dread and anxiety if I closed my eyes or had them open, if I walked or sat still.

Back at the house, as expected, Jennifer's car sat on the driveway. Before heading inside, I looked at my eyes in the sun visor mirror, trying to convince myself they did not look puffy, bloodshot or sad. I would wait and see what she had to say, see what she knew before offering the information that it was actually over.

I entered, my key turning in the lock prompting Jennifer to emerge from her studio down the hall.

Henry raced toward Jennifer, excited to see her there, his gallop rewarded with affectionate words and stroking.

'How are you doing, Eddie?' Jennifer asked me from the studio doorway.

'Fine,' I lied.

'That's good. You look shaken, I am sorry about that.'

'I am okay,' I replied, not wanting to say too much at this time.

'Shall I make tea? Looks like you could do with one,' Jennifer offered.

I nodded my agreement.

We entered the kitchen. Jennifer lifted the kettle to

check the water level inside, and I lifted Henry's bowl and filled it with water for him to quench his thirst.

We stood with our own thoughts, the sound of the kettle boiling blocking out any embarrassing silence.

'You sure you are okay, Eddie?' asked Jennifer as the kettle cut out.

'Yes I am,' I stated again.

'Sally's gone?' she asked.

'Yep, she left a note,' I said absent-mindedly.

'And you are okay with that?' she enquired slowly, as if choosing her words carefully.

'The note's there.' I gestured toward the work surface in front of her. 'It was a bit strange to receive it, though,' I added.

'You just left it there?'

'Why wouldn't I?'

'Of course, of course,' Jennifer replied hurriedly.

'You can read it if you want,' I suggested, happy to keep the conversation away from the reason Jennifer was here.

'No, Eddie, I wouldn't dream of it, it's of a personal nature.'

'It only states that she is seeing her brother about those bloody solar panels again. I don't understand why that warranted a note.'

'Sorry?' she said, lifting a brewed teabag out of a cup with a spoon.

'She's out all the time, but never leaves a note, so I don't know why today is so special.'

'May I?' she asked, nodding toward the paper.

'Sure.'

Jennifer picked up the note, while still balancing the

discarded teabag on the spoon. She read it quickly and dropped the teabag back into the cup with a splash, and uttered, 'Shit' as the scolding drink caught her fingers.

It was my turn to ask if *she* was okay. She replied yes, but seemed suddenly flustered. She reread the note over and over and I sensed this had somehow, for reasons I did not understand, distracted her from confronting me about Cerys. She sipped at her tea repeatedly and thoughtfully, attempting to drain the hot liquid as quickly as possible, and made the excuse, through blowing over and slurping the tea, that one of her dogs had a grooming appointment as her eventual reason to make a hurried departure. She left the house, her mind obviously preoccupied – perhaps she had had a change of heart, I thought.

I walked into the hallway, wishing I had had a change of heart myself at the beach and was now looking forward to the excitement of lying with another woman in a few short days. Instead, I felt lonelier than I had ever imagined it possible to be.

Chapter 15

In the Kitchen at Parties

I spend a large proportion of my time in strangers' gardens. Similar to dogs, I believe a garden reflects an image of its owners, their outlook on life. From the neat borders packed with colour-coordinated -consciousflowering blooms, to the towering leylandii surrounding a plot like a living prison wall, each gives an insight into a person. Invariably, those with majestic floral displays and swinging, solid wooden garden furniture tend to scrutinise their invoices, in some cases requesting an itemised breakdown of the costings before paying, normally in full, but begrudgingly to some extent. In the shaded gardens, where only the ridge tiles of the neighbouring house are visible and the borders are an arid, acid-filled wasteland, to secure eye contact with the owner is an achievement; to be invited inside an improbability.

Then there are the gardens where the family pet uses the entire grass area as its toilet of choice, selecting, supposedly at random, areas to defecate in multiple times a day. Despite my request on the phone beforehand that an area is clear for the inflatable to sit, I regularly have to hose down and clean the base of a bouncy castle in Clifford's yard, the foul smell caught in the water spray making me want to retch. I guess these people simply see life differently to me and have trouble dealing with words like 'consideration' and 'respect'. I am not sure when or how a collection of garden gnomes or comical ceramic figures dotted around a garden can ever be classed as acceptable, but I have seen plenty of examples and many that are the main focal point of the entire space. This type of person breaks my mould of characterisation, as they cannot be collectively defined, but they do have one trait in common: they are all slightly odd!

But today, seven days after last seeing Cerys, I couldn't tell you which type of garden I was standing in, or any detail about the owner.

I had tried to reconnect with Sally, but failed. A person has to be with you both physically and mentally for a relationship to work.

Hooking up the generator to the second bouncy castle of the day brought, as always, the excited cheer and expectant gasp from the birthday child and their closest friends – those selected few, the elite ones with special passes, the ones invited prior to the party, before the masses. But today I did not see the excitement in their eyes, nor sense their anticipation of wanting to jump, tumble and flip before the inflatable had reached its full height. It was the same with the earlier drop. I knew they had perfect weather for it, I could feel the sun on the top of my head and no breeze through my shirt, but I couldn't register that this equalled clear blue skies above me and a hanging yellow sun for the remainder of the afternoon and evening; the time when the grown-ups enjoy their own party in the garden with the selected parents who have been invited to stay seated, as the day's heat remains trapped in the air, sweet with the aroma of chilled wine, honeysuckle and the sound of children edging toward exhaustion.

With the generator breathing a steady stream of life into the inflatable, I headed for the van. My phone rang in my pocket as I slipped the keys into the ignition to head away.

Who was it, I wondered as I retrieved the mobile? Maybe Cerys – no, it couldn't be, she didn't have my number. Sally? Jennifer?

'Mary?' I answered.

Down the line, I heard the sigh in her voice and knew the reason for her call.

'He's gone, Eddie,' she said quietly.

'Mary, I am so sorry,' I said. 'Where are you?'

'I am still here.'

'Let me get there.'

'No, I am going to head home. I need to bathe, I need to sleep, I need some space,' she replied honestly.

I understood. Grief was attacking her in the way designed only for Mrs Mary Wilson, widow.

'Come around later, Eddie,' she added. 'I just need a bit of time.'

She hung up, and I sat with the phone to my ear. My mind tried to reason it was for the best as I placed the phone in the door pocket. But it wasn't for the best at all – he was gone, we were left; how could this ever be explained away as being right? This man who lit up a room with his presence and innocent excitement for life was gone. The hands that could almost hide a pint glass would never be fumbling for the correct change at the bar again. He would never be tinkering in his yard in his torn, stretched, ill-fitting navy blue jumper, or checking the ewes up on the hillside. Even though two summers had passed, there was always hope in my heart that I would again see him bouncing on an inflatable with flailing arms and his childlike giggles expressing his delight.

But with Mary's call, this hope was extinguished. I would never again, when dressed as Clive the Clown, be requested by him to throw my hat and ginger wig high into the air and catch them on my head. I would miss his quick mind and his teasing of Mary, their jibes and bickering shown to be nothing more than playful banter, proven by his request to be with her alone at the end, showing how deeply he loved her. I would miss him; I would really miss him.

I picked up the phone and called Sally's mobile; it went straight to voicemail. I tried a further four times, calling at three-minute intervals, but each time the result was the same. On the fifth time, I simply said, 'Clifford is gone' and hung up.

I jumped out of the cab and knocked on the front door of the house, hearing for the first time today the shouts and laughter of the children from the back garden. I knocked again, and when no one responded, I wandered down the side alley and into the garden. The girls played happily, ignoring me, the man who brought the bouncy castle barely fifteen minutes ago. They had made up a circuit, involving the use of a hula hoop to skip with, a scooter to traverse the garden perimeter and the inflatable to dive on as a finale.

Turning to the house, I knocked firmly on the slightly ajar kitchen door. Through the glass door, I could see party preparations in full swing: sausage rolls and chicken nuggets being placed in the oven, bread being buttered and bags of crisps being poured into huge bowls by a team of adults.

'Would you get that, Trish? Bloody cheek, I didn't think he wanted paying until pick-up,' I heard the birthday child's mother utter, not realising, I am sure, in her pre-party, slightly stressed state, that I could hear her.

'Can I help you?' Trish asked me, opening the door wide.

'Sorry to bother you, can I borrow a phone directory please?' I replied. 'I can see you are busy, and I wouldn't ask, but I urgently need to contact someone,' I added as my explanation.

'Hang on,' she said, and slipped inside. 'He wants a phone book,' she relayed.

'What?'

'I don't know, said he needs to contact someone.'

'Hallway table, Trish.'

She returned, phone book in hand, and flashed a half-smile in acknowledgement of my gratitude before heading back inside.

'I'll leave it by the front door,' I called into the kitchen.

But my words were not heard, or possibly quite simply ignored.

'Kirsty, do you want equal jugs of orange squash and blackcurrant?' pondered Trish loudly from inside the kitchen.

Chapter 16

Everything Changes

I pulled up outside the address taken from the phone book, looked out of the passenger window and surveyed the handsome detached Victorian house. It had the look of a 'proper' house about it, the kind a child would draw, with symmetrical windows left and right, top and bottom, and a front door plumb centre of the brickwork front. A prunus tree sat to the left, casting shade over the gravelled frontage. All that was missing was smoke rising from the single chimney to complete an image that could take pride of place on any refrigerator door.

I walked across the gravel, enjoying the satisfying crunching sound each footstep made, and pressed the doorbell for a single long tone, noting as I stepped back my reflection in the jet-black glossed front door.

As I waited for an eternity for my call to be answered, I noted the absence of any other vehicle and suddenly questioned why I had come here. I felt foolish, not prepared to draw attention to myself by ringing the bell a second time. I turned to go, to retreat to the van, the gravel under my feet once more, when I heard the sound of a lock being opened from within. I turned back and witnessed the door open and a slight, bespectacled man, markedly older than I was, standing on the threshold. He wore a dress suit, but no tie. In his vision, I felt drawn back, and as I walked to the house, I realised he wasn't as old as he had appeared. It was the hair that caused him to seem older; it was pure white, cut smartly, but pure white nonetheless. Stood now in front of him, his glasses, though probably needed, were worn equally as a fashion statement. They fitted the image of a Germanic corporate professional type. Not that I had actually seen any in my time, my knowledge being drawn entirely from TV and magazine advertisements for performance cars or audio equipment.

'Mr McKenzie?' I asked.

'Yes, can I help you?' he replied.

'Sorry to bother you, but is Sally Dungiven with you?'

'Who?'

'Sally Dungiven, she comes here every Saturday – changed to afternoons lately,' I stated.

Ignatius McKenzie looked at me thoughtfully and calmly for a while.

'Mrs Dungiven, you say?'

I nodded in response.

'She hasn't been here for a while now, months I believe,' he said. 'Why, is there something wrong?'

My head started to spin; all the doubts and signs I had ignored crashed into my mind at once: the never-ending negotiations for her honey contract, those hours spent with her brother working on 'Eco-Lites', and now the absence of her car, the final fatal sign. I had to get away.

'I apologise; I must have been mistaken. I am sorry for troubling you,' I said, and turned on my heels.

'Wait! Please stop!' he commanded.

And I found the sound of his voice made my feet stop dead involuntarily in the gravel. The fact Sally was not here, and had not been for some time, slip away and seem irrelevant. involuntarilyI turned and walked back toward the front door of the perfectly proportioned home of Ignatius McKenzie, not knowing why I was doing so.

He looked at me intently, his stare boring into mine. I tried to avert my eyes, but his mind seemed to command them to respond to a message I could not hear and I met his gaze once more.

'You seem deeply troubled. I can see a sadness walking with you. Come in for a chat?' he said, trying, I felt, to pull my soul out through my eyes.

'No, no, I am fine,' I eventually said.

His expression changed from one of intense concentration to one of concern.

'Please, I think I can help you,' he insisted quietly.

And with these words I felt myself stepping in through the door frame.

'Come in, come,' he instructed with an open palm and a smile as he closed the door quite some time after I had entered and then bolted it shut, an action that left me feeling wary.

I don't know what I was expecting, but inside the house was conventional. No stuffed ravens, skulls, piles of leather-bound books, dark wood panelling or gloom in sight. Instead, natural light flooded the space in which I stood through a floor-to-ceiling gable-shaped window, through an open door at the far end of the hallway and through a lesser-sized, but still substantial window located at the top of the stairs. The walls were painted in natural, light colours and the wooden floor was covered with a terracotta rug. A single oak table was pushed to the wall, topped with a marble sculpture. The whole area seemed peaceful and serene.

'We'll go in here,' he indicated, opening a door halfway along the hallway.

I stood, looking into the room opening before me.

'Please, after you,' he added, raising his hand again in welcome and direction.

I entered the room. Again, natural light filled the space, this time from French doors, which looked out onto a mature, well-loved garden. Inside the room, the walls were a cool green; a cream carpet lay on the floor. I quickly glanced at a bookcase that ran the entire length of the wall opposite, but I could not recognise any of the books on display, nor fathom their subject matter.

Ignatius McKenzie ushered me to a seat, one of two opposite each other beside an unlit, open stone fireplace. I opted for the chair with a view of the garden and sunk down into its comfortable cushions. The white-haired man took the seat opposite me.

'You must be Mr Dungiven?' he asked, crossing his legs.

I nodded. I still didn't know why I was here, but equally, now inside, I didn't feel the desire to leave.

'I don't normally make a habit of this,' he stated suddenly, 'inviting a stranger into my home, but I think you were brought here today.'

I didn't understand at all. I had driven here to find Sally, to tell her that Clifford had died, to share in that grief. She wasn't there, she couldn't release my grief, but still I sat in this tranquil room, not looking out onto the garden, but instead transfixed by this man's blue-eyed stare. Or perhaps, in truth, I couldn't face the fact that Sally had not been there.

'Do you believe in an afterlife, Mr Dungiven?' Ignatius McKenzie asked suddenly.

I was taken off guard and didn't answer. He stared straight between my eyes.

'What do you think happens when we leave our physical bodies?' he pressed.

'We die. We are gone. We no longer exist,' I replied flatly.

Ignatius nodded. 'That explains the physical aspect. What about the energy that was the person, the very essence of that person? Does that go? Does that no longer exist?'

A rushing sensation swept over me. My mind fell clear, I felt vulnerable and I no longer desired to be in the house.

'I do not understand what you are saying, or why you are saying it. I only came to see if my wife was here. She isn't, so I think I should leave,' I said, standing up.

'Please, please don't go.'

I stood, trying to not react to his voice.

'I can help you,' he stated with a gentle smile.

I did not respond.

'I am obliged to help you,' he reasoned.

'Obliged to help me?' I repeated, drawn in by his words, though trying to ignore them.

'Yes. This is my duty. It will not cost you anything, but it will give you something.'

And again, I felt rooted to the spot by the sound of his calming voice.

'This sadness you feel, it doesn't have to be there, it really doesn't. You need to let it go, move forward, stop tormenting yourself.'

'What sadness?' I questioned, again managing to wrench myself from the spell of his voice.

'The sadness only a parent can feel.'

I stared at him, trying to free my mind of thought, trying to protect myself, but I was left with the feeling again, the same I had experienced on the steps: that he was reading me, that he knew, despite my best efforts, what I would think next.

'Please sit down.'

Unable to summon back the desire to leave the room, I chose again to take my seat and tried and failed once more to seek out the garden beyond the French doors.

'What is your first name? It is so much easier when we are relaxed.'

'Eddie.'

'Good strong name, Eddie.'

'What is easier?' I asked.

Ignatius McKenzie ignored my question. 'Eddie, I know about your loss,' he said.

I said nothing, but wondered how on earth he knew about Clifford.

'It's the hardest thing, losing a child. We are wired to be outlived by our offspring. Our essence cannot understand when this doesn't occur.'

I still did not respond; instead, I looked at the ground, suddenly angry that Sally had divulged our personal tragedy to this man.

'Don't be angry with Mrs Dungiven, she didn't divulge much. She was here to make sense of her father departing,' he said, again seemingly understanding my thoughts.

I still said nothing.

'With you it is different, Eddie,' Ignatius suggested, looking fleetingly to my right-hand side. And then he went quiet.

'Different?' I eventually asked.

'You weren't alone when you entered here.'

'Sorry?'

'When you came in, you weren't on your own.'

'I don't understand.'

'I don't wish to alarm you, but there isn't an easy way to put this.' He paused and took off his glasses.

Again, I reverted to saying nothing.

'When I opened the door to you earlier, you had a spirit child standing beside you, a young girl, around ten years of age.'

I laughed in disbelief and shock.

'Impossible,' I reasoned.

'It's true, Eddie; she's back again just now, in the room.'

'Where?' I asked, feeling uneasy and frightened.

'Standing to the right side of your chair,' he replied, nodding his head in that direction.

I turned my head and looked at the empty space to my right, then gazed back at Ignatius McKenzie.

'I think she is the reason you are here. I don't know if she is going to speak to me. Sometimes they do, sometimes they don't, I never know.'

'And she is standing right here?' I gestured with my hand.

'Yes, right there.'

My focus returned once again to the empty space bedside my chair.

'She does want to speak,' he said, regaining my attention. Ignatius closed his eyes. 'Say again, please,' he said, a slight smile on his face.

I was transfixed, unbelieving but caught in the moment.

'Rebecca? Is that correct? Your name is Rebecca?'

Sally must have told him this, I thought, *and now he mocks the memory of our only child*, but despite this, still I couldn't move.

'She says she likes the dog, she strokes him when he sleeps under the breakfast bar in the kitchen,' continued Ignatius.

'What is the dog called?' I blurted out, ready to project my anger to an even higher level, to prove he was a fake, *he must have noticed dog hairs on my trousers* I thought, *an easy connection to make.* ,

'Say again please, Rebecca?'

Ignatius McKenzie nodded slowly, his eyes still closed.

'She says he is called Henry. 'She is showing me a doll now.called Mandy,it's her favourite.'.'

Again, this information must have come from Sally;,
–We bought the rag doll, Mandy, when Rebecca had chickenpox when she was three; she carried it, ate with it and slept with it for the rest of her life.

At this point, with no self-control, the anger dissolved painlessly from my mind. I started to want to believe he really was in communication with our dead daughter. Maybe, I reasoned, those times Henry looked up suddenly from his slumber under the breakfast bar, it wasn't actually a distant noise I couldn't hear that forced him to stare into space.

'Clown? Is that correct, clown?' asked Ignatius.

I looked down at the empty space to my side and felt a cold chill run down the entire side of my body. Imagination is a powerful thing.

'She is scared of a clown with ginger hair. She really doesn't like it.'

'Is the clown there with her?'

'No, no, she sees it with you. She is telling me it makes you sad, it makes you cry. She wants you to stop being sad, she wants you to stop crying.'

I didn't reply, afraid of what I would hear if I did.

'Rebecca wants to know why you don't use the fairy bouncy castle any more, why you always look at it before you turn off the light,' he stated, drawing out my fears anyway with or without my input. 'Does that mean something to you, Eddie?'

I didn't reply. How could Sally know about this? She never came to the lock-up in Clifford's yard, never saw me load the van using the sack truck, had no idea that the pink fairy castle, Rebecca's favourite, had sat unused and collecting dust for all these years. It broke my heart to see it every day in its packed-away state. I had no idea what emotion would be unleashed if I brought it out again into the world, inflated it.

'Eddie, I sense someone else is with her now.'

'Here in the room?' I asked.

'No, not in the room, they are with her.'

'I don't follow. Has she left?'

'Someone has joined her in the spirit world.'

Ignatius McKenzie suddenly laughed out loud. A genuine laugh that caught him off guard.

'Eddie, Rebecca has clambered onto a bouncy castle,'

he said, his eyes still closed slightly. 'She has been joined by someone. A man, a huge man – she has taken his hands and they are bouncing together. Up and down, up and down. He is an older man, but he is giggling excitedly like a child!'

I sat, stunned, believing this man, in a way I couldn't understand, had made more sense of my grief in a matter of minutes than I had achieved in seven long years.

'What is your name please, sir?' Ignatius probed.

I wanted to shout, 'Clifford, I am here, it is me', but I remained silent, a sense of peace and fear flowing equally into me.

'He doesn't want to speak, sometimes they don't. I think he is too interested in bouncing!' he said with a smile.

Suddenly, his face changed, a slight frown appearing on his brow, indicating puzzlement.

'What is it?' I asked.

'Rebecca is showing me something, but it isn't clear,' he answered. 'Try again, please. Bless her, she is so good, she keeps showing me a car. A blue car, over and over and over, does that make any sense to you?'

I replied no, and kept my real thoughts to myself.

'She is telling me it is important, over and over, but they are not to blame.'

Still I did not answer.

'Whoa! One at a time, please, one at a time,' Ignatius blurted out.

'What is it?' I asked again, completely drawn in now, speaking without choosing my words.

'There are lots of people around her who have suddenly joined her. All wanting to speak, to come through – the problem is, they are all talking at the same time, but I can make out that they look after Rebecca. They are all very excited to make contact. It's just a wall of noise – think of an audience before a concert performance, it's like that.'

I looked on, trying to understand what he had heard inside his head, in contrast to the quiet and calm of the room.

'Eddie, I am losing her now. All I can say to you is that she is surrounded by love and is very safe.'

And with these words, I felt my eyes fill with hot tears and my vision blur.

'She's gone. She's cocooned in love,' said Ignatius McKenzie simply.

He opened his eyes, blinking quickly with the look of confusion of someone waking from a dream.

He smiled at me and I smiled back. I felt as if I too had awoken.

'Is she still here?' I asked.

Ignatius shook his head. 'Do you understand what has happened? She was here because of your sadness, Eddie – she couldn't move on until you had a level of acceptance in your heart. Does that make sense?' he said.

I nodded. 'What now?' I asked.

'I think our time together is over. I think you can move on, content with the knowledge that Rebecca is safe. When you think of her now, it will be positive, happy memories, just as it should be.'

'I have one question,' I said.

Ignatius nodded.

'Who are the people with Rebecca?'

'The crowd at the end?'

'Yes.'

'I couldn't say for definite, there were so many of them all speaking at once. But within that group will be relatives, multiple generations of grandparents, aunts, uncles, cousins and friends with a link to you or Rebecca.'

The knowledge of family members I had never met, or others I could barely remember from my past, actively supporting Rebecca welled up as contentment, a sense of relief inside me. Equally, Clifford's death seemed acceptable. To imagine him not as a weak shell, with a tube full of oxygen forcing his body to inhale, but instead bouncing, carefree, too busy to know I was there, made me smile inside. And my beautiful, beloved daughter at peace, surrounded with love, showing me it was all right to let go. In my mind, she had taken hold of my hands which had been closed tight in fists for so many years, and one by one coaxed the fingers to extend outward, to splay them out to their full extension, and with that action, had released tension, fear, grief and guilt. I understood it was all right to move on; it was the thing to do. Yes, still remember, always remember, but don't live with your mind in the past. Nothing stays the same, we need to adapt and we need to accept change. If we do not, our entrenchment will collapse upon us and smother our future that is there to grasp, forcing us to focus with ever-greater concentration on events that have come and gone which we cannot undo. Events that cruelly sever the link forward, bury it so it can no longer be found or seen, however much we try.

Ignatius McKenzie stood up.

'Please forgive me, I can feel extremely tired after a session like this, it can be very draining,' he said. 'I feel I need to rest.'

'Certainly, I understand,' I said, standing up.

We walked out of the room and into the hallway in silence.

'Thank you,' I said at the front door.

'For what?'

'For doing this.'

'I didn't do anything,' replied Ignatius McKenzie, unbolting the door. 'Rebecca did all the work; she sought me to speak to you. She must have a reason for doing so at this time, but that is for you to understand, not me.'

'Well, I still want to thank you,' I repeated, stepping out of the door.

'Just one thing, though,' said Ignatius. 'Rebecca was insistent about the blue car. She kept showing me it over and over. Try to think in the coming days – hopefully this means something to you.'

As before, I denied any recognition and felt sure that for once, he wasn't able to read my mind.

'Well, it's strange, people from the spirit world would not pass on information without a reason,' he stated, his eyes boring into me once again.

'I'll have a think,' I answered.

Ignatius McKenzie thrust out his palm toward me. 'Goodbye, Eddie.'

'Goodbye,' I said, shaking his hand.

I crunched across the driveway toward the van and heard the door close and lock behind me. I took my phone out of my pocket. I had lost track of time and was surprised to discover I had only been in the company of Ignatius McKenzie for thirty minutes; it seemed a lot longer, hours in fact.

I drove away with my mind at last full of memories and no regrets.

I remembered Rebecca learning to ride a bicycle. Her determination to succeed fuelled by her best friend, Abby, flaunting her pink, sparkly and tasselled bike on the pavement outside the house, her deliberately slow ride by, intended to draw attention to the sudden lack of stabilisers on the rear wheel. Each time Rebecca fell, she got back on, even when she had to bite her lip to stop herself from crying. I told her many times I could put the stabilisers back on, but each time she shook her head. With each practice, I ran beside her, my hand held strong against her back, until suddenly she got it, my hand lessened the pressure on her back and I ran with her, ready and prepared if she need my support.

She loved the recorder. We loved her enthusiasm, but the noise was dreadful; when her fingers moved into the position for middle C we winced, knowing what was in store!

I took her to her first movie, just her and me. It was a cartoon, lots of colour, simple story and songs. She never took her eyes off the screen for the duration of the film, even when searching for her oversized (and overpriced) fizzy drink held in the armrest of her seat; instead of sight, she used her hand and mouth to locate the protruding straw. I believed the experience would prepare her for later the same year and her first live stage show of her favourite TV characters.

It didn't prepare me, though. I already had an idea that a theatre full of sugar-saturated preschool children can become very excitable, but I was not aware that the central character, when appearing onstage, would whip them up into a frenzy with his cheery 'Hello, girls and boys!'

The shrillness of the children's collective 'Hello!' back surprised me and forced me to adopt a look of pain as the decibel count increased.

I then looked on in disbelief as from the stage, he shook his head and said, 'I can't hear you – I said hello, girls and boys!' and encouraged them, with his hand cupped to his ear, to shout even louder and harder. Upon reflection, he may not have been acting and actually *was* unable to hear them, as performing this show twice a day for three weeks could have perforated his eardrum!

Rebecca loved it, loved the shouting out, loved the songs and the actions she, along with the others, was encouraged to repeat, and she adored telling the hero character that the villain was in close proximity to him.

She wiggled and pulled her first wobbly tooth at every opportunity for two weeks, before the wide-eyed look of shock crossed her face and she removed her hand from her mouth and held up the tiny pearl between her first finger and thumb for inspection. That bedtime, on instruction, she placed the tooth under her pillow in anticipation of the tooth fairy's arrival and cuddled up to Mandy the rag doll. At our bedtime, it became apparent that she had moved the tooth from underneath the edge of the pillow, as we had shown her, and instead placed it in the centre, directly under her head. Trying to locate, extract and substitute the tooth with coinage without waking her proved challenging and I froze on a number of occasions, my hand under her head as she stirred.

In the morning, she came into our room early to show us

the coins, but didn't behave as excitedly as we expected. We quizzed her and asked if anything was wrong. She replied she had moved the tooth so the tooth fairy would wake her up when she took it and she was disappointed she hadn't seen her. To see her, we learned, was everything to her. I kept all the subsequent teeth I could as they were discarded, a total of eighteen, kept in a matchbox in my wardrobe. We know for certain that one was lost in a park, when Rebecca tripped and fell and the tooth landed in undergrowth, overrun with brambles and nettles. To her relief, the tooth fairy came anyway, tooth or no tooth to take. The other we presumed she swallowed in her sleep, as it had become loose and as before, we saw her fingers encased in her mouth, moving and wiggling the tooth, willing it to dislodge during her bedtime story. The next morning, we noticed the vigorous probing had stopped. We looked inside her mouth but couldn't be sure which tooth, if any, had been lost, as by this age she had multiple gaps and loosening teeth in her mouth. We asked her if her wobbly tooth was still there, but received the answer an eight-year-old would present – a shrug and a skip away.

For Rebecca's first Christmas, we bought her a push-along pony, set on wheels and with a handle at the rear for her to grip, to aid learning to walk; she had started to toddle in the October. We had to actually wake her in the morning. We carried her downstairs; she rubbed her eyes and was extremely grumpy on being woken. Sally sat her on her knee, while I tore the wrapping paper off the enormous box, hiding the toy inside. As the paper rustled, Rebecca stopped crying and looked on in interest as I withdrew the pony for her. She clambered off Sally's lap and patted the flank of the toy with a giggle, looking at Sally and me. Yet, within moments, she had tired of this and instead picked up the ripped wrapping paper and began to drop the pieces into the now-empty box. Each time we lifted her behind the pony, she crawled back to the box and continued to place objects inside – once all the paper had been picked up, she added Christmas tree decorations, the TV remote, magazines and her other gifts, which Sally and I had helped her to open. This activity continued until mid-morning, when she fell asleep, leaning against the side of the box.

Two Christmases later, when Rebecca had a fuller understanding of the whole experience, we got creative. We purchased some fake snow and when Rebecca had finally drifted off to sleep on Christmas Eve, I brought in my wellington boots from the garage and stepped into them at the fireside. Sally sprinkled the substance around the outside of the boots as I stood there and we giggled as I walked a step and saw the imagined effect of Santa's footprints outlined by snow materialise. Sally repeated the process until I was standing by the sofa, where we would distribute Rebecca's presents before we retired to bed.

The reaction in the morning was as expected, with lots of squealing and laughter from downstairs waking us up. We repeated Santa's footsteps from the fire to the sofa for the next five years; it became a Christmas tradition and was received with the same excitement, time after time, although Rebecca never questioned why Santa's boots were covered in snow when it had never snowed on Christmas Eve in her lifetime.

However, in the year that she died, she didn't mention Santa at all, didn't write a letter to him and didn't ask, 'I wonder what Santa will bring me?' Perhaps her maturing mind had finally worked out, along with her peers, the flaws in the myth spooned to her from her earliest memories, and perhaps she was now too grown-up to speak about such childish notions. Whatever the case, we would never know the real reason behind her silence.

The driveway was empty when I arrived home, and I heard from inside Henry's claw-clips on the tiled hallway floor as I found the lock with my key. I opened the door and was greeted with his frantic tail-wagging; so severe was the movement that his entire rear end moved in his excitement. The house was void of human presence; just Henry circling around my body, his tail never ceasing its swinging; as always, his unconditional greeting made me smile. I patted his head and tickled his ears and moved into the kitchen to allow him out into the garden to relieve his bladder.

He ran outside and I watched as he performed his doggy ritual of sniffing and examining particular areas of foliage and grass, before moving on to another area and urinating immediately, without any requirement to check its scent.

I gazed out and wondered, as I has been prone to do before, what was actually running through his mind. I leant against the door frame and felt comfortable in this safe, familiar environment. I could manage the recent events – the conversation with Cerys, Mary's phone call and the revelations of Ignatius McKenzie – here in this space.

I turned back into the kitchen and noticed the envelope sitting on the worktop, in the same place as Sally's note had been the previous week. On the front she had simply written, *Eddie*.

I picked it up, ripped it open and began to read.

Dear Eddie,

This is the hardest thing I have ever had to write. I don't really know where to begin, but by the time you read this, I will be gone. I have known you for so long, from that wide-eyed youth that spilt those drinks down me, to the middle-aged man, set in his ways, I lived with for years.

You have been a constant in my life for all of this time, Eddie. When I first met you, I knew I wanted to spend my life with you, to grow up and then grow old with you. To live out our dreams, to share many, many, moments of laughter and happiness when we would be blessed; the best side of life shown to us. Equally, I truly believed we would comfort and protect each other in times of stress and sadness.

But reality is so different; we had no idea our world would be shattered, destroyed so clinically that dank, rainy November afternoon seven years ago. For years I have held this to myself, but I now have to say, you let me down, Eddie.

That first night, when I tried to make sense of the initial knock on the door from the two constables, the removal of their hats as they sat down in the living room and the pained expressions on their faces as they prepared to speak to me. I thought something had happened to you; that you were injured or hurt, that they held some news so terrible they had to visit me in person to explain. But then you walked into the room, confused and startled, moments after they had torn out my heart with their words and you just stood there – you left me in the arms of a policewoman, a stranger, when it was you I wanted to take all the pain away, to tell me it was going to be all right, to tell me our angel was safe and well.

And in the months that followed when I pleaded with you to fease my mind, to agree she looked peacefully asleep when you identified her in that cold, clinical place where they put her, you remained silent. The sleepless nights, the days without food, the darkened bedroom, the white coffin – your response was always silence, when all I wanted was for you to hold me, to take the weight from my heart, even for a short while, and tell me everything was all right. When the white car was found with the dented nearside, when the driver was breathalysed, when he was found to be drunk, you remained silent, refusing to blame him; instead you listened to his tale of the blue car that caused him to swerve, that caused him to take away our angel, the day she visited her friend on her own for the first time, that day our lives were destroyed. The times Rebecca came to me, talked to me, our beautiful daughter standing at the side of the bed, you dismissed completely as tricks played by my mind, as a mother's grief forcing me further into myself and away from you.

I did always love you, Eddie; I just wanted you to love me equally in return. I swear, as months became years I never lost my yearning to be touched by you, desired by you and wanted by you – but you never did, and instead, I clung pathetically to any scrap of affection from you as a sign that it could still work, that you still felt the same. I cannot be sure when I finally gave up all hope, but I did; it died slowly, then it just couldn't be seen at all.

Eddie, this is so difficult for me to write and I have tears streaming down my face. I cannot continue to lie to you or myself; it isn't fair on either of us. I have found someone. Someone who makes me feel wanted, desired, like a woman free to be expressive, and who is good for me. I wasn't looking for this, it just happened a few months ago. I finally feel supported, protected and understood – all the things I have wanted for so long from you.

Please do not try to find me; if a part of you still does love me, you will let me go, let me be happy. I do not want anything from you, Eddie – the house, the car, everything is yours; I will pick up the rest of my clothes at a later time. All I want is to be at peace with myself, to be surrounded by happiness, to feel like a fulfilled woman, and though it kills me to say it, after that November night, you were no longer able to provide these things for me.

Please take care of yourself; you too deserve to be happy.
Sally.

I read the letter over and over, losing track of time, until Henry's bark alerted me to the fact that he was still outside in the garden, staring in at me, and the night had closed in, my eyes adapting to the twilight as I read.

I let him in, put food in his bowl and traipsed out into the hall and up the stairs, not really knowing where I was going or what I was going to do. I got under the covers of the bed in the half-light. I heard a rustling sound as my hands formed into fists once more and I realised I still held the letter tightly in my palm.

Chapter 17

The Queen Departs

I do not remember Sunday. Not because I was a drunken mess, I just cannot recall the details. I know that mid-morning, I got up and let Henry out into the garden. He remained there for the day until I brought him in and gave him some food. I know I returned to bed and stayed there until the darkness of night returned. I know this was the case until Monday afternoon.

During this time, I checked my mobile regularly, wishing for Sally to make contact, to answer the questions I had flying around inside my mind. But the phone did not respond to my desire. At one point, I even called my mobile from the landline, telling myself that a weak signal was the reason I had not received any contact. But as my mobile burst into life as I entered the last digit of its number into the phone beside the bed, I knew this wasn't the case.

Early Monday afternoon, in the silence, the doorbell rang out loud and prolonged. I lay on the bed. There was a pause and the noise was repeated. Still I did not attempt to move. The bell was rung for a third time, followed by banging on the door itself. Whoever it was wasn't going to go away. From the doorstep, it must be obvious that someone was in the house, with the Party King van parked on the driveway. The phone beside the bed suddenly rang. I sat up, simply staring at it, noticing my breathing had quickened as it abruptly rang off. My mobile suddenly rang; a number I didn't know was displayed. I stared at it as it eventually went to voicemail. The doorbell rang a fourth time, one long, final, continuous blast. It went quiet. . I wanted to go the window to see if they had definitely gone, but did not want to be seen. As I contemplated my move, my mobile bleeped with a message. I opened it and was surprised to read, *Eddie, it's Jenny – I am outside and I am not going anywhere.* I sensed by her persistence that she was telling the truth. I got up, stretched my frame as I moved to the bathroom and splashed cold water onto my face. I looked at my reflection, water running down my cheeks and off my chin, and saw my features in the mirror, puffy and pale, my eyes bloodshot.

Descending the stairs, unsure of what I was going to say to her, I stopped dead as a memory exploded into my mind from nowhere. I remembered Jennifer's sympathy regarding the note Sally had left me, and her subsequent shock when she realised the actual content. That time in her studio with Phoebe the toy poodle, she had wanted to speak to me, but was so angry after Henry destroyed her equipment that she couldn't. It made sense now; she knew about this, she knew Sally was leaving and had known for some time.

I exhaled deeply and walked on toward the front door and registered Jennifer's form through theglass. My hand pulled down the lock, opened the door and removed the barrier between us.

Jennifer studied my face closely, gauging from my appearance how to address me.

'Oh, Eddie,' she said, biting her bottom lip.

I must have looked worse than I imagined.

We stood in silence, me avoiding her eyes, looking at the ground, while I sensed Jennifer continued to stare at me.

'Can I come in?' she eventually asked.

'Sure.'

I moved aside to allow Jennifer to enter the house, still staring downwards. In the kitchen, we stood in silence, avoiding eye contact.

'You knew?' I asked flatly, staring out of the window into the garden.

'I knew both of you were unhappy,' replied Jennifer cryptically.

'What does that mean?'

She didn't answer, just gazed at the tiled wall.

'But you knew she was seeing someone?' I finally asked.

Jennifer looked up at me. 'Yes, I knew,' she admitted.

'And you didn't think to tell me?!' I roared at her.

'Eddie, it's not my place to tell you.'

'I think it is!'

Jennifer shook her head.

'What about that time you said you wanted to talk to me?'

'Sorry, when?'

'When Henry wrecked your studio chasing that poodle Phoebe around. You said you wanted to speak to me but didn't.'

Jennifer nodded her head in recollection. 'I admit; my instinct was to say something to you,' she said, 'to give you some idea of how unhappy Sally was. But Henry's destruction ruined that thought. Perhaps it was fate causing the distraction, telling me not to become involved.'

'You should have told me. It was your obligation,' I argued.

'No it wasn't, it's your marriage and Sally is my friend. I listened to her, told her to think carefully, but to ultimately make sure what she was doing was right for her and for you.'

'For me? How can it be right for me? She has left, she hasn't tried; she's run out.'

'Eddie, she did try, you know she did – she tried for years,' she said, turning toward me.

She looked at my hand and I followed her gaze. I hadn't realised I had picked up the letter again before I came downstairs.

'This was the letter you thought you would see last week when you came round?' I asked.

Jennifer nodded.

'You can read it if you want,' I offered again, as on Saturday.

'No, it's personal, not my place to,' stated Jennifer.

'Why did you come around, then? To rub my nose in it?'

'Eddie, that's unfair to say,' she protested.

'Is it? Is it really? You came round on Saturday and when you didn't see the scenario you expected, you left very quickly. Go on, read it!' I yelled, holding out the letter at arm's length, as my hand began to tremble.

I screwed up my eyes and saw stars, and felt hot liquid start to form behind them. I lowered my arm and in my blindness, felt Jennifer standing closer before me, felt her embrace, felt her hand rubbing my back in a soothing circular fashion.

'I came because I thought it was wrong, after all these

years, for her to leave you via words on paper,' she whispered gently, as my body and breathing relaxed.

I rested my head on her shoulder, content for her to take the weight of this pain for a moment, content just to breathe.

Minutes passed until Jennifer pulled back from me slightly, forcing me to look up, but I refused to meet her eyes.

'Eddie, look at me,' she said sternly.

I eventually obliged.

'We all deserve to be happy, Eddie. If both people in a marriage are unhappy and cannot find a way out of that, it stands to reason one will find happiness elsewhere before the other.'

She said no more, she didn't have to, and I replayed the words Gus had said to me those short weeks ago among the Whispering Rocks – *Sally deserves to be happy too*.

What would I be doing now if I hadn't witnessed Clifford and Mary's long-standing love in the hospital ward? I would probably be shopping for new boxer shorts, a new shirt and shoes. I would have already checked my nose thoroughly for unsightly nasal hair and clipped the hairs under my arms to a neat length to ensure any redness or soreness would have disappeared by Wednesday and my time in an airport hotel with Cerys Sindon.

'You do seem pretty together.' lied Jennifer 'Are you really okay?' she added.

I nodded, keeping my thoughts to myself.

'Are you eating?' asked Jennifer, glancing at the kitchen clock.

I shook my head.

'Well, you need to eat something.'

She headed to the fridge and retrieved eggs, ham and salad as I watched.

'Omelette?' she offered.

'Okay.'

Ten minutes later I ate the food as Jennifer went through my diary for the week and cancelled all my appointments via the house phone. In fairness, there were only a few; the weeks before the schools break for the summer holidays are always quieter.

'Have you met him?' I asked later as I washed up.

Next to me, Jennifer shook her head and glanced at the clock once more.

'Do you know anything about him?' I quizzed.

Again, she shook her head.

'You must know something. Is he tall, short, young, old, thinning on top, a drinker, a smoker, into sports, self-employed? She must have told you some detail about him?' I argued.

'Sorry, nothing.'

'I know she is gone, I am just curious, that's all.'

Jennifer remained silent.

'I am sure Sally will be forthcoming when she is ready,' she eventually replied.

'I bet she will,' I hissed.

Jennifer was poised to answer, when the doorbell rang. She stepped into the hallway quickly and looked at the front door.

'That's Faruk,' she said after studying the figure deformed behind the frosted glass.

'Who?'

'The man I worked with at the animal rescue centre. He was waiting for me outside.'

I didn't speak.

'We have started to date,' stated Jennifer, building on her earlier comment.

'Oh, I see. That explains you not being around on Saturday evenings then.'

Jennifer gave a half-smile. 'It's early days yet.'

The doorbell rang again.

'Will you be okay, Eddie, if I leave? I told Faruk I would be…' She trailed off, not finishing her sentence.

'Only ten minutes?' I offered, and smiled.

'No, I didn't mean…' Jennifer started to say.

'I am teasing you, Jennifer!'

'But I shouldn't have said it,' she protested.

'I am fine; think I have cried until there is nothing left in me, and I feel better after the food and what you said about being unhappy.'

'I feel awful now! Will you be all right?'

'Don't be silly, it made sense.'

'Will you really be all right?' she repeated.

I put my hands up and told her again that I was fine. 'Seriously, you go. Thanks for coming, I appreciate it.'

'I hate leaving you like this,' Jennifer said.

'Don't keep your date waiting!' I said with a grin.

She gave me a hug and whispered for me to be kind to myself, to give myself a break.

'I am sorry it is like this, Eddie, but it will be for the best in the long term, for both of you,' she added as we parted.

As she got to the door she stopped.

'You must have a good memory, Eddie.'

'Why is that?'

'I didn't remember the name of that poodle,' she said.

I couldn't tell her the reason I recalled that yappy creature's name so easily. And as she closed the door behind her I knew exactly what I had to do, and who I had to see.

I showered, shaved, put Henry out and was on my way in twenty minutes.

The track was dry as I swung into it; there had been no rain since April and it had taken its toll on the landscape. The house was so far up the winding private lane that it wasn't visible from the main road; probably the reason he bought it, I mused. I had been here on only a few occasions over the years, and never without Sally. Today would be a first. I did not remember being here before at this time of year. I didn't recall the giant beech and chestnut trees full of green cover that filtered the light as they rustled audibly in the faintest of breezes that provided temporary relief from the growing humidity. Nor had I seen the climbing red and yellow roses covering a circular frame to the left of the house, which had now come into view around the last bend of the lane. The house suited its surroundings; it looked right there, like it truly belonged with its whitewashed walls, green-painted window frames and asymmetrical style.

I knocked at the door and listened to the birdsong that filled the air as I waited. I knocked again; there was still no response. His car was parked in front of the garage – I was quite sure he wouldn't go anywhere with it – and a pair of wellington boots with a fine layer of dust on the toes sat next to the side door hinted at recent use.

I walked around the side of the house and wandered into the rear garden. It was beautiful. A perfect lawn, lush thanks to a continuous feed of moisture soaked under its surface, stretched to an area of mature trees. The grass looked so healthy, I presumed, due to a blatant disregarding of the district hosepipe ban imposed in the past few months in an effort to conserve water. But who would know in this place that the law had been breached, that something was wrong? Flanking the lawn on both sides lay deep beds; full to bursting with speckled colours, examined and probed by countless honey bees.Behind the flowers an avenue of trees acted as a border to the property, through which, the ripening golden barley in the fields beyond could be glimpsed.

I headed toward the mature trees at the end of the garden and once under their protection, remembered they marked roughly the halfway point of the garden. Here were planted out vegetable plots, four huge quadrangles of raised beds containing ripening produce, some visible in the muggy air, the branches and stems bending, already heavy with fruits or flowers; others, with only their green foliage on show, lay hidden and incubated by the warmth of the cocooning soil. And as with the flower beds behind the trees, honey bees busied around, buzzing as they foraged.

A wall of hawthorn acting as a windbreak marked the end of the vegetable plot, and through an arch cut into them I could see outhouses marking the very end of the garden. The three single-storey buildings were positioned in a half-hexagon shape, and as I neared them, I remembered a sunset I had witnessed before here, looking west over the barley fields that stretched to the horizon.

I saw him seated through the bank of windows in the smallest building, concentrating on a task, and strode to the door, suddenly rushing, suddenly anxious and ready for confrontation. I twisted the handle of the wooden door but it stuck, resulting in a mere rattle instead of a dramatic entrance I had intended. I tried it again, gripping it more tightly, but still it would not open. I tried a third time, with my shoulder pressed against the wood, and suddenly I was through. As the door opened, I stumbled gracelessly into the room, the force knocking me off balance. I stood up straight and calmly closed the door behind me, which shut without sticking. The room was full of a stifling heat.

The smell of toxic glue also filled the air, and I stared at him as he continued his task I had witnessed outside unabated. Laid out upon a bench was a half-built model of a Lancaster bomber. The grey plastic shell looked nothing like the painted image on the front of the box for the kit, which also sat on the table. In his hands he held a wheel and a length of thin plastic, which he was pressing together with his fingertips.

'What do *you* want?' he asked, not looking up at me.

This situation had caught me off guard. 'I didn't know you made models,' I said, forgetting what I had come to say.

The anger I had felt leaving my house, the desire for confrontation and my embarrassment on entry had dissolved and I was truly surprised to find Sally's brother Greg hunched over, enthusiastically pursuing a child's pastime before me. I looked around the room; along the bench four other models had already been completed, their bodies transformed with paint in camouflage patterns and transfer stickers displaying ensigns and numbering. I had to admit they looked impressive, more in keeping with the illustration on the box fronts than his current work in progress. I didn't recognise the other aircraft, but by their markings and propellers, I judged them to be from the same era as the Lancaster.

'Are those the wheels?' I said, looking at his hands.

'Landing gear,' he sighed.

Still he did not look at me. Instead he set down the landing gear, glanced at the instructions in front of him and reached for a grey frame which held as yet unassembled pieces.

'I said, what do you want?' Greg Dixon repeated.

'What did you mean the other night?'

'What other night?'

'At the golf club, you asked if I knew where Sally was. What did you mean by that?' I spluttered.

'What night are you talking about?' he said, finally looking at me.

'The Lombarders' ladies' night.'

He stared at me blankly.

'At the golf club,' I added.

He nodded slowly and turned back to his model-making. 'Didn't see you there,' he responded.

I stood, my eyes burning into the side of his head. 'You asked me if I knew where Sally was that night,' I repeated, not content with his answer.

'Did I?' Like I say, don't remember you being there.'

'She was planning to leave and you knew about it,' I stated simply.

'Did I?' he repeated.

The anger came to me; made me move toward him

seated at his bench, it took control of my thought process, forcing words out of me.

'Put that thing down and show me some respect!' I yelled into his face.

Greg calmly put down the model pieces he was handling and swung around to face me.

'You arrive at my home uninvited, have the audacity to burst into my private workshop, almost taking the door off its hinges, yell into my face and demand *I* give *you* respect? I suggest you get rid of that anger, either get laid or join a gym. Get off my property, you excuse of a man,' he said calmly.

I stood my ground. 'You knew she was seeing someone else!' I yelled. 'And yet you didn't tell me.'

'I still don't know what you are talking about. But if I did, why would I tell you?' He leered up at me.

'Because it would be the right thing to do!'

Greg Dixon stood up. 'You know what, I am glad if, as you say, she has found someone else, I always knew she could do better than you. God knows she had many chances, too.'

'What does that mean?' I said, suddenly feeling very hot in the room.

Greg chuckled to himself and walked toward a bank of windows at a right angle to the door.

'You really have no idea, do you?' he said, stopping and looking at me before opening a fanlight window to allow some of the trapped, humid air to escape the room.

I said nothing.

'I don't know how to put this,' he began, 'but I know of, let me see, at least five affairs she has had down the years,' he added with relish in his voice and a smile on his lips. He looked at me as I tried to remain still, my fingernails digging into my palms with force. 'Oh, I thought you wanted to know!' he said, his hand covering his mouth in mock surprise.

He suddenly adopted a quizzical look and rubbed his chin. 'Actually, come to think of it, it must be six. There was definitely an accountant, a painter and decorator, and two firemen. Can't remember the others, but they were years ago now.'

I stood still. 'You are lying,' I spat.

'Oh, and of course there was Trafford, the supermarket buyer, most recently. Lot younger than her, but had good prospects, solid corporate man – not sure what happened there, but then I haven't seen her in ages.'

'I know you are lying – she was here on Saturday, talking about those solar panels of yours,' I said, feeling crushed on hearing the name of the buyer again. I recalled Trafford to be the same name Sally had once mentioned casually as being a lunch date, before insisting she had told me about him. I had felt uneasy at the time but dismissed it. Only now, in this stifling hothouse, did I wish I had reacted differently.

'Nope, she wasn't here. Haven't discussed those panels for months, didn't even get off the ground,' he said.

'What about the hives? She checks the hives,' I added, clutching at straws.

'So she tells you! Not inspected in weeks. Surprised those things haven't swarmed.'

I looked at the ground.

'Oh, I remember one of the other guys now. You know him, that rich, pompous idiot Gus Eastley. He moved here to be near her, she said he was the—'

I don't know where it came from, but in an instant my fist connected with the right side of his jaw and stopped his speech. He stumbled backward, clutching his chin, while his tongue protruded, red with blood. He dabbed at his tongue with his fingers and looked at the blood, before rubbing his reddened jaw.

'Get out of here before I have you arrested,' he hissed in my direction.

I took the few steps to the door, opened it, ventured outside and closed it behind me. Under dark, murky skies, I processed what Greg had revealed to me. He had to be lying. Sally had always been with me, always by my side. *But she wasn't when I worked as the Party King or Clive the Clown, was she?* I argued. But no, I dismissed this – I would know, I *knew* her.

But the revelation about Gus; how could I explain that away? That first time I met him in Malacy's and they were cosied up at the bar on my arrival; the way he had never revealed why he had moved to the area; his background was so far removed from here, but I always put his silence down to him just being him. Then there was the fact that he had gone away this week, the same time Sally had left – was this coincidence? Had they met up? Were they in Italy together right now? My mind refused to picture any more and instead recalled the punch I had just unleashed, and guiltily took pleasure in how satisfying it had been.

Initially I couldn't place the sound that came from my right; I wasn't able to put it in context. The desperate scream from the workshop moments later was the trigger. I spun around to witness a rapidly moving trail heading into the building via the fanlight window Greg had opened moments before.

Looking in through the front windows I could no longer see Greg. Instead a human-shaped mass of insects had replaced him, covered him and continued to grow in size with the stream of new arrivals. He wiped them from his face with bee-covered hands and screamed again, only for his features to disappear as quickly as he had revealed them, and to be replaced by yet more bees that muffled and then silenced his screams with their continuous buzzing. I twisted the door handle to get him out of the building, but the catch was again stuck. I tried again and again and again, but still the door would not open. I resorted to kicking the door and then the frame, but to no avail, and all the while, the sound of the bees became louder and louder.

I looked in again through the window and found the bee-covered form of Greg Dixon now lying on the floor, motionless.. His arms, legs, torso and head were no longer outlined, but instead were hidden under a crawling, violently vibrating mass. I reached for my phone, to call for help, but was presented with *no signal available* on the screen in this remote place and kicked the door again, this time in desperation. All I could do was watch in horror through the window as the attack continued unabated. I needed to summons help quickly.

. prophecy -apass

I ran through the gap in the hawthorns, through the vegetable and flower gardens and back to the house. The side door was open and I ventured in to get to the phone in the hallway.

On my call being answered, my request sounded bizarre to me; I couldn't imagine what the emergency services operator was thinking as she repeated back, 'Your brother-in-law has been attacked by swarming bees, but you cannot get into the building to help. You think he is dead. Is that correct, Mr Dungiven?' she stated.

I merely said, 'Yes' in reply.

'Okay, the police and paramedics are on their way, and an apiarist,' she said before hanging up.

As I put down the phone, I couldn't help but notice the piles of glossy brochures on the hallway table and the mock-up solar panel model all embossed with a distinctive *Eco-Lites* logo. It didn't look to me as if the business had not got off the ground, as Greg Dixon had claimed.

The police arrived first, two officers. One jogged down to the end of the garden on my instruction and disappeared from view behind the trees, en route to the outhouse, while the other spoke to me outside the garage. His questioning, though in a friendly manner, was probing as to who I was, what my address was, my relationship to Greg Dixon and why I was there, and throughout this I was extremely conscious of him glancing at my reddening right knuckle as we spoke. I tried to remain calm, to remain level-headed, to not reveal I had struck Greg.

His colleague returned, slowly walking, as the paramedics arrived. He shook his head as he neared us.

'He's unconscious, slight pulse,' he stated matter-of-factly.

'What about the bees?' his colleague asked.

'Just a few around him, dead – had to smash a window to open the door from the inside, it was stuck shut.'

'But no swarm?' the other officer asked, looking at me.

'No, like I said, just a few around him – his face is swollen and red, though, where he has been stung.'

'All over his face?'

'No, just on one side.'

I looked on, observing the conversation, trying not to blink, trying to not touch my face, trying to not move at all, to not show any sign of nerves.

'Which side?' the officer asked quickly.

'The left part of his face.'

'Not the right, definitely the left?'

'Yes, the left. Probably didn't know he was anaphylactic,' the policeman who had gone to investigate suggested.

'Possibly,' the other officer replied, again looking at me. 'Let the paramedic boys work on him,' he added, as the ambulance crew locked the stretcher into position and wheeled with purpose down to the end of the garden, accompanied by the first policeman.

We both watched in silence as the party moved beyond the trees.

'Can you please make sure you remain available, Mr Dungiven? We may need to interview you at a later date at the station,' the policeman informed me.

'Certainly,' I replied, wary of revealing too much, but I knew I had to say something to him. 'Can I ask a question?' I added, dreading where it would lead me.

The officer looked at me.

'Who informs his family of this? Do you want me to do it?'

'That would be normal procedure.'

I nodded.

'Is there a reason you cannot do this?'

He had me, and it was so easy. My blank expression and innocent questions must have spoken volumes to him.

'I am separated from his sister,' I revealed, dying inside as I made the words form in the open for the first time.

'I see, that's different then,' he said. 'But I will still need you to be available, though,' he added.

I held his stare, nodded and headed to the van.

'Incidentally, Mr Dungiven, when did you separate from Mr Dixon's sister?' he asked calmly.

I stood with the keys to the van in the door lock.

'Recently,' I admitted, not turning around.

'How recently?'

'Saturday,' I replied.

He remained silent and I opened van door.

'I would like you to come down to the station with us now, Mr Dungiven,' he requested, as I placed my foot on the step of the vehicle.

It was turning into a day of firsts. I had never been in a police car or been interviewed in a police station before, I certainly hadn't been witness to a person covered in vibrating bees, close to death and I had never been hugged by Jennifer Rees before.

After a drive in silence to the police station, I was ushered into an interview room and in that enclosed environment, I believed I had some understanding of how Jennifer felt when she was brought in and forced to watch the footage of her rescue dogs being torn apart by Elliot Wallace's 'boy'.

The waiting was the worst element. I sat in the small room with a uniformed police constable standing by the only door, who refused, despite several attempts on my part, to engage with me. I asked for water a number of times and he ignored me on each occasion. At least my reddened fist had reverted back to its normal condition.

Several hours passed in this manner, until the door opened and two officers walked in and sat down noisily. Without looking at me, one of them quickly introduced himself and his colleague; so quickly that I forgot their names the moment he stopped speaking. They both looked up and asked why I was at Greg Dixon's place earlier.

I had had hours to think about this, sitting in this room, and had decided that a half-truth would be the safest course to take. I reasoned they probably knew about Sally leaving, the officer at the scene having briefed them, I assumed. With this in mind, I explained I had gone to Greg's on the off chance he knew why Sally had left; I needed someone to talk to about it, I lied. But when I arrived, finding the house empty, I wandered down to the outhouse where I found him covered in bees inside, but was unable to open the sticking door to get him out. That was when I called the emergency services.

They asked why I didn't break the door down to get him out. To which I replied what that I had told the operator that I had tried, but couldn't. down . They rapidly countered by questioning how hard did I really try to get in. I admitted I maybe could have been more forceful, but was worried the noise and commotion of breaking down the door would agitate the bees further. They.asked what was different about breaking the door down and just going in – the bees would be agitated either way. I again repeated that the bees would respond more to sudden noise than to someone moving in quietly. This drew in response a question of how I knew so much about the behaviour of bees, and I advised them that

I had picked up the knowledge from Sally – they were, after all, her bees, from her hive.

The officers looked at each other and then at me. They advised me that the apiarist had informed them that all the hives were full and content. I looked blankly at them, to which they retorted, with a level of sarcasm, that if I did know anything about bees, as I said, I would know that a swarm would not return to a vacated hive. They could therefore only conclude that I had exaggerated the number of bees I had seen, as Greg Dixon, now in a coma, had indeed fallen into anaphylactic shock, caused by the stings of the small amount of insects seen lying dead on the floor by his face. I wanted to argue my case, that I knew what I had seen, but before I spoke, I was advised there would be no further questions and I was free to go. It felt like such an anticlimax, but I knew I shouldn't argue; I should simply leave.

I stood up and paused, weighing up whether I should ask a question, if I should disclose the detail that I had held for over a week in my mind.

The two men in front noticed my hesitance to leave.

'Yes? Was there something else?' the main interviewer asked me.

'I have some information,' I offered.

'Information? What about?'

'It's about Elliot Wallace,' I added, standing my ground.

The police officers looked at each other, then up at me.

'Elliot Wallace?'

I nodded slowly, wondering if I was going to regret my statement.

'Please take a seat, Mr Dungiven,' the second interviewer

said. PC Osborne could you get us some drinks?' he added to the uniformed office by the door.

'Is tea okay for you, Mr Dungiven?' he said, looking at me.

Chapter 18

Home Truths in a True Home

Mary looked lost. I knew she was riding that journey of emotion that grief forces you to endure. The infrequent moments when a small well of euphoria teases you that everything will be fine, that everything will be all right, only to be repeatedly replaced by the crashing enormity of loss that draws your breath away.

It was the morning of Clifford's funeral and the first time I had seen Mary in over a week. A fine surrogate son I was, I thought to myself. I had called her after my time in the police station to see how she was coping, to check the time of the funeral and to volunteer for whatever still needed to be arranged. But she had performed all the tasks herself, said it had helped her to keep busy. She mentioned the funeral director was a friend of Clifford's – *everyone* was a friend of Clifford's – and he had made it as easy as it could possibly be for her. She did ask me to perform one task, one that I was pleased to do. Mary wanted me to arrange the pallbearers for the coffin.

'It is what Clifford would have wanted,' she said. But she looked lost.

Last night, I had paid my respects to Clifford in the chapel of rest. He didn't look like Clifford lying there; he didn't look like he was asleep, he looked like a waxwork caricature. He looked hollow-cheeked, with slightly protruding front teeth; he had clean, clipped, sparkling and polished fingernails, no longer ingrained with grime and dirt from tinkering with his farm machinery. He was gone. As I gazed at the corpse in the open coffin, unsure of what to feel, the image of him happily jumping and laughing with my dear Rebecca on an inflatable came bouncing into my mind, and with it, drew a smile tight across my face. Ignatius McKenzie, in his consulting room overlooking the mature garden, had planted an image in me that I now realised would be replayed over and over, and a comfort to me at times I required it.

Ahead of the funeral, I explained to Mary, as she scanned the room, that Sally was absent due to illness. It wasn't the time or the place to reveal the true reason, nor was it the correct setting for me to confront Gus. Although, the fact he was there should have alerted me that my suspicion that he was with Sally in Italy was incorrect – no one could be that brazen, to turn up to a funeral, could they? He arrived back only this morning and came straight from the airport to Mary's, via his wardrobe for a suit, white shirt and black tie. I hadn't contacted him; I presumed Mary must have done.

The look on his face on entering was one of simple shock. Mary acknowledged him and asked brightly if his 'team' had won the horse race. He shook his head and admitted they hadn't even come close, and I sensed he was struggling with the normality Mary's questions invited. I took Gus to one side and asked quickly if he would be a pallbearer, and he readily agreed. After fulfilling Mary's request, I retreated to the other side of the room, turned my back and looked out of the window toward the hill, where the sheep grazed contentedly. In my mind's eye, I saw Clifford striding purposely through the heather toward them, with Ben, his Border collie, faithfully by his side. I wanted distance between Gus and myself, not only to confront my own personal grief, but equally to ensure I didn't say anything out of turn to him, not here, not at this occasion.

Through the window I watched as a hearse silently glided to a stop in the yard, followed by a gleaming charcoal-grey limousine. The hearse's glassed flanks were bursting with bouquets of colour, to such an extent that it was impossible to be certain Clifford's coffin was actually inside.

'Flowers,' I said to myself with shame.

The passenger door of the hearse opened and a figure got out; his suit was immaculate and his black shoes gleamed, similar to the shine from the limousine. He walked with purpose toward the farmhouse, resting a top hat in the crook of his right arm. He was in through the front door and I turned away from the window as, quietly and with considerable respect, the funeral director entered the room. He made no eye contact with any of the mourners, but merely wandered over to Mary and touched her gently and with dignity on the forearm. Mary looked at him, sensing what he was about to announce.

'It's time, Mary,' he said simply, and Mary nodded, bit her lip and followed him out of the living room.

Once she left the room, the rest of us departed too. Outside, in the yard, the funeral director placed his hat on his head with a fluid motion and took a walking cane handed to him by the driver of the hearse, who now stood solemnly by the side of the vehicle. He took his position at the front of the hearse, ready to lead the procession as tradition dictates.

Clifford's funeral was a private affair; I do not wish to discuss it further.

Later I sat alone at the bar in Malacy's, nursing a pint, the other mourners quietly engaged in conversation in small groups, their voices murmurs, hushed tones continuing the sobriety of the day.

'Can I join you?' a voice asked me softly.

I nodded as Gus took the stool to my left. My heart raced.

'Give us Clifford's usual, Malacy.' Gus gestured toward the optics.

Malacy smiled, reached for two glasses and readily filled them with Clifford's choice of spirit – Morgan's Spiced, enjoyed when his body could not hold any more bitter and he felt the urge to sing. He placed the drinks in front of us, as Gus took out his wallet.

'No, they are on me, boys.' Malacy waved in Gus' direction.

We thanked the barman as he sought the attention of the next customer.

'Clifford,' said Gus simply, raising his glass upwards.

I repeated the toast as we downed the amber liquid in unison. As the raw burn hit our throats, a wince appeared simultaneously across our faces.

'Bit of an acquired taste, isn't it?' rasped Gus.

I coughed and nodded in agreement.

We sat in silence, our thoughts our own. It was obvious, sitting there, that Sally hadn't left me for Gus; that seed of malice planted in my mind by Greg Dixon had no right to exist, and yet it seemed to grow stronger. I was sure I would be able to tell. There would be signs – a scratch of the nose, avoidance of eye contact – in fact, there was no way he could sit with me, toasting our deceased mutual friend, if my wife had met him in Italy, flown back and was now waiting for him to finish paying his respects.

And then, after looking around the bar, he asked me the question in an innocent tone.

'I didn't see Sally at the funeral, is she here?'

I didn't answer, but merely stared ahead and the seconds ticked by.

'Eddie, is everything okay?' he asked, rolling the empty glass in his hands.

'She's gone,' I eventually answered flatly.

Gus stopped turning the glass and looked at me. 'Sorry?' he said.

'She's gone, left a note; said she doesn't want to be found.'

I stared deliberately into his eyes to gauge any reaction to my words, words that sounded as raw as they had done when I first digested the note.

'You must find her, Eddie, I will help you,' he insisted, moving from his stool.

He seemed panicked, agitated on hearing my words. It was first time I remembered seeing Gus Eastley flustered.

'No, she was very clear, it's over, for lots of reasons, reasons I cannot go into. Said she will come back for her things,' I confessed.

'Oh, right,' he replied, looking relieved as he sat back down.

'What does that mean?'

'I mean, I thought you were telling me she had...' He trailed off.

'She had what?' I asked, my fear taking control of my suspicions. I wanted to ask him outright, there and then, what he knew about Sally leaving.

'It's okay, Eddie, it doesn't matter.'

'You don't know who he is, do you? Everybody else does,' I blurted out suddenly.

'Who who is?'

'The person Sally has left me for.'

'Why would I know that?' Gus replied, somewhat unconvincingly in my eyes.

'Because her brother knew all about it, along with her friend Jennifer – thought you might too.'

'I don't really like where this is going,' Gus confessed.

'Do you not?' I asked, knowing I was losing control, directing my frustrations at the wrong target.

'No, or your tone,' Gus answered, rising from his seat.

'Well, her brother said there had been many, how can I put it, "liaisons" over the years, you included, apparently.'

Gus stood up to leave as I looked straight on. He leaned in towards me.

'It's been a difficult day and you are stressed; let's just leave it there.'

'Don't patronise me, Gus,' I breathed at him through gritted teeth.

He looked shaken, wounded by my words.

'Come on, Eddie; we go back years, don't we?' he said, just trying a reasonable approach.

But I ignored him and instead allowed the seed to push its roots further into me, to take full control.

'Actually,' I continued, 'it was in this very bar, wasn't it, when I first met you, cosying up with my wife? All makes sense now.'

His face changed in an instant, and a dark frown I had never seen before formed rigidly across his brow.

'Who was it telling me at the Whispering Rocks a few weeks ago that they had met somebody? Somebody that made you feel, I believe your phrase was "alive"?' he hissed into the side of my face, his voice still controlled, but the anger he felt now visible in his eyes.

I went to reply, to tell him of my decision to make the marriage work, but he continued.

'You both were unhappy, unhappy for years; the whole thing was a lie, a farce – one of you had to make the move to leave,' he said, echoing Jennifer's words to me. 'Perhaps you are just sore, your stupid pride is dented because Sally dared to go first. You are nothing but a sad, pathetic hypocrite,' he spat at me.

'Gus–'

He put his hand up to stop me speaking. 'I don't know what her brother said, or anyone else, but for what it's worth, I have never been close to Sally in that way. She and you were my friends.'

'*Were* your friends?' I questioned.

'I am going to say bye to Mary. I'll see you around, Eddie,' he said, his voice revealing the hurt he held inside.

And he turned and walked away.

I contemplated calling after him, to tell him I was sorry, but in a split second the protocol of the occasion took control and instead I just felt my face burn. I wasn't sure if it was the after-effects of Clifford's toast or the anger and embarrassment I now felt toward myself.

The burning slowly subsided, replaced by the acute anxiety which can only be driven by loss. I sat and looked at my reflection in the mirror behind the bar. In the space of a week, I had chosen to end something before it had begun, lost my wife, a good friend and now another.

I smiled at my mirror image – *I thought things were supposed to happen in threes*, I thought. I sat on and on, feeling guilty that my own predicament was taking precedence over supporting Mary, but I didn't dare to move, I couldn't face having to explain, now the day was drawing to a close, the absence of Sally.

People were starting to leave. It is always the same: a trickle soon becomes a flood, all looking to not be the last person to depart; the last person, guilt-ridden, knowing they are the one leaving the grieving spouse to face the first night alone with the empty ache, now that the corpse is at restlife.

I contemplated finding Mary to offer my final condolences, but she found me.

'Thanks for coming, Eddie,' she said behind me, and squeezed my arm. 'And thanks for organising the others to…' She trailed off, remembering, I sensed, the image of her husband's body carried aloft.

I placed my hand on top of hers in response – words were not necessary, were not needed.

Mary smiled to herself and went to speak to me, but stopped herself. I guessed at this, the tail end of the day, she knew Sally's absence wasn't due to illness, but didn't know how to broach it.

I waited, ready to craft a response.

'I've been very naughty,' she said finally, taking me completely by surprise.

'Naughty?'

Mary nodded and smiled. 'Since Clifford's been gone, I've let Ben and Alfie into the house.'

'I don't follow, Mary,' I stated, but feeling content with the subject matter.

'You know he had a thing about animals being in the house, he said it spoilt them, but I always felt sorry for them, outside in the barn on a filthy winter's night.'

I laughed as I remembered his thoughts on Henry being inside. 'He has a fur coat for a reason,' he would argue to me.

'At first, just during the day, they seemed restless,' Mary continued. 'I let them come and go, but now they are sleeping in the kitchen all night. He'd have a fit if he knew!'

'Yes, he would,' I laughed.

'They have taken to it straight away, not a peep out of either of them.'

'What about the others, the Jack Russells?' I asked.

Mary shook her head at the suggestion. 'No, they are happy in the barn and the yard, they do their own thing. And besides, they weren't that close to Clifford. But the other two followed him everywhere – up onto the hills, when he tinkered in the yard, or headed into town for anything. Having them inside is like he is still...' She trailed off again, and again she didn't need to finish the sentence. Her light-hearted approach was to no avail; it had still been hunted down by her grief.

'Thanks for the flowers, too,' she said quickly, changing the subject.

I felt my face flush as I recalled that moment of gazing at the hearse earlier that day. In my self-absorbed state, I had not even considered purchasing a bouquet, a fact Mary would discover when she sought comfort from the array of flowers at the grave in the days to come.

'Although, I know Sally bought them!' she stated.

I gave a guilty smile as I waited for Mary to ask *the* question. But instead she drifted off into her own space, her own world, and as the time dragged slowly by, only our eyes making contact, the emphasis for me to continue the interaction became intolerable. Ignatius McKenzie jumped into my mind, and the revelation he had shared with me. It appeared the perfect time to pass the message on to Mary that Clifford was fine; was back to his old self, not the dissolving shell we had recently witnessed. But my mind would not allow the words to form, to burden Mary with a cruel image she had not been privy to herself. Evidently, my subconscious mind had decided that four departures in a week were enough; a fifth would be positively careless.

'I will give you a ring tonight and see you tomorrow, Mary,' I said, giving her a hug.

'Thanks again for organising what you did, Eddie. No need for the call though, I'll be fine,' she replied over my shoulder, and then broke away.

She held my face in her hands and looked at me intently.

'Life goes on and life is good,' she whispered.

I held her gaze, not blinking. She didn't seem to be trying to convince herself with these words.

'Shouldn't I be the one saying this to you?' I eventually replied.

'Perhaps.' She smiled, lowering her hands slowly from my cheeks.

I smiled back.

'I just think you need to hear it more than I do, Eddie,' she reasoned.

Chapter 19

After the Storm

Life did go on, but it was not good, far from it. I merely blundered through a void. Each day seemed unrewarding, indistinguishable from the next.

I did try to get on; I headed into the mountains on three separate occasions over the past eight weeks. Their beauty remained, as did the glorious silence held within. But I found as I climbed that I had to stop regularly to draw breath and to answer the screaming from my lower legs. I couldn't believe my fitness levels had deteriorated so rapidly in just over two months; it must be the lack of conversation, limited though it used to be, that left my brain bored and susceptible to discomfort.

Even when the summit was reached, the usual sense of achievement deserted me. When I was with Gus we would spot distant landmarks far below, or just sit and talk, or watch for hares and buzzards, and all the while feel a degree of accomplishment at sitting as high as it was possible to go. But on my own, I stood and watched for mere minutes before a voice reasoned with me that it was time to head home, though for what purpose was never made clear to me.

Over the past few weeks I have improved my culinary skills. I have had to. There are only so many ready meals we should have to eat in our lifetime; not only for the health of our bodies, but for the well-being of our bank balances too. My repertoire is mostly made up of basic, one-pot dishes, but is tasty and hearty in delivery.

Henry approves of them too; in fact, he eats more than I do at present, as after cooking I do not really relish the prospect of eating alone. As I sit down, he moves next to my breakfast stool and looks up at me, licking his lips expectantly.

I usually make enough food for two or three days; I follow recipes for four people and am not as yet confident enough to reduce the quantities for a single portion. This means the second and third days' meals are reheated in the microwave. Perhaps I am not free of ready meals just yet.

Henry had all of the meal yesterday, as instead, I digested the contents of the letter that greeted me from the doormat when I arrived back at the house. I read the letter as the microwave whirred into life and stopped rereading as it gave notice of its completed task with a resounding 'ping'. The page revealed that Sally wanted to divorce me, or rather, she had instructed a firm of efficient-sounding solicitors to tell me her wishes. They informed me that if I was in agreement, 'proceedings', whatever they entailed, could be over in a matter of weeks. However, if I contested, they had *more than enough evidence of unreasonable behaviour* against me dating from throughout the marriage, which would be cited in court. They urged me to seek legal advice and trusted I would decide to take the easy option for all concerned and not contest the petition at this difficult time. The letter concluded with a notification that Sally planned to move her personal possessions out of the property in a week's time and that it would be appreciated if I was not at the house at this time.

After reading that, I lost my appetite. It made sense, but it seemed sudden and rushed; the countless years of unhappiness did not now seem enough to justify this outcome. I had no control, and what was 'unreasonable behaviour'? I felt I had failed.

We could have talked, but we had had years to do that. Besides, the drift had occurred slowly, like someone ageing or gaining or losing weight – you do not notice the change while living with them until the person you once knew is all gone.

I wouldn't contest, why should I? As Gus had told me, we all deserve to be happy. But was my life happy, standing again in the kitchen, ready to prepare food once more for myself? I had answers, but no plan for where I went to next.

I looked at Henry as he plodded toward me.

'Chilli con carne tonight, boy,' I said, as he wagged his tail in approval. 'You haven't tasted it yet,' I added, nodding at his tail. 'Besides, I think onion is bad for you.'

I struggle with onions. Whichever way I approach preparing them, my eyes always stream. I've tried all the 'cures' – wearing sunglasses, chopping under an open window, placing a wet metal spoon between my teeth – but nothing alleviates the symptoms. They say peeling away the layers of an onion is like revealing a person's character. Not sure what this says about me, as with the first crisp, dry layer removed, I am reduced to tears.

I selected an onion I hoped wouldn't be vicious. I picked up the knife and cut through the top. With the first layer of skin discarded and the onion sliced in half, my eyes began to smart.. By the fifth cut, the sting had forced my eyes to close, the resulting tears burning even more as I screwed up my face, searching for relief.

The doorbell rang, directing Henry to forget about his forthcoming dinner and revert to his role of reluctant guard dog with a deep but half-hearted bark.

I ignored him and the doorbell and kept on chopping, now operating by touch alone, as I was rendered blind by tears.

The doorbell rang again, three times in quick succession.

Guess I should answer it, I thought to myself.

I wandered through the hallway, rubbing my eyes with my shirtsleeves. As I neared the front door I sniffed hard as my nose became affected too.

I opened the door and focused on the threshold through watery eyes.

'Cerys?' I asked for confirmation, not wanting to rely on my blurred vision.

'Eddie, are you okay?' she replied anxiously.

'Yes, I am fine.'

'You don't look fine.'

I glanced at my reflection in the hallway mirror and for the first time saw my bloodshot eyes peeking through swollen, puffy eyelids. My cheeks were moist and glistening where my tears had decided to settle. Frankly, I looked a mess, but my heart pounded hard in my chest at the sound of her voice.

I heard her making a fuss of Henry, who had joined me at the front door, and sensed her tickling his ears.

I turned back to Cerys. 'I've been chopping onions!' I stated with a smile.

'Liar!' she replied, looking up. 'Anyway, I wasn't talking about your eyes; you've lost a lot of weight.

I shrugged my shoulders. 'I am fine,' I repeated.

She continued to stand on the doorstep. She, in contrast to me, looked lovely, despite my blurred vision.

'Sorry, please come in,' I finally instructed, opening the door fully.

Cerys hesitated, choosing her words. 'Is it okay? What about your wife? I shouldn't have come,' she added quickly, before I could answer.

'Wait!' I called as she turned to leave. 'You said that once before on the beach – there must be a reason you came,' I said, as she stood still. 'And no, Sally isn't here,' I added.

She continued to wait.

'Please come in,' I said gently, my eyes finally clearing.

Cerys stepped inside, into my house, my domain, for the first time.

I closed the door and we embraced, briefly, awkwardly, in the hallway.

'Come through, I'll make tea,' I said, unsure what else to say.

In the kitchen Cerys spied the half-chopped onions on the board.

'You really were chopping onions!' she giggled. 'You should try a wet metal spoon in your mouth to stop the eyes thing.'

'Doesn't work,' I dismissed, flicking the kettle switch on.

'Your garden is lovely,' she commented, ignoring my response.

I followed her gaze through the French doors and saw the garden with fresh eyes. Eight weeks of neglect had encouraged it to revert to a more natural state, and as the heat of summer had given way to the softer light of autumn, warm golden shades had spread across the garden.

'Where are your wife's bees?' she asked.

'The hives are at her brother's place,' I replied, handing her a mug of tea.

'Oh,' she said, blowing over the surface of the drink.

'How did you find the place?' I asked quickly, changing the subject from Sally.

'You always forget you have a ruddy huge van advertising the Party King – I just needed to locate it parked up. I knew you were the other side of the mountains, so that narrowed down the search.'

'Did it?'

'No, I was being sarcastic.'

It had been a while; I wasn't in tune with her at all.

'How long were you looking for?' I asked.

'A week or so.'

'I see.'

'I had a cover story.'

'Sorry, what do you mean?'

'In case your wife answered the door, I had a cover story prepared.'

'Right.'

'I intended to say we were renting a property with my sister over the summer and it was my nephew's birthday – I was driving by and saw the van and wondered if we could book a magic show. All very spontaneous.'

'"Just driving by"? It took you over a week to find the place. Not very plausible, is it?'

'You are wrong – I was going to state that I was lost and found this place by chance, very plausible in my eyes.'

'"Renting a property over the summer"?' I repeated.

'Yes.'

'But it is autumn now, look outside.'

'You are splitting hairs, Eddie – anyway, the cover story wasn't needed, as you are here. Where is your wife? When do you expect her home?' Cerys smiled.

Something switched inside of me.

'What do you want, Cerys, and why the fascination with Sally?' I asked curtly, banishing her smile.

'Because last time we met, you made it very clear you wanted to stay with your wife.'

I rolled my eyes.

'I am not knocking this,' she continued. 'I was just resigned to meeting her today.'

'What do you want, Cerys?' I asked again, pouring my tea down the sink in temper.

'Eddie, I need to talk to someone and you are the person who knows me best. If you had opened the door, I was going to start with this, but your appearance threw me. I am sorry for mentioning your wife, but now I am here, in her environment, it is a lot harder than I thought it would be.'

She paused, as if choosing her words carefully.

'I don't want to impose, but can we go somewhere else? But if your wife is coming home soon, or it's not convenient, I can just leave,' she said sadly.

'Sure, let's go out,' I replied.

'Thanks, Eddie. Maybe we can go to the beach, bring his lordship here, if he can behave during waking hours yet.'

'No, he can't,' I responded with a smile, as Henry looked

on, knowing he was the point of discussion. 'We could head out for lunch?' I offered quickly.

'Looks like you have something already planned?' said Cerys, nodding at the pile of half-chopped onions.

'Was only dinner prep,' I said, picking up the board and throwing the onions into the pedal bin.

'What about your dinner?'

'I can do it later.'

'I feel awful imposing.'

'Don't, it isn't a problem.' I smiled at her. 'I just need to change my shirt,' I added, and walked out of the kitchen.

'Don't change on my account – look at what I am wearing,' she shouted after me.

True, Cerys wore the clothes I had seen so many times before – baggy fleece, jeans and boots – but I was sure she hadn't had the same shirt on underneath her fleece for three days as I had.

Once upstairs, I selected a cleaner shirt, worn only once before being hung back in the wardrobe, unwashed.

'Do you do a lot of cooking, Eddie?' she asked as I re-entered the kitchen.

'Yes,' I replied, picking up my set of keys.

'Your wife is lucky,' stated Cerys.

'Shall we go?' I suggested, ignoring her comment.

Cerys patted Henry goodbye and followed me through the hallway. I held the front door open for her to pass through and held her gaze for a second too long.

'Where to? Best you lead, Eddie,' said Cerys as we reached her Range Rover.

'No, let's just go in yours,' I replied.

'Travel together, you mean?'

'That was the idea.'

'Are you sure? What about——?'

'The neighbours?' I interrupted. 'Can you see anyone else here?' I added unnecessarily.

'No, I was going to say, what about your wife? How will you explain where you've been when the van is here when she returns, but you are not?'

'Just open the door of this beast!' I commanded.

'Assertive, Dungiven, nice!' she said, unlocking the vehicle with a bleep. 'I'll drop you off near the house, don't want to make it difficult for you later,' she said, turning the engine over.

'You like seafood, don't you?'

'Love it.'

'Let's try the Blue Cafe,' I said.

Cerys shook her head.

'You don't know it?'

She shook her head a second time.

'How long...?'

'Have I lived here?' she said, completing my sentence. 'Not long enough, obviously,' she added, smiling.

'It's about thirty minutes' drive.'

'Next to the sea?'

'You do know it, then?' I teased back.

We drove in silence; the scenery didn't require any commentary. It was strange to be actually moving in this car that I had spent so much time stationary in, and to witness Cerys driving – it was like meeting someone for the first time.

'Twenty minutes,' said Cerys as we pulled into the Blue

Cafe car park. 'You must drive very *s-l-o-w-l-y*, if this takes you half an hour,' she added playfully.

'Ha, ha,' I replied sarcastically.

The restaurant was only a third full, the lunchtime rush drawing to a close, and we had our pick of window seats to choose from that looked over the water, the vista flanked on the left by the mountains.

We ordered the food quickly, both deciding on mussels and string fries, which we knew to be fresh as the waiter pointed to the small boat in the bay pulling up lines, the sister ship of which, he explained, had landed ten minutes before. The boats hadn't been out yesterday, he said, on account of bad weather, but today was ideal, and once the catch was landed, the shellfish would be cleaned and cooked.

I realised I still didn't know what Cerys wanted to talk about, and prepared to ask when she interrupted me.

'It's lovely here, Eddie, do you come with your wife?' she said, staring out at the view.

The same feeling I had experienced in the kitchen returned with her words.

'Cerys, Sally has gone,' I stated flatly, moving my head to take in her view of the bay.

'Gone?'

'She has left me.'

I felt a touch on my wrist and looked down to see her hand there.

'I am sorry, Eddie,' she said softly. 'When?' she asked, looking at me.

I gave a little laugh. 'Last time I saw you on the beach, I came home to an empty house and a note.'

'Not a great day, then?'

I smiled. 'I received a letter yesterday from a solicitor, notifying me that she wants a divorce.'

I fell silent as our food arrived.

'Is it what you want?' asked Cerys when the waiter had gone.

I thought, choosing my words before replying.

'I don't have a choice,' I said.

'Is it what you want?' she repeated.

'I feel like I am a failure, I feel stupid, and I feel like I want to sign the papers and close my eyes and let it pass me by.'

'I am sure it is normal, Eddie, it's a form of grief.'

I looked at her quizzically.

'Something is gone that was there, that was standard, and what is left behind is grief,' she explained.

'I think I knew it was too late, that too much time had passed to bring it back. But I didn't want to be the one that admitted it. Trying to mend it made me somehow feel better.'

'Somehow made you not to blame?'

I nodded.

We sat in silence.

'We should eat,' I instructed, looking at the bowls of fresh, steaming mussels.

We each took one first mouthful, and commented on the taste to each other before continuing to eat in silence.

'I wasn't going to tell you,' I eventually admitted, 'but you kept mentioning Sally, so I felt I had to.'

'I am sorry. I guess I just wantedto connect to your life.'

We finished the course in silence. I was unsure exactly how she felt about my life.

'I am as bad as you, Eddie, trying to keep things to myself,' said Cerys, scrunching her napkin in her hand.

'Is that what you want to talk about?' I replied.

She turned her head out to sea once more.

'Where do I start?' she said, in the same tone she had used on the beach that day I learned about Phoebe's disappearance.

I remained silent, letting her speak.

'Cole has been arrested,' she said flatly.

'When? What for?' I stammered.

'I don't know how to say this,' she said, biting her lip.

'Go on,' I encouraged, now holding her wrist.

'He's an accessory.'

'An accessory?' I asked. Cerys was quiet. 'To what?'

Cerys remained silent.

'Cerys?' I probed, trying to reconnect with her. 'Cerys?'

She turned to face me, composed, ready to speak.

'He has been arrested as an accessory to dog fighting,' she revealed.

'Dog fighting?' I replied, trying to sound surprised and hide the guilt I felt for not warning her.

I must have been convincing, as she continued to explain.

'That time I went to Amsterdam, I felt terrible checking in at the airport, because I was supposed to wake up with you and we both know what happened to that plan.'

She stopped speaking, and the words hit me hard.

'I arrived,' she continued, 'tired and miserable, only for Cole to inform me he had to return urgently – the earliest flight was that afternoon. I was furious with him, but he said he had an emergency at one of his shops that he had to

326

attend to. I should have been suspicious when he rejected my idea of flying back too and instead insisted I stayed and took in the sights for the day. He assured me he would be back in thirty-six hours. He can be very persuasive.'

She had stopped speaking again. My mind replayed her opening words over and over and refused to let them go, knowing I should be concentrating on the serious content.

'We argued, we *really* argued, it was horrible, until he left the room and headed to the airport early, leaving me alone. In the empty room, my stomach reminded me I hadn't eaten, so I ordered room service, selecting the most expensive breakfast combination to spite him!' She stopped and gave a little laugh in my direction.

I smiled back, ignoring the fact that she had deviated from her husband's arrest.

'To be honest,' she continued, 'I really had come to see Amsterdam on my own – Cole wasn't interested in the place; it was all about business to him. I took time over the meal and spent the rest of the morning taking a canal cruise and visiting the Van Gogh Museum; the afternoon was spent in Anne Frank's house and then it was a toss-up between the flower market and the flea market, but to be honest I was sick of flowers at this point, so bric-a-brac won. I finished the day with an early-evening meal in Chinatown. I was in bed by 10pm and slept really well, and was woken at eight by the bedside phone ringing. It took me a few moments to understand the significance of the call. It was Matthew Gorham, Cole's solicitor.' She paused and took a sip of water.

'His solicitor?' I repeated.

Cerys nodded. 'Yes,' she said, after swallowing the

liquid. 'He told me Cole had been arrested at a secret dog fight and had now been charged.'

'I am sorry, Cerys.' It was my turn to speak with compassion.

'Don't be,' she responded curtly. 'He was watching dogs being ripped apart and betting on the outcome. Dogs, Eddie – he got what he deserved,' she said, searching for my eyes with her own. 'I am sure that's where Phoebe went: ripped to shreds,' she surmised.

'No, I am sure that isn't true,' I countered, trying my best to sound convincing, to keep the vile conversation I had overheard by my van from my thoughts.

'Really, Eddie? He wouldn't divulge where she had gone, I asked him repeatedly, but he would never tell. Just said she was his dog, his property and I knew this.'

'Why not ask him now? At this time, when there is nothing to hide?' I suggested.

She shook her head. 'I don't want to see him,' she said.

'Isn't that awkward?'

'I have no desire to see him again,' Cerys replied honestly.

'Is he staying somewhere else, then?'

'Sorry?'

'I am not sure how bail works,' I confessed.

'He wasn't granted bail,' she said flatly.

I looked at her, surprised. 'I thought…'

'He would be released on bail?' said Cerys, finishing my sentence.

I nodded.

'Matthew Gorham told me during that first call that due to the people involved, bail had been denied. Extremely unsavoury characters involved in organised crime, by all accounts, who would possibly intimidate witnesses or worse, or even flee the country if released from custody.'

I had no idea such a shadowy world of violence and intimidation could exist in my community.

'You said that first call – have you spoken to him again?' I asked. 'I don't know your husband, but I am sure he is not part of some criminal underworld,' I added.

'I've had many calls from his solicitor, asking me to speak to Cole. But I really don't want to. What is there to say? He was caught and filmed watching and betting on two dogs destroying each other in a barn. Why should I speak to him? I have found out a few details though, through Matthew.'

'Oh?' I replied.

'The police got a tip-off from a member of the public that the fight was going to take place. They didn't know when or where, but knew the names of likely attendees. Why Cole's name was put forward, I don't know – guess he *must* be part of an organised crime syndicate. Goes to show: you can live with someone, but never really know them.'

In my peripheral vision, somebody walked toward the table.

'Would you like to see the dessert menu?' the waiter asked brightly.

'No, no,' we replied too forcefully in unison and he hurriedly retreated, leaving our empty bowls in front of us.

'How do you know this?'

'Know what?'

'That he was named, and that he is part of a crime gang?'

'Matthew said his was one of the names put forward along with Elliot Wallace's. I was introduced to him at the Lombarders' ladies' night. Think he is the organiser – sounds like he's been arrested before, or so Matthew Gorham said. I *knew* there was something wrong about him when I met him.'

that your husband is fully involved

I sat back silently, not wanting to offer any indication of my knowledge of or involvement in Cerys' situation.

'I am grateful that someone went to the police – this had to be stopped,' she continued, 'but I now know our every movement was monitored; we were under constant surveillance.'

'That must have been really hard to deal with. I am really sorry,' I offered.

'Why are you sorry? It wasn't your fault.'

'I can imagine—'

'You don't understand, Eddie, what it feels like knowing you have been watched twenty-four hours a day, but at the time, you had no idea it was actually happening,' Cerys interrupted sternly.

I was shamed into silence.

'I am paranoid now. Any contractors that I see parked up, I instantly wonder if they are really what they seem. I crossed the road yesterday to avoid a man cleaning a shop window,' she said eventually, a semblance of her usual tone restored.

I merely nodded an acknowledgement.

'They must have seen us leaving the house together, him on his own or me alone; seen us in the garden, inside the house, by the windows, in the bathroom showering and washing. They must have followed on every car journey, every shopping trip and even parking at the airport – they tracked him all the way to and from Amsterdam,' she said.

She paused, letting me take in the words.

'Lately, I've convinced myself they went through the bins and removed any personal details, and also entered the house, checking and removing correspondence, gaining evidence, though logically, I am quite sure they didn't. But all of this defies logic, so I decided last week to check his filing cabinet in the study, make sure nothing was missing – I wasn't entirely sure what I was looking for, but I discovered a lot.'

'What do you mean?' I asked.

Cerys closed her eyes and exhaled audibly. 'It's all a lie.'

'Sorry? What is a lie?'

'The entire life he built. The shops, the house, the cars, the motor cruiser, the watches, the jewellery – none of them were owned by him, none.'

I wanted to speak, but Cerys continued.

'Letters hidden in the study showed the level of debt he had accumulated over a considerable period of time, and how repayment plans and loans were in place to cover them. The whole thing is a mess and out of control.'

'You must be able to get help or advice,' I said.

'Who from?'

'The lenders – which bank is it? We could do this together.'

Cerys stared at me and touched my hand gently. 'Eddie, there is no bank involved,' she revealed wearily. 'The letters are from extremely dubious-sounding companies, registered mostly in Costa Rica; the loans and terms seem complex.'

I felt foolish, really foolish. She smiled, looked at me and squeezed my hands. As I had earlier, Cerys now held my gaze for a moment too long.

'I've a plan, though,' she revealed.

'What's that?'

'My mother left me a property in her will; I've used it for occasional weekends down the years. It's a small place, a long way from here, on the opposite coast. It's right on the edge of sand dunes, but has no guarding mountains, just endless sand flats, enormous skies and ever-changing light.'

'Sounds lovely.'

'It is – look out of the lounge window and you often find seals lying up near the shoreline. It's as if they are sunbathing!'

I smiled at the image.

'I am going to go there,' Cerys said.

'Okay.'

'It's safe,' she added quietly.

I reflected on her words and thought again about my involvement in leading her to this current state of mind. It was me, my responsibility; I had informed the police regarding the dog fight. I could have stopped at naming Wallace, but spontaneously – and eagerly, I shamefully admit – I offered her husband's name too. The pain resulting from my actions was clearly evident on her face as she sat in front of me, but without my involvement, would the true extent of her husband's financial problems have been revealed to her in time? Would she have had time to act, time to protect herself before businessmen from San Jose came looking to recover their investments in any way they deemed appropriate? It is easy to justify our actions by latching positives to them.

'When will you go?' I asked.

'As soon as I can,' she replied. 'I'm packing up at the moment, but not sure what I can or cannot take – I do not know what is paid for,' she added with a sarcastic smile.

I smiled back. 'I could help you,' I said, squeezing her hands in mine.

Cerys looked at me.

'With the packing,' I added by way of an explanation.

Cerys didn't answer me, but rather seemed lost in her own thoughts.

'That's really kind, Eddie, when did you have in mind?' she finally said.

'Now?' I said excitedly. 'Pay the bill and go?' I suggested with a laugh, drawing the attention of the waiter we had previously banished with my raised arm.

'Okay!' she laughed back. 'I was thinking next week, but now works too!'

The waiter returned quickly with the bill; we were the last diners remaining in the restaurant. I checked the figures and reached for my wallet to pay.

'We should halve this, Eddie,' said Cerys.

'It was my suggestion to go out to eat,' I replied.

I took out banknotes to pay for the meal, included what I considered to be a reasonable tip and handed it to the waiter. I commented again how good the mussels had been.

'Always the best after a storm,' he said. 'Turmoil seems to intensify the flavour.'

He turned and walked to thet bar area, joining his fellow waiting staff who sensed the shift was finally ending.

'Thank you,' said Cerys.

'What for?' I probed.

She smiled at me, as our eyes made prolonged contact for a third time.

'Shall we go?' I suggested.

Chapter 20

Eebiss

We drove with the sun heavy in front of us, guiding us, starting its daily search for the western horizon. I knew this road well, but had never had cause to stop; it was always used as a means to arrive somewhere else, an alternative to avoid tractors and slow-moving trucks on the main routes.

Cerys slowed as she approached a high brick wall to our left. She swung the car to face beech gates edged with brushed steel, and when on the driveway, pressed a fob on her key ring to activate the movement of the gates. As we passed through, a slate plaque to the left identified the house, in gold lettering, as *EEBISS*.

'Here we are,' she said, applying the handbrake.

I'd had a vision of Cerys' home in my mind, but from the outside, this was far beyond what I had imagined. It made self-congratulating self-builders, all smug smiles and bare feet in glossy magazines, appear to the living in the bad side of town.

She opened the oak front door and pushed a code into the alarm box on the wall. With the alarm safely silenced, we moved through the porch, the floor space revealed being vast.

Natural light spilled in through two large glass gables,

but the late-autumn warmth could not penetrate into the heart of the open-plan structure; the tiled floor and double-height ceiling proved too challenging for a dying sun and the house was cold.

I was always led to believe that a house had to have many rooms, defined separate compartments designed for a specific purpose. I hadn't entered a property like this before. The bare white walls stretching to the angled roof and the empty shelving units seemed to expand the area yet further, and my eyes were drawn, as intended, I presumed, to a wood-burning stove positioned as a focal point in the centre of the space. Its brushed steel exterior and flue rising up through the roof mirrored the edging of the beech gates outside. Around it were positioned four cream leather sofas, their backs covered with coloured throws of luxurious-looking wool.

'Lovely house,' I stated unnecessarily.

Cerys did not answer.

I followed her to the far end of the house, to the kitchen area. The units were arranged in a horseshoe, surrounding an island that housed a sink and a hob. The units were of a reflective white material with no visible handles, and in contrast, the work surfaces were of black granite.

'Would you like a drink?' asked Cerys, pushing one of the units to reveal a refrigerator hidden inside.

'Sure, what do you have?'

'Fruit juice, sparkling water, or I can make a hot drink – tea, coffee – if you prefer,' she replied.

'Tea would be great.'

'Earl Grey, masala, green?' she asked.

Before I could make my choice, Cerys interrupted me.

'Or we could have this,' she said, revealing a bottle of chilled Chablis. As I looked on, she fully retrieved the bottle and gently shook it from the neck as way of coaxing my decision from me. 'Opened it last night, I need a drink to face more packing,' she confessed.

I nodded in agreement.

'Glasses in the cupboard next to you, Eddie – just push the front, same as the fridge, it will open.'

I pushed as instructed and found the cavernous space almost completely empty.

'Last two,' I stated, retrieving two delicate-stemmed wine glasses.

Cerys poured the liquid, releasing the familiar satisfying glugging sounds as the wine moved from vessel to vessel.

'I've packed all the other glasses away; stored them in the garage. I only need two with just me here; they are one thing I know I definitely bought.'

'Cheers,' I stated brightly, raising my glass toward hers.

She responded by clinking my glass with her own.

'Really good to see you, Eddie,' she said, before bringing the glass to her lips.

'You too.'

I sipped at the chilled wine and felt the coldness travel through me.

'I noticed the walls and shelves are bare – I thought you would have a lot to pack?' I said.

'Did all that already; I've stored everything – books, painting and sculptures – along with the drinking glasses. There are a number of original pieces he bought out there, but I am not sure if they are valuable, or even owned by him.'

'You should keep them just in case!' I laughed.

'That's why I moved them out of sight – you never know, they could be my pension!' Cerys smiled.

'You're not going to leave them in the garage, are you?'

'Course not; I've arranged to put it all in storage in two weeks' time, so I really need to get organised. I haven't even touched upstairs,' confessed Cerys.

'Upstairs?'

Cerys looked at me quizzically.

'I didn't think there was an upstairs,' I explained, pointing at the vaulted ceiling.

'Did you think I've got a hammock up there?' she said, pointing upwards. 'Lowered by a clever usage of pulleys?' she added.

Before I could answer, she had picked up the wine bottle and was heading for the whitewashed wall facing us in the kitchen area.

'C'mon, I'll show you.'

I followed, glass in hand.

'Aren't we supposed to run at this with a luggage trolley to get through?' I asked.

Cerys giggled and pushed the wall at a spot known to her, her action releasing a catch that triggered an unseen door to open inwards, revealing another area, at first glance roughly the same size as the one in which we stood.

Beyond the door was a structure of mainly glass, which opened up on a view taking in rolling hills and the mountains on the horizon. Again, it was double-heighted, and this time the glass reached up the apex, forming a glass roof.

Running to the right side of the apex were four heavy oak doors set in a white wall. Between the central doors, the wall was bisected by a white, open-riser staircase jutting straight from the wall, the steps of which appeared to have no apparent source of support, but instead seemed to simply float. The stairs led to a mezzanine level fronted by oak balustrades and a rail.

'Steam room, gym, home cinema, studyo,' said Cerys, reading my mind as we passed the first oak door.

'Thought you were showing me the pulley system for your hammock?'

She smiled but ignored my comment, instead she pointed at the doors in turn, stating, 'Not used, never used, not used by me, room I never want to enter again.'

I was sure the order of rooms matched her previous explanation, but I could have been mistaken.

'Not being rude – you have all this natural light in here, but aren't the rooms a bit dark?' I suggested. 'I guess for the cinema, you would want it dark, and the steam room doesn't really matter,' I added.

Cerys said nothing, but pushed a switch on the wall, which instantly prompted the 'white wall' to change and reveal glass, that allowed natural light to flood the rooms.

'Wow,' I said simply, transfixed by the change and equally by the substantially equipped gym.

Cerys stepped onto the staircase in silence. I followed, my mind processing the treadmills and the rowing and weightlifting machines as I ascended the stairs, intrigued as to what would be discovered on the second level.

Reaching the top, the oak rail was lower than I expected, standing waist-height, the wood grain beautiful and invitingly tactile. The mezzanine floor revealed a similar set of oak doors as below.

'Can I press the magic button, Cerys?' I asked, feeling like a ten-year-old as I spied a switch in the centre of the white wall.

'Of course, but it's not a toy, don't break it!' she commanded, a mock sternness in her voice.

I pressed it and felt the same wonder as I had downstairs as the rooms within were exposed.

'That is one of the most amazing things I have ever seen,' I confessed.

'I said before to you that I didn't care for all of this, even less so now that I know it's built on a lie, but this is one thing that I really appreciate and never tire of.'

I nodded in agreement.

'Waking up to a darkened room and revealing that framed view with the flick of a switch is truly a privilege and a pleasure, Eddie.'

'I'll take your word for it, I believe you,' I said.

Now exposed, not all the rooms were bedrooms; one was a bathroom, another was a dressing room, and both appeared kitted out to the highest spec available. Judging by the brown cardboard boxes on the floor and the black bin liners and clothes arranged on the bed, one of the bedrooms had evidently seen more packing activity than the others.

'Where do you want to start?' I asked, turning to Cerys.

'In here.' She gestured toward the bedroom with the packing boxes.

We entered the room and Cerys took my now-empty wine glass from me and placed it with her own on an oak unit.

'We need a top-up before we start,' she said, and refilled the glasses. 'Thanks for doing this, Eddie, you are a good man,' she added.

With her words guiding the way, I rubber-banded back

to that first encounter on the beach and Cerys turning around to address me on the duckboards.

'It's fine,' I volunteered.

As well as a bed and bedside tables, the room held a number of units, cases and a huge wardrobe, all oak and all in pristine condition.

'We need to clear all the shelves and cupboards. Just put all the clothes in the bin liners, anything else in the boxes – no need to sort,' she said.

I moved toward the wardrobe and reached for the handles, preparing to reveal the contents inside, while Cerys opened a cupboard. I glance over to her and saw rows of files and boxes piled into the space.

'Feels strange to rummage through your clothes,' I confessed with a laugh.

'Why, worried what you might find? You're okay, my bondage dresses are downstairs with my whips!' replied Cerys with a straight face. 'Anyway,' she added, now smiling, 'I do not recall giving the go-ahead for any "rummaging" to occur in the first place.'

'Fair point,' I muttered.

'It's just old stuff, Eddie, that I cannot bring myself to discard,' Cerys said, as I scooped the first armful of clothes from the rail inside.

We worked quietly, at a steady pace, until different garments that were in stark contrast to the dresses, skirts and tops came into my view.

'What are these?' I asked instinctively, as I held the hanger up for her inspection.

Cerys turned around and caught sight of the outfit. 'My whites,' she stated flatly.

'Your whites?'

'From catering college, long time ago now,' she said.

'You were a chef?' I asked, impressed.

'Trained to be one, but never got there though – long way from it, in fact.'

I remained silent.

'I met Cole when I had just started working as a commis chef, but he thought the whole thing was stupid, so I stopped,' she added, filling the void.

'What, just like that?' I wondered.

'Pretty much, I was young and not in a good place, remember, my dad had recently died. Cole was very good at making my dreams and ideas seem whimsical to me – his strength and drive were what I needed, he said.'

'That's not right.'

Cerys shrugged. 'He provided everything. Couple of years after we married, to fill some of my time, I started to bake and decorate cakes. Had a real flair for it, all my passion came flooding back and I decided to start up a business from home, doing wedding and birthday orders – there definitely was a gap in the market, but again my plans were dashed by Cole.'

'But why?' I asked.

'I told you before, he can be very persuasive.'

'I've never fully known what you mean by that,' I stated.

'Once your confidence is gone, it's hard to accept you can do things,' said Cerys.

I still did not understand fully. To me she was one of the most quick-witted, gregarious, fun and confident people I had met in my lifetime. I couldn't imagine her not standing up for herself, unable to control every aspect of her life. I supposed it was this lack of self-belief that kept her trapped in the marriage, when it was obvious from my position, looking in, that she should have left a long time ago. At this point, my self-righteousness was justifiably cut short, as my mind recalled my inability to bring to a clean end my own particular circumstances. Who was I to judge another's personal story?

'I've got some photos here somewhere,' she said.

Cerys moved to a new cupboard, lifted a pile of blankets and revealed a large cardboard box. She placed the box on the bed and took off the lid; the action dislodged a significant number of photographs from inside and they slide out onto a white duvet trimmed with blue flowers. Each image captured similar subjects.

Cakes, lots and lots of cakes, it wasn't until I picked up one of the photographs and examined it that I appreciated the work that had produced this creation. Delicate pink iced roses climbed the side of the cake, topped with a pure white iced bow that had the texture and shape of a silk ribbon and gave the illusion that the ends could be pulled and the bow would unravel into a single strand. Another was a four-tiered cylindrical creation of colourful stripy and star-covered icing; a red clown's hat made of marzipan, complete with yellow flower, crowned the cake. Yet another was in the shape of a Ducati motorbike, another a mermaid, her tail held thirty degrees in the air.

'These are amazing,' I said, sitting down. 'How do you begin to make something like this?'

Cerys smiled.

'You should start again.'

'Maybe,' she replied. She sat next to me and rummaged in the box. 'Looking for my favourite one,' she explained.

Her efforts spilt the majority of the remaining photographs from the box onto the bed.

'Here,' she said triumphantly, retrieving a shot of a pink-and-green turreted fairy castle, 'this took an age to build.'

But my eyes had been distracted.

'Who is this?' I asked, holding up a picture that had been revealed of a young woman, her elfin features emphasised by heavy rouge applied around her cheekbones and pouting red lips. Her eyes were heavy with black mascara and her face was framed by short, spiked, shocking purple hair.

'Give me that,' she said, laughing, while trying to grab the picture from my hand.

I moved my hand up and away from hers and looked at the picture more closely.

'Is that you?' I asked.

'Give it to me,' she commanded, as I rose from the bed.

I held the photograph ever higher. 'Take it,' I teased.

Accepting the challenge, Cerys jumped up onto the bed and stood up in one fluid motion and reached down, trying to pluck the image from my grasp. Taken by surprise, I moved my hand away too slowly and she took hold of the side of the photo. I held the other side tightly.

Our tussle and laughter brought instability and I lost my balance, falling forward onto the bed, the picture still caught between my fingers.

I landed on Cerys, my face resting on her stomach, my arm draped over her thigh. And all the time our laughter continued and the picture remained shared between our hands.

The laughter slowed as we regained our breath and was eventually replaced by slight giggles. I think we both realised at the same time where and how I lay, my face so close to the zipper of her jeans, my hand on her thigh.

I sat up quickly, letting go of the picture, deciding it to be the appropriate action, only to be followed by Cerys.

'Why stop?' She smiled.

And in a moment we kissed, gently at first, barely registering contact, but soon the wild abandonment we had succumbed to in Cerys' white Range Rover, parked behind the dunes, returned. We lay down side by side, kissing frantically, our movement crinkling and dislodging the photographs onto the floor. I reached up and cupped a breast in my hand, an action I had longed to perform on so many occasions, but due to the loose-fitting fleece she wore, initially it wasn't entirely clear what was flesh and what was material, but judging by her quickening breath, the fleece was evidently thinner than it felt. Encouraged, I unzipped the fleece and raced my hand under her T-shirt; reaching upward, I touched the underside of her bra, my action causing Cerys to break away from kissing.

'Let's go into the other bedroom,' she suggested.

We leaped off the bed and rushed into the adjacent room; for whatever reason, I was not aware. Once inside, I manoeuvred Cerys so she was standing with her back against the glass wall, and we continued to kiss, lost in passion. I moved my lips to her neck, the caresses gentle, but her response intense. She pulled me closer to her, our thighs pressed together, her hips rocking slightly back and forth, forcing me to draw deeper breaths. I slipped off her fleece and quickly pulled her T-shirt up and over her head and threw it behind me, while her fingers moved nimbly on the buttons of my shirt. Her bra was delicate, ivory lace, and her breast within roundly shaped. I reached around her back with one hand and unclipped the clasp instantly; surprised I hadn't fumbled clumsily at the task before needing my second hand in a supporting role, or worse still, letting Cerys take responsibility.

Exposed, her breasts were beautiful, full and heavyp. I took each breast in hand and moved my mouth over a nipple and lapped and nibbled, drawing it toward the back of my mouth, before repeating on the other. Cerys had my last button undone and moved her hands up to my shoulders to push my shirt away. I now regretted eating the quantity of bread I had with my mussels earlier, concerned my stomach may appear bloated for that all-important first impression. If it was, Cerys didn't seem interested at all. She lifted my head and walked me backward to the bed, guiding me into a sitting position on the edge.

She quickly removed her socks and jeans, leaving her in a black thong ,and straddled me. We started to kiss again; the feel of Cerys' breasts against my chest made my groin throb with a lustful pain. Cerys seemed to sense this and moved her hand downward to stroke the front of my jeans, reaching for the button flies. I in turn hooked my fingers around her thong at the hips and pulled, encouraging her to rise up to allow the garment to be removed. Cerys duly obliged and lifted herself from my lap, and as I drew the black material down her legs, she revealed a small, neat area of dark hair and emitted a musk that caused my groin to tighten even further.

We scrambled up onto the bed; Cerys positioned herself on her back, as I lay on my side next to her. We smiled at each other. I moved my hand slowly down her arm, her stomach and rested at the top of her legs, which she parted slightly at my touch. I We resumed kissing as my hand ventured downwards, searching for and finding the wet warmth that gave way effortlessly to my fingers. Cerys moaned through our kiss as my fingers moved still deeper.

Suddenly she pulled away. 'Get these off,' she said, tugging at my button flies again. I jumped off the bed and carefully removed my jeans and pants, and before I could get onto the bed again, Cerys turned and rolled over onto her stomach, facing me, and took me into her mouth, her hands gently guiding the entry. I felt her tongue circle and flick the tip, before she settled on a steady rhythm. She finally withdrew, placing a kiss on the tip as she did.

'Reach into that drawer, we don't want any accidents, do we?' she said, nodding at the bedside cabinet to my right.

I opened the drawer and was confronted by a layer of foil-wrapped squares, and felt dismayed as all held a bold and proud *XL* in the centre of each packet.

'Never used these before,' I confessed, removing a condom from the drawer.

'Never?' replied Cerys, sitting up.

I shook my head shamefully, knowing my hardness was rapidly deflating, bewildered by the daunting size and issue of application of the contents of the foil.

'Here, I'll do it,' she said, reaching out her hand.

Cerys ripped open the foil and removed the coiled condom from inside. Shequickly squeezed it, turned it around and positioned it on my tip, before firmly pushing towards me. She began to stroke me back into hardness, her hands cupping my testicles as she did so.

'Wow, you are filling that well, Eddie,' she giggled,

looking into my eyes and moving her hand quicker as I regained full hardness. 'Now, come over here with that big cock and fuck me,' she whispered urgently, moving onto her back, spreading her legs wide apart.

Her words made my entire body tingle and my groin throb uncontrollably, as I positioned myself on top of her. With one push, I felt the slippery warmth envelop me as I sank down to my hilt. We stayed in the position for a few moments, smiling to each other, enjoying the sensations, before instinct took hold and gentle movement soon grew more hurried until I eventually cried out, followed by our joint laboured breathing, then silence. We remained still, as we had previously, smiling and enjoying the sensation, wishing for it to linger as my hardness retreated.

'Best we take that out,' she eventually advised.

I pulled out from inside her and as I did, found the condom now only half on. I peeled it off entirely and held it up, looking at the trapped liquid inside.

'You are such a bloke, Eddie, admiring your load!' Cerys teased.

It wasn't that at all. I was wondering how all the effort, all the chasing, the euphoric highs, the crashing lows, the emotion-sapping guilt could culminate in this seemingly insignificant pale fluid that was cooling, separating and dying before our eyes.

Cerys took the condom from me, tied a knot in the end and placed it on the floor. I lay on my back (my ego, at least, remained inflated) and was joined by Cerys, who snuggled into the crook of my arm and laid her head on my chest, as I stroked her hair. We basked in this afterglow and drifted between dozing and being awake, neither speaking, neither making a sound as our bodies and emotions returned to normal.

Suddenly, Cerys propped herself up on an elbow, her cheek resting on her hand.

'We should run away!' she exclaimed.

'You are, you are going to your mother's place,' I said.

'No, *really* run away.'

I laughed at the suggestion.

'I am serious,' said Cerys.

'Where to?'

'Anywhere!'

'Anywhere?'

'Yes, anywhere!'

I laughed again.

'Where would you like to go to?' she asked.

I thought for a moment. 'South of France,' I offered.

'Not very exotic, Eddie!'

'I've always wanted to go.'

'Why?'

'I like the thought of the afternoon in a sleepy medieval village, where all there is to do is listen to the abbey bells chiming on the hour, watch doves soaring overhead and see the warm sun dancing on the surface of a contented stretch of river.'

'If you put it like that, I suppose,' said Cerys respectfully, 'but I was thinking further afield – Patagonia, Myanmar, Kerala.'

'Really?' I said, my suggestion now feeling somewhat foolish.

'Yes, I was thinking more of experiences that will change your life – landscapes, atmospheres, environments, food, music and cultures so different, so removed from what we are used to. The whole of Europe is lovely, but it's just that, lovely; I don't think it would change the way you view the world; it will not make you see things from a different perspective.'

'Okay, let's go to Kerala,' I said spontaneously.

'Is that your choice?'

I nodded, a smile on my face.

'It doesn't have to be there specifically.'

'How long shall we go for?' I said, ignoring her statement.

'However long we want to – a month, three months, a year; we can just make it up, it's that simple!'

'It's not that simple though, is it?' I stated.

'Why not?'

'What about the practical things? There is the business, for one thing, and my commitments to the schools; Henry, what will happen to him? The divorce, the settlement; so many things.'

Cerys laughed and held my face in her hands.

'What is it?' I asked through her laughter.

'You called it a business, that's the first time I've heard you say that. That's good, really good.'

She was correct: I had never used the term before; subconsciously I hadn't thought my activities could in any way compete with her husband's, until now.

'You are missing the point, I cannot just suddenly leave it,' I argued.

'Again, why not?' she repeated.

'Because…' I trailed off, unable to articulate my reasoning.

'Do you have a mortgage, Eddie?'

'What?'

'Do you have a mortgage; do you need to work to meet payment obligations?

'No, there isn't a mortgage any more,' I admitted.

'So that isn't a reason not to go then, is it?'

'I have to remain visible to keep the bookings coming in.'

'Eddie, when we come back, people will still have birthdays, will still want magic shows – we can pick up then.'

'You say, "we"?'

'Of course, I will support you. Build a website, adverts in local papers, handing out flyers – we can do whatever it takes.'

I was taken aback by her suggestion, astounded by her offer – but why wouldn't I be, with only years of isolation to compare it to?

'What about the loss of earnings? I don't have a lot saved,' I said.

'Eating, sleeping and travel, all can be costed reasonably. Think of what you would spend in a week here being easily spread over a month there, or if we are really clever, we could budget to make seven days' money last six or even eight weeks.'

I digested what Cerys had said.

'Anything is possible, Eddie, anything,' she said.

'What about Henry? I can't just leave him,' I stated, knowing my argument was becoming weaker and weaker.

'We can make arrangements. Maybe Mary would take him for you until you return. Or your wife's friend, I can't remember her name.'

'Jennifer,' I offered.

'Yes, Jennifer – I am sure they would love to have him, maybe take it in turns if we go for a long time. If not, we will work it out some other way; as I said, anything is possible.'

'You are forgetting the divorce – how can I leave with that progressing?'

This was my final argument, the final roll of the dice, the last chance to keep me within familiar bounds and secure in conformity.

'Do you plan to contest?'

I didn't answer.

'Eddie?'

I shook my head lightly.

'Good answer,' she replied. 'Especially after this,' she added, retrieving the used condom and waving it in front of me.

Cerys let the condom go, her swing perfectly timed for it to land in my lap. We both looked down as it hit its target and began to laugh.

'Anyway, will take at least six weeks for our visas to be processed; I am sure the divorce could be nearing completion by then, and if it isn't, well, we can wait until it is.'

'Maybe,' I reasoned.

Cerys noticed my changing mood. 'You are both unhappy, Eddie, have been for a long time; at least there are no children to consider in all of this, or any creditors from Costa Rica.'

She was correct, but I still felt the nagging pang of failure I had developed as reaction to Sally's solicitor's letter.

'In any case, I think it's time you got rid of that,' she said, pointing at the used condom. 'Why don't you reach into that drawer again to ensure you have definite grounds for divorce as a backup plan?' she added, and winked at me.

I smiled and duly complied with the instruction, the feelings of failure banished as recent memories took the lead in mind and body.

This time our foreplay was more leisurely; the passion was still in abundance, but the urgency had diminished.

I moved to mount her again, but Cerys stopped me.

'Not here,' she said.

'Okay,' I responded, not knowing where this was leading.

Cerys slipped off the bed and took firm hold of my hardness in one hand and walked out of the room, still gripping me tightly, giggling. I followed her out to the mezzanine. She stopped at the rail, the waist-height, tactile oak rail, and bowed before it, spreading her hands over the grain as her fingers curled around the rail.

'Fuck me here,' she ordered.

Her command hardened me still further and I pushed inside her from behind, forcing Cerys to give a low moan at my entry and a deep contentment to sweep over me that I hadn't experienced at any time before. Again, we built to a steady rhythm, Cerys' ever-louder cries echoing around the white walls and glass, until I abruptly lost my momentum as I reached to squeeze her breasts. But the sensation surprisingly remained the same, as I felt Cerys moving back and forth independently and despite me.

I stood still, feeling her working me, drawing me to orgasm with her movement, while in front of us through the glass, the sun threw pinks and crimsons over the entire western sky as it dipped below the mountains, still just visible in the twilight. Suddenly, Cerys cried out loudly and her body contracted and shuddered; the action triggered my own spasm and I groaned in satisfaction, thrusting now again, until the sensations had completely ceased. I removed myself from deep inside her, pulled off the condom and again examined the contents, much to Cerys' amusement. It was the most pleasurable climax that I had ever experienced.

We staggered back to the bedroom and drifted into a deep, contented sleep.

Later, I awoke to the sound of the lavatory being flushed and Cerys returning to the bed. As before, she laid her head on my chest.

'What's your thing, Eddie?' she asked later.

'Sorry?'

'What's your thing, your turn-on? I am guessing it is me talking dirty, my words had the desired effect!' she said.

I laughed and felt a pang of embarrassment; it was true, the words had turned me on and were a new experience for me, but it wasn't 'my thing', as Cerys put it.

'It was you pushing back on me, out there,' I said, nodding my head toward the balcony.

'Oh, you are a dirty boy. You liked that, did you?' she cooed.

I nodded, remembering the sensation. 'What about you?' I asked.

'Oh, I thought mine was obvious. I love being fucked out there over the rail! I love the thought of being seen by the world outside, drives me crazy,' Cerys confessed.

'You say that a lot.'

'Say what?' teased Cerys.

'You know what!' I said.

'I just like the word! In context, you understand.'

I was puzzled, though. 'I thought you felt vulnerable, though, knowing you had been under surveillance, and then we are out there,' I said, again nodding outside the room.

'To be honest, Eddie, that is the first time I have been out there,' she explained, replicating my nod. 'I thought about it loads of times, fantasised, but never acted on it. I feel safe with you, it feels right with you – together, we protect me from the fear,' she added.

Her words were touching, honest and they lingered in my mind.

'Is there anything you really regret, Eddie?' she suddenly asked me.

'Sorry?'

'In life, is there anything you regret?'

'Not doing this sooner!' I laughed, kissing her cheek.

'I am serious,' she said, hugging me. 'Anything you wish hadn't happened, something you would change if you had the chance?'

The obvious subject began to come into focus in my mind, but as the image formed, so too did Ignatius McKenzie's words resound inside of me. *She is cocooned in love*, I heard, and the sentence ushered in positive memories of Rebecca to replace thoughts of the lifeless body laid on the slab that I witnessed on that dank November evening.

'Nothing springs to mind,' I eventually said. 'You cannot undo what has been done.'

'That's true. But sometimes an event stays with you, a time when you wish you had behaved differently.'

'That's just guilt; we all feel it from time to time,' I mused.

'But what if that memory makes you shudder, no matter how hard you try not to blame yourself?

'Go on,' I said quietly.

'I want to tell you something. No one else knows this, not even Cole,' she said.

'Okay.'

'Eddie, you are the only person I can really be me with, I am worried you will judge me.'

'I won't, you have my word,' I said, feeling a level of trepidation at her build-up.

'I think I told you how I met Cole, in a florist's shop.'

I nodded in response.

'The rain was torrential as I left the shop, and I was struggling to locate my car keys when he sent me a humorous text asking me to dinner, then another and another in quick succession. I didn't respond until I was in my car, and replied simply with, *Okay*.'

'And?'

'And, I was flattered, naturally, but I wanted him to respond to my text. Don't forget, I was young – this was my purple-hair stage, and I was sitting proudly in my first ever car, Bessie, and a stranger had just bought me flowers and had now invited me to dinner; such things didn't happen to me.'

'Bessie?'

'Yes, that was her name, my car's name.'

'Okay.' I smiled, not for the first time in my life failing to understand why people name their cars.

'I text him again, just before I pulled away. As I drove, I kept an eye on my phone, waiting for an alert. Minutes passed of driving through the rain and checking the phone, driving and checking, driving and checking. I didn't know the area very well and due to my lack of concentration, I took a wrong turn; on a bend, the road forked without warning to the left. As my phone finally buzzed, I wasn't worried that I didn't know where I was heading, or about the poor visibility due to the constant rain – being lost was of secondary importance, reading the new message was paramount. I remember laughing as he told me to stop being bossy.'

Cerys stopped speaking and looked at me tersely, before looking out toward the darkness.

'What is it?' I asked.

'Please don't judge me,' she requested again.

And for a second time, I promised I would not. A silence fell into the room which only Cerys could break.

'We carried on texting, rapidly; he asked what food I would like – Italian, Greek, Cantonese. I replied that I really didn't mind. I hadn't really experienced anything other than home-cooked food at that time,' she said.

'I remember – it was seen as adventurous, then, eating out?' I smiled.

Cerys nodded and returned my smile. 'The dark road gave way for some street lighting,' she continued, 'but the darkness returned on the other side of the few houses lining the pavement. I had no idea where I was, but thought I must meet a main road soon. Another text arrived, telling me he would pick me up at 8pm that night.'

'You hadn't told him where you lived?' I asked quizzically.

'No, that was the point. I adored the forwardness, and was answering when it happened.'

Cerys stopped speaking and looked at me, her gaze haunting, replaying an event unknown to me in her mind.

'I was extremely happy, giggling as I texted back – I was completely caught up in the moment and I didn't see it.'

'See what?'

'The other car. It was my fault; I had drifted to their side of the carriageway, more interested in texting than concentrating on the road. They swerved to my left to avoid me, but I felt them clip my side. I slammed on the brakes and stopped violently as they passed the rear of my car. I just sat breathing heavily, still on the wrong side of the road, the sound of the windscreen wipers swishing through my gasps. When I looked in the rear-view mirror I saw their brake lights flick on and the interior light come on as they opened the door of their vehicle. I decided I didn't want any confrontation, so I pulled away. I shouldn't have, I should have faced them.'

'You had no idea who was in the car, though – you could have been attacked, beaten, or worse,' I reasoned. 'Yours was a normal reaction, anyone would do the same.'

Cerys just looked at me.

'I don't understand why you think I would judge you,' I stated.

'I don't know, Eddie; I thought you would judge my mental stability,' she replied.

'Why would I do that?'

'I have a horrible feeling of anxiety, of dread when I think about the incident, which is often, even now. I have no idea why, but I have an urge to return there after all these years.'

'Why don't you do that, then?'

'Eddie, I have no idea where it was – I have tried to find it on so many occasions, but I was driving at night in the rain, it could be anywhere. And throughout this, this gnawing anxiety has stayed with me; it isn't as if anyone was hurt or died, so it has never made sense why I feel like this.'

I looked at her, stunned by the torment she had kept hidden.

'See, you think I am crazy!' she suggested in response to my silence.

'Not at all, I don't think you are crazy, and why are you to blame? You could blame your husband for insisting on your number, for texting you; your friend for not organising the funeral flowers herself. Where do you stop? No, I am just trying to think of a way I can help you.'

'I think you already have. It is strange, but telling you, sharing it with you seems to have dulled the guilt and the urge I've felt to apologise for all these years. Thank you,' she said, kissing my cheek lightly and squeezing me tightly.

'Maybe you just needed to offload, to focus the event into perspective,' I said, kissing her cheek in return.

We didn't speak any more of the subject after that; Cerys genuinely appeared to be uplifted, a huge burden taken from her., We got dressed and continued to pack her belongings into the boxes and black bin bags.

Later, as we approached my house in her Range Rover, singing loudly to her music, a clear coldness suddenly rushed over me.

'The incident with the car, when was it?' I asked.

'What?' laughed Cerys.

'That rainy night, when was it?'

'Years ago,' she shouted above the song.

'No, I mean specifically *when* was it?'

'Couldn't be sure what day, but definitely November – it sticks in my mind because of the funeral being in the month of the dead.'

We pulled up on my driveway and Cerys turned off the ignition, cutting the music with her action, but not my thoughts.

'Why these questions, Eddie? It's okay, I really think I am fine about it all now. It is strange, though, to carry this around for so long and then speak openly about it, but the hold on me has evaporated,' she said.

'I was just curious when it was,' I said, unbuckling my seatbelt, preparing to leave the vehicle.

'You sure we can't just bring Henry back with us?' asked Cerys, content with my explanation.

She had already suggested this as we pulled out of her driveway, so that we could wake up together in the morning. I had countered that we could stay at mine, but Cerys had refused the offer.

'Like I said, this is his home; he'd be a nightmare outside his own environment,' I told her.

Cerys leant over and kissed me firmly on my lips, her hands either side of my face. Her mouth left mine and softly covered my cheek in kisses, before stopping on my jawline.

'I love you, Eddie Dungiven,' she whispered gently into my ear.

The words sent a shiver and tingle down my spine, and a spinning sensation that popped inside my head and forced a huge grin across my face.

'I love you too,' I said into her hair.

We parted and smiled at each other, studying each

other's faces as we had done behind the sand dunes in the past summer months.

I opened the passenger door and illuminated the interior.

'See you tomorrow?' asked Cerys as I stepped outside.

'That would be lovely,' I replied.

Cerys smiled and blew me a kiss.

'There was one thing,' I blurted, speaking without thinking.

Cerys stopped as she was preparing to blow a second kiss in my direction. 'Go on,' she said.

'What colour was Bessie?'

'What, my first car?'

I nodded.

'Why, blue of course; thought they went well together, Bessie Blue,' replied Cerys cheerfully. 'Why do you ask?'

'No reason, just curious,' I said again.

Chapter 21

Toward the Land of Cranes and Buffaloes

The screen held the information, but kept it hidden, kept it a secret from me. It held all that I sought to trigger my next move. I stood, chin pointing upwards, head tilted backwards, studying the bank of monitors suspended from the ceiling, checking and double-checking; a singular search in a crowd of strangers, united in a task.

Relax and shop, I read again from the monitor.

I could do neither.

I didn't require an array of obscurely named vodka-based spirits, wrapped designer chocolates finished with a red satin bow, or, despite what the impeccably dressed demonstrator preached, a multi-functional, multi-holed universal electrical charger, compatible with all six continents. I certainly didn't need to purchase an eye-wateringly expensive raffle ticket on the flimsy chance that on entering a draw I could win the pristine super-car gleaming on the podium ahead of me. I am sure the accompanying photographs stuck on a display board of your 'average middle-aged man of the people' past winners, all huge smiles, raised arms and clenched fists, would encourage some to partake, but I was merely left wondering how on earth they had gotten the vehicle into this position – one storey up, with no obvious entrance – in the first place.

I couldn't relax. The voices of so many people preparing to travel to so many places around the globe were amplified in the contained environment. My mind churned, and all the events that had carried me to this point jostled for attention.

That random call from Mike Saunders to book me for the Lombarders' ladies' night – why did he have a copy of a network magazine published three years ago? The overheard conversation from behind my van, and Greg Dixon's comments about Sally on the same night – why did they occur? Why did Greg remain in a coma, unable to wake, unable to rage about my punch to his jaw and confirm my dismissed account of the swarming bees covering his form? Why had I to witness the demise of Clifford and the love he shared with Mary to understand I should be happy? And through all this, always just a thought away, were Ignatius McKenzie's piercing blue eyes. I still did not fully understand what occurred that still afternoon in his quiet study, overlooking the mature garden, but he had changed me utterly. The need to change the unchangeable buried within had been replaced by a feeling of acceptance. And finally, the pain of the divorce, leading me through sadness, from failure and the past, had all sprung from that early-morning encounter on the beach with Henry, all those months ago, when Cerys Sindon entered my life.

My thoughts returned to the now and my anxiety regarding the whereabouts of my newly purchased backpack, chosen with the help of Cerys, who insisted a 'top-loader' was not a practical choice. I smiled at the thought of the clothing and array of practical items it contained, that up until yesterday, at no point in my life had I ever considered necessary to pack. What if it was lost on arrival? What if it was damaged and couldn't be carried? What would I wear?

All my questions were met by a giggle and rejection from Cerys as I closed the outer zip.

'Imagine! What would you do, Eddie?' she teased.

I imagined and panicked, voiced my concerns, told her that her teasing was making me cross, which merely seemed to fan the fire of ridicule yet further.

'Tell you what, you could borrow some of my clothes – you'll have to go commando though, I guess!' she offered.

The lunacy of my prickliness dissolved as she extracted a pair of fetching pale pink shorts, complete with sequin trim on the front pockets, from her own bag.

'Try these,' she said, tossing them over to me.

I could do nothing but laugh.

'Eddie, we can kit you out very easily – a few shirts and a pair of fisherman pants. Done,' said Cerys.

'So why are we taking all of this?' I replied, pointing at my near-full backpack.

'So you can take me to some posh restaurants in style!' she gushed.

After we had finished packing and I had checked my list of items for a third time, Cerys suggested we go for a walk before the shy sun dipped and drew a close to the short winter day and I departed to spend the night at Mary's. We headed out with Henry over the sands – not our familiar beach by the mountains, but with a backdrop of an expanse of sand, capped with enormous skies and ever-changing light, in front of the small house Cerys' mother had left her in her will. The seals had yet to draw their bulk up from the water ahead of the winter storms, leaving the entire beach for Henry to chase his own agenda, his own route, as we strode out.

Contrary to what I had feared, Henry had adapted effortlessly to his new surroundings, sleeping contentedly that first night in front of the wood-burning stove, and had slumbered there each night since in its warmth and glow.

I had helped Cerys move into the place, coincidentally on the same day Sally had requested to remove her belongings from the house, and I hadn't really gone back in the past few weeks. I knew I had to return at some point, knew I had to check off the items listed by her solicitors as removed, but I didn't want to face it now, didn't want to seek closure under someone else's direction. I was surprised she had included the *Book of Perfect Brilliance* on her list, thinking it had been lost years ago – perhaps Sally had kept it in a secret place, a place only she knew.

With Cerys' encouragement, the week she moved in, I called in to see Gus to make my peace with him. It was a difficult experience to knock on his front door, and after several attempts and an anxious wait, he had not answered. I left a phone message and a text stating I had popped by and signed off with my desire to meet up, but I have not received a reply. I hope to reconcile with him, but only time will tell if he feels the same.

Cerys and I had agreed to meet only at the departure gate; a romantic gesture signalling the beginning of an adventure, our adventure – although, as a practicality we had, on booking the flights, secured our seats together – after all, romantic notions would have no place in the experience if one of us was squeezed between a pair of formidable 'two-seat' passengers for the forthcoming journeyeleven and the other was discarded in the woeful seats beside the rear toilet cubicle.

Despite our agreement, I had tried to locate her during my time as part of the laboured, moving beast which is the check-in queue. I did the same through the security area for a while, until I felt my regular 360-degree glances around the room could be viewed as suspicious behaviour and draw unwanted attention from special government personnel hidden behind the mirrored glass wall. And now, here in this maelstrom of noise, lights, information and people coming from all directions, I admitted defeat.

What if when I got to the gate she wasn't there? What if she had been delayed? What if she had had a change of heart, and decided that upon reflection, she couldn't go?

I would have to board on my own, travel to my first adventure alone. What would have been a memorable, shared experience of movie-watching, progress-plotting and excited conversations, instead would manifest into a miserable journey of barely warm, processed, tasteless food; defective airline earphones performing in monotone through one ear; and sudden, violent tugs of the back of my headrest as the person behind used my seat as leverage to propel their excessive bulk into a standing position, the process repeated regularly to control their descent as they returned from their numerous 'comfort breaks'. And without question, the seat in front of me, and from my perspective, the only seat on the entire aircraft, would be reclined fully within seconds of the seatbelt light switching off, and my personal space would be instantly halved as the aircraft hurtled still upwards, in blind search through the darkness, for its cruising altitude.

In essence, every negative aspect of airline travel would be magnified into mild despair by my own company over the long journey.

The screen lit up with a message. *Please wait* replaced its previous demand.

I stood and obeyed. The words began to flash, to pulsate, and as I scanned I realised it was the only one to do so. One final flash, and without warning the words vanished entirely.

Faruk had picked me up from Mary's that morning and driven me the two hours to the airport. It was hard to imagine the necessity of the lightweight summer clothes that I stood in when my breath hung visibly in the air as I said goodbye to Mary and a thick layer of ice covered the windscreen of her Land Rover parked in the yard.

Henry had travelled with Cerys and me last night when she dropped me off at Mary's farmhouse before heading to an airport hotel. He couldn't hide his excitement on seeing Mary again, the back half of his body moving from side to side as he wagged his tail at every syllable she uttered in his direction. I had concerns about Henry's interaction with Ben and Alfie, her Border collies, and momentarily regretted taking Mary up on her offer of taking care of him while we were away. But it was unfounded, as after an initial wariness from all, the three soon settled down together on the kitchen floor. Perhaps they sensed they would be living as a pack for a reasonable time. Or perhaps Henry had changed.

Mary appeared well, but she had lost some weight – she

said she didn't bother cooking for herself every night; she didn't get hungry and didn't like eating alone. I remembered how that felt. But tonight was an exception, as she happily feasted with me on the beef stew she had slow-cooked, starting from late that afternoon. Sitting at the kitchen table, talking with her as I had done on so many occasions, I regretted not spending more time with Mary since Clifford's passing, but life goes on regardless, or in spite of our good intentions.

Mary thought Cerys seemed nice; it was the first time they had met and it was a brief, cordial exchange. She didn't really say any more and she didn't mention Sally, just vaguely stated that she didn't understand young people today. I wouldn't categorise myself as young, but concluded that Mary disapproved of the situation.

I thanked Faruk a number of times for driving me while en route to the airport – the round trip was, after all, four hours out of his day – but each one of my statements was waved away as unimportant and resulted in a 'No trouble, any time, Eddie.' His driving style could be best described as 'relaxed' – his fingers barely gripped the steering wheel, his elbow rested on the window and he weaved from lane to lane with little or no notification of his forthcoming actions to the other drivers he passed. His mind seemed preoccupied, and he spoke about Jennifer *a lot*. How she had changed his life, given him purpose – I thought the same was evident for Jennifer, judging by the weight she had lost and the huge smile she was giving in the photo he proudly displayed on the dashboard, but I let it pass. She seemed so happy, the thing we all deserve.

As we pulled up in front of the terminal, Faruk told

me to try to visit a retired colonel he had heard about who lived in a run-down bungalow. The colonel was known to happily invite travellers in to share afternoon tea and tales of a long-lost world on his shaded veranda, and to snooze in wicker colonial chairs until the evening brought relief from the relentless sun.

He repeated the colonel's name again, and the town where his bungalow was located, in deliberate syllables.

'Don't forget,' he said to me.

As I exited the car and retrieved my backpack from the boot I tried to put money into Faruk's shirt pocket to reimburse him at least for his fuel, but he removed it quickly and slapped it back into my hand.

'You will do the same for me one day, Eddie, maybe to take us on honeymoon!' he laughed.

I admitted defeat and stepped back, as he jumped back into the driving seat. He honked the horn twice and was away, pulling out into the flow of traffic without warning.

Once inside the terminal building I instantly forgot the name of the colonel and the location of his veranda and colonial chairs.

The screen finally gave me the instruction: *Gate 001* appeared. Following direction from the overhead yellow signs, it soon became apparent that Gate 001 was not in close proximity to the hubbub I had been immersed in. As I walked, ranges of gate numbers frequently branched off to the left or right, until only individual gates were left to choose from, counting down sequentially.

Uninvited, the subject that kept occupying me and which I kept pushing away returned – Cerys' blue car and that rainy November evening. I knew I could take her to the place where Rebecca was knocked down – I would find it by instinct, the stretch of road was burnt into my memory – but would Cerys remember the place? Would it even *be* the same place, or would a false memory play with her, manipulating her recollection to form a connection that wasn't there? But what if it was the place and her eyes betrayed her – how would I feel, how would I react?

I had told Cerys about Rebecca on the beach with Henry the day after I had been to Eebiss. The timing and location seemed somehow right. She had listened quietly as we walked across the sand, my eyes focused firmly on the mountains that faced me. I explained she had been hit by a car and had died of her injuries, and until recently I hadn't been able to move on. I didn't mention Ignatius McKenzie, or his revelations.

Cerys stopped walking, turned to face me and held her arms out. I buried my face in the nape of her neck and felt her arms close around me as the last remaining strands of grief were squeezed gently from my being.

Back at the car, while we waited for Henry to lap his water, Cerys asked if I had any photographs of my daughter. I told her no, which she was surprised to hear. When pressed further, I confirmed there would be some at the house, stored away, quite like her cake photos or the one from her catering college days. She suggested that when I returned to the house I should retrieve some, frame them and place them in a prominent spot of my choice in her mother's house on the shore of the endless sand flats, sky and ever-changing light.

I did not know if I should ever mention to Cerys the

blue car noted by the driver who killed my daughter – would it make any difference if it remained unspoken, the possible connection never pursued? Would revealing it change everything? That instant gut feeling I voiced at her confession of guilt remained: where do you stop applying the blame?

Gate 001 – Mumbai finally greeted me at the far end of the airport. Half the seats were already occupied and I had no idea how my fellow passengers had got here before me. As I looked around to find Cerys, still nervous in case she had had a change of heart, my phone rang in my pocket. I extracted it and didn't recognise the number.

'Hello, Eddie Dungiven,' I said.

'Hello?' replied the female caller.

'Hello, Eddie Dungiven,' I repeated.

'Is that the Party King?' the voice asked, confusion in her voice.

'Yes it is; how can I help you?'

'I would like to make a booking for a child's party.'

'Okay, but I am not around for a while – I am actually at an airport,' I revealed.

'Oh, this is for early summer,' she replied. 'You provide bouncy castles?' she added.

'Yes, we do.'

'Excellent – my daughter is a very girly girl, would you have anything like that?' she asked.

'We have a large fairy-princess castle with pink towers and battlements that we could supply.'

'That sounds perfect!' she replied happily. 'Can I book it, please?'

'Certainly, just text over the date and time and I will hold it for you.'

'Oh thank you, she will be so pleased!'

'No problem,' I replied.

'Enjoy your break, where are you flying to?' she asked.

But before I could answer, there was a tap on my shoulder. I didn't think I was speaking too loudly, didn't think somebody would complain, and I span around ready to confront an unnecessary dispute, but instead found Cerys standing before me, a huge, warm smile on her face.

We kissed as I cut off the phone call, my interest solely on her.

'Did you bring it?' she asked excitedly, breaking away.

I reached into my bag and removed a bottle of grapefruit seed extract and waved it playfully in front of her.

There was sudden activity at the gate.

'BA flight 139 to Mumbai is now ready for boarding through Gate 001,' the ground crew informed us.

The words forced all the waiting passengers to automatically stand and pick up their flight bags and begin to shuffle toward the gate.

'Will the passengers seated in rows thirty-five to forty-five *only* step forward with their boarding passes for inspection and passports open at the photo page?' came the response to this mass movement.

When our turn came, we greeted the gate attendant warmly as she checked our details, our smiles in sharp contrast to the stern images in the passports we offered to confirm our identities.

Once airborne, with the ground falling rapidly below us, the engines carried the weight of the full fuel tanks and the heavy expectations of those on board.

But neither of us could settle; Cerys fidgeted with her

pillow, placing it behind her head, then her back, then her head again, before discarding it onto the floor. I took the bottles of water from my hand luggage under the seat in front of me and stowed them in the rear pocket. Sitting back for mere moments, I suddenly bent forward again to search and rummage through the same bag for my MP3 player, only to remember I had previously placed it in the same pocket as the water. I didn't need it; I just wanted to know it was there in case I wanted to use it. I took one of the water bottles out and offered it to Cerys, who shook her head in reply and instead took out the entertainment console from its bracket in front of her, which had suddenly grabbed her attention. At this rate, with this level of nervous energy spent, the coming hours will be a major endurance test , I thought.

But we did settle; the relief that we had made it, that we were flying to meet the sun as it dragged the darkness behind it, contented us.

And as I expected, in unison with the seatbelt sign on the flight deck switching off, the seat in front of me reclined fully with a violent thud.

Cerys clasped her hand to her mouth and buried her head in my shoulder, trying to smother her laughter.

'See,' I hissed, pointing at the TV screen now inches from my chest. My actions merely made her stifled laughter even harder to control.

She eventually looked up at me and said, 'In just under eight hours, Eddie, we will land in a place that will bombard your senses. The noise, the chaos, the sheer amount of people and the total disregard of personal space are unprecedented. The heat, the vibrant colours all around and the direct questions delivered with huge, warm, genuine smiles are not anything you will have experienced before. You can read every guidebook, every travel blog, every brochure, but nothing will prepare you for that initial shock that is India. You can either embrace it and go with it and discover something too precious to ever describe with words, or you can fight against it, loathe it and hone in on its imperfections as your sole memories.'

And I have to admit that after an age waiting to clear immigration and being safely reunited with my panel-loading backpack, Cerys' prediction was proven correct, as the doors opened to reveal a scene I would never have been able to imagine.

Life had changed.

I was happy.